Paper Hearts

Paper Hearts

KAY COVE

Page & Vine
An Imprint of Meredith Wild LLC

Editing by Michelle Morgan at Fiction Edit
Proofing by Judy Zweifel at Judy's Proofreading
Cover Design by K.B. Barrett Designs
Art by Aga Olario

Paperback ISBN: 978-1-964264-31-8

DEDICATION:

This one is for the performers—the ones who learned early that love was something to be earned, and never stopped auditioning.

For everyone who got so good at being what others needed that you forgot what you actually wanted.

Take back your stage. *The approval that matters most is your own.*

EPIGRAPH

"Until you're ready to look foolish, you'll never have the possibility of being great."

- James Carse

Prologue Charlie

He wanted me?

"Spence," I wheeze, rising to the very tips of my bare toes. "This one." I give up when the pain of my big toe grinding into the hard concrete becomes too much. I point upward at the jumbo black bin with a neon-yellow lid—the only tub we haven't torn apart like ruthless scavengers.

"I forgot what a shortcake you are when you're not in your bedazzled stage boots." My big sister Spencer nudges me out of the way with a gentle hip check. She puts her extra three inches of height to good use, and when she rises to her tiptoes, she's able to wriggle the tub free from where it's lodged on the wire rack. "I'm pretty sure this is just old clothes, Charlie. Tubs are clothes, blankets, and shoes. All the scrapbooks were in brown moving boxes."

I shake my head stubbornly. "No, there's gotta be more somewhere in—"

Thud!

She drops the bin in front of my feet. In a normal garage, that would've caused a dust cloud, but this is Nate's—my adoptive dad and big sister's husband—brand-new work garage. The epoxy floors are clean enough to eat off of.

I look to the left, eyeing the candy-apple-red antique sports car with the hood popped. "Nice of Dad to share his new working garage with you to store all of our mom's stuff."

The space is massive. It could hold an additional four cars even with the wall of organized boxes, bins, and tubs—evidence of our sentimental hoarding. When Mom passed away, Spencer tucked all of her belongings into a storage unit. From what I remember, the owner of the unit ensured it was free, taking pity on two orphaned sisters. It wasn't until Spence and I moved to Las Vegas, and she met and married Nate, that we finally had a home big enough to comfortably store all our sacred memories.

Spence has way more than me. She was eighteen when Mom died. I was only five. I should be grateful she remembers so much and I have someone to tell me the stories, but sometimes I resent her for having thirteen more years with Mom than I did. Even though people say I'm Mom's spitting image, I feel like a stranger wearing her face. That's why I can't let go of a single shred. It's only paper, but it's all I have. I'm clinging to scraps...it's all I have. I'm clinging to scraps while my big sister has whole memories.

Dropping to my knees, I grab the yellow tub lid and yank. Finally, the satisfying snaps of the plastic dislodging echo around the room. "Blankets my ass," I grumble, as the tub reveals its treasures—an entire bin full of loose papers and photographs.

I hold up a list, waving it triumphantly in the air. "See?"

A sweet smile overcomes my sister. God, she's pretty, especially when she smiles. Curvaceous. Thick, long dark hair, and soft brown eyes. The most beautiful, effortless tan. We look nothing alike. Spencer's dad is Cuban. Mine? He's nonexistent. I never knew the guy, and he never wanted to know me. The cheating bastard. He wasn't there when Mom needed him. He wasn't there when I needed him. He's a ghost I will never let haunt me.

After gracefully dropping to the ground next to me, Spencer folds her legs and begins to sort out papers and pictures. "Mom must've never gotten the chance to organize all these. Look at this one." She hands me a snapshot of Mom in a flowy, floral dress with spaghetti straps, standing next to a brawny man in pitch-black sunglasses. They're posing in front of a for-sale sign. And behind that stands a small cottage-type house, meager but charming.

"Mom and your dad?"

Spence nods slowly, her eyes shifting as she gets lost in a distant memory. "Mom's pregnant with me here. They bought this house for me."

I examine the handsome man in the photograph. His jet-black hair gleams in the Florida sun, and his tan—just a few shades deeper than Spencer's complexion—stretches across broad shoulders that strain against a crisp white guayabera shirt. His giant brown loafers peek out from beneath pressed khaki pants, completing the quintessential Miami look of a man who knows exactly who he is in the world. His face is partially obscured by those onyx sunglasses, making him seem both present and somehow unreachable at the same time.

"How old were you when he left?"

"Two." Her eyes fall to her lap. "He found someone else. Love was a game of leapfrog for him. Jumping from one woman to the next. It broke Mom. She really loved him." Her voice drops to a whisper. "Legend has it, he's still out there man-whoring around, ruining women's lives."

I pat my sister's knee. "I'm sorry. Poor Mom...poor you."

"Hey, we were stronger for it." Reaching over, she taps the top of the picture. "Mom figured it out and raised me in that house, all by herself. She did it again when you came along. She always found a way to make the impossible possible. I learned to live by that mantra. It's why even though everyone with a brain cell said I had no business keeping custody of you when she passed, if she figured it out once...well, so could I." Her shoulder nudges mine playfully, knocking me sideways. I topple from my kneeling position onto one hip, then cross my legs like hers. The concrete feels less punishing this way.

"Do you regret it?" I ask, half-heartedly, looking around the two-thousand-square-foot garage only a stone's throw away from the mansion I moved into when I was eleven. Obviously, it worked out.

"Regret what?" she asks mindlessly as she continues to riffle through the tub, pausing on a photograph that catapults her back to what seems like a whole other lifetime.

"Keeping me."

She turns her head to face me, her lips pursed and one eyebrow raised. "Once." She can't hold her scowl long, her teasing smile curling at the corner of her lips.

"Humor me. When did you consider dropping me off at a fire station?"

"When you were seven, we were so broke, I could barely afford our apartment but I won a gift card to Sephora from work around Christmastime. I could finally buy some nice makeup for myself." She holds up her pointer and middle finger together. "I left you alone for *two minutes*, just to start dinner and you used my brand-new Tom Ford eyeshadow palette for watercolor paintings on the wall. *Ooooh*, I wanted to..." She chokes the air, conveying her frustration but she pairs it with a soft chuckle. "Back then, sixty dollars for one makeup palette was ludicrous."

"I don't remember our lives being so bleak. I never felt poor. I was always okay, Spence."

She wets her lips before rubbing them together. "Then I did a better job of shielding you than I gave myself credit for."

The obvious answer is my billionaire adoptive dad saved us. But that's not the whole story. My big sister was my rock. We survived because of her. Because of how much she loved me.

Spence shakes her head like a dog with wet ears in the universal sign for, *let's change the subject*. "And now look at us. *Look at you, mega pop star.* You could wipe your ass with our old rent money."

"Yeah...look at me," I mutter bitterly.

The humor wipes clean from her face. "What's that tone?"

"Nothing," I mumble, trying to busy myself with the papers again, but Spence, as usual, refuses to let it go.

"How's the tour training going? You must be working hard." She pats my thigh, feeling the firmness of my quadriceps that wasn't there last year.

"I rehearse six hours a day, five days a week, and I still look like an ostrich on stilts when I dance."

It doesn't matter how much they dumb down the choreography, I can't keep up. But in my defense when I started this whole thing seven years ago, I said I was a singer-songwriter. Not a dancer. Not a grand performer. Not some blonde, Barbie icon who would fool tens of millions of fans that she's perfect... that she's happy.

"A world arena tour of this size has been your dream since you signed with Domino Records, right?"

Wordlessly, I shrug.

"You're allowed to change your mind."

I scoff this time.

"As much as I'm enjoying your caveman responses, do you want to actually tell me what's going on?"

"Claire's pregnant." I say it like a full sentence, as if Spencer is supposed to understand.

"I'm aware of that. She's my daughter."

I cackle. "Our family is so twisted. You're my half sister. Your husband is my adoptive dad. My dad's other adoptive daughter was my childhood best friend before she became my sister. Your sons are technically my nephews yet they call me 'sissy' and basically we're eligible to be on *Maury* any day now."

"Yeah, our family sounds like a complicated math problem, but that's beside the point. What do you mean by 'Claire's pregnant'? Are you upset she's on bed rest and can't go on the tour with you?"

"*No.*" My eyes pop into wide circles. "I'm not that selfish. I'm happy for her, and I really want this baby to make it all the way. I'm just...lonely. Claire's been with me on every tour. This will be the first one she sits out. She's due when I'm scheduled to start the European leg."

"Well, what about me? I can be your assistant this year."

I sigh heavily, stretching out my legs. "You have Eli and Remy to care for."

"They can come. Nate too," she insists. "If you need your family, Charlie, we're here."

"A four-year-old and six-year-old have no business being stuck on a tour bus, or catching endless flights to the corners of the world. I just want what's best for your kids."

"What's best for my kids?" Spencer asks in a tone as soft and sweet as a toasted marshmallow.

"Simplicity. That's what I wish for the people I love most. Peace...and beautiful, simple things. Like home-cooked Sunday dinners and little babies that smell like graham crackers and lavender bubble bath." I loved those precious moments with the boys when they were toddlers. It wasn't that long ago but the memories have already begun to fade.

"I hate to break it to you but they smell less like lavender and more like feet and dirty laundry these days. They are going to lose their minds when they find out you're here visiting. Uncle Dex took them to play laser tag but they'll be back soon. How long can you stay?"

"Just tonight. I have to get back to rehearsals. The tour kicks off in less than three months."

Spencer tucks a thick tendril of her curly hair behind one ear. "You came all this way from LA for one night for this?" She taps the side of the bin with her knuckle. "What are you looking for?"

"More paper hearts," I admit.

They are little love notes from Mom. When she was diagnosed with cancer, she started documenting, afraid the clock was running out. Mom had always been a crafter, full of old-school creativity in the form of calligraphy and pressed flowers. She used photographs and letters to keep me company from beyond the grave. For years she tried to squeeze a lifetime of motherhood into a collection of scrapbooks. I love the pictures, the lines of lyrics from her favorite songs. But my favorite parts are the paper hearts—love notes of encouragement, or just sweet sentiments scribbled onto various kinds of paper cut into Cupid's favorite shape. I plucked them from the scrapbooks and trapped them in a keepsake box like little fireflies I could keep alive forever. Precious specs of light to guide my path.

Eighteen years later, I've not only read them all, the messages are etched into my mind and heart. I could trace the curve of her handwriting in the air from memory. The paper is creased, worn, used far past its purpose. I'm desperate for fresh inspiration. I need more of her voice, breadcrumbs to follow through this forest of disappointment that has become my life. A life I desperately wish I had lived differently. But now it's too late. I don't belong to myself. I belong to the label, the machine, the money...the world. But those little paper phantoms stick to me. They remind me of a precious, simple time—when I used to belong to my mother.

"All right, I'll dig through all of this with you, but we're going to need coffee."

"Chai tea?" I plead.

Spencer smirks in my direction. "Why? Worried about the caffeine stunting your growth? Because the damage is done."

"Hilarious," I deadpan. "You know I don't like coffee. I'm recently open to matcha though."

"That I can do."

"Thank you, sister," I singsong.

She scrambles to her feet, but her foot must be asleep because she winces and stumbles, grabbing the side of the tub to steady her. It's not sturdy enough. She tips it, sending papers everywhere, skating across the epoxy floor like a gold-medal performance at the Winter Olympics.

"Ah, dammit," she breathes.

We both drop to our hands and knees, collecting the scattered documents, photos, letters, bank statements. There's so much junk in here it's kind of exciting. After all these years, more moments of Mom to uncover. I pick up an orange letter envelope that slid farthest away and stand up with it, my curiosity piqued after seeing the name. "I thought Mom went by Beth. She hated when people called her Bettany."

"She did." Spencer drops a stack of paper back into the tub, holding out her hand for the letter. "The only people who called her Bettany were her parents."

"I guess Grandma or Grandpa wrote her a letter."

Spence shakes her head. "Not likely. They were estranged. Mom emancipated herself at seventeen. I never even met her mother and father." She slips her finger under the flap and frees the letter, unfolding it as she reads. Slowly, almost ominously, my sister's eyes widen as they shift from left to right, gobbling up the words like she's starving. "*Oh*," she whispers.

"What...What is it?"

Lips parted, Spencer presses the letter to her chest, and her eyes lock on to mine, unblinking. Filled with a look I rarely ever see on her face: *Fear.*

My growing anxiety forms a knot in my throat. "*Who is it from*?" I ask again more insistently.

She wets her lips, reluctant for some reason. "I didn't know," she murmurs. "I swear I didn't know."

I step forward, worried Spencer may go big-sister-protector on me and try to shield me from some disturbing revelation that is definitely mine to discover. Quick like a cobra, I snatch the letter from her grip before she can get rid of it.

Dear Bettany,

It's been months and I'm tearing myself apart trying to figure out what to do next. I've dialed your number until my fingers ache, but you won't pick up. So here I am, resorting to your favorite medium—letters—because maybe this time you'll read my desperation.

I have no excuse good enough. The ugly truth is that I fell in love with you while I was still married. I know how it sounds—shameful, reckless—but from the very first moment I saw you, I lost any power to stop it. I fought it, honest, but loving you felt like breathing.

If there's even a sliver of hope that you're not done with me, I promise I'll fix this wreck I've made. I'll go to my wife and tell her I'm leaving, that I'm a coward for falling so hard for someone else, that I'm filled with shame. I'll stand there, head bent, voice trembling, and admit that love hit me like a hurricane and knocked me off course. I'm bewitched, consumed...obsessed. The thought of a life with you and our baby terrifies me with how much I want it. I'd do anything to win you back, because as much as I love you, I'll love that baby in your belly ten times more.

Please don't take her away from me. We could be a family again. I can put the pieces back together. I'll prove my loyalty to you, to Spencer, and to our daughter. Even if it takes every breath until my dying day, I will show you I can be gentle with your heart. I've never been this man before—a liar, a cheater. No. This, I swear, is love in its rawest, most twisted form. But it's true love.

What more do you need me to say? What must I do? You want the moon? I'll crawl across the sky to bring it down. The stars? They'll all be yours. My heart? You already have it—every beat.

Please.

Please.

Please.

I know I may never hear from you again. Just writing that

makes my chest hurt. I feel like I've already lost you, and the thought makes me hollow with grief. If this is truly over, I will respect your choice. I'll learn to let go somehow. But I need you to open one more letter on the way: it unlocks a trust fund for our daughter. Half of my retirement, saved for whatever she might need.

Promise me you'll tell her someday not just what I did, but how fiercely I feel about her. I have wonderful sons, but I always dreamt of a daughter. I even promised my mother on her deathbed that if I ever had a little girl, I'd keep her name alive. Whatever name you choose, will you whisper to her that I would've named her Charlotte? That each night I tuck my boys into bed, I'm wishing I could tuck in my baby Charlie, too?

I'm rambling because I'm terrified of silence. I don't know what else to say...only that I'll never stop hoping.

And I'll never stop loving you.

Liam

I read the letter again, and then again, before finally meeting Spencer's watering eyes through my own veil of tears.

"He wanted me?" I croak, my knees beginning to wobble as the letter crumples in my shaking hands.

My dad loved me. He wanted me.

And she kept him from me.

I. Can. Save. This.

Three Months Later - New York

The ringing is faint, coming in and out of focus. I tug on my earlobe aggressively, our signal, praying stage production sees my plea. *Something is wrong.* When no one responds, I pull the mic from my lips for two seconds, just enough to mouth, *sound check, feedback...feedback.* I missed a line, but the crowd roars in support when I give them confirmation I'm not lip-synching. It's energizing to hear the praise...for a millisecond. But the moment the mic is near my lips again, the ringing comes through once more, *louder* and even more distracting this time.

I fucking knew it. A cold dread floods my stomach, a repeat of the feeling I had mere hours ago when I realized Mom's box of handwritten notes was sitting in a hotel dressing room three states away...or maybe crushed at the bottom of a dumpster by now.

My throat tightens, but not just from the loss. It's more complicated than that now. Three months ago, I would have given anything to have that box in my hands—my mother's voice, her love, her little paper promises that I was enough. But three months ago, I didn't know she was a liar. I didn't know that every "I love you" was written by the same hand that kept my father from me. That every heart-shaped scrap of encouragement came from a woman who died letting me believe I was unwanted.

I still need those paper hearts. That's the sick part. Even knowing what I know, I'm desperate for them. I want to reach into that box and pull out her sacred words of wisdom and pretend none of it matters—that love can exist alongside betrayal, that comfort can come from someone who stole your whole identity before you were even born. But I can't unknow what I know. And now, I'm standing on a stage in front of forty thousand people, reaching for a mother who maybe never existed at all.

Now, I'm cursed. How could I forget to pack the single most important item in the world to me? The universe is making me pay for my epic carelessness, and no doubt an equipment malfunction at the beginning of the biggest show I've ever done is just the beginning of my punishment.

Or maybe this has nothing to do with the box. Maybe I've been cursed since before I took my first breath—the product of an affair, wanted by a father I never knew existed, raised on an origin story that was pure fiction. My whole life I thought I was the girl nobody chose. Turns out I was the girl someone fought for, and my mother said no. What kind of karma does that create? What kind of cosmic debt do you carry when your entire identity was built on a lie someone else told?

Or maybe I should focus on this goddamn concert I'm performing that has earned in the eight digits. *Maybe I should stop ruminating on what could've been and do my fucking job.*

Stupid faulty earpiece, a flesh-colored nub of plastic and wires that's supposed to be my salvation. My fingers twitch with the urge to yank it from my canal, to feel that satisfying *pop* as suction breaks. But it's my last thread to sanity in this chaos—the only way I can hear the music beneath the wall of noise. Without it, my own thoughts would drown in the tsunami of screams, a hundred thousand voices crashing against me from every corner of the stadium, bouncing off steel beams and concrete, until there's nothing left but vibration.

The lights are blinding, the massive white-hot spotlight

circling overhead like a SWAT team. Sweat pours into my eyes, glazing over my thick eyeliner, threatening to make a mockery out of the infallible waterproof makeup that's caked on my face like a double coat of paint. The sting is unbearable; I can only find relief when I clamp my eyes shut to jump an octave and hit the money notes that gave my career a fighting chance against the endless sea of competition. I'm only twenty-three and yet there are about five hundred viable candidates begging my label to replace me, daily—all younger, prettier, blonder, thinner. The only thing I have going for me is my four-octave range, nearly flawless pitch, and a relentless work ethic.

I could do this performance in my sleep. Actually, I have. My home security cameras have caught me during more than one insomnia-induced episode of sleep dancing—a product of being so nervous about first rehearsals with the professional dancers pledging a year of their lives to my tour. They believed in me, but all I saw was my awkward, uncoordinated movement that made *Sesame Street* look like a Broadway production. So I practiced relentlessly. Morning, noon, and night—and apparently also while I slept. After nearly four months of hellish dance training, at minimum six hours a day, I'd say I'm moderately better. Enough to scrape by. Enough to make this world tour happen which is all I've been dreaming about since I could understand what a dream was.

But when I fantasized about my name in lights and the roar of cheers from the crowd, I never imagined this tug-of-war inside me—one moment riding high on the validation I've craved as far back as I can remember, the next drowning in painful fatigue that makes me question if I even want this anymore. I survived the first week of my world tour in Las Vegas, performing at Dad's hotel where his proud smile from the front row both steadied and suffocated me. Those shows felt manageable, almost safe—my family cushioning the feeling of failure.

This week feels different, though. It's only the third show. I have thirty-eight more to go this year, and I'm already losing momentum. Am I too hyper-aware that I'm still singing the same damn songs I wrote when I was seventeen, or does *everyone* imagine how embarrassing this is? The world grew up but I stayed stuck. I haven't written a damn thing worth humming along to in years.

When I'm too tired to form a cognitive thought, muscle memory carries my legs to my marks. Step, step, crossover, step. Pop out my nonexistent ass. God, I hate this move, but the fans go nuts every time. Slow squat, then a sensual lean on my most sturdy backup dancer's shoulder. Eye contact with camera two, the one that feeds the jumbotron. Pause for dramatic effect while my mind screams to just keep moving. Another ass-pop that makes me feel like a trained monkey. Two steps back, away from the crowd I both need and resent.

I've rehearsed this so many times. It should be easy. *This is my job.*

It's only the third song in a two-hour set, and my body is already betraying me, muscles screaming like they've been wrung through a meat grinder. Everything inside me has collapsed—my stomach a barren crater, my thoughts ricocheting off the walls of my skull like stray bullets. The stage beneath me could dissolve into nothing and I'd float away, untethered, into the black rafters. The crowd's screams drill into my brain, each one a physical assault, while the feedback from this broken earpiece feels like someone's jamming an ice pick directly into my eardrum.

I drop the mic again, my fingers trembling as they release the cold metal. "Sound check," I scream this time, my throat burning raw with desperation. But no one reacts—not the sound engineers hidden in shadows, not the dancers gliding around me in perfect formation. The reedy whine drowns everything, even my own voice, until all I can hear is that piercing electronic shriek boring into my skull. Ah, fuck it. I dig my fingernail under the flesh-colored plastic, feeling the suction break with a painful *pop* as I yank out the damn thing. The earpiece flies from my sweaty palm across the polished black stage, skittering under the feet of my backup dancers like a wounded insect. I break free of their synchronized circle, my costume sequins catching harsh light as I rotate my pointer finger in frantic circles, the universal signal to keep going. Their eyes widen but they never miss a beat. We're improvising now.

I take three deep breaths as I catwalk to the edge of the stage.

"How's everybody doing tonight?" I yell into the mic over the band. "New York City! Look at this turnout. Thank you! I love you guys. Best city in the whole dang country."

The words taste like cardboard in my mouth. I just said that in Vegas. I'll say it in LA, Atlanta, Houston, and Orlando too. Part of me hates this script, this pretending that tonight is special when it's all a transient routine—but God, when they scream back, when their faces light up believing I mean it just for them, I need that rush more than my next breath. This industry isn't about making great music like I once thought. It's about being liked and adored while balancing on a pedestal that feels like home one minute and a guillotine the next.

I try to focus on the crowd to stabilize my sensory overload. The front-row audience members are close enough I can sort of make out their faces. They all paid half a year's rent to be eye level with my bedazzled boots marching up and down the stage designed in the shape of a stiletto. *At all costs.* I can't let them down.

It's frigid cold tonight in the outdoor arena. My nude tights are paper-thin even in the twenty-degree weather because we couldn't add any extra inches to my thighs. I have about sixty production cameras on me...*how many pounds does that add?* My leotard, skintight, strapless, with half my ass exposed is doing nothing to keep me warm, the leather fringe feeling like little whips against my near-frozen skin every time I spin around.

I wipe the dripping-cold sweat from under my eyes and take a deep breath to find the music again. It's like untangling Christmas lights, trying to separate the blaring cheers from the melody. *Focus, focus, focus.* But I can't find it.

Fuck, *fuck*. Now I'm panicking.

"I'm so happy, everybody." My voice sounds hollow even

to me, the lie tasting like rubber on my tongue. "Thank you for being here. Thank you for"—I swallow hard, forcing a smile that feels like it might crack my face—"making my dreams come true." *Dreams? Nightmares? Both?* "We're going hard tonight! All your favorites!" The crowd erupts in whoops and screeches while my heart hammers against my ribs like it's trying to escape. *Where the fuck is it? Where is the melody?*

Forty thousand sets of eyes, cameras demanding composure, noise loud enough to drown out an airport runway—this would break any sane person. But after seven years as Charlie Riley, America's sweetheart, voice of a generation...am I even sane anymore?

I feel a large hand on my shoulder and breathe out in relief. Omar, the production manager, dressed in black head to toe, blending in with the darkness of the midnight sky, finds my eyes. He gives me a kind smile as he makes quick work of popping a new earpiece in. He takes a deep breath, instructing me with charades to do the same.

"I got it, I got it," I whisper-shout with my mic pointed at my shoes. I give him an enthusiastic thumbs-up. The moment my earpiece is back in, it's muted bliss. I find the melody, just in time for the chorus, and belt it out like I was born for this very moment.

Midnight kisses, our tongues twisted
We're frozen in a sunset,
Where the sea meets the sky
And all I see is you and I

Oh, no, shit.

The line is all I see is *you in my mind.*

Dammit. It's fine. I was a little disoriented. I catch the chorus on the song title.

It was all perfect, in hindsight.

Shit. Another blunder.

The line should be *it was picturesque in hindsight.*

What is wrong with me tonight? *Hindsight* is my most popular song. My first platinum record. The lyrics every one of my fans has etched into their hearts. Oh, they are never going to let me live this down. The impending social media roasts start flashing in my mind no matter how hard I try to block them.

It's clear she doesn't write her own songs. She can't even remember the lyrics.

All that money and Charlie didn't even sing my favorite song. Such a waste of money.

I'm not sure why I was ever really into her. She's not even that good live.

And that's when the ringing in my ears begins again. This time, more aggressive; a high-pitched drilling craters through my skull, drowning everything else in its metallic trill. My right knee buckles like wet cardboard, sending me stumbling three steps to the left, my ankle rolling outward, barely contained by my knee-high Barbie-blue boots. The spotlight catches my falter in merciless white clarity. Forty thousand faces gasp in unison, their collective "ooooh" rolling toward the stage like a wave, their phones raised higher to capture the precise moment Charlie Riley's performance derails into spectacular, shareable disaster.

It's all right. I can salvage this. You know what? We'll run it again. I'll tell the band we'll run it from the top. *I. Can. Save. This.*

But my lungs seize, each breath coming in tiny gasps that don't reach my chest. My knees wobble and my legs are pasta-soft. The stage seems to tilt five degrees left, then right. My fingers tingle, numb at the tips. The ringing pierces higher, drowning the bass line, the roar of the stadium, until all I hear is that silver needle of sound. The mic slips in my sweat-slick palm. Shit! The choreography...*what comes next*? The lyrics...*what song is this*? The crowd's faces all blur into a single gaping mouth, teeth bared, ready to swallow me whole.

"Fuck!" The word explodes from me like a grenade, thankfully not into the mic, though I can already imagine the slowed-down TikToks dissecting my lips forming that four-letter bomb. Front row, third seat from the left—a girl, maybe eight, wearing my tour shirt, clutching her mother's hand. Her innocent face slams into my conscience. America's sweetheart doesn't curse in front of children. America's sweetheart sings radio edits and smiles through pain and never, ever lets them see the cracks in her perfect plastic veneer.

"I'm so sorry, everybody," I say, pulling the heavy mic to my dry lips. "Bear with me...um...we're just going to try this again..."

I pull out the earpiece again, wanting relief from the alarm assaulting my skull. It's in this moment I realize the ringing isn't coming from my earpiece. I can't escape the sharp, persistent wail breaking through the barrier of my own self-control. *Breathe, Charlie, breathe.* Dark spots cloud my vision like ink splotches blending together to completely blind me. I can't blink them away.

This time when my knees buckle, I can't ground myself. My hips meet the wooden floor so hard the pain reverberates up my spine. I try to get up, but my legs won't listen. Dripping tears find the droplets of sweat and mix together in a cruel cocktail of helpless chaos.

No, no, no. Get fucking up. Finish the damn thing.

And for a minute, I think I've willed my body to move, but it's not of my own fruition. Strong arms scoop me up, and I recognize the smell of Omar's soap. We hugged earlier and I thanked him for everything. He promised me it was going to be a legendary show. One for the history books. His promises were wrapped in sandalwood and amber and just two hours ago I felt like I was on top of the world.

Omar marches down the runway, away from my center mark.

"Put me down," I plead through broken tears and chattering

teeth. "I have to finish the show."

"Charlie, you're ghost white and shaking out of control." He looks down, meeting my eyes. I see panic and fear in his chocolate irises. "It's over. You're done."

"Please...*please*?" But I know he's speaking the truth, because I try to push off of him but none of my limbs are working. I can only feel the chill of the icy night on the side of my cheek, so I press it against his warm chest, surrendering to the harsh reality.

I think of the paper hearts. How before every show, I used to close my eyes, reach into that painted wooden box, and pull one out at random. How her words would wash over me like a blessing, like armor, like proof that even though she was gone, she was still watching. Still believing in me.

I don't know what those hearts mean anymore. Were they love letters or guilt offerings? Encouragement or compensation for the life she stole from me? I've been carrying her voice with me for eighteen years. Now I don't know if I ever really knew her at all.

The armor has cracks in it now. And tonight, I finally fell through.

I failed.

It took seven years, three studio albums, one platinum record, over a hundred shows, and one sold-out stadium to finally break me.

"It's going to be okay, Charlie," Omar says. "We're almost there. The medics are here."

But I know a lie when I hear one. He's doing what everyone does—trying to soothe me with empty promises. Nothing about this is going to be okay. I'm careening off the road at a hundred miles an hour with no brakes and no steering wheel. And there's nothing I can do about it. So I just close my eyes and let the ear-splitting whine become my final melody of the night, hitting that gruesome note with perfect pitch as the curtain falls.

Chapter 2

Taio

Trying to outrun a ghost that lives inside my own bones.

It's been three years since I've been here.

The Marionette's brass handle curls beneath my fingertips, cold and smooth as antique coins. The doorman clears his throat, his charcoal peacoat buttoned to the collar, a cloud of breath hanging between us in the February air. Behind the frosted glass, silhouettes of waiters glide between tables, carrying silver trays held high above their shoulders. A woman's laugh spills out when someone exits—sharp, practiced, like the clink of crystal against crystal.

I check my reflection in the window, smoothing the lapels of my sports coat with sleeves two inches too long. Four years ago, I would've had it tailored for a perfect fit. The new me doesn't give a rat's ass. I have heavier things on my mind than pristine attire that screams, *I don't look at prices on the menu.*

I used to walk through these doors comfortably, like this uppity restaurant was a second home. Mom loved this restaurant. We always started with an artisan charcuterie tray with a warm brie. Every birthday, anniversary, graduation, or celebration dinner was here at the Marionette.

I can't remember ever frowning here. All the memories quilting together as I stroll down memory lane are warm and happy. But that might as well be a different life now.

I'm here on a mission and it's anything but pleasant. I ball up my trembling fist and draw in a deep breath.

It's like a job. Put on your mask. Treat it like any other Friday night.

Except it's not. And I can't.

I push through anyway.

The heat hits me first, then the smell—butter and wine and something floral from the massive arrangement in the foyer. A string quartet plays somewhere in the main dining room, the notes floating over the low murmur of conversation. Everything is exactly as I remember it: the cream-colored walls, the crystal chandeliers casting soft stripes of light, the subtle clink of silver against porcelain.

I make it four steps before the maître d' materializes.

"Good evening, sir." His smile is polished and professional, but his eyes have already conducted a full audit—my shoes, my watch, the cut of my coat. I pass, apparently, because his smile doesn't waver. "Do you have a reservation?"

"I'm meeting someone at the bar."

The smile tightens almost imperceptibly. "I see. And the name on the reservation?"

"I don't have the name. She made it."

Now the smile is glacial. The maître d' shifts his weight, positioning himself between me and the dining room like a bouncer at a club I'm not cool enough to enter. "Perhaps you could describe your party? I'd be happy to check if they've arrived."

Translation: I don't believe you belong here, and I'm two seconds from suggesting you try the burger joint down the block.

Three years ago, I would've given him my father's name and watched him scramble. James Wilkes, table twelve, the usual. Back when "the usual" meant a corner booth and the entire staff knew my dad took his whiskey neat, my mom liked hers on the rocks, and I was the shameless chump who could only take his whiskey sour.

Now I'm just another guy in a nice coat who might be lying

about having plans to sneak into one of Manhattan's most elite and exclusive clubs.

"Taio."

The female voice comes from behind the maître d', and his posture shifts instantly—shoulders dropping, smile warming, the full performance of deference.

"Mrs. Carrington." He practically bows. "My apologies, I didn't realize—"

"He's with me, Gregory."

I watch her approach through the gap in the maître d's defensive stance. Anne Carrington, fifty-three, in a regal navy dress. Her blonde hair is swept up in a twist, though I can see the darker roots at her temples where she's due for a touch-up. She's thinner than I remember. The angles of her face are sharper, the hollows beneath her cheekbones more pronounced.

Three years of stress will do that to a person. *Three years of frantically rebuilding what my father stole.*

"Of course, of course." Gregory—who apparently we're on a first-name basis with now—steps aside with a flourish. "Right this way, Mrs. Carrington. Your table is ready."

Anne reaches me first, and for a moment we just look at each other. Then she does something that catches me off guard—she pulls me into a hug. Brief, but warm and maternal.

"You look too thin," she murmurs near my ear. We both know this is a lie. I lost a lot of weight right after the scandal broke loose, but I'm at least twenty pounds of muscle heavier than when I last saw Mrs. Carrington and her daughters. But it's just the thing people say to convey, *I'm worried about you.*

"You're one to talk."

She laughs, a short exhale that sounds more tired than amused, and loops her arm through mine. We follow Gregory through the dining room, past the tables of power couples and business dinners and old money pretending to be modest. I keep my eyes forward. I don't want to recognize anyone, and I definitely don't want anyone to recognize me.

The table is tucked into a corner, semi-private, with a view of the park through frost-laced windows. I pull out Anne's chair before Gregory can reach for it—old instincts, the ones my mother drilled into me my entire childhood. I would beam when she'd call me her little gentleman. I wore a three-piece suit and pocket square for Halloween when I was six. I was always destined to have a very different life than I ended up having.

"Your server will be right with you," Gregory says, setting leather-bound drink menus in front of us. "Can I start you with some wine? Perhaps the Montrachet you enjoyed last time?"

"Just water for now, thank you." Anne doesn't even glance at the menu.

I wait until Gregory retreats before I speak. "You didn't have to do that."

"Do what?"

"Rescue me from the maître d'. I had it handled."

"You had it handled?" She raises an eyebrow. "Taio, he was about thirty seconds from calling security. You can't just wear a sports coat in here. You need a formal suit jacket. I didn't agree to have lunch with the riffraff today."

"I didn't mean to—" I stop, because her lips are spread and her teeth on display. I realize from her wide smile she's teasing me. It's so familiar that something in my chest twists painfully. After all, half the memories I have at this restaurant include Mrs. Carrington, her husband, and two daughters, one of which I thought I'd spend the rest of my life with.

A server appears with water and a practiced speech about the evening's specials. Anne orders a champagne—Cristal with an orange twist, her go-to for as long as I've known her—and a second one for me before I can object.

"You need to eat something," she says once the server leaves. "Order whatever you want. My treat."

"Thank you, but I'm fine. I ate before I came."

A lie. I gulped down a chalky protein drink four hours ago but that's it. My stomach is rolling at the smell of warm French bread and honey butter. My mouth waters remembering how juicy and flavorful the ribeyes are here, but there's no way I can order anything on this menu on Mrs. Carrington's dime. I promised I'd pay her back, not take even more from her and her family.

"Taio." Her voice softens. "Please."

"I didn't come here to eat, Mrs. Carrington."

She sighs, but she doesn't push. That's one of the things I always appreciated about Anne—she knows when to let something go. Unlike her husband, who holds grudges like family heirlooms. I invited both Mr. and Mrs. Carrington to this lunch. Only one of them showed. Mrs. Carrington didn't even bother to offer an excuse. We both know the truth. I remind Richard of my dad, so he's going to hate me until his dying breath, maybe beyond.

We sit in silence for a moment, the string quartet filling the space between us with something melancholy and classical. I study the tablecloth, the weave of the linen, the small imperfection near the corner where a thread has come loose.

"How have you been?" Anne asks finally. "And don't say 'fine.' I want a real answer."

"Busy."

"With?"

I make an honest mental list. *Escorting. Screwing strangers for money...a lot of them around your age. Visiting my father in prison. Missing my mother. Trying not to drown in the disappointment of my life.*

"Work," I say. "Staying busy."

She watches me for a long moment, her gaze shrewd. Anne Carrington is a lot of things, easily fooled is not one of them. She knows I'm not telling her something, and she knows I know she knows.

But she lets it go.

"How's your father?"

And there it is. The shift I've been bracing for. The temperature at the table drops ten degrees, even though nothing visible has changed.

"He's...the same. Taking classes. Reading a lot." I reach into my coat, fingers brushing the envelope I've been carrying against my chest like a secret. "Actually, that's why I wanted to meet."

I pull out the envelope and slide it across the table. It's thick—not as thick as I'd like, but thick enough. Five thousand dollars in hundreds, rubber-banded into a neat brick. I straighten my shoulders and add, "That's all I have right now after Dad's legal fees. It's rightfully yours."

Anne looks at the envelope but doesn't touch it. "Taio..."

"I know it's not much. Especially compared to what he took." I have to force the words out past the knot in my throat. "But it's a start. There's more coming. I just need a little time."

"Sweetheart." She reaches across the table and covers my hand with hers. Her skin is cool, her rings catching the candlelight. "Where is this coming from?"

"It doesn't matter."

"It matters to me."

I pull my hand back gently, wrapping it around my water glass just for something to hold on to. "I've never lied to you, Mrs. Carrington. Not in the twenty years you've known me." I meet her eyes. "I don't want to start lying to you now. So please don't ask me where the money comes from."

Something flickers across her face—concern, maybe, or pity. I hate both options.

"Are you safe?" she asks quietly.

"Yes."

"Are you doing anything that could get you hurt? Or arrested?"

Define hurt. "No, ma'am. Nothing illegal."

Well, *technically,* not illegal. I'm legitimately employed through Rina's very legal business. What we do off the books is borderline...questionable, but once I've paid back every penny Dad owes and get him out of prison, then I'll properly admonish myself for my gigolo behavior. Until then, the hustle lives.

Anne holds my gaze for a long moment, searching for the

lie. I keep my face neutral, my breathing even. I've gotten good at this—the performance of calm when everything inside me is screaming.

Finally, she nods. "Okay."

That's it. No interrogation, no lecture, no demands for details. Just *okay.* I don't know if that makes me feel better or worse.

The server returns with our champagne—two crystal flutes, each with a perfect spiral of orange peel curled against the side. Anne murmurs her thanks, waits for him to leave, and takes a slow sip.

"I spoke to your mother a few days ago," she says.

The champagne I just swallowed turns to thick sludge in my stomach. "Oh?"

"She called to wish Joy a happy birthday. They talked for almost an hour." Anne traces the rim of her glass with one finger. "She asked about you."

"Oh? And what did you say?"

"I asked her why she was asking me how her son was doing." Anne presses her lips together, and in a very un-Mrs. Carrington-like fashion, plants one elbow on the table. "Why aren't you speaking to your mom?"

I shrug. "I'm not...not speaking to her. I just happen to be busy every time she calls." I fight the urge to roll my eyes at my lame excuse. I'm busy. My phone is never charged. My service is crap. The time difference. I was at the gym. The endless excuses worked for about the first three months after Mom moved away. By now she knows what I'm full of.

"Well, I told her you invited me to this lunch." She pauses and raises one eyebrow for dramatic effect. "I promised my best friend that when I saw her only, beloved son, I'd ensure he'd call. Don't make a liar out of me, Taio."

"Yes, ma'am. I'll call her." *Ah, dammit.* My first ever lie to Mrs. Carrington. "I'm glad you two were able to stay friends."

"Naomi had no idea what your dad was up to, Taio. Neither did you. We don't hold either of you at fault."

The corner of my lip twitches, maybe a warning that I shouldn't open up this can of worms, but before I know it, the words are out. "Then why isn't Mr. Carrington here?"

She takes an exaggerated sip from her champagne. "Because Richard is a dimwit who struggles to separate the sin from the sinner. He sees what was lost, he's not thinking about who stole it."

"He's not alone. I think that's the majority's opinion." I take a long drink of champagne, letting the bubbles burn my throat. "My mom wanted me to come with her. Start over in Tokyo like the last twenty-seven years of my life didn't happen. But I couldn't just abandon my dad when he needed me most."

"And staying here, cleaning up his mess—that's better?"

"He's my dad."

It sounds pathetic even to my own ears. A child's argument. *He's my dad.* As if that explains anything. As if that justifies the choices I've made, the things I've done, the person I've become.

Anne is quiet for a moment. Then: "You know I love you, Taio. I've known you since you were six years old, following Alaina around like a puppy, trying so hard to impress her father." A sad smile crosses her face. "You were so nervous the first time you told me and Richard that you and Alaina had decided to go steady. I mean, I couldn't believe how time flew. You went from wetting the bed at my house so many times to dating my teenage daughter in the blink of an eye."

"I mean I don't think it was *that* many times," I mutter, a little embarrassed for six-year-old Taio.

"What your father did was unfathomable. He stole from us, from everyone who trusted him. Richard will never forgive him—you know that. But I don't blame you. I never have." She leans forward slightly. "And I don't want to see you waste your life trying to atone for his mistakes."

I don't have an answer for that, so I change the subject. "How's Joy?"

Anne's expression shifts—still soft, but with an undercurrent of something heavier. Worry, maybe. "She's...sixteen. You know how that goes. Moody and dramatic. Convinced that no one in the history of the world has ever suffered as much as she has."

"Charming." I smirk.

"Indeed." Anne takes another sip of champagne. "Although, she did have quite a night a few weeks ago. I took her to that concert—you know, the pop star she's been obsessed with? Charlie Riley?"

The name rings a vague bell. Blonde, I think. Young. One of those ubiquitous faces that shows up on magazine covers at the grocery store. "What about it?"

"Well, the poor thing collapsed on stage. Right in the middle of her set. She just went down like a robot powering off. They had to cancel the whole show."

"Geez."

"We paid a fortune for those VIP tickets, right up against the front barrier. Charlie could've sweat on us that close." Anne shakes her head. "Joy said she didn't care and claims she was '*so over*' Charlie Riley anyway. You know how teenagers are. But I know she was devastated. We'd been saving for months."

The guilt twists deeper. Three years ago, Anne wouldn't have thought twice about VIP concert tickets. Three years ago, I could've bought them myself without checking my bank account.

"I'm sorry that happened. Is there another city you could see the show in?"

Anne's hair, glued down by hairspray, doesn't budge as she shakes her head, almost violently. "From what I understand, the entire tour is canceled until further notice. Such a waste. And it was the last thing she needed after getting her Stanford letter."

My eyebrows shoot up. "Stanford? She already applied?" Joy and I always got along great. I treated her like a little sister because that's what she was always supposed to be. Going to Stanford was her absolute dream.

"She got her early admission letter last month."

"That's amazing. Go Joy! But why don't you seem more excited?"

"We were." Anne's smile doesn't reach her eyes. "For about three days. Until we sat down and really looked at the numbers."

I already know where this is going. I can feel it coming like a train in the distance—the low rumble before the impact.

"Out-of-state tuition," Anne says quietly. "Room and board. Books, travel, living expenses. We're looking at almost a hundred thousand dollars for the first year alone. We're maxed out on loans, and with the savings gone..." She lets the silence finish the sentence.

With the savings gone. Because my father stole it.

"I'm out of retirement," she continues. "Did I tell you that? I'm back at the firm three days a week, trying to rebuild what we lost faster. But at our age, and with Richard's health..." She stops, composes herself. "Right now, we just don't have anything to spare. Joy is looking at scholarship opportunities at an in-state school. It'll be okay."

I feel sick. Physically, genuinely sick like I might have to excuse myself and find a bathroom.

"How long do you have?" My voice sounds strange. Deeper and sharp, like I'm trying to close a business deal. "If she accepts admission, when is the first payment due?"

"Fall. August, technically, but there are deposits before that. She'll lose her spot in April."

"Tell her to accept."

Anne blinks. "I'm sorry?"

"Tell Joy to accept. I'll get the money."

"Taio—"

"I mean it. The hundred thousand, the full year—I'll get it." I'm talking too fast, making promises I have no idea how to keep, but I can't stop. "Just tell her to accept. I'll figure it out."

Anne stares at me like I've lost my mind. Maybe I have.

"Sweetheart." Her voice is gentle, careful, the way you'd talk to someone standing on a ledge. "That's very kind, but...do you have any idea what you're saying? A hundred thousand dollars by fall? On top of everything else you're trying to do?"

“I’ll find a way.”

“How? And please don’t tell me it’s from this mystery job you won’t explain.” She gestures at the envelope still sitting between us. “You just handed me five thousand dollars like it was nothing. That’s not nothing, Taio. That’s months of work for most people. What are you doing?”

“I told you, I can’t—”

“I’m asking because I’m worried about you.” Her voice cracks slightly. “Do you understand that? I’m not angry, I’m not judging you, I’m *worried*. You look exhausted. You’re sitting here promising me a hundred thousand dollars like you’re going to pull it out of thin air, and I don’t—” She presses her fingers to her lips for a moment. “I don’t want you to sacrifice yourself for us. That’s not what I want. That’s not what anyone wants.”

I don’t know what to say. The champagne has gone flat in my glass. The string quartet has shifted to something so soft, it’s almost mournful.

“Is this what you’re going to do with your life?” Anne asks, and there’s no judgment in her tone, only sadness. “Spend it trying to fix your father’s mistakes? Because I have to tell you, sweetheart—what he took from people, it’s in the millions. Tens of millions. You could work yourself to death and never make a dent.”

“I know I can’t pay everyone back.” My voice is rougher than I intend. “But I’m starting with you. The people who mattered most. The people who were our friends.”

“And then what? What happens when you’ve ruined your health, your future, your chance at a real life—and there’s still more debt to pay?” The way she keeps bringing up my health, I know Anne thinks I’m running drugs. I wonder, if I told her I’m an escort, if that’s better or worse than what she’s imagining.

“I don’t know.” I stare at the table. “I’m just trying to take it piece by piece. That’s all I can do.”

Anne is quiet for a long moment. When she speaks again, her voice is different. Softer. She holds my gaze, bracing me for something.

"Alaina is engaged."

The words hit me like a rogue homerun ball straight to the chest. I feel my face freeze, while my whole body goes rigid as I process what she just said. Engaged. Alaina. *My Alaina.* Except she's not mine, and hasn't been for three years.

"Congratulations." It comes out mechanical. "To the whole family. That's...that's great news."

"Taio."

"Who's the guy?"

"His name is Bradley. He works in tech—something with apps, I don't fully understand it. He's nice. Stable." Anne hesitates. "Safe."

Safe. Unlike me. Unlike the son of a thief.

"That's good." I force my mouth into something resembling a smile. "That's really good. She deserves to be happy. The Plaza, right?"

The Plaza. I remember Alaina talking about it on our third date—how she'd walked past it as a kid and decided right then that's where she'd get married someday. I'd filed it away, the way you do when you're young and in love and convinced you'll be the one standing next to her at that altar.

"We haven't gotten that far," Anne continues quietly. "We're still waiting for the dust to settle... Money and such."

"She could get married in a parking lot and still be the most stunning bride anyone's ever seen," I say.

Anne reaches across the table and takes my hand again. This time I don't pull away.

"I didn't tell you to hurt you," she says. "I told you because I don't want you to think...I don't want you to carry some hope that if you just pay back enough money, if you just fix enough of what your father broke, she'll come back. She's moved on, Taio. And you need to, too."

I nod, not trusting my voice.

"Can I tell you something? Off the record—not as Alaina's mother, but as your friend?"

"Sure."

Anne squeezes my hand. "Real love stands through the fire. It doesn't run when things get hard. It doesn't leave when the money disappears and the name gets tarnished." Her eyes are shining now, bright with unshed tears. "You deserve someone who will stand next to you through anything. Not someone who flees when things get uncomfortable."

"Like my mom did."

The words hang in the air between us. Anne doesn't answer. She doesn't have to.

I pull my hand back slowly, reaching for my champagne, buying time to collect myself. The liquid is warm now, the bubbles long since dissipated, but I drink it anyway because I need to soothe my dry throat.

"Three years ago," I hear myself say, "I had a ring for her."

Anne's eyes widen, then narrow, her face caught between shock and something harder to read—pity, perhaps, or regret. Her fingers tighten around her glass. "You're kidding."

"No. I made a reservation at this restaurant. This exact one. I was going to bring you and Mr. Carrington here, ask for your permission, do the whole thing properly. The way she deserved." I gesture vaguely at the room around us. "I was going to sit right here and promise you I'd take care of her forever."

"Taio..."

"Dad got arrested four days after I made the reservation. I canceled it from the police station while I was waiting for him to be processed." I laugh, but there's no humor in it. "Kind of forgot about it until just now, honestly. Being back here."

Anne doesn't say anything. She just looks at me with those sad, knowing eyes, and I wonder if she's seeing me as I am now or as I was then—the kid who showed up at her door with flowers, treated their daughter like a princess, always so desperate to prove he was worthy.

That kid feels like a stranger now.

The server approaches, larger dinner menus in hand, and

Anne waves him off with a small shake of her head. But she flags him back a moment later.

"Two more champagnes, please. With the orange twist." She looks at me. "We're going to have a proper toast."

"I should probably go—"

"Taio Wilkes, you are not leaving this restaurant until you have another round with me. You evade everyone we know, including your mother. You won't tell us where you live, where you work. You won't let anyone help you. You're a ghost. So if all you're offering is a drink every couple of years, the least you can do is make it two."

I don't have the energy to argue. And part of me—the part that remembers what it felt like to belong somewhere, to be part of a family, to sit at tables like this with people who loved me—doesn't want to leave.

The champagne arrives, fresh and cold, the bubbles rising in delicate streams. Anne lifts her glass and waits for me to do the same.

"What should we toast to?" I ask.

She tilts her head, considering. I already know what I want to say. The words are sitting on my tongue like a bruise.

"To what could've been," I offer, raising my glass to the woman who should be my mother-in-law.

Anne holds my gaze for a long moment. Then she lifts her own glass a fraction higher. "To what *should've* been."

We drink, then say our goodbyes. I hug Mrs. Carrington tightly and make promises I don't know if I can keep: *Yes, I'll call my mom. Yes, I'll call if I need anything. Yes, I'll call before another two years go by.*

I have to all but run from the table to prevent myself from suffocating inside all the memories of the life I used to know. The one sometimes I still want.

The cold hits me like a wall the moment I step outside.

February in New York is the kind of cold that finds every gap in your coat, every inch of exposed skin, and punishes you for daring to venture outdoors. My breath fogs in front of my face as I stand on the sidewalk, trying to remember which direction leads home fastest.

The champagne is warm in my stomach, but it does nothing to touch the ice spreading through my chest. *Engaged. She's engaged.* The words keep circling, vultures over roadkill.

A hundred thousand dollars by fall.

Real love stands through the fire.

Like my mom did.

I shove my hands in my pockets and start walking, no destination in mind. Just movement. The city blurs around me—headlights, storefronts, people rushing past with their collars turned up against the wind. Everyone going somewhere. Everyone with somewhere to be.

I stop at a crosswalk and pull out my phone.

The screen is too bright in the sudden darkness, the sun plummeting into the southern half of the skyline making five o'clock the new midnight in a brutal New York winter. I squint at it, thumbs hovering over the keyboard, and type out a message to my boss, Rina.

I need more work ASAP...

I delete the message before sending it because she'll have questions and I don't have the energy to explain why I just promised a hundred thousand dollars to pay for a concert I never saw and a college I'll never attend. All for a girl who I'll never get back.

I pocket my phone and keep walking.

The wind picks up, sharp enough to make my eyes water. I tell myself that's why I'm blinking so much. That's why my vision is blurry, why my throat feels thick, why my chest aches like someone's sitting on it.

Just the cold.

Just the wind.

Just another night in a city full of strangers, walking toward nothing in particular, trying to outrun a ghost that lives inside my own bones.

Chapter 3
Charlie

I can't tell if this is a happy or sad song.

The penthouse bed sprawls before me like a pristine white desert, king-sized multiplied by two, with its crisp Egyptian cotton sheets stretched taut over a mattress that barely registers my weight. Six people could lie star-shaped across it without touching fingers, which only amplifies the empty feeling in my chest as I sit here, a solitary island in an ocean of too much space.

I'm sitting cross-legged in the center of it, still in the overly fluffy hotel robe I put on two days ago, my phone lying on the duvet in front of me like a grenade with the pin pulled. The heavy blackout curtains are drawn tight against the Manhattan skyline, sealing out even the thinnest ribbon of light. Beyond that fabric barrier lies a sixty-story drop, glass-walled skyscrapers catching the sun like massive mirrors, and eight million people going about their day. It's a breathtaking view all the way up here in the stratosphere of wealth, but I've been in this hotel for two weeks. Stalled. Unwilling to look at the city that watched me crumble under the spotlight, forty thousand phone cameras capturing every second of my public unraveling.

"...and honestly, Charlie, the response has been better than we expected."

Sage's voice floats up from the speakerphone, calm and measured. That's what I pay her for—to be the steady hand when everything else is chaos. She's been my publicist since I was nineteen, and she's never once raised her voice at me, even when I've given her plenty of reasons to.

"The usual trolls are out of course," she continues, "but the overall tone is concern. People are worried about you. That's not a bad thing. It humanizes you."

"Great." My fingers find a thread escaping from the duvet's edge, and I pinch it between thumb and forefinger, working it back into the fabric like I'm trying to erase evidence of imperfection. "Glad my public breakdown is good for my brand."

"That's not what I—"

"I know." I close my eyes. "I'm sorry. I didn't mean it like that."

Marcus interrupts, his voice sandpaper-rough from what I'm sure has been a marathon of damage-control calls since my meltdown. "The label's been breathing down my neck, Charlie. I hate to ask, but I need to give them something right now. A timeline, a statement, something...*anything*. What do you want to do?"

"Marcus," Sage scolds. "We called to check on her, not to talk shop."

"Well, shop is my job," he snaps back, exhaustion sullying his mood. "You take care of her, and I take care of her bank account."

"I want to refund everyone," I cut in before their bickering escalates.

Silence on the line.

"Everyone who was at the first New York show," I clarify, even though I know they understood me the first time. "They paid to see a concert. They didn't get one. I want to give them their money back."

Marcus sighs—a long, exhausted exhale that tells me exactly how this conversation is going to go. "Charlie, that would bankrupt the tour. We've already canceled two more shows while you're recovering."

"I don't care."

"You should care," he grumbles. "We're talking about millions of dollars. Tens of millions actually. These are sold-out stadiums. The venue fees alone—"

"Those people saved up for months to see me. Some of them probably couldn't afford it in the first place."

I picture the faces in the crowd, the ones who worked double shifts just to afford nosebleed seats. The college kids who chose my show over textbooks. The parents who surprised their daughters with birthday tickets. And what did they get? Me, crumpling to the floor mid-chorus, leaving a packed stadium in stunned silence.

"And they saw you," Marcus adds. "After you left, they streamed the Vegas performance. Most of the crowd stayed. Everyone got a free drink ticket."

"That's not good enough. How is that fair? They deserve—"

"Charlie. They knew the risk when they bought the tickets." His voice has shifted into business mode, the one that makes me feel like a product instead of a person. "There's a clause in every purchase agreement. No refunds, no exceptions. It protects us from exactly this kind of situation."

"It doesn't feel right."

"It doesn't have to feel right. It has to keep the tour alive."

My mouth opens to protest, but the words die somewhere between my brain and my lips. Something hot and tight builds in my throat, and I press my fingernails into my palms until they leave half-moon indentations.

"Cancel it," I say quietly. "I'm done."

"Cancel what?" Marcus asks, his tone sharpening.

"The tour. All of the shows. I don't want to postpone. I want to cancel." I take a breath. "I need some time, Marcus. To focus on my mental health. To figure out what's going on with me lately. I can't just—"

"Charlie," he says, gentler now, which is somehow worse. "I had a call with the label this morning. A long one."

I wait.

"This tour is the only thing keeping you relevant right now.

Album sales are down. Streaming numbers are flat. The label invested heavily in this tour because they believe it's the path back to the top." He pauses. "If you pull out, they're done."

"Done?"

"Done investing in you. Done promoting you. Done, period." Another pause. "They'll drop you, Charlie." His voice catches, and I hear him take a breath. "Look, I hate even saying this. I don't want to be the one who—" He stops. Starts again. "The label sees you as...replaceable. God, that sounds awful. But they think it's easier to manufacture some TikTok nobody than resurrect a has-been. Especially one that's...struggling. I'm on your side here, I swear. I fought for you in that room. But I promised I'd always shoot straight with you, right? Even when it kills me to do it? This is the reality. If you walk away from this tour, you walk away from all of it."

I press my palm flat against the duvet, grounding myself in the texture, the coolness of the fabric. Perhaps I should be crying, but my tear ducts have officially gone on strike—probably unionized while I was sleeping. Good for them.

"Okay," I hear myself say. It's strange—"okay" wasn't the response in my mind. Somewhere between my brain and my vocal cords, *fuck this* turned into *okay*. "*Okay*," I repeat, just to hear how it sounds. "I'll figure it out. Tell them I'll be ready for Boston next week."

"Are you sure?" Sage's sweet voice massages the silence. "Canceling Boston won't break the tour. We can get you another couple weeks—"

"I'm sure." I drag the back of my hand across dry cheeks. "I'm fine. Really. I'll be ready. Just make sure we get an extra rehearsal in beforehand, okay? I want everyone there—dancers, singers, the whole crew. We'll run it until my feet bleed."

I meant it as a joke, but it wouldn't be the first time I've left bloodstains inside those rhinestone-crusted boots.

We say our goodbyes. Sage tells me to stay off social media, and promises to handle the press. Marcus ensures me he'll go back to the label and shove my comeback down their throats so hard they'll choke on all my success. Then the line goes dead and I'm alone again in this enormous bed in this enormous room in this city that suddenly feels like a cage.

The thought of stepping back on stage makes my stomach twist into knots that would impress an Eagle Scout, but what choice do I have? The show must go on, as they say. Even when the performer has nothing left.

I think about calling Claire.

My phone is right there, her contact just a few taps away, and I know she'd answer. She always answers, even now, even when she's supposed to be on strict bed rest with a pregnancy that her doctors keep calling "high risk" in voices that make everyone around her nervous.

But that's exactly why I can't call.

Claire is in bed because she's growing a human being. She's creating life, nurturing it, protecting it with every breath she takes. Her stillness has purpose. Her rest has meaning.

I'm in bed because as much as I want to fix myself, I don't understand what broke. It wasn't the letter. No, I was broken long before that secret reared its ugly head. That particular truth might've been the final nail in the coffin, though.

But I don't want to start a conversation I know I can't finish. So I don't call Claire. Instead, I pick up my phone and open my text thread with Grayson.

The last message is from two weeks ago, right after the collapse. A single line from him: *Heard what happened. That sucks.*

That sucks. Two words. No follow-up, no check-in, no "are you okay" or "do you need anything." Just *that sucks*, like I'd told him I got a parking ticket instead of having an epic breakdown during a live performance.

I stare at the screen, thumbs hovering, trying to figure out what I even want to say. What I want from him. What I ever wanted from him in the first place.

Three months ago, I thought I liked him. We met at a party

in LA I didn't want to go to—some industry thing where everyone was trying too hard to look like they weren't trying. I liked his laugh. It was a raspy bark, probably the consequence of thousands of bong hits. But it sounded so unpracticed. So un-charming and I liked that because it felt real.

We went on three dates. Dinners at places with waiting lists, walks on beaches closed to the public, the kind of performative romance that looks perfect in paparazzi photos. The conversations were short and empty. His eyes were on his phone more than on me, even when I wore my sexiest little black dress. He's no Price Charming, but I'm twenty-three. There's no time like the present to settle.

I almost spread my legs for him and offered up my most sacred secret. Thank God I surprised him that night at his place and interrupted him in bed with another woman. She was one of at least three in his rotation. It woke me up to reality.

I never gave him grief about it. What was the point? We weren't official. We hadn't made any promises. And honestly, part of me was relieved because what if I'd gone through with it? What if everything I'd been waiting for, everything my mom told me to wait for was...*this*? A constantly baked, self-important dimwit of a man who thinks the phrase "that sucks" is empathy.

No. The grass has to be greener somewhere else. Disney and Hallmark have to be pulling story ideas from some sort of real experience, right?

Grayson and I should've had a clean break but then the photos surfaced. *Grayson and Charlie, America's hottest new couple.* It was overinflated celebrity gossip nonsense, but suddenly my ticket sales exploded. People who hadn't thought about me in years were buying albums, streaming songs, following my every move. It helped his career too—gave him a softer image, made him seem like boyfriend material instead of the Hollywood dickwad everyone suspected he was...because he is.

I made a deal with the devil. Or Sage did, anyway. Our oh-so-loving relationship is mapped up in a stack of paperwork as thick as my fist. A PR relationship, carefully staged and managed, lasting until the end of my world tour. We'd be seen together at events, post the occasional Instagram story, sell the fantasy of Barbie and Ken to a world desperate to believe in something perfect and beautiful.

It was a savvy business move, and I figured fake-loved would feel better than being real-alone.

Now I'm not so sure.

Hey. How's the press tour going?

I watch the three dots appear almost immediately. At least he's responsive when it's convenient for him.

Grayson

Crazy busy. Back-to-back interviews all day. Did a late-night appearance last night. You see it?

No, I'm sorry. I was asleep. How did it go?

Grayson

Killed it. Had 'em eating out of the palm of my hand. The host asked about you actually. Played the concerned boyfriend card. You're welcome.

Thanks.

Grayson

No prob. Hey I gotta run, car's here.
Talk later?

Sure.

He doesn't ask how I'm doing. Doesn't mention the collapse, the canceled shows, the fact that I'm alone in a hotel room trying not to drown. Just *talk later*, which we both know means *talk never unless the cameras are watching.*

I set the phone down and stare at the ceiling.

Maybe this is why I feel so hollow. I've been living my life through old memories of love—my mother's paper hearts, the fantasy of what Grayson could have been—instead of making new ones. I'm a full-fledged adult and I've never really been loved. Not romantically. Not in a way that felt real and present and *mine.*

I'm starting to wonder if I ever will be.

When my phone rings again, I almost don't answer. But then I see the name on the screen—*Dad*—and something in my chest loosens just a little.

"Hey, sweetheart." Nate's voice is warm, familiar, the auditory equivalent of a warm hug. "How are you holding up?"

"I'm okay." The lie comes automatically. "Just resting."

"Mmm." He doesn't sound convinced. "Spencer called me this morning. She wanted to fly out, but I told her to wait until you asked. Didn't want to overwhelm you."

"Thank you." I mean it. I love my big sister, but the thought of her hovering right now, watching me with those worried eyes, makes me want to crawl under the covers and never come out.

"She FaceTimed me this morning. The boys made you a card," Dad continues. "Eli drew what I think is supposed to be you on stage, but it looks more like a yellow octopus. Remy scribbled blue in the corner because he knows it's your favorite color. He said it's asshat art, but I think he meant abstract art."

Wrong. My favorite color is orange. But I laugh—a real laugh, the first one in days. "Tell them you showed me and that I love it."

"I'll do better than that. I'll bring it when I see you."

"Looking forward to it." The momentary reprieve of talking to one of my favorite people in the world dissipates and the heavy sullenness returns.

He lets the silence breathe, waiting for me to offer something, but when I don't he continues. "I'm calling with good news, by the way."

"Oh yeah?" God, he better not bring up the stock market. No one cares when a billionaire gets even richer.

I can hear the smile in his voice. "We found your box, Charlie."

I gasp like the message hit me with a physical force. I sit up straighter, my heart pounding deliciously hard. "What?"

"You left it in the dressing room in Vegas. First night of the tour. You must've forgot to pack it back up."

Oh. Of course. I was so tired after that set I could barely stand. I grabbed my phone and nothing else.

"Who found it?" I ask, not that I really care. It's found. That's all that matters.

"Housekeeping, I believe. When they did the deep clean of the dressing room. They didn't know what it was but they had the good sense to call my assistant. It's already on the way to you. It'll be there tonight. I wanted to surprise you but—"

"You suck at surprises." I smile so big that my cheeks ache. I've been Nate's daughter since I was eleven years old. Never once did I get a gift from Dad on my actual birthday. Always a few days early when he was bursting at the seams. He was way too excited to hand me the world.

"Yeah, well. I wanted to cheer you up, kid. You have me worried."

"Dad..." My voice cracks. The salty-tear reservoirs have now replenished. But the fat droplets racing down my cheeks are from relief, pure and overwhelming. "I thought it was gone. I thought

I'd lost her forever."

"Charlie, your mom is in your heart. Not just scribbled across notes. You'll never lose her."

I know he gets it. Maybe it's why we bonded so fast. Nate has trauma too from losing the most important person in his life. He understands what it means to have his heart turn cold. But he found a reason to come back alive—my sister, Spencer.

Where's my reason? Who's coming to save me?

I feel guilty asking these questions. I'm loved, so why don't I feel it? I'm successful, but why doesn't success feel powerful? I'm talking to my dad, but how come...the title feels a little different now? I feel the guilt twist in my stomach like a knife because Nate is the best father I could have ever prayed for. He chose me. He raised me. He loved me without condition or hesitation.

He was the only dad I knew until three months ago when I found out he wasn't the only father who wanted me. Who loved me.

Now Nate shares the title "Dad" with a man named Liam who begged my mother to let him be part of my life. And she refused.

I think about the contents of that box. All those little love notes, all that encouragement and warmth. Written by a woman who looked me in the eyes my entire childhood and lied about where I came from.

"Charlie? You still there?"

"Yeah." I wipe my face, pulling myself together. "Sorry. I'm just...thank you, Dad. Thank you so much."

"I'm having it couriered, should arrive in a few hours. I wanted to check on you and bring it myself, but I'm still in Singapore with your grandfather—this development deal is taking longer than expected."

"It's okay. I understand."

"I'll be back by next week. Maybe in time for your next show? Do you want me there?"

"Of course I do," I breathe out. "Right by me in the tents."

"You got it, sweetheart. I'll be there."

We talk for a few more minutes—about the deal, about the boys, about Spencer's new obsession with some true-crime show, and our shared annoyance that Claire made us wait so long to find out the gender of the baby. By the time we hang up, I feel almost human again. *Almost.*

I call down to the front desk.

"Hi, this is Charlie Riley in the penthouse. I'm expecting a messenger tonight with a package for me. It's extremely important. Can you please send them straight up when they arrive? I don't want it sitting at the desk or getting misplaced."

"Of course, Ms. Riley. My shift is over in an hour but I'll leave a note for my team. We'll send them right up. Can we send up any refreshments or perhaps dinner for you? The steakhouse has a lovely filet on special tonight."

"No, thank you. But I appreciate it."

"Okay, well, please let us know if you change your mind. If there's nothing here you'd like to eat, we'll send someone out to retrieve whatever you please."

After thanking her once more, I hang up and take a breath.

The box is coming. Mom's voice is coming. And maybe—just maybe—I can figure out how to hold both truths at once. The love and the lie. The comfort and the betrayal.

Maybe I don't have to choose.

Needing to stretch my legs, I venture to the living room. The grand piano sits in the corner, gleaming black beneath the soft overhead lights. It's a Steinway—of course it is; Dad's hotels don't do anything halfway—and I've been staring at it for weeks now, working up the courage to sit down.

I haven't played since before the collapse. Haven't sung, either, except in my head, where the lyrics loop endlessly like a song stuck on repeat.

But my fingers are itching. And the silence in this room is becoming an unbearable weight on my chest.

So I walk over. I sit down. I lift the fallboard and rest my hands on the keys, feeling the cool ivory beneath my fingertips.

And I play.

I don't feel like playing one of my songs. Instead, I sing a cover I've loved for years. "Stay," performed by Rihanna and Mikky Ekko. I can't tell if this is a happy or sad song. All I know is there's something raw and aching, about holding on and needing someone and wanting to be saved by something bigger than yourself. This is the kind of song that makes you feel like the artist reached into your chest and pulled out something you didn't know was there.

My voice comes out husky and rough, wrecked from rehearsals, performances, crying, and dehydration. But my fingers don't falter. They know this song by heart. They move across the keys with a fluency that feels almost separate from me, like my body remembers how to do this even when my mind has forgotten why.

The tears return somewhere around the second verse. They slide down my cheeks and drip onto my hands, onto the keys, and I don't stop. I keep playing, keep singing, keep pouring out someone else's heartbreak because I don't know how to access my own.

That's the thing, isn't it? This song was written from something real. Raw emotion, lived experience, the kind of pain that leaves scars. The artist who wrote it knew what it felt like to need someone so badly it hollowed you out. To be the broken one. To need rescuing.

I've never felt that.

I've been sheltered my whole life—first by my mother's illness, then by Spencer's fierce protection, Dad's money, then the bubble of pop stardom that keeps me safe and suffocated in equal measure. I've never been in love. Never had my heart broken. Never experienced the kind of devastating, soul-deep emotion that births songs like this one.

I'm a doll. Perfect on the outside, hollow on the inside. I can perform other people's feelings flawlessly, but I've never really been alive.

The song ends, and I sit there with my hands on the keys, the final notes still hanging in the air.

I love singing. I've always loved singing. But playing in private rooms was never enough for me. I wanted to be seen. I wanted to stand on stages and feel the roar of the crowd and know that I mattered, that my voice meant something, that I wasn't invisible.

I got exactly what I wanted.

And I've never felt more alone in my life.

But I can't stand the silence, so I draw in a deep breath, and start from the top. I play it again, and again. And one more time.

Until the music drowns out the blaring nothingness in my mind.

Chapter 4

Taio

The grace of a panther and the entitlement of a trust-fund baby.

Living alone is mostly hell, but there's a certain freedom in heating up a Hungry-Man at four p.m. while still wearing yesterday's sweatpants, with no witnesses to your decline except the walls.

Well. Almost no witnesses.

Black Cat sits on the kitchen counter—a place he knows he's not supposed to be because his furry ass is not welcome where I prepare my food. I'd scold him but nothing works. He likes water sprayed in his face. Shaking a penny can just riles him up. And he thinks "Bad Cat" is a compliment. I feel his glowing yellow-green eyes transfixed on me as I peel back the plastic film on my Salisbury steak to vent my frozen meal before nuking it in the microwave. I glance up to see him staring with the intensity of a food critic at a Michelin-starred restaurant. He tracks every movement of my hands, whiskers twitching in what I can only describe as disappointment.

"Don't judge me," I tell him. "You eat right out of a can."

He blinks slowly. Judgment rendered.

I found Black Cat four months ago, yowling in the alley behind my building like someone was murdering him with a rusty spoon. He used to be scrawny, matted, feral as hell—the kind of cat that would sooner claw your eyes out than accept a belly rub. I made the mistake of leaving a bowl of tuna on my fire escape, thinking I was doing a good deed for a wild creature who'd move on by morning.

He did not move on.

He moved in.

I refuse to name him because naming him would mean admitting he's mine, and I'm still clinging to the delusion that he's a free spirit who chose to crash at my place temporarily. Any day now, he'll remember he's a wild animal with places to be and disappear into the urban jungle from whence he came.

Any day now.

The name "Black Cat" was supposed to be a declaration of my apathy. He's not my pet, just a passing stray. Except it stuck like gum to a shoe. Now when I say it, his ears do that radar-dish swivel thing, and he makes this chirpy half meow that sounds suspiciously like he's correcting my pronunciation. So much for maintaining emotional distance.

The microwave whirls to life, and I shuffle my ass to the couch to wait—the same couch where Forrest and I used to demolish entire pizzas while arguing about NFL playoff contenders and whether the DC Universe is superior to Marvel. For the record, it is. He's wrong. I'm the literary critic here. There's something enthralling about the hauntingly beautiful broody heroes from DC.

The apartment feels too big without him, which is ridiculous because it's a shoebox even by Brooklyn standards. But when you've shared barely seven hundred square feet with your best friend for two years, his absence leaves a crater.

Not that I begrudge him. Forrest left the business when he found love. Real love, the kind that makes a guy a simp who moves to a brownstone with a woman to play house, and somehow finagles her father's blessing despite the fact he's a former escort. He built this beautiful, traditional family lifestyle for his four-year-old who says "Daddy" like it's the highest praise. I'm happy for the guy. He deserves every bit of it.

I just miss the bastard. He's never around anymore.

The microwave announces my gourmet feast with a pathetic little ding. I extract my plastic tray of sadness and shuffle the five steps to what the rental listing generously called a "dining area." It's barely enough room for a coffee table with one wobbly leg propped up by a Stephen King paperback in front of my couch that sags in all the wrong places.

That Stephen King novel came from my other best friend, Saylor, who thought he was doing me a favor when he discovered I "read books." Little did he know it would serve me better as furniture repair than entertainment. These days he's well aware of my actual preference: romance novels, stacked in precarious towers beside my bed. I started devouring them after the one-two punch of my father's perp walk on the local news, and then finding Alaina's side of the closet cleared out. Something about watching fictional people get the endings I never would became its own kind of therapy.

Black Cat leaps from the counter to the couch in one fluid motion, landing beside me with the grace of a panther and the entitlement of a trust-fund baby. He stares at my Salisbury steak.

"No."

He stares harder.

"You have your own food."

He puts one paw on my thigh. Gentle. Almost polite. The audacity.

"Fine." I tear off a corner of the mystery meat and hold it out. He sniffs it, recoils, and gives me a look that clearly communicates: *I expected better from you.*

"Yeah, well. Join the club." I only eat well when my clients are paying for it. Every spare dime I have goes to Dad's legal team who apparently want my nonexistent firstborn child to chip a few years off from his sentence.

I eat in the dead silence, annoyed by the sound of my own chewing, trying not to stress about the promise I made to Anne Carrington three days ago. A hundred thousand dollars by fall? What the actual fuck was I thinking? I said the words like they were nothing, like I had that kind of money sitting in a sock drawer somewhere. Like I wasn't already drowning in my father's debts with no life raft in sight.

Joy deserves to go to Stanford. She's worked her entire life for that acceptance letter, and she shouldn't have to give it up because my dad decided to play Robin Hood in reverse—stealing from people who trusted him and keeping it all for himself.

But a hundred thousand dollars.

I set my fork down, appetite gone. And not just because the gray-ish mystery meat is scalded on the outer rim and still a little frozen in the middle.

Releasing a deep exhale, I force myself to think about anything else outside of the pressure of my impossible promise. Unfortunately, my brain—the traitor that it is—immediately swaps out one form of self-torture for another.

My phone is right there on the coffee table, and I know I shouldn't. I know it's self-destructive and pointless and will only make me feel worse. But my fingers are already moving, already typing her name into the search bar, already pulling up the profile I swore I'd never look at again.

Alaina Carrington.

Her profile picture is new. She's on a beach somewhere—Turks and Caicos, maybe, or one of those other places that rich people go to feel richer—wearing a white sundress and laughing at something off-camera. She looks happy. Genuinely, radiantly happy in a way I'm not sure I ever made her.

I scroll down.

There he is. Bradley. The fiancé. And as advertised in the vacation photos, this guy isn't just rich. He's Scrooge McDuck rich.

He's exactly what I expected: clean-cut, strong jaw, the kind of guy who probably played lacrosse at some Ivy League school and summers as a verb. His arm is around Alaina in every photo, possessive but casual, like she's always been his.

Met the love of my life three years ago today, his caption reads. *Can't wait to make her my wife.*

Three years ago.

That math doesn't sit right in my stomach. Three years ago, Alaina and I were still together. Three years ago, I was planning to propose at the Marionette with her parents' blessing. Three years ago, I thought I knew exactly what my future looked like.

Did she meet him before or after she left me? Did our timelines overlap? Was she already falling for Mr. Lacrosse while I was picking out rings and rehearsing speeches and believing we had a future?

I scroll further. Engagement photos. More vacation photos. Photos of them at restaurants that look suspiciously like our old spots. There's one of them at a rooftop bar I used to take her to—*our bar*, the place where we had our first real date where I made it clear I was no longer interested in playing ball in the friend zone. He's kissing her cheek in the same spot where I told her she was the one. I study the image closer...How can she laugh for the camera like that when the ghost of us is surrounding her?

A vise clamps around my ribs, squeezing until I can barely breathe.

I slam my phone down. Self-destruction has a rhythm—first the search, then the scroll, then the crushing weight in my chest as I'm reminded exactly why I scrubbed her from my digital life, why that diamond sits in some stranger's jewelry box, and why I've tried to surgically remove two decades of memories like deleting corrupted files.

But some nights, the masochism wins.

I close the app before I spiral any further.

None of it matters. She's moved on. Anne told me to move on. Everyone keeps telling me to move on, like it's as simple as *deciding*—like I can flip a switch and stop loving someone I've loved since I was six years old.

Black Cat head-butts my elbow, which is his version of emotional support. I scratch behind his ears and he purrs like a motorboat with a cold—raspy and gurgled. He probably needs a vet visit for that raspy purr, but there's something about filling out paperwork with my name in the "owner" field that I'm not ready for. We have an arrangement—I provide the tuna, he provides the judgment—but making it official feels like tempting fate. The minute you start calling something yours is usually when the universe decides to take it away.

"You know what we need?" I ask him.

He doesn't answer. He's a cat.

"We need to take the edge off."

I haul myself off the couch and dig through the kitchen cabinet where I keep my stash—a small tin of gummies I bought from my favorite dispensary last month. I don't excessively partake, but tonight most definitely calls for chemical assistance.

I pop one in, just one, because I'm not trying to end up on my kitchen floor having an existential crisis. Then I glance at Black Cat, who has followed me into the kitchen and is now sitting expectantly by his food bowl.

"Oh, you want some too?"

He meows, flashing his fangs. Demanding little gremlin.

I pull the catnip from the cabinet and sprinkle a modest amount over his untouched dry kibble that he'll only tolerate if fish isn't on the menu. The second the catnip touches down on his meal, he attacks it like I've given him the feline equivalent of a five-star meal.

"Just a little. You have to make this last," I tell him, putting the container away. "We're on a tight budget starting immediately."

He ignores me, too busy drowning in his drug-laced dinner to acknowledge my financial concerns.

I return to my Hungry-Man tray, now all the way cold and even less appetizing. But in about half an hour the cardboard-textured Salisbury steak and mashed potatoes with the consistency of wet cement will look gourmet. The brownie, inexplicably, is solid. I enjoy that dessert even without any cannabis coercion.

My mom would be horrified.

She used to make the best katsu curry—crispy pork cutlet over rice, smothered in a sauce she'd simmer for hours. The apartment would smell like spices and home, and I'd come back from class to find her humming in the kitchen, an apron tied over her work clothes.

I haven't had her cooking in three years. Not since she decided that putting an ocean between herself and the wreckage of our family was the only way to survive.

I try not to blame her. She stayed as long as she could, weathered the arrest and the trial and the public humiliation. But everyone has a breaking point, and watching your husband get sentenced to federal prison while reporters shout questions about your complicity will test even the strongest marriage.

She begged me to come with her. Start fresh, she said. Leave the past in the past. But I couldn't abandon my dad. Even after everything. Even knowing what he did.

So she left, and I stayed, and now I eat Hungry-Man dinners alone while my cat gets high on catnip beside me.

Living the dream.

I choke down the last edible bites of my meal, pitch the plastic tray in the trash, and sink back into the couch cushions. My paperback waits where I left it. I smile at page 73 of my current read featuring the standard-issue grump who owns a failing bookshop and the relentlessly cheerful florist moving in next door. Pure formulaic escapism at its finest. Absolute relief from the unpredictable mess of my actual existence.

I'm three chapters in, just getting to the part where the florist accidentally destroys the bookstore's window display with an errant delivery truck, when my phone buzzes.

Then buzzes again.

I return to my book until I can no longer ignore the explosion of notifications.

Groaning, I pick it up. My phone screen is lit with notifications from the agency group chat named Off the Books, our sad attempt at witty subterfuge that fools exactly no one.

Group Chat: Off the Books

Rina

Emergency request. Anyone available tonight? 2K in cash. Client is a divorcee hosting a passion party. Needs a plus-one who can look pretty and pretend not to be intimidated by vibrators.

Saylor

Are vibrators supposed to be intimidating?

Cam

There's one called The Detonator. Trust. It's intimidating.

Saylor

Curiosity buffering.

Forrest

Why the hell am I still on this group chat?

Cam

The Detonator is two-prong. Perfect for DP. And the vibration is so powerful, it's the closest thing you'll get to the strength of a sybian.

Rina

Can we stay on track? Who's available tonight? I need to tell the client a yes or no, NOW.

Theo

How much?

Rina

2K, Theo. Read up for God's sake.

Theo

No, I meant for The Detonator.

Forrest

SERIOUSLY. How do I leave the group chat? I exited but the messages keep coming through.

I let out a laugh, imagining Forrest's wide-eyed panic as these messages pop up on his phone while Sora, his girlfriend, peers over his shoulder. She's a good sport. She's probably giggling along at his embarrassment.

Saylor

Sorry, Rina. I'm out. Promised Mum some quality time.

Cam

I'm out. Literally on my way to a job.

Forrest

Since the messages won't stop...I'm out. BECAUSE I'M IN A RELATIONSHIP AND NO LONGER DOING THIS SHIT.

Saylor

Forrest, can you ask Sora which one is the good Korean BBQ place? I have a hankering.

Rina

 Theo? Taio?

Theo

I'm catching up on Game of Thrones and I have warm soup belly. I'm out.

Rina

I am thoroughly regretting all of your Christmas bonuses. Saylor, please?

Saylor

Sorry, boss. Priorities.

Cam

Mama's boy.

Saylor

Proud of it, mate. And I'm a mama's boy who knows your address and could pound you into a pulp.

Cam

...

Cam

Sorry, that was autocorrect. I meant "noble loving son."

Saylor

Attaboy.

Rina

FOCUS. I need a warm body in a sports coat at the Elusive Hotel in two hours.

All right, that's enough of that. I call Rina directly instead of responding to the group chat.

She picks up on the first ring. "Please tell me you're saying yes."

"I'm saying yes, conditionally."

"Oh thank God." She exhales through the phone. "You're saving my ass, Taio. This client is a referral from one of my best customers."

"Not for two thousand though. Four, minimum. And she can have me all night."

She's silent for a moment. "I'm going to pretend I didn't hear that because the job I have for you, from my *very legitimate, law-abiding* business, is just companionship for a party. I would very much like to stay in the dark of your dirty off-the-books dealings. But out of curiosity, why are you suddenly so greedy?"

I take a breath. "From now on, I need you to call me directly with any jobs. All of them. Before they go to the group. I want first right of refusal on everything."

Silence on the line. Then, "That's a big ask."

"I know."

"The other guys won't like it."

"They don't have to know."

More silence. I can practically hear her calculating—weighing my value against the potential drama, running the numbers on my reliability versus the hassle of preferential treatment.

"What's going on, Taio?" Her tone is softer now. "Are you in some kind of trouble?"

"No. Nothing like that."

"Then what? You've never been this hungry before."

I think about Anne Carrington and her sad smile. Joy's Stanford letter. The hundred thousand dollars I promised like a fool.

"I just need to make some money fast," I say. "It's...a family thing. I can't really explain."

"Your father?" Rina asks defeatedly.

She's got an incredible legal mind, once a tenured professor at Columbia Law. And while she likes to pretend she's Meryl Streep in *The Devil Wears Prada*, she's wildly compassionate, and far more den mother than pimp. We met when I approached her for help about my dad's case. She pored over the case for weeks trying to find anything that could help. Unfortunately she said going to trial would be useless. The case was open and shut. My dad did the crime and he would absolutely do the time. She recommended a plea deal.

His current lawyers disagreed. We went to trial. We lost, but they haven't stopped working. Appeal after appeal, and it's becoming clear they're just hustling me. But everyone clings to hope—even false hope—when they are desperate enough.

"Not exactly," I finally answer.

Rina is quiet for a moment. "You're not doing anything stupid, are you? Gambling? Drugs?"

"No. I promise. It's nothing illegal."

"You know I'm here if you need—"

"I know, Rina. Thank you. I'm good. It's just...I made a promise to someone. And I need to keep it."

She sighs. The kind of sigh that says she knows she's going to regret this. "Fine. First right of refusal. But please be discreet, or I'll castrate you, so you have to keep it squeaky clean."

"Fair enough." But I shield my dick with an open palm as if her threat is imminent.

"I'm texting you the details now."

Elusive Hotel. Wear a sports coat. "I can read. I got it," I say too eagerly, already heading to my bathroom to take a record-fast shower.

Rina continues anyway. "The client's name is Margaret. She's forty-two, recently divorced, and according to my notes, 'looking to sow her wild oats.' Be charming. Be complimentary. And please don't make fun of anything she may buy at the party."

"I would never."

"You absolutely would. I've seen you roast a woman's shoe collection for twenty minutes."

"*In private.* Not to her face. And those were Crocs, Rina. Rows of *bedazzled Crocs.* I stand by my choices."

She laughs despite herself. "Go. Get ready. You have less than two hours. Oh and I forgot to mention, she's a little shy and needs your help picking up her contribution for the party."

She's shy yet she's hosting this party? Hmm. Okay.

"Contribution?" I ask Rina.

"Yes. From what I understand, this is one of those parties where everyone brings a toy and leaves with a different toy."

"What kind of unhinged White Elephant is this?"

"Hell if I know. But pick up whatever item you please within a one-hundred-dollar budget. She'll reimburse you when you arrive. There will be a key at the front desk waiting for you. Head right up to the penthouse."

"The toys we're bringing are all unused, right? Like new and still in the box?"

"Dear God I hope so."

With that, she hangs up, effectively avoiding any more of my questions that she either does or does not have the answer to.

I look at Black Cat, who has finished his catnip-laced dinner and is now sprawled on his back in the middle of the kitchen floor, paws in the air, absolutely vibing.

"One of us is having a good night," I tell him.

He doesn't respond. He's ascended to a higher plane of consciousness. His eyes are half closed, his purr rattling through his entire body like a faulty engine. I envy him. No existential dread. No hundred-thousand-dollar promises hanging over his head. No hurting over the feline who dumped him after he lost his money. No father in prison who we might have to excavate with a reenactment of *Shawshank Redemption*. Just catnip and kibble and the simple pleasure of existing.

Must be nice.

The edible is starting to kick in—just a gentle warmth at the edges, nothing too intense—as I race through the world's fastest shower. The hot water helps clear my head, and by the time I'm toweling off, I've almost convinced myself this is a great idea. Step one in a twelve-step redemption plan where I keep my promises and restore myself to my prior palatability in society.

I dig through my closet for something presentable, which takes longer than it should because my wardrobe has significantly deteriorated since my trust-fund days. I sold everything name brand I owned after Dad's scandal for a little survival money. The sports coat Anne commented on at dinner is now the nicest thing I own—a navy number I bought secondhand from a consignment shop in Brooklyn. It's quality, just not new. I pair it with dark jeans and a black button-down, check my reflection, and decide I look like someone who could plausibly be invited to a passion party of the elite.

THE SEX SHOP is a fifteen-minute walk from my apartment—a place called "Sinfully Seductive" that I've passed approximately four hundred times without ever going inside. The neon sign flickers in the window, promising *Tasteful Adult Novelties* and *Discreet Packaging* which at least suggests I won't have to carry a giant dildo down Fifth Avenue in a see-through bag.

Inside, the store is surprisingly aesthetic. Clean shelves, soft lighting, a bored-looking employee with green streaks in her hair who barely glances up when I enter. It's nothing like the seedy backroom vibes I expected.

"Can I help you find something?" Green Hair asks, not looking up from her phone.

"I need a gift. For a party."

"Bachelorette?"

"Passion party."

She finally looks at me, one eyebrow raised. "Passion party. Fancy. What's your budget?"

"Hundred bucks."

"Okay, so mid-range. You want something practical or something that'll get a laugh?"

I think about Rina's instructions. Be charming. Don't make fun of anything.

"Practical," I decide. "Something...I don't know. Classy? My friends mentioned something called The Detonator is all the rave."

Green Hair snorts in laughter. "Do you want classy or The Detonator? Two different things." She leads me to a display case near the back, gesturing at the options like a sommelier presenting a wine list. "Budget friendly is bottom shelf. Mid-range is eye level. Top shelf is where you'll find The Big D—our nickname for The Detonator."

"You have a nickname for it?"

Wide-eyed, she nods. "It's that popular. Believe me, you'll be the hero of the party."

I lock eyes with the box. Intimidating indeed. Its phallic girth and length alone are enough to make any grown man feel unbearably insignificant. Not to mention it's like a two-headed hydra, threatening to demolish you from the inside out.

"It only comes in black?" I ask. "Is there something less aggressive-looking like...pink?"

"We keep a twenty-four-carat-gold limited edition in the back." She reaches for the key hooked to her lanyard. "I'll have to unlock it."

"How much?"

"For Goldie? Two thousand."

I snatch up the box in front of me. "Black it is."

She smirks. "Wise choice. Gift-wrapped?"

"God, no. Just your most subtle bag."

She rings me up and slides the toy into a brown paper bag with glittery-gold cloth handles. "Do you want me to input your name and number? We have a loyalty program and a huge variety." She plants her elbows on the counter, scoots forward, and drops her voice to a whisper which is unnecessary because we're alone. "We have taint stuff. Top of the line."

My slow, heavy blinks aren't answer enough for her, so I have to add a pointed, "Hell no, thanks," before sliding my bag off the counter and exiting.

"Come back anytime." She's already back on her phone before I reach the door. "The loyalty program has generous rewards if you change your mind," she calls out as I exit the store into the frigid early February air.

Back on the street, I check my phone. Rina's prior text with the hotel name glows on the screen:

Rina

FOCUS. I need a warm body in a sports coat at the Elusive Hotel in two hours.

The Elusive is all the way across town. There's no time to be cheap and hoof it. Nor do I feel like navigating the subways. I hail a cab, mentally noting that when I offer to stay overnight with this client and set my fee, I include the cost of this ridiculously overpriced cab ride.

I'll get half of what Rina booked, so that's one grand. If I ask for another three to stay the night, that's four grand from one night. Not terrible. It's four percent of Joy's tuition. Four percent closer to keeping my promise.

The cab drops me off in front of the Elusive Hotel, a sleek tower of glass and steel that screams money so loudly I'm surprised the doorman doesn't demand to see my tax returns before letting me inside.

The lobby is all marble floors and modern art—the kind of abstract sculptures that serve no purpose other than intimidating you with their ostentatiousness. A massive chandelier hangs overhead, dripping crystals like frozen raindrops. Everything is very white, very clean, very designed to make people like me feel like we don't belong.

The front desk stretches like a runway, all gleaming marble and brass accents, but only one person mans the station—a young woman so entranced and unnerved by whatever's on her computer screen that I have to clear my throat twice before her eyes flick up to acknowledge me.

"Oh, I'm sorry, sir." She shakes her head, and her neat ponytail glued down by hairspray doesn't budge. "How can I help you?"

Her eyes dart between me and the screen, clearly eager to get back to whatever emergency she's dealing with.

"I'm expected in the penthouse."

She opens her mouth, her brows pinching in confusion. Before she can question me, a sweeping realization overcomes her expression. "Ah, yes—you're delivering a package to the penthouse?"

"Uh...I guess?" I thought I was a guest, but maybe Margaret is going out of her way to be discreet with the hotel staff. Not the worst idea since she invited a bunch of her friends to an esteemed hotel to what I sincerely hope will not escalate into an orgy.

A chirpy ding of a notification pulls her attention back to her screen once more. She lets out a small roar of frustration and puts one hand on the receiver of her desk phone. With the other, she fetches a black keycard and sets it on the counter between us. "The elevator all the way down the hall leads to the penthouse. There's a small foyer and then just ring the bell by the double doors. You can't miss them."

The receiver is already wedged between her ear and shoulder as she dials like she's angry at the phone. Glancing up one more time, she flashes me a hurried smile. "Anything else?" she mouths.

"Nope. Thank you." Effectively dismissed, I collect the key and head to the elevator bay, locating the only one that leads to the "P Level."

The elevator is mirrored on all sides, which means I get to watch myself ascend in infinite recursion—an endless hallway of Taios in sports coats, all of them clutching brown paper bags containing giant black vibrators, all of them wondering how their lives ended up here.

The edible has settled into a comfortable hum, taking the edge off without making me stupid. I wish I was back home, cozy with my book. Splurging on takeout that's actually edible. I wish I was anyone else, doing anything else because while I know escorting, outside of winning the lottery, is the fastest way to dig myself out of the hole my dad made, I'm so tired of this shit. There's a fatigue in me that goes so far past physical.

But I don't have time to wallow. The elevator ride is brief, the steel box slingshotting to the top floor. The doors open onto a private foyer, and that's when I hear it.

Piano music. Soft and melancholy, drifting through the penthouse door like smoke. And beneath it, a voice—husky and raw, singing a vaguely familiar song. Except this rendition is harrowing. It's that Rihanna track, the sad one, the one that plays in every movie when someone's having an emotional breakdown in the rain. The one included on every single playlist of an angsty romance with a third-act breakup.

But this version is different. Stripped down. Intimate. Even more harrowing if that's possible. Like whoever's singing it means every single word.

I stand there for a moment, frozen, listening. The voice artistically cracks on a high note—not from lack of skill, but from emotion. From something real and aching underneath the melody. *Margaret has some singing chops.* Holy hell. That's great. An easy icebreaker for the woman I just might end up in bed with tonight. I decide it's the very first thing I'll say to her. *Hi, Margaret, I'm Taio. Nice to meet you. Your voice is devastatingly beautiful. How long have you played piano?*

I step up to the penthouse door, my knuckles finding the wood with three hard knocks before I remember the doorbell. I hover over the blue-lit button but drop my hand when the piano stops. She heard my knocks.

Footsteps approach.

The door swings open, and my prepared smile dies on my face.

I'm expecting Margaret. Forty-two. Recently divorced. Looking for a confidence boost.

Instead, I'm staring at a face I swear I've seen on about a million tabloid covers lately. I stand frozen, silent, my brain making the Windows 95 shutdown noise as I wonder if that gummy was stronger than I realized and we've entered a THC-induced hallucination where celebrities materialize like I've summoned them through some accidental pop culture séance.

But why the fuck would my brain conjure up...*Charlie Riley*?

And while we're at it, this isn't an easily recognizable Charlie Riley. She's as far from "glam" as she can get.

She's standing in the doorway, also silent, wearing an oversized Tweety Bird T-shirt that hangs just above her knees, her blonde hair scraped back in a messy ponytail that's more "gave up" than "effortlessly chic." Her eyes are red-rimmed. No makeup. She looks exhausted and young and nothing like the polished icon I've seen on billboards.

She looks human.

She also looks at the brown paper bag in my hand, and her entire face transforms with relief. To my surprise, her eyes begin to water.

"You earth angel," she breathes out, stepping back to admire the plain-ass paper bag properly. "You have no idea how important it is to me."

I open my mouth, but nothing comes out except a small choking sound. Charlie Riley is standing here looking at me like I'm her savior because I brought her The Detonator for her passion party. Surely a woman worth hundreds of millions has an entire staff who could discreetly acquire whatever battery-operated appliance her heart desires?

What the fuck is happening right now?

"Um, sorry, I just was expecting...Is Margaret an alias?"

"Huh?" She cocks her head to the side like a confused puppy. Then she holds out her hand. "No, I'm Charlie. It's nice to meet you...?"

"Taio Wilkes," I answer. *Oh weird.* Normally I give a pseudonym but the truth slipped right out.

I wrap her small hand in mine, accepting her handshake, but the moment our palms touch she flinches. "What?" I ask, examining the hand she rejected, looking for evidence of suddenly onset oozing sores.

"Your hands are freezing," she says.

"Oh, right. It's bitter cold out." I nod over my shoulder vaguely gesturing to "out."

"You don't have a coat?"

I tap my lapel. "Dress code. I don't have an appropriate winter jacket that goes with this."

I vigorously rub my right hand against my thigh, feeling the friction warm my stiff fingers through the thin fabric of my dress pants. Then I awkwardly transfer the bag to my other hand, the weight of The Detonator swinging slightly as I repeat the process, watching my pale knuckles gradually flush pink with returning circulation.

"Well, thank you." She reaches for the bag, but I step back. No way I'm letting her open this until I offer an explanation. What that explanation is, I don't know yet, but as soon as the puzzle pieces of this bizarre encounter settle, I'll think of something.

She rolls her eyes. It's brief, but I catch a glimpse of her annoyance. "You recognize me and now you want a tip, don't you?"

"What?" I ask, genuinely confused.

Her smile turns sweet and warm. "It's *okay*. I get it, truly. And you deserve one, freezing your tush out there to hand-deliver my box. Here, come on in." She waves me into the penthouse then disappears down the hallway.

I enter the luxurious space, nearly tripping over my own feet when I spot the glossy black grand piano dominating the corner of the living room. Well, that explains the singing...I think. My brain is still buffering like dial-up internet. I've heard Charlie's radio hits—all processed within an inch of their digital lives, sounding like an auto-tuned Alvin and the Chipmunks covering a Disney Channel soundtrack. I didn't know she could sing *like that*.

Soft thuds on the hardwood floor alert me to Charlie's return before she banks left in the hallway and returns to view, carrying a thick wad of cash in her left hand.

"Are you okay?" she asks, frowning at me now, head tilted once more. "You look kind of pale. Do you want some water or soda or something before you get going?"

Get going? Now I'm thoroughly convinced this is some sort of mix-up. But the edible has chosen this exact moment to hit a little harder, and all I can manage is: "You're *Charlie Riley*, the pop star."

She blinks. "Yes. We've established that. And you're Taio, the courier my dad sent." She holds over the wad of twenty-dollar bills and notices my surprise. "It's okay. I'm feeling generous today. And I'm not kidding"—she points to the bag in my hand—"that is the most valuable possession I have. I thought I lost it. Thank you for returning it. Swap?" She wiggles the money in her hand, urging me to take it and to hand over the bag in exchange...

Courier? What the hell?

Oh, wait.

Are we role-playing?

Lots of celebrities book escorts under fake names. Maybe the entire passion party was some type of ruse and Charlie Riley wanted me here, with a toy so we could...*play all night*?

"Don't you want the money?" She shifts her weight to her other foot, crossing her arms and suddenly looking at me suspiciously. I scan the room for hidden security team members, a little surprised this mega star is here alone. But of course—if Charlie hired me for what I think she hired me for, no way she'd want company for that.

This all makes sense now. Okay, it's showtime.

"Oh, I want the money," I answer, dropping my voice to a honey-sweet baritone. "But I want to earn it first. So, Charlie...or should I say, *Margaret*, what would you like to do tonight? It's your choice but if the passion party was just an excuse, I'd still love to have dinner and get to know you a little better first before we move on to...dessert. If that's what you want?"

She blinks at me like her eyelids are heavy. Her lips relax into a half-moon, almost a frown. "I know all of those were words, yet none of it made sense. I just want my package."

I pump my brows at her. "Your *package*?"

"Yes." She points in the vague direction of my crotch. "Do you need a signature?"

I set down the bag and unbutton my sports coat so I have the freedom to cross my arms over my chest. "The deal you signed with Rina already bought my full discretion. You can trust me, I promise. I know you have status, but there's no funny business here. Rina runs a very legitimate, professional business. Me, on the other hand? Well, let's just say the real fun begins once I clock out."

She squints one eye. "Rina is your boss?"

"Yes. She's who you were texting about tonight."

Charlie shakes her head. "No, that'd be my dad. He's the one who hired you guys."

Oh that's pretty fucked up. "Your *dad* hired me...for you?" I ask to clarify.

"Either him or my sister. She usually handles the admin stuff. She was his assistant for so long that I think it just stuck even after they got married."

Full. Stop. I take a small step backward trying to collect my thoughts. I get it—I've encountered some freaky shit in my line of work, but this...this is next level.

"So, your dad and your sister are married and they hired me together...for you...for tonight?" I glance at the ground where the bag sits. "And asked me to bring you this package?"

"Don't judge," she balks, crossing her arms to mirror me. "He's my adoptive dad."

"It doesn't make this situation better. Just less illegal," I argue in a mumble.

Charlie clutches the sides of her temple with open palms and growls. "Okay, I'm not one to dismiss the help or anything, but may I please just have my package and you can go? I'm very busy and I have to get back to my shitstorm of a life." She juts her thumb over her shoulder to the piano.

"I heard you outside," I blurt out.

"Oh," is all she responds with.

"You sounded really great. I'll be honest, I've heard your music before, and I would've never expected you could sing like that. It was so—"

"Masculine, husky, soulful, depressing, not easy to sing along with?" Charlie interjects, arching one brow. "Or so my label says."

"Um, no—none of those things. The word angelic came to mind."

Her lips spread first, then her reluctant cheeks bunch into half spheres. It's almost like she's unwilling to smile at my high praise. "My label likes to keep my brand young. It takes a little auto-tune and me, singing like a chipmunk in the studio, but..." She shrugs. "It keeps me relatable to the younger demographic, I suppose. I rarely get to sing like I want...like I can."

"That's the most ridiculous shit I've ever heard. Why would they want to cover up a voice like yours?"

"When it comes to mainstream music, it's more about what looks good than what sounds good. Most days I'm more of an actress than a singer. That's showbiz for you." She winks at me and holds her hand out, asking for the bag again.

"You're really eager to get started," I say with a scoff of disbelief. This is really happening. There's no turning back now. "Okay, well, I guess we're skipping dinner."

"Huh?"

"We can eat after. I just have to make it very clear that you hired me through Rina for my company. If you're enjoying our time together and want me to stay on my own accord, that stays off the books. Cash only. Half upfront, the remainder when we're finished. Condoms are non-negotiable. Anything is on the table, except for non-consensual role-playing. Light spanking is okay, but I don't like to inflict pain. It's not my style." I show her a warm smile. "Don't let my frame fool you. I'm way more of a lover than a fighter. I hope that's okay." I remove my sports coat and lay it on the back of the sofa. It's only when I'm unbuttoning my shirt that I see Charlie's big blue eyes snap open as if a sweeping realization popped like a bubble in her mind.

"What's in the bag?" Charlie asks quietly, a smirk growing on her face.

Reading her expression, I'm suddenly a little uncomfortable exposing The Detonator. "Um...what exactly do you think is in this bag?"

"Up until ten seconds ago I thought it was a small wooden box, hand-painted with little hearts." Her voice drops low. "It's valuable, but only to me. It holds notes from my mom. Good luck charms if you will. She died when I was little. I lost it in the dressing room at my last performance. My dad, who owns the hotel, just let me know his staff found it and overnighted it. But you're not a courier, are you?"

Oh shit.

Shitastic hell.

Fuck my actual life.

"I…" My voice comes out strangled. "No."

She advances, hand outstretched, still asking for the bag that is now the gigantic purple elephant in the room. I bend down to scoop it up, dead set on ensuring that she never finds out what's inside, but the flimsy handle betrays me, ripping the paper bag in half. The Detonator topples out, stopped by the tips of Charlie's manicured toes.

She bends down to pick up the box, her justified look of horror growing as she rotates it in her hand. It takes about three seconds for the chaos to register on her face and her eyes snap to mine in a look that is all shock and simultaneously full of curiosity.

Oh, kill me now. Please.

"Taio, are you an…?"

"Escort?" I finish her sentence because she seems reluctant to. "Yes."

She pinches her eyes closed and drops her head. "You thought *my dad* hired you? Seriously?"

I hold up my hands. "I don't judge. I was going to recommend serious, invasive family therapy, but I would never judge."

She rises and I lift my palms higher in surrender as if her pipsqueak self is capable of attacking me and inflicting serious damage. I take a large step back, seriously contemplating fleeing.

She points the box at me menacingly, like it's a weapon. "Is Taio your real name?"

"Actually, yes."

Her eyes narrow. "Okay, Taio. Start explaining."

Chapter 5
Taio

This is not the start of some fairy-tale story.

Charlie Riley is pointing a two-pronged vibrator at me like it's a loaded weapon, and honestly? I've had worse Tuesday nights.

"Start explaining," she repeats, and there's steel underneath the exhaustion in her voice. "Now. Please," she adds, taking the time to add manners to her demand.

"Okay. Um, I don't know. My boss—Rina texted me about a job tonight. A woman named Margaret, recently divorced, hosting a passion party at the Elusive Hotel penthouse. I was supposed to be her date. But I get here and..." My wrist does this sort of lazy roll so I'm gesturing toward Charlie but not pointing at her in accusation.

Her brow quirks again, a soft round arch. She should be freaking out. I am a strange man in her apartment, so how come blatant curiosity is sprawled all over her expression? "Margaret?"

"That's what Rina said. Margaret. Forty-two. Looking to"—I clear my throat—"sow her wild oats."

I brace myself for her wrath, mentally rehearsing my "*I swear I'm not a creep*" speech while calculating how many steps to the door. Instead, Charlie unleashes this laugh that sounds like a lumberjack gargling bourbon—deep, rough, and weirdly satisfying. It's like watching a chihuahua bark with James Earl Jones's voice. Honestly? Extremely hot in a way I'm not prepared to examine right now.

"And you thought...Margaret was...me?" she manages through her heaves of laughter. "And I thought you were a delivery boy. What're the chances?"

"Whoa, hey. Delivery *man*," I correct, tapping my imaginary name badge. Her laughter is infectious—like a TikTok dance craze you swore you'd never do but suddenly find yourself practicing fervently in the bathroom mirror. "Not to be the guy giving stranger-danger lectures while holding a vibrator, but most women would've already pepper-sprayed me into next Tuesday. You know, after the whole condoms-are-non-negotiable opener. You seem pretty at ease, have you done this before?"

She places her hand against her heart like she's worried about an attack. "You're asking if *I* have ever ordered an escort?"

"Half my clients are celebrities. All of them rich. Most of them could buy and sell small countries before breakfast. When you're that loaded, paying for company is like ordering room service—just with more orgasms and fewer club sandwiches."

A wicked smile crosses her face. "Which celebrities? Spill the tea."

I snort-laugh like a startled bull. She's still holding the vibrator while wearing Tweety Bird pajamas and wants celebrity gossip like we're at a slumber party. "Sorry to disappoint, but I'm under a strict privacy clause. No exceptions. I could sleep with your mother or best friend, and you'd never ever find out."

Her shoulders relax and the sadness in her eyes returns. "You actually can't. My mother's dead and I don't have a best friend. My sisters, maybe. But both of them are happily married."

I scratch the back of my neck. "Yeah...happily married isn't exactly my target audience."

Her lips flinch into a barely there smile. "Right."

We stand there in silence for a moment. Her in that ridiculous Tweety Bird pajama shirt, hair that looks like it survived a cage match with a leaf blower, clutching a vibrator, waving it around as she talks like she's about to signal a commercial flight to its appropriate gate. Then there's me, trying to subtly re-button my shirt, my secondhand sports coat in my periphery, hands still raised like I'm being mugged by a cartoon character. If my life were a GPS, it would be saying "recalculating" right about now.

Then her expression shifts. The exhaustion is still there, but something else creeps in underneath—suspicion. Calculation. The look of someone who's been burned too many times to take anything at face value.

"How much did they pay you?" she asks quietly.

"What?"

"Oh come on, *Taio*, if that's really your name. Nothing about this is believable. But I'm a good sport, and you know what? You're as much a victim as me. I bet they offered you a golden unicorn to catch me in here"—she twirls around—"like this. Looking like the next big meltdown in the line of pop queens like Britney, Christina, and Shaylin. Well, news for you, buddy—I'm not drunk. I'm not doing drugs. I'm not smacking puppies. There's no story here. I was just exhausted, okay? Tell your bosses that. The most irresponsible thing I've done is ignore hydration to the point there is sand in my veins. That's it. No scoop, no story. We'll be announcing my return to the tour shortly."

She points at my chest with an angry resonance. "And don't you dare spin this story like I answered the door half naked, either." She lifts up her long shirt to flash me a pair of pink spandex. "I'm wearing bottoms, and in my defense, I thought we were going to have a three-second exchange. As far as my hair..." Charlie's eyes shift left, then right. "Well, I don't actually have an excuse for that. This is just kind of what it does after a nap."

Now that she's mentioned it, there is a strand defying gravity and standing upright and center like it's trying to catch a lightning strike. I close the gap between us in two small steps and smooth her frayed hair. She doesn't flinch, she doesn't move away, but I catch her sucking in a breath and holding it until I retreat a pace backward. "There you go. Right as rain. Now, who do you think I work for?" I ask, trying to contain my humor.

"*New York Post*? TMZ? CelebNow, maybe?"

"Hmm." I nod my head in consideration. "And you think I'm doing some kind of exposé on your concert from two weeks ago?"

She pulls her gaze from mine, her toes suddenly fascinating as she wiggles them against the hardwood floor. "They'll call it—'Pop Princess Charlie Riley: From Stadium Tours to Sex Toys'? Complete with unflattering photos and some quote from my third-grade teacher about how I always had 'attention-seeking tendencies.'" She tosses the vibrator onto the coffee table like she's ditching evidence at a crime scene. The thing springs to life, buzzing with the fury of a chainsaw powered by ten thousand horses. *Christ*, that's not a sex toy—it's a power tool.

"I'm just gonna turn that off." I do this awkward side shuffle that probably makes me look like I'm crab-walking to a bathroom emergency. The box is one of those impossible plastic contraptions designed by sadists who hate human fingernails. After wrestling with it like a dude trying to unhook a bra one-handed in the dark, I finally extract the mechanical beast. Three wrong buttons later—each one cranking this thing up until it's practically levitating—I finally find the off switch, which is hilariously a frowny face. I set it back down on the coffee table carefully, trying not to provoke the damn thing.

"I find it charming you don't really know your way around a vibrator." Her smirk has returned and I breathe out in relief.

"Charming? Well, perhaps that's because as I said...I'm not a reporter, Charlie. I'm an escort."

"Oh, please. I've been in this circus since I was sixteen. You vultures are getting creative with your disguises. The hot escort angle?" She gives me a mock applause with one hand. "Chef's kiss. Truly inspired. *Almost* tempted."

"It's not an angle—" I stop short. "Wait. Tempted, you say?"

"Almost tempted," she clarifies, poking out her tongue at me which sets a little butterfly free in my chest. *Oh, gross, Taio—knock it off.* Stop flirting. This is not the start of some fairy-tale story. This is you stalling and missing out on four thousand dollars that you desperately need.

"Charlie, you have my word," I emphasize. "I'm not a reporter, I swear. It sucks that's the conclusion you jump to because it's happened before, but I assure you—that's not what this is. I won't tell a soul about your uh...quirky attire, and the graveyard of takeout containers you have behind you." I point over her shoulder to the open kitchen. "But maybe crack a window, a little fresh air... your call. But tonight I either got hustled or I'm at the wrong hotel. Either way, I need to figure it out, so it's been very nice to chat, but I have to get going."

She rolls her eyes. "To report back on me to your handler?"

A small wave of annoyance rolls through me. *Why won't she believe me?* I return to her, our toes touching, hovering over her the way a tree looks at the grass. Ignoring my better instincts, I grab both of her hands in mine, wrapping around her small fists like a tight swaddle. "My name is Taio Wilkes. My dad is James Wilkes—serving a twelve-year sentence at Otisville for a white-collar felony. It's public record, you can look it up. I really am an escort...because of that. Because I'm trying to get him out and put my family back together. So, now that you have my deepest, darkest secret, I need you to keep it. Just like I'll keep yours." I release her fists and hold out my hand. "Deal?"

"For real?" she asks.

"For real."

She shakes my hand with more gusto than seems appropriate at the moment. "I won't tell a soul." She says it like a soldier accepting her mission.

I disentangle my hand from hers, pull my sports coat off the back of the sofa, and make for the exit. Hand on the door handle, I can't help but steal one last look. This version of Charlie Riley—messy-haired, cartoon-shirted, vibrator-wielding Charlie—is infinitely better than the airbrushed pop princess plastered across billboards. She's real. Human. Talented. And infinitely interesting because I have about a hundred more questions I'd like to ask her. But I'm out of time, and it's a damn shame I'll never see her again.

I point to the piano. "For the record, I would pay good money to go to a concert and hear you play like that. Good luck with the rest of your tour. You're going to do great. Don't forget—hydrate."

She doesn't respond. Just looks at me with those big, sad eyes.

I make myself leave.

The elevator descends, and I use every floor to wonder what the hell just happened.

I should be calling Rina. I'm officially late now. I should be begging for forgiveness, explaining the mix-up, salvaging whatever's left of my professional reputation. Instead, I'm standing here, reluctant to return to reality because I'm still thinking about Charlie Riley's deep, rumbly laugh.

The elevator hits the lobby. I pull out my phone, ready to face the music—

And that's when I see it.

A small wooden box, sitting abandoned on the concierge desk.

I stop walking.

The desk is unmanned. The lobby is nearly empty. And there, like someone just set it down and walked away, is a box exactly like the one Charlie described. Hand-painted with little orange hearts. Old, the colors faded with age. Small enough to hold in both hands.

Notes from my mom. She died when I was little.

Some lazy courier saw an empty desk and left it there. Didn't wait. Didn't care. Didn't understand that this little painted box might be someone's entire world.

My phone buzzes in my pocket like an angry hornet trapped in denim. Ah, crap. It's Rina. The digital firing squad has arrived, locked and loaded, ready to berate me before I can even devise a half-decent excuse.

"Hey, Rina."

"Where the hell are you?" Oh, she's murderous. "Margaret is livid you're late. Are you okay?"

"I don't know what happened. I'm here at the Elusive. She's

not staying in the penthouse." I pick up the box. It's lighter than I expected.

"Why are you at the Elusive? That's Midtown. You're supposed to be at...*Oh shit—*" A pause. Scrolling. "Oh, for fuck's sake. Autocorrect. Yep, there it is. Sorry, Taio. I don't normally make mistakes like that. You're supposed to be at the Eloise. Other side of the city." She exhales sharply. "Okay, that's on me. But, Taio, you can still make it if you hurry. We'll have you arrive fashionably late and can still salvage all this—"

"Tell Margaret I'm sorry. I can't make it tonight." I fight the urge to open the unlocked box and satiate my curiosity. But now that I've met her, and I know what this is and what it means to her, it feels wrong.

"What? I already talked her up to double the price *for you*. Do you understand? You begged me for first right of refusal and now you're—"

"I know."

Silence.

"Rina, I'll call you tomorrow to accept my verbal lashing, I promise. But I'm serious. Something came up. I have to go."

I hang up. Turn off my phone. Swivel on my heel. Before I know it, I'm marching right back to the elevator bay.

I'm an idiot. A complete, certifiable idiot.

But I'm already in the penthouse elevator, box cradled in my arms like a baby. Already swiping the keycard for coveted access to the most elite guest in this hotel. Already picturing the surprise on her face when I roll in like some poor man's Prince Charming, hand-delivering this talisman like the hero she never asked for.

The numbers climb.

This is insanity. My brain's been hijacked by one too many romance books. I silently vow to detox with at least one Brandon Sanderson fantasy beast before I completely lose my man card in the land of big romantic gestures, bedroom eyes, and happily-ever-afters.

The elevator doors open.

And there she is.

Charlie. Standing in the foyer, flushed and out of breath like she just sprinted a 5K in flip-flops. Still rocking that ridiculous shirt with the most gigantic Tweety Bird you could ever conjure up. *And fuck's sake*, she's clutching The Detonator in one hand like it's a damn TV remote she absentmindedly grabbed while rushing to catch the UPS guy.

"My box," she breathes out.

"Someone left it on the front desk." I hand it over promptly.

Lost in a moment of nostalgia, she runs her free fingers over the faded painted hearts. "That was really nice of you. I guess you ended up the delivery man after all."

I nod. "And fully open to tips. Big tips. Like four thousand dollars to help me make up for the night I just lost out on."

Carefully tucking the box under her arm, she points at my chest with The Detonator, the bottom arm dangling around menacingly. "Hey, that was your choice, buddy. You could've walked right past."

No, I couldn't. Not with those tears in your eyes.

I make eye contact with the vibrator and immediately regret it. "I see you two have bonded. Did you already put that thing to good use in the five minutes I've been gone?"

Her jaw drops like a cartoon anvil, and she fumbles the vibrator like a hot potato between her hands before unintentionally turning it back on again. She slaps it against the chest of her shirt, clutching it desperately and using Tweety's giant head to muffle the vibration. "No. I wasn't. You forgot it. I figured I'd..."

I raise an eyebrow, a smile tugging at the corner of my mouth. "You were coming after me?" I tease, gesturing at the vibrator still clutched against Tweety's face. My heart does a small, unexpected flip.

We stare at each other just listening to the awkward vibrations, pretending we don't know where that sound is coming from.

"Well, I'm here. What did you want?"

She shrugs. "Truthfully, I don't know. I just um...never

mind." She hands over the vibrator like it's painfully embarrassing to do so. "I hope you have a nice date...or party...or wherever you're going." She waves the big black two-dicked sex toy in the air. "And I sincerely hope there are no fatalities because of this thing tonight."

God, I can read her like my favorite book.

I run a hand through my hair. "Job got canceled. The client's pissed. Doesn't want to see me. And now, I'm finding myself very available tonight." My voice comes out rougher than intended.

She shakes her head, her hair catching the amber light from the sconce behind her, making her whole head glow. "I need another secret," she says, fingers tracing the worn edges of her box. "Collateral. Something really embarrassing. Because I'm about to drop another big one on you."

The elevator door beeps—a shrill, impatient sound—and attempts to murder me, steel jaws closing on my shoulder. I jam my elbow against the rubber edge, wincing at the pressure. Charlie steps backward across the plush carpet, making room for me to stay in her orbit.

"Okay. Um..." I step fully into her space, the doors finally surrendering behind me. "I got high with my cat tonight. Like, those were my actual plans this evening until I got the call about a job."

She stares at me, her bright blue eyes widening beneath those impossibly long lashes. "Yeah, that's definitely embarrassing, but I need something deeper. Much more vulnerable." Her lips quirk up at one corner. "Like I need to know if you had a bad circumcision, or have a ridiculous tramp stamp with dolphins or something."

I drop my arms and shake out my shoulders, letting out a long groan. "Uhhh, fine. Okay, here's a big one. The only woman I ever loved left me when my family lost our wealth. It took me three years to stomach that, but tonight I think I just found out that she might've been cheating on me before shit hit the fan. So there's a possibility she didn't just leave me because of money. It's very possible she just didn't want to be with me. It's kind of...messing with my head. I tell everyone I'm over it, but I cried. Not bawled like a baby, but there was a single, glistening manly tear."

The pity permeates her eyes, her head doing that slow tilt, the way someone looks at a three-legged puppy.

"Is that worthy enough?" I ask.

She nods. "Yes. I'm sorry."

"And now you? What secret did you want to swap?"

"I came after you," she admits.

I duck my head, nodding along as I gesture to my abdomen. "I mean, I get it."

She cackles. "You cocky son-of-a-gun. I meant I came after you because I had questions. Whatever your client was going to pay you, I'll match it. I'll pay you more."

"For what, exactly?" I ask. I could've sworn on my life this girl has a boyfriend. I'm sure of it. The guy looks like the doppelgänger of a twenty five-year-old Brad Pitt. "You have sex questions?"

Her nod is so small it barely registers. "Sort of."

"So you want to hire me for tonight?"

"I don't know. I don't ever do this. I always thought this is against the law, but I just..."

I take a step closer, close enough for our body heat to wrap around each other. "You're interested?" I rake my top teeth over my body lip, the universal symbol for, *just ask for what you want.*

"I must sound absolutely off my rocker, right? I don't even know you. You were a total coincidental accident."

I tuck a strand of hair behind her ear, pairing it with a sweet smile. "Sometimes good things are born out of accidents."

"You can't tell anybody?"

I shake my head. "Not a soul. That would hurt us both."

"And if I don't like it, can we stop?"

"Of course," I say gently. "Absolutely. It's all about you. We'll talk numbers, then you just tell me what you want."

Her gaze skips away for a beat, then slowly comes back to meet mine. "And what if I don't know...what I want?"

I try to read the pained expression on her face which seems to say yes and no all at once. I don't like the ambiguity. I step back, giving her space. “Charlie, I’m not into pressuring you, or anyone. If you’re asking me to stay, then I’ll stay. If you’d prefer I go, I’m a ghost. It’s up to you.”

“I want you to stay, I just don’t know what I want because...” She clamps her eyes shut. “I’ve never done it before.”

“Done what?” I eye The Detonator again. “Been with an escort?”

“Had sex, Taio. I’ve never had sex with an escort...or anybody. I’m a virgin.”

Full. Fucking. Stop.

Charlie Riley—pop star, tabloid fixture, woman in crisis—looks at me with those big, tired eyes and makes a choice. “And I’d like you to stay.”

Chapter 6 Charlie

I seem to have this pesky virginity I can't get rid of. Would you mind?

I just told a complete stranger I'm a virgin and basically asked him to take care of that for me. Like I'm returning a defective waffle maker to Target. *Excuse me, sir, I seem to have this pesky virginity I can't get rid of. Would you mind?*

This is fine. Everything is fine. I'm definitely not having a complete mental breakdown in front of the hottest man I've ever seen in real life while wearing a slouchy, cartoon pajama T-shirt while clutching a vibrator that has enough horsepower to jumpstart a Toyota. Totally normal, run-of-the mill evening. Nothing to see here. Just your average girl-meets-boy story. Except instead of a cute coffee shop meet-cute, I'm casually offering my virginity to a professional sex-haver like I'm struggling to get a pickle jar open and his thick, muscular arms are the magic solution.

I swear he was *not this hot* fifteen minutes ago.

I mean, I noticed he was attractive before—in a vague, objective way, the same way you'd notice a nice painting or a well-designed lamp. But now that I'm actually looking at him, now that my brain has apparently decided to fully process visual information for the first time tonight, I'm realizing that "attractive" doesn't quite cover it.

He's gorgeous. The kind of gorgeous that makes my brain short-circuit like I've just licked a 9-volt battery while standing in the rain. The angles of his face are model-like, and his sharp jaw could probably slice cheese with ease. His lips look like he's been sucking on one of those cherry popsicles that stain your tongue for days, and his eyes are so dark yet sparkly, it's like looking into tiny galaxies. And sweet baby giraffe, is this man tall. I'd need NASA's help to kiss him without developing serious neck strain. My five-foot-three self would need a stepladder, a trampoline, and possibly rocket assistance just to boop him on the nose.

I've spent twenty-three years following my mother's advice about waiting for true love. Saving myself for someone special. Someone who would see me—the real me—and choose me every time.

And now I'm about to throw all of that away. Why? I'm not sure, but lately my virginity feels like some kind of bouncer at club Grow The Fuck Up Already, and I'd really like to kick that bastard to the curb so I can finally get in. I'm tired of being treated like a child. Hiring an escort is the antithesis of childish behavior...or so my logic says. My loyal brain is working overtime to make this make sense, because it doesn't. But on the other hand, the last time I can remember actually wanting a man was...never.

This is either rock bottom or the beginning of something. I genuinely cannot tell which.

Taio stands in the entryway like a sculpture that wandered in from a museum, patiently waiting through my silent, category-five mental hurricane. The ticking of the wall clock sounds like a time bomb counting down to social catastrophe. When the awkward lull stretches so long I swear I can see the houseplant growing in real time, he finally asks, "Where do you want me?"

"Um..." My eyes ping-pong between the couch and the hallway leading to my bedroom, which suddenly seems miles away. He reads the panic on my face like I'm a neon billboard flashing: *Virgin in Distress.*

"I meant to sit and talk, Charlie. I'm not asking you what piece of furniture you want me to bend you over."

I palm-smack my forehead so hard I probably leave a cartoon-worthy red mark. "Oh, right. Well, first should I..." I gesture vaguely toward the hallway, my arm flopping like a dying fish. "Shower? Change into something sexier? Burn this Tweety Bird shirt in a ritual sacrifice?"

"Whatever makes you comfortable," he says with the faintest hint of a smile as he retreats to the couch, his long legs folding gracefully into my cramped living space. "And I like the shirt. Team Tweety over Sylvester any day. You look good in it. Very girl next door."

"You like 'girl next door'?" I ask, my voice catching. Part of me wants to believe he finds me genuinely attractive—that beneath the professional veneer, there's something genuine. But another part whispers this is just his job. Does Taio actually get to choose who he sleeps with? Or does he just smile and nod at whatever's in front of him? I picture him checking his watch when I'm not looking, calculating his hourly rate while I fumble through my first time.

"I like you."

I pout at him. "Oh, please. You can't possibly know that yet."

He winks at me. "I can, and I do. I mean, I don't have a ring in my pocket or anything, but you're funny, nice, and so refreshingly down-to-earth. I'm happy to be here."

"Okay," I chirp out uncomfortably as if his compliments might eat me alive. "I'm just going to go..." I don't finish my sentence, I'm already gone, bolting toward the master bathroom like my T-shirt is on fire. Which, metaphorically speaking, it should be. No one in the history of seduction has ever successfully gotten laid while dressed as a cartoon canary.

I slam the bathroom door behind me and catch my reflection in the mirror.

Oh. *Oh no.*

It's worse than I thought. The shirt is even more aggressively yellow under the bathroom lights. My hair is somehow greasy and dry, just really doing the most to cover all bases. My face is a topographical map of exhaustion—dark circles, blotchy skin, the general pallor of someone who hasn't seen direct sunlight in weeks.

This is the face of a woman about to have sex for the first time? This is the body I'm offering to a man who probably sleeps with supermodels on a regular basis?

Triage. I need triage.

I rip the ponytail holder out of my hair, wincing as it takes several strands with it. Finger-comb. Finger-comb harder. Okay, that's...marginally better. Not great, just better. I can settle for that. Now, onto makeup. I dig through my toiletry bag with the frantic energy of a surgeon looking for a scalpel. Foundation—no time. Concealer—can't find it. Mascara—yes, that'll help, mascara makes everyone look more awake and alive and less like a sleep-deprived gremlin—

I yank the wand out of the tube and jab it directly into my eyeball.

"*Fuck!*" I roar with an intensity that surprises even me.

Pain. Immediate, searing pain. My eye floods faster than the *Titanic* taking on seawater, and each blink feels like sandpaper coated in whiskey. The mascara spreads in an artistically questionable black river, transforming my under-eye area into what can only be described as a raccoon's attempt at goth makeup after three espresso martinis.

I try to fix it with my finger. This transfers mascara to my other eye somehow. Now I have two black smudges. I look like a sad panda who lost a boxing match.

I grab a tissue and scrub at the mess, but the mascara is waterproof—of course it's waterproof, I only use the industrial-strength kind for tour—and all I'm doing is smearing the disaster across a wider surface area.

I stop. Hands braced on the sink. Staring at the catastrophe in the mirror. I look like a clown. A sad, exhausted, sexually frustrated clown who is definitely not about to seduce anyone tonight. A hysterical laugh bubbles up in my throat. Or maybe it's a sob. It's hard to tell the difference lately.

I hear my mother's voice in my head. *What are you doing, Charlie? Tell him to leave. This is absolute madness. This isn't you. I know you're lonely, but this isn't the answer.*

"Charlie?" Taio's voice, soft through the bathroom door, chases my mother's warnings away. He follows with a gentle knock. "You okay in there?"

No. I am absolutely not okay. I am the opposite of okay. I am the dictionary definition of not okay, illustrated with a picture of my raccoon face.

"Fine," I manage. "Just...technical difficulties."

A pause. Then, he asks, "Can I come in?"

I should say no. I should fix my face, find something silk to wear, emerge looking like the confident, sexy woman I'm pretending to be. Instead I hear myself say, "Yeah."

The door opens. Taio takes one look at me and his expression does something complicated. Something flickers across his face, frustration that melts instantly into softness. Now there's only pity in his dark eyes. He doesn't laugh. Doesn't tease. Just walks toward me like he's approaching a wounded animal.

"Here," he offers quietly. "Let me."

Before I can protest, his hands are on my waist, lifting me onto the bathroom counter like I weigh nothing. The marble is cold on my bare legs. He's standing between my knees now, close enough that I can smell him—something warm and clean, soap and skin with a rich, spicy hint underneath. Intoxicating. Teasing. Yet, so familiar for some odd reason.

He reaches past me for a washcloth, runs it under warm water, wrings it out. Then he cups my chin with one hand, tilting my face up toward the light.

"Close your eyes," he murmurs.

I close them. Feel the warm, damp cloth against my skin as he gently—so gently, you'd think he was cleansing a butterfly's wings—wipes away the mess I made. His other hand stays on my chin, steadying me. The bathroom seems to shrink around us, the air growing thick with something unspoken as he traces the cloth along the curve of my cheekbone.

This is more intimate than anything I've ever experienced. A man I barely know, cleaning mascara off my face in a penthouse bathroom, treating me like something precious instead of something broken.

I don't know what to do with that.

"Why tonight?" he asks, still dabbing at the smudges under my eyes.

"I normally wear mascara. I was trying to—"

"No. Sex, Charlie," he clarifies with a little chuckle. "Why do you suddenly want to have sex tonight? You've waited how many years?"

"Twenty-three." I don't offer anything else right away. The question feels bigger than he knows.

"You can open your eyes."

I do. He's close—so close I can see the flecks of gold in his dark irises, the slight furrow between his brows. He's looking at me like he actually wants to know. Like my answer matters.

"I let it get too big, I think."

He cradles my knee so gently, I find myself craving the pressure. A new kind of desire bubbles beneath my belly button. Something definitely different. Far more powerful than my usual anxiety and nerves around the opposite sex.

"What does that mean?"

"The idea of sex. I let it get to be this big, scary, ugly, hairy monster of nightmares. Honestly? I don't really understand the appeal. Getting that close to someone has to be the most awkward, uncomfortable thing. I never understood why everyone is so obsessed with it."

He blinks at me like I just said the world was flat. "I think once you try it, you'll see why everyone seems to like it."

"Not the physical, Taio," I whisper-whine; it sounds like a deflating balloon animal. "I've orchestrated my own standing ovations, thank you very much. It's the whole...soul-naked thing. Trusting someone enough to let them see you...*really see you*. I thought all the stuff my mom wrote me was lived experience. Like she understood love on a deeper level and wanted me to experience that too. I've had my mom on this pedestal for so long. I wake up every day, and when the internet hates me, or I'm splattered across some tabloid nonsense that is so ridiculous everyone gobbles it up without thinking twice, I remind myself that the only person I have to impress is her. If my mom is proud of me, I'm all right. But then I found that letter." I duck my head, shaking it slowly.

A teasing smile gleams on his face. "Let's circle back to that part about orchestrating your own standing ovations, because I'm dying to hear more about *that*, but in the meantime...what letter?"

"I found a letter," I hear myself say. "Three months ago. From my biological father."

Taio's hands still, but he doesn't pull away. Just waits.

"I never knew him. My mom told me he didn't want me. That he was just some guy who got her pregnant and disappeared. My whole life, that was the story. Unwanted. Abandoned. And fuck, I hated him. I thought he was a selfish, cowardly piece of..." I swallow hard. "Then I found this letter, and it turns out, he begged her. Begged her to let him be part of my life. He wanted to leave his wife, raise me, be a family. And my mom said no. She kept me from him."

The words are coming faster now, spilling out like water through a crack in a dam, then a broken levee, then a biblical flood that could drown cities. I get it's ridiculous—like wearing-a-ball-gown-to-buy-milk ridiculous—but isn't that the whole glorious point of an escort? For one night, he's mine. All mine. My personal emotional hazmat team, contracted to wade through my radioactive feelings without judgment. We're bound by the beautiful secrecy of it all, two strangers passing like ships in the night, except one ship is paying the other ship an obscene amount of money to solve its ship problems.

The danger of it thrums through me like electricity.

"I'm sorry. Believe it or not, I understand what it feels like to be lied to by a parent when you trust them with everything."

"Your dad?" I ask.

He gives a half-hearted, one-shoulder shrug. "Enough about me. How do you feel about your mom, now?"

"She lied to me. She went to her grave *knowing* she was going to keep lying to me. All those paper hearts she left me—all that advice about waiting for true love, believing in myself, keeping my heart open, taking chances—it was all hypocritical bullshit. I could've had a different life. Simple. White picket fences. Sunday dinners. Having a baby without having to plan a pregnancy around a world tour. Making homemade cupcakes for my kid's school's bake sale. Maybe those things would've been enough. Maybe if my mom wasn't dead, and my dad wasn't kept from me, I wouldn't have needed all this"—I wave my hands in the air, gesturing to God knows what—"to fill the void. Every damn day I wake up and wait for strangers on the internet to tell me how I should feel about myself and I just..."

I growl out in frustration now, speaking more to myself than Taio. "I am so sick of myself. And I have no one to blame but me. I chose this career. Sold my soul for it, it would seem. And now I hate it? I hate performing, I hate being a star. I just want to be on the ground, bare feet in the grass. I want to experience life and love like everybody else. Maybe that's why I can't write a damn song to save my life. Ironically while the world thinks I have everything, I actually have nothing worth singing about. That's why I collapsed on stage. I couldn't perform for one more second. Finishing that performance felt physically impossible. But starting next week, I have to do the impossible, thirty-four more times."

Taio sets the washcloth down. His hand finds mine on the counter, warm and steady.

"So you think sex will make you feel more human?" he asks carefully. "Like the rest of us?"

"Am I out of my mind?"

Taio shakes his head. "I don't think so, at all. I think you're lonely and looking to connect with someone." He cradles my cheek, his hand so big it could palm my entire face like a basketball. It's mostly smooth and warm, but callused in places I wouldn't expect. The kind of hand that could build something or break something. "I also think it's okay if you're mad at your mom. It doesn't mean you don't love her."

I give him a small nod. "Thanks for saying that."

The air grows quiet between us, the tension thick as pudding. The bathroom suddenly feels like a snow globe someone forgot to shake—two tiny figures frozen in a forever-looping moment. I realize if I don't make the first move, then we won't move.

I reach for the hem of my shirt. My hands are trembling, but I'm committed now. I'm doing this. I'm taking control of something for the first time in years—

Taio's hands cover mine, stopping me. "Charlie."

"What?"

He's looking at me with those dark eyes, and there's something in his expression I can't name. Not rejection. Not pity. Something gentler than both.

"Let's not rush," he says. "Let's not do this."

It lands like a slap. Heat floods my face—embarrassment, shame, the specific humiliation of being turned down by someone you're literally trying to pay for sex.

"I thought—you said...Is it the money? Because I'll pay whatever."

"I know what I said." His hands are still on mine, warm and steady, his thumb tracing an absent figure-eight pattern across my knuckles like he's trying to soothe a spooked animal. "But that was before I knew what you were actually asking for. I think I can give you what you need. Come with me."

He helps me down from the counter, and I follow him out of the bathroom on shaky legs, not sure what's happening but too wrung out to resist.

He leads me through the penthouse to the wraparound patio I've barely used since I got here. The outdoor space is massive—bigger than most city apartments—with a fully stocked bar, string lights draped overhead, and a view of Manhattan that demands a seven-figure income. The air hits my flushed skin like a splash of ice water, Manhattan's midnight frost slipping under my thin shirt and raising goose bumps along my arms. It's miserable cold, only survivable because of all the patio heaters.

Taio walks straight to the bar like he owns the place, ducking behind it and surveying the bottles with a critical eye.

"You bartend too?" I ask, settling onto one of the outdoor barstools.

"Jack of all trades." He grabs a shaker, some bottles, starts pouring with practiced ease. "When you're trying to make rent in New York, you learn a lot of skills. I bounced for clubs, waitered, bartended, anything to scrape together a little money before—"

"You became an escort?"

He nods. "Yeah. This pays better than all of those combined."

I watch him work—bottles flipping, ice clinking, liquid arcing in precise streams. He's showing off a little, and I find myself smiling despite everything.

"What's that?" I ask as he slides a bright pink drink across the bar.

"Something fun. You look like you could use fun."

I take a sip. It's sweet and tart and goes down dangerously easy. "That's really good."

"This bar is *very* stocked. Who keeps vermouth on hand?" He grins, already making himself something darker.

My eyes drift across the patio, taking in details I'd ignored before. The outdoor sectional with its mountain of pillows. The firepit. And tucked in the corner, a karaoke machine with a microphone still attached. "There was a bachelorette party booked in this suite before me. They got kicked out early to make room for a VIP guest." I stare into my pink drink. "Me. I'm the VIP guest who ruined someone's bachelorette party."

"I'm sure they got upgraded to somewhere nice."

"Probably. But still." I sigh. "I hate that narrative. The spoiled rich brat who takes whatever she wants. I've spent my whole life trying not to be that person. Ever since Nate adopted me, I've tried so hard to be grateful. To deserve what I have. To not be a burden or a disappointment or—"

"Charlie," Taio cuts me off, not unkindly. "Can I ask you something?"

"Sure."

"Is the real problem with performing that you're more worried about what everyone else thinks of you than what you think of yourself?"

The question lands somewhere deep. I open my mouth to deflect, to make a joke, to do the thing I always do when someone gets too close to the truth.

Nothing comes out.

Taio gestures toward the karaoke machine. "Why don't you sing a song the way you like to. Not the way your label tells you you have to."

"What?"

"Your real voice. The one I heard through the door when I first got here." He comes around the bar, drink in hand, and settles onto the outdoor sectional. "Sing for an audience of one. No label. No fans. No judgment. Just you, and me, and whatever song you want."

"That's—" I shake my head. "Uncomfortable."

"More uncomfortable than sex with a stranger?"

"Yes. Obviously yes."

He just looks at me, patient and steady, like he's got all night. Which, I guess, he does.

"Fine," I grumble. I drain the rest of my drink for courage and walk to the karaoke machine on legs that feel like jelly. The screen glows blue in the darkness as I scroll through the song options. Pop hits. Classic rock. Broadway standards. None of them feel right.

Then I see it.

"Hallelujah."

My hand hovers over the selection. I haven't sung this song since I was eleven years old. One of Dad's charity galas—the band canceled last minute, and I filled in. I remember standing on that stage, so small the microphone stand had to be lowered all the way, singing the words I barely understood to a room full of adults in fancy clothes.

It was one of my mom's favorite songs. She taught it to me. We used to sing it together in the kitchen while she made dinner, her voice a rich harmony with my five-year-old squeals of delight as I tried to hit the high notes.

I remember how music used to make me feel. Before the label. Before the brand. Before I became a product to be packaged and sold. Before every note had to have a return on investment. Music used to feel like magic.

"This one," I say quietly.

"Yeah?"

"I don't need the screen. I know the words by heart." I select it before I can change my mind.

"Then that's the one." Taio settles deeper into the cushions, giving me his full attention.

The opening notes fill the patio—soft, haunting, familiar as my own heartbeat.

I close my eyes. Take a breath. And sing.

Not the pop princess version. I sing it like a broken person, because I am. I sing it like it hurts, because it does. The real me. The sadness I've been stuffing down for years because someone in a suit didn't know how to market the real me.

The first verse comes out shaky, rusty from disuse. But by the chorus, something shifts. The tightness in my chest loosens. The words stop being words and become something else—prayer, confession, release. I'm not singing for forty thousand strangers. I'm not performing for cameras or critics or fans who might turn on me tomorrow. I'm singing for a man on a couch who showed up at my door by accident and stayed on purpose.

I'm singing for myself. Testing my vocal range, dancing through the octaves, leaping up to hit the high notes, and letting the low baritones settle deep in my chest.

I turn around to see the city glitter below me, eight million lives humming along in the darkness. The stars burn above, faint but persistent through the light pollution. And I pour everything into this song—the grief, the anger, the loneliness, the desperate hope that somewhere inside me is still a person worth knowing.

By the time I reach the final hallelujah, I'm shaking. Tears are streaming down my face again, but these feel different. Cleaner somehow. Hopeful release.

I let the last note fade into the night air. The silence that follows is terrifying. I turn back around, afraid to open my eyes. Afraid to see boredom, or pity, or worse—nothing at all.

"Charlie," he says like a command, and I look.

Taio is staring at me like I just cracked open the sky.

His lips are parted. His eyes are bright. He looks...undone. Swept away. Like he's seeing me—really seeing me—for the first time.

No one has ever looked at me like that. Not once in my entire life. I haven't wanted them to. It felt like too much pressure.

"I was pitchy on the first verse—"

"Stop," he says. "Voice of a fucking angel. Don't you ever doubt it. Sing it again? Please?"

"Again?" My voice comes out hoarse.

He smiles, slow and warm, and something in my chest blooms. "I could listen to you sing all night."

So I do.

I sing "Hallelujah" again, because I'm not ready to let go of this feeling yet. And this time, as the melody wraps around me, something new starts to emerge. Fragments. Phrases. The ghost of a song I've never heard before.

Paper hearts and frozen time...
This stranger made his secrets mine...

The lyrics surface from somewhere deep, unbidden, unexpected—like artifacts washing up on a shore I didn't know existed within me. They come complete: melody, harmony, bridge, and all. I file them away while my mouth continues forming the familiar words of "Hallelujah," but my mind is already spinning in a new direction, chasing this sudden gift, this fragile thread of creation that appeared the moment I stopped performing for them and started simply singing for him. It feels like waking up after years of sleepwalking through my own career.

Taio is inspiring me. Just by being here. Just by listening. Just by looking at me like I'm worth his time even without a return on investment.

I finish the song, and the silence that follows feels sacred somehow. Like we've built this fragile, beautiful thing between us, and any sudden movement might shatter it.

I set down the microphone. Walk toward him on unsteady legs.

Taio stands, meeting me halfway. And then his arms are around me, pulling me into a hug I didn't know I desperately needed. I melt into it, the way ice cream dissolves on a hot summer day, all the sharp edges softening. The warmth of his chest radiates through my thin shirt, a furnace against the night's chill. The steady thump of his heartbeat against my cheek becomes a metronome, more reliable than any backing track I've ever sung to. His chin rests lightly on the top of my head, and I feel sheltered, like a small bird tucked beneath protective wings. How long has it been since I've been held like this? Not the quick, perfunctory embraces from publicists or the calculated hugs for photo ops, but like *this*—this genuine connection of two bodies finding comfort in each other's presence.

I understand now. It's obvious I'm not having sex with Taio tonight. It's why he hasn't brought up the money. Like a tortured hero, it seems he's trying to save me from myself. But we did take a massive step forward. Because this hug? It's bigger than sex.

It's intimacy.

We stand there near the balcony ledge, wrapped up in each other, the city sprawled beneath us like a blanket of stars. I close my eyes and breathe him in and think about paper hearts and frozen time and the beginning of a song I can't name yet. I'm not ready. I just want to stay here, wrapped in his arms.

And then I see it.

A flash of light, bright and brief, from somewhere in the darkness beyond the patio.

Then another.

My body goes rigid. Taio feels the change immediately.

"What?"

I pull back, practically shoving Taio away, my gaze scanning the shadows, the rooftops, the windows of the buildings across the street.

Another flash. And another.

Camera lights. Unmistakable. Coming from somewhere I can't pinpoint, capturing everything—me in my Tweety Bird shirt, wrapped in the arms of a strange man on my private patio, tears still wet on my cheeks.

"Charlie?" Taio asks, concerned now. "What's wrong?"

I can't answer immediately. My throat has closed up.

How? Fucking how? The paparazzi found me.

"We were just photographed," I breathe out.

"Okay. I'm sorry, but don't you get photographed a lot?" he asks innocently.

"You don't understand...This is going to be all over the internet tomorrow." I hang my head in shame. "And I have a boyfriend."

Chapter 7

Taio

This wasn't part of the plan. I wasn't part of the plan.

"I just want it on record," Cam announces, adjusting his mask for the fifteenth time, "that when you said 'guys' night,' I pictured a bar. Maybe a steakhouse. Possibly a strip club if we were feeling inspired. Not..." He gestures at the open field around us. "Whatever the hell this is."

"Strip club's still open, Cam. Feel free to see yourself out." Forrest points to the arena entrance with his pen, not looking up from the tactical map he drew on a napkin. An actual tactical map. With arrows and positions and what I think might be enemy sight lines. "A plan builds trust. Trust builds cohesion. Cohesion wins battles."

"We're not in a battle. We're grown-ass men playing paintball in Jersey who had to get dressed in a gym locker that smells like old cheese and a tire fire."

Forrest taps his temple, eyes still glued to his unimpressive map. "The battlefield is a state of mind," he murmurs.

Cam turns to me. "He's been like this for twenty minutes. I'm starting to worry."

"Hawk?" I ask. Forrest actually makes eye contact with me. "Is Sora letting you out of the house enough? You know...like for fresh air?"

"Is Hawk like a cool battlefield nickname?" Cam asks,

suddenly looking intrigued. "Do we all get nicknames?"

Saylor materializes beside us, crouched low behind a stack of inflatable barriers, already in full tactical mode. "His name is Forrest *Hawkins*, you eager-ass puppy. No one is getting cool ops nicknames. We're not taking a blood oath. Quite frankly, your presence here is optional, especially with all the bellyaching."

"Harsh, Say," Forrest adds.

"He did just call him a mama's boy two days ago," I mumble.

"Right." Forrest turns his gaze to Cam. "Sorry. Justified."

"Do we at least head to a bar afterward and get our drink on?" Cam asks.

"*We* are." Forrest points to me, Saylor, then himself. "Jury's still out on if you're invited. Let's see if you hit your targets first. I'm going to test our radios." He paces a few feet away.

Saylor, being a good sport, picks his walkie-talkie up in full support of Forrest's over-the-top leadership.

"Bravo Team, this is Alpha Leader." Forrest's voice crackles through the cheap walkie-talkies he insisted we needed. His back is turned but he's standing ten feet away. We can see him clear as crystal against the dusky sky. "What's your twenty?"

"We're right here, Hawk. Turn around and you're looking right at us," I gripe, my tone suddenly matching Cam's because I'd like to be doing anything else than playing paintball today. I'm too distracted, worried about the growingly menacing headlines that have been swarming, just as Charlie predicted two days ago.

"Radio protocol—" Forrest starts. He's interrupted by a loud grumble from Cam.

"I swear to God, if you say 'radio protocol' one more time, I'm defecting to the other team."

"Great. Do it. Gives me a really interesting target," Say gripes.

I should be paying attention to this. I should be fully immersed in the primal art of pelting strangers with neon-colored paint projectiles while Forrest channels his inner G.I. Joe, complete with unnecessarily intense hand signals and useless information on military equipment. This is our sacred ritual. When we're playing paintball, we're no longer grown men with real problems and responsibilities. We don our plastic armor that makes us look like we're acting out a scene in *Call of Duty*, and pretend for a couple hours that the solution to all our shitty baggage is annihilating the opposing team.

Even after Forrest abandoned our apartment and the escort business for domestic bliss, the ritual remained. We're friends who've seen each other at our best, worst, and most ridiculous. This is supposed to be an escape, but I'm chained and trapped by the guilt of what happened on that balcony. I shouldn't have touched her. I shouldn't have gift-wrapped her for the wolves with their telephoto lenses and clickbait headlines.

Charlie was clearly barely holding herself together with tape and prayers. I just set her world on fire in the worst way.

"Taio." Forrest's voice cuts through my spiral and suddenly I'm staring at his boots. "You with us?"

I rise, then huddle into the team circle with all the renewed enthusiasm of a cat being forced to attend its own birthday party. My paintball gun dangles from my fingers like an overcooked noodle. "Yeah. Sorry. What's the plan?"

"Cam takes left flank. Saylor takes right. You're with me up the middle. We breach in thirty."

Cam blinks. "I don't know what any of those words mean."

Forrest rolls his eyes so dramatically his entire head follows the motion, like a human-sized bobblehead. "Just go left and try not to get shot."

"Which left?"

"There's only one left, Cam," Say grunts out.

"There's also a right. And a middle. And frankly, I'd rather be at the bar around the corner, which is south."

Forrest pinches the bridge of his nose, trying to control his exasperation. "Just follow Say. Do what he does."

Saylor nods with enthusiasm. "Right in front of me, mate. *Like a human shield.*"

"Fine. But I want it noted that I'm here under protest."

"Noted. Now move."

We move. Or rather, Forrest and Saylor move with the fluid precision of men who take this way too seriously. Cam wanders vaguely leftward, looking like a man who just time-traveled and is trying to orient himself with this strange new world. I move like someone whose brain is three miles away, tangled up in memories of a cartoon Tweety shirt and a voice like heartbreak.

A paintball whizzes past my ear. Then another. The enemy team has spotted us. Easily. Probably because Cam is walking around like an inflatable tube man.

"Get down, we're made," Saylor warns about a second too late.

I take a hit to the shoulder. The impact stings—a sharp bloom of pain that'll leave a bruise tomorrow.

Another hit. Chest this time. I roar more out of frustration than anything. Ten seconds into the match and I'm sat? What the fuck?

"Taio's down!" Saylor shouts. "Hawk, it's the three of us. Let's just—" He stops short and I hear a cry of agony coming from my distant left. "Shit. Just two of us," Say says through the radio. "Cam just got pelted."

"Just leave me, bro," Cam pleads through the radio with mock theatrics. "Finish the mission."

"Yeah, we were going to, buddy. Ty—you good?"

"Yup, just headed to the loser bench," I answer defeatedly.

I raise my hands and trudge toward the dead zone. Cam joins me approximately two minutes later, having been cornered behind a barrier and shot repeatedly while yelling "*I surrender, I surrender*" to opponents who clearly didn't care.

Cam collapses onto the bench beside me, clutching his neck like he's been hit by a sniper rather than a paintball. "This is a war crime," he declares, voice pitched uncannily like a toddler who was denied ice cream. "That jackass in the blue mask saw I was surrendering and shot me anyway. *In the neck!* That's fucking illegal." He yanks his collar down dramatically. "Look at this monstrosity. It's bad already, isn't it?" The welt is indeed impressive—angry red with a purple center, pulsing like it's trying to communicate in Morse code.

"No, man. You can't even see it," I lie, just to stop his whining.

I'm already on my phone, scrolling through headlines with a growing knot in my stomach. The news has gotten worse since I checked this morning. *Much worse.*

CHEATER CHARLIE: Pop Princess Caught in Secret Tryst

Grayson Hayes "Blindsided" by Girlfriend's Balcony Betrayal

Mystery Man Identified? Internet Sleuths Hunt for Charlie Riley's Secret Lover

That last one makes my blood pressure spike, but when I click through, it's just speculation. Someone thinks the mystery man might be a backup dancer. Someone else is convinced it's her bodyguard. A third theory involves a member of a boy band I've never heard of.

No one's identified me. My head was ducked during the hug—chin tucked against the top of Charlie's head, face hidden from the cameras. All the photos show is my back, my shoulders, the dark shape of someone who could be anyone.

I'm safe.

Charlie is not.

#CheaterCharlie is trending. So is #FakeBarbie and #GraysonDeservesBetter. The comments section is a dumpster fire of strangers competing to say the cruelest thing about a woman they've never met.

The game ends with a shrill electronic wail. Forrest and Saylor trudge back to us, their uniforms dirt-splattered but free of paint. Their smiles are triumphant. They've somehow clinched victory despite being down to half strength almost immediately. Forrest's face carries the smug satisfaction of a general who's just conquered a small nation, while Saylor's already dissecting our failed strategy with military precision.

"If you two hadn't abandoned your posts so quickly, we could've dominated them completely," Saylor says, pulling off his mask.

Cam rubs his neck welt. "Stupid game you guys take way too seriously," he mutters.

"All right, chump. Go put your big-boy pants on. We'll take you out for a beer now." Forrest ruffles Cam's hair like a child. Cam swats him away and we all head to the locker room. The space is cramped and smells like rubber and old sweat. Cam is already lobbying for his favorite bar that he's been grumping about all afternoon. Saylor is half listening, stripping off his gear with practiced efficiency.

I'm on my phone again, and this time my face must give something away.

"Mate." Saylor drops onto the bench across from me. "What's got you so twisted up? You've been somewhere else all day."

I don't answer right away. I'm reading Grayson Hayes's official statement—a carefully crafted bit of press manipulation designed to make him look like a wounded saint. His statement reads like a PR master class: "Charlie and I request space during this difficult time. We appreciate your understanding as we navigate these personal challenges away from the public eye."

But the ambiguity might as well be Charlie's social death sentence. The comments are a flood of support for her apparently jilted beau. *Poor Grayson. He deserves better. She never appreciated what she had.*

Forrest drops onto the bench beside me with a grunt, tugging at his bootlaces. I catch him exchanging a look with Saylor—that silent bro-code communication where eyebrows do all the talking.

"I can see you two," I mutter. "Subtlety isn't your strong suit."

Forrest claps a hand on my shoulder. "Sora's locked away working on her manuscript, and I don't get Koda back until next week. My schedule is wide open for whatever existential crisis you're having."

Instead of answering, I flip my phone around and hold it up.

Forrest squints at it. "The singer?"

"Yeah.

"Read the headlines."

Forrest scans the article, then hands the phone to Saylor.

"Okay, so she cheated on that douchebag who is ruining the Marvel remakes, by the way. Cheating is hardly news in Hollywood, mate. Did you place a bet on this couple or something?" Say asks.

"She's not cheating," I answer flatly. "Because they're in a fake relationship."

Forrest lifts his brows so high they nearly disappear into his hairline, his expression shifting from confusion to concern like someone watching a friend claim they were abducted and probed by aliens. "And you care because?"

"I'm the guy in the photos. I caused this."

"Come again?" Forrest asks.

An eavesdropping Cam stops rubbing his neck and swivels around. Saylor's jaw drops as he zeroes in on the picture on my phone. "No way, mate. You're way too tall to be this guy. Are you sure it's you?"

"That's because I'm practically folded in half. Charlie barely comes up to my shoulder." I tap the blurry image on my screen. "But yeah, that's me. I know because *I was there*. We weren't—it wasn't what they're saying. She was upset, I gave her a hug, that's it."

"How did you end up in Charlie Riley's penthouse?" Cam asks accusingly.

"Why? Jealous?"

"Uh, yeah. I'd leap with that. How is she?" he asks.

I have to bunch my fist like I'm squeezing an invisible stress ball to avoid wrapping it around Cam's neck. Mental note: petition

Rina for veto power on group chat additions. I can't control who she hires, but this human embodiment of a participation trophy needs to stay approximately thirteen zip codes away from me.

"How did this happen?" Forrest says. "Rina doesn't like celebrity clientele. Too much risk for gossip."

"Charlie wasn't a job," I explain. "She was a..." What exactly was that? Wrong place, wrong time? Or exactly where I needed to be with exactly the right person? How do you categorize a head-on collision that leaves no wreckage, just endless unanswered questions? "I was at the wrong hotel. Autocorrect of all things. We met, and we...talked. She sang outside on the patio which maybe is what invited the cameras."

Cam pries my phone from Saylor's death grip and examines the image. "That doesn't look like talking."

"It's complicated," I huff out.

"Like you guys were talking in your underwear?"

"I'm fully dressed, and she's wearing clothes. A pajama shirt and..." Well, I'm not going to say tight little pink spandex that I wanted to peel off her like a banana out loud. "Shorts."

"It'll pass. It always does. Impossible to make you out in this photo, mate. You'll be fine," Say offers, firm in his resolve.

"I wasn't worried about me," I admit. "I can't imagine she's taking this well."

"Have you talked to her?" Hawk asks.

I shake my head. "After we saw the cameras going off, she snuck me out of the service elevator and I basically fled the scene. She was terrified. I didn't want to stress her out anymore. I did exactly what she needed. I disappeared. I don't know how to get a hold of her. I'm sure she's not checking her social media at the moment. I doubt she's still at the hotel. I mean I could swing by, maybe?"

"Don't you think you two being seen together would make things far worse?"

I nod solemnly. "Fair."

Hawk pats me on the back, all chummy and supportive.

"Her people have people. They will handle it. That's what they do. There's an entire army of protection around Charlie Riley. She'll be fine. Don't beat yourself up."

"I know." But they didn't meet the girl I did. So broken, hopeless, and very much alone. What good is an army if they can't stop her from drowning in her own head? Who's treating her like a person, and who is treating her like a product? Are those paper hearts her mom left going to be enough? I can't help but worry because for better or worse, we had a moment. An exchange of vulnerability that somehow tethers us to each other and has left me with all these damn questions.

"All right, beer o'clock." Cam slams the locker after collecting his stuff. The welt is angrier than ever and I know he's going to screech like a baby bird when he catches a glimpse of himself in the mirror.

"I'm going to take a rain check," I say, holding out my hand until Cam returns my phone. I pocket my phone carefully like it's a bomb that'll erupt at any moment. "Black Cat's probably planning my murder."

"You still haven't named that thing?" Hawk asks.

"Black Cat *is* his name."

"That's a description, not a name. A pet should have a real name," Saylor adds.

"He's not my pet. We're cohabiting, not bonding. Any day the call of the wild is going to whisk him right back on the streets of Brooklyn." But not even I believe that. Black Cat is getting a little thick, like a few new-relationship-happy pounds, which makes me think this drifter thinks we're in some sort of commitment situation. He's wrong. I don't do that anymore.

"Didn't you buy him a heated blanket?" Say asks. "I remember because you used my Amazon Prime account."

I glower at Saylor for calling me on my bullshit. "It's February in the Northeast. I'm unattached, I'm not a monster."

We say our goodbyes in the parking lot—Forrest and Saylor reluctantly agreeing to one beer with youngblood over here.

I climb into the back of my budget Uber that arrives right on time. A tiny Corolla that can barely contain me. I have to bend my legs like a wilted spider to fit in the back seat. Once I'm somewhat situated, I go back to my own internet sleuthing, pulling down on the screen, hoping for new articles related to my "Charlie Riley" search. To my surprise, a new one posted barely five minutes ago. I lunge to the CelebNow article, hungry for the details. Headline:

Charlie Riley Cancels Boston Show: "Personal Reasons" Cited

The first few lines of the article speculate that the entire tour is canceled and Charlie is dragging out the inevitable for attention. My chest tightens. Again, that's not true. She told me she wanted to finish the damn thing, to show up for her fans, to reignite her passion for performing. This wasn't part of the plan. *I* wasn't part of the plan. And now? She's worse off for knowing me.

I should've gotten her number. Should've thought past the moment. But everything happened so fast—the boyfriend bomb, the fake-relationship explanation, the awkward goodbye, the elevator ride where I convinced myself it was cleaner this way. Ships in the night. A collision that was never meant to last.

So why do I feel responsible?

And why did that goodbye feel like a beginning?

Black Cat is stationed by the door when I get home, his grumpiness radiating.

"Hey." I toss my keys on the counter. "Miss me?"

He meows—a sound that roughly translates to: *My dinner is late. You'll be hearing from my attorney.*

"You have an automatic feeder. You're literally the least neglected creature in Brooklyn." But the kibble won't cut it. He wants his wet food, served on his stainless-steel platter, the bougie little beast.

Another demanding meow.

"Fine," I grumble, fully recognizing who owns whom. I don't

have a cat, I have a furry overlord.

I fork tuna into his bowl and watch him attack it like it's personally wronged him. Even with Black Cat's coos of appreciation between the satisfied smacking sounds while he eats, the apartment feels too quiet. Too small. *Too alone.*

I check my phone again and am disappointed to see #CheaterCharlie still trending and on the rise. I read the comments, looking for the unsung heroes defending her, urging the trolls not to jump to conclusions because hugging someone isn't a crime. But the unsung heroes are buried under the avalanche of hate and negativity. All of this over a hug...No wonder Charlie hates the spotlight. It never highlights the good. Only the unhinged.

I have to get in touch, somehow. I need to figure out a way to help, or at least promise Charlie she has my discretion. I should—

Knock, knock.

I freeze. No one knocks. The building has a buzzer, and my friends would've texted before they showed up to make sure I had beer.

Another knock. Sharp. Impatient.

Who the fuck?

Trying to keep my footsteps quiet, I make my way to the door and check the peephole.

A woman. Tall, angular, red-brown hair pulled back in a tight, low ponytail. Structured blazer. Silk blouse. The kind of understated elegance that indicates she's important. Even her posture radiates authority—arms crossed, chin lifted, the expression of someone who bills by the hour and deeply resents every second she's wasting. Oh fuck—she's giving lawyer vibes. Maybe she's here on Charlie's behalf to serve me a gag order. Hiring an escort can't look good for her reputation, but I'll just calmly explain nothing happened and no money changed hands...

I slowly pull open the door. "Yes?"

Her eyes sweep over me, cataloging the paint-speckled jeans, the rumpled shirt, whatever haunted expression I'm currently wearing. The assessment takes two seconds. I don't pass. "You've gotta be kidding me," she mumbles under her breath. "Taio Wilkes." She says my name like a statement, not a question.

I answer anyway. "That'd be me."

"I'm Sage Hilston, the head of Charlie Riley's PR team." Her eyes narrow, her tone is ice, wrapped in smooth silk. "We need to talk. Or, more accurately, you need to listen."

Chapter 8
Taio

You should work on your negotiation skills.

My brain is sending emergency alerts to every nerve ending—slam the door, change your name, flee the country—but I swallow hard and wave Sage into my apartment with all the enthusiasm of a man inviting in a tax auditor.

She crosses the threshold like she's entering a crime scene, carefully assessing and cataloging every detail for future evidence. Her eyes sweep across the cramped living room, lingering on the secondhand couch with its suspicious stains, the coffee table propped up by a Stephen King paperback, my dog-eared romance book with the pink flowers I forgot to hide, and the general ambiance of "man who has given up on impressing anyone."

From his perch on the kitchen counter, Black Cat arches his back at the sight of Sage, releasing a hiss that is undoubtedly full of cat cuss words.

I gesture toward the kitchen counter. "Meet Black Cat. Don't take the hissing personally—this is him being sociable."

Sage's eyebrow arches. "You actually named your cat...Black Cat? Seems lazy." She unsubtly glances around my moderately tidy, could-be-worse apartment.

"It's not lazy. It's quantum physics. Until I give him a real name, he exists in a state of both being and not being my cat." I shrug. "You know...like Schrödinger's cat."

"I don't think that's what Schrödinger's cat represents." The words drip with judgment.

"Fair enough." My smile feels tight across my face. "Drink? I should warn you"—I retreat toward the kitchen, grateful for the excuse to put furniture between us—"my options are limited to..."

I open the fridge and face my barren food desert—a half-empty Tampico jug and three beers huddled together like the last survivors of the apocalypse. A single slice of American cheese curls at the edges like it's trying to escape the Tupperware container that I've been afraid to open since Forrest moved out. I sigh.

"If you're feeling nutritious, I have orange juice, or beer if you prefer?"

Sage peers around me at the fridge's sad offerings. Her expression somehow manages to convey disgust without moving a single muscle. "You're calling Tampico, orange juice? And nutritious?"

"It has vitamin C."

"It has corn syrup and delusion." She straightens. "Water, please."

"Excellent choice." I grab a glass from the cabinet—the only one without a chip. "Would you like tap, or tap?"

Her smile is tight-lipped. "Surprise me."

I fill the glass and hand it to her. She accepts it like I'm offering her a biohazard sample, holding it with two fingers as far from her silk blouse as possible.

We move to the living room. I drop onto my couch—the one that sags in the middle like a defeated sigh—while Sage perches on the very edge of the armchair across from me, knees pressed together, posture immaculate. She looks like a woman who's never touched a piece of furniture that cost less than four figures.

"How can I help you?" I ask. "And also, how did you find me, stalker?"

Sage doesn't answer. Instead, her eyes narrow to slits, and I watch her entire demeanor shift from "reluctantly tolerating this situation" to "about to verbally eviscerate you."

"Let's talk about you first," she says.

"Okay, what exactly do you want to know about me?"

Her eyes grow wide. "Oh, I already know everything about you, Taio," she says in almost a hiss.

"What the fuck does that mean?" I return her scowl.

"It means this adorable little accidental meet-cute story that Charlie concocted to protect you for some unapparent reason? I'm. Not. Buying. It. So I did some research. And I dug up every single piece of dirt you and your family were trying to bury. A prior prince of New York, his family worth tens of millions, and then poof." Sage claps her hands together. "Turns out your wealth was stolen, your dad's a felon, your mom ditched her married name and moved out of the country, leaving you here to live like..." She gestures around my sad apartment. "This."

"Careful," I warn.

"Oh, I get it. I believe all the articles that said you and your mom were none the wiser. Honestly, Taio—it was a shitty situation and I'm sorry. But no way being an escort is paying all those legal fees. No way you have enough to pull yourself out of bankruptcy. Seems like all your problems could be solved by blackmailing...oh, I don't know—a pop star arguably worth nine figures?"

"Blackmail?" I balk. "What the hell?"

Sage uncrosses her arms and leans forward, her index finger directed at my head. "I already know who you are, Taio. Now, I need to know what you want. What you're *planning*."

Each word lands like a punch. I feel my jaw tighten, but she's not done.

"Let me be clear—Charlie Riley is not my daughter, but she might as well be. Because I am the mama bear that will rip you to shreds if you try to hurt our girl. She's innocent. Not just of this bubbling scandal, but Charlie *is innocent*. She's probably the only young twenty-some in the industry who isn't snorting lines or shooting up on ketamine. She doesn't party or sleep around. She cares deeply about her craft, legacy, family, and all of the people she loves. You're hand-plucking the petals of the most beautiful, delicate flower." Sage lowers her gaze, swaying her head side to side, suddenly overcome by emotion. "She's been through enough. Pick someone else. Anyone else. Someone more resilient. She's not prepared to play your stupid games and win your stupid prizes."

"You done?" My nostrils flare as I try to control my ragged breathing.

"Not yet," Sage continues, her voice dropping to something even more vile. "If you come after her reputation, we'll come after yours. And we're so much better at it, let me assure you of that. I will destroy you. Not threaten. Not warn. *Destroy.* There won't be enough left of your reputation to fill a thimble. We'll come after you for extortion, harassment, trespassing, whatever it takes to throw you in a cell right next to your father."

I'm on my feet before I realize I've moved. "Get out."

Sage blinks. It's the first time I've seen her look surprised.

"Excuse me?"

"You heard me." I point to the door. "We're done. Meager as it may be, this is my home. You're not going to walk into my own home and insult me like this with your false threats and blatant lies. Tell Charlie, despite the unfathomably unpleasant company she keeps, our pact still stands. Her secrets are safe with me. Now, get out."

"What secrets?" Sage asks, the sharp edges suddenly gone from her voice.

"Well, if I told you, they wouldn't be secrets anymore, would they?"

She rises, then lets out a deep exhale. Instead of moving to the front door like I suggested, she settles into the sofa chair, making herself comfortable. "I asked you what you wanted, and I didn't give you a chance to answer. I'm sorry. It's been a very stressful couple days for all of us. Charlie especially."

Finally allowed to speak, the question on my mind barrels out like a river breaking through a dam. "How is she doing?"

"You're worried about her?"

"Well, I caused this, right? I mean that hug was the extent of it. Charlie and I didn't...Even if they find out who I am and what I do, I can honestly say Charlie never hired me. If I need to make a public statement, I will." Or, at least I didn't *let* her hire me, but we can keep that tidbit out of the media.

Sage doesn't move. She studies me for a long moment, her expression unreadable. "You'd do that? There'd be implications. You know that much attention would have law enforcement looking into your client history, just to make an example out of you. Everybody who gets close to Charlie falls under extreme scrutiny. It's why she prefers to be alone."

I shrug. "I'm nearly at rock bottom. What's dropping one more foot, you know? If it helps her, I'll do it."

Something shifts in Sage's face. The attack-dog posture softens, just slightly. She looks at me like she's seeing me for the first time—not as a threat to be neutralized, but as an actual person. "She won't get out of bed," Sage admits. "She's still here in New York, still in that penthouse, afraid to leave. Yesterday there was a small mob outside of the hotel with signs. The internet is demanding a public apology. They want her to grovel, to admit she's a cheater, to confirm every terrible thing they've decided she is." She pauses. "Except they don't know the truth."

"Even the truth isn't the truth," I say, lowering myself back onto the couch. "Her relationship with Grayson—that's fake too. A PR scheme. One you cooked up, I'm guessing."

Sage doesn't deny it. "That's how this industry works. Narrative is everything. Truth is whatever we can sell."

"And right now you can't sell anything that helps her?"

"I had an idea yesterday, but I thought I'd be confronting a slimy escort with blackmail and extortion on his heart. I had no idea you'd be such a..."

I narrow my eyes. "Such a what?"

"Simp," she says.

I roll my eyes. "And the insults continue," I say through gritted teeth.

"No, I meant it in a good way. You could be a real asshole, but instead you want to help? I—"

"Should maybe stop assuming everybody is the enemy?" I jump in.

"Taio—when it comes to fame? Everybody *is* the enemy. Until they're not. So, you really want to help? Because that idea I mentioned..."

"All right, I'm all ears. Let's hear it."

She reaches into her briefcase and pulls out a stack of papers, sliding them across the coffee table toward me.

"What's this?"

"An employment contract." She taps the top page. "Effective five weeks ago. It says you were hired as Charlie Riley's personal bodyguard."

I pick up the papers, scanning the official-looking letterhead, the dense blocks of legal text. "I was?"

"You were. That's why you were alone with her in the penthouse that night. That's why the cameras caught you embracing—you're paid to protect her, to be close to her. Was it a tender moment? Perhaps. But it was strictly professional. A bodyguard comforting his client after a difficult evening."

It's clever. I have to admit that. It explains everything without requiring anyone to believe anything scandalous.

"This might actually work," I say slowly.

"It will work. But only if you sell it." Sage leans forward. "If we release this story and then you disappear, people will assume it's a cover-up and we cooked this story up—"

"Which you did."

"—which we did, yes. But we need it to look organic. Which means we need you to actually play the part."

"Play the bodyguard?"

"For the rest of Charlie's US tour at minimum. You don't leave her side. Every public appearance, every show, every airport arrival and hotel departure. We need a hundred more photographs of you being exactly what we say you are: her bodyguard. Attentive. Professional. Protective."

I stare at her. "You want me to go on tour with Charlie Riley."

"I want you *to be seen* going on tour with Charlie Riley. There's a difference." She pulls out her phone. "Grayson will release a corroborating statement. He'll say he personally hired you to keep Charlie safe while he was busy with his own press tour. Very thoughtful of him, right? Very devoted boyfriend." Sage rolls her eyes like she's disgusted at the idea of Grayson and it makes me like her slightly more. "It makes him look good, it explains your presence, and it gives Charlie the cover she needs to get back on stage without being crucified."

"And then what? After the tour?"

"When the time is right, we stage a very public termination. Nothing that will make you look bad, just an explanation as to why you're no longer around. You go back to your life, Charlie continues with the European leg of the tour, and this whole mess becomes a footnote."

"How long are we talking?"

"Four months. Maybe a little more."

Four months of pretending to be something I'm not, following Charlie Riley around the country, living in a world I don't belong in? Eh...

But then again, four months of being near her...

"How am I supposed to work?" I ask. "My actual job. The one that pays my rent."

Sage's fingers hover over her phone screen. "What's your email address?"

"Why?"

"Because I'm contacting our finance department to collect your banking information and arrange a deposit." She looks up at me, utterly matter-of-fact. "Four months of dedicated service. By Charlie's side, twenty-four seven. Name your price."

Name my price?

I think about Joy Carrington, seventeen years old, holding a Stanford acceptance letter she can't afford to use. I think about the promise I made to Anne at the Marionette—reckless, desperate, convinced I'd figure it out somehow. I think about the number that's been burning a hole in my brain for weeks.

First-year tuition, room and board. The full amount.

"A hundred thousand," I say.

I expect Sage to flinch. To brace herself for negotiation. To laugh in my face and tell me I'm out of my mind.

She doesn't blink. She types something into her phone, taps send, and looks back up at me like I just asked for spare change.

"Done. You'll have the paperwork within the hour." She stands, smoothing her blazer. "Pack your things. Whatever you need for four months on the road. Report to the JFK private tarmac by ten o'clock tomorrow night."

"Tomorrow night?"

"We're taking a late flight to Miami. Charlie's next performance is in four days. She's missed a few shows, but the tour continues." Sage picks up her untouched water glass and carries it to my kitchen sink, because apparently even in crisis mode she has manners. "A car will be here tomorrow to pick you up at nine thirty. Don't be late."

She's halfway to the door when I stop her. "Sage."

She turns.

"Honest answer. How high were you willing to go?"

For the first time, something like a smile crosses her face. It's small, barely there, but it transforms her whole expression.

"Two hundred and fifty thousand," she says. "You should work on your negotiation skills."

The door clicks shut behind her.

I look at Black Cat. He's still on the counter, watching me with those judgy yellow eyes.

"No," I tell him. "You're not coming."

His meow is wretched and pathetic.

"You could stay with Forrest? Koda loves animals. You'll be forced to wear bonnets and have tea parties, but their place is huge, and warm, and there'll be tuna for days."

If looks could kill...Black Cat would be charged with my

murder.

"Fine," I grumble out. "But you better be on your best damn behavior."

I pull out my phone and log into Saylor's Prime account, looking up overnight litter box solutions for private planes.

Yeah, that doesn't sound ludicrous at all.

This is fine. I'm just abandoning my entire life for a third of a year, all for a girl I've known for about five minutes.

What could possibly go wrong?

Chapter 9

Charlie

Or just don't sleep with your staff...Your call.

The windows of the SUV are tinted pitch black, a shield between me and the frenzy outside. I press my fingertips to the cool glass, feeling the subtle vibration of bodies moving beyond it. Probably for the best I can't see clearly. There was a time when I craved those camera flashes—each burst of light like a hit of something addictive. *Click. Click. Click.* Little dopamine explosions that told me I mattered, that I was doing something right.

God, how I lived for that validation. Each flash a confirmation: Yes, you're worthy. Yes, you're talented. Yes, you matter.

Now my stomach tightens at the thought of stepping out there. When did it change? When did those same flashes start to feel like tiny daggers instead? They don't capture me anymore—they capture versions of me. Versions that get picked apart, dissected, judged. A wrinkle here. A blemish there. Too thin. Too fat. Too much. Not enough.

I draw my hand back from the window, examining my own reflection in the dark glass instead. The cameras don't just document; they contradict. They take the self I've carefully constructed and they twist it, distort it, until I barely recognize myself in the headlines the next day.

But blaming cameras is like blaming a knife for a stabbing. They're just tools—cold, mechanical things with no will of their own. They point where they're told to point. They capture what they're aimed at. They're extensions of the people who wield them.

And people...

People are the real problem.

The driver clears his throat, catching my eye in the rearview mirror. "I've counted twelve of them so far," he says. "And more arriving."

I inhale deeply, my ribs expanding against the tight fabric of my top. Ready or not, those cameras are waiting. I shouldn't be surprised. We're the ones who tipped them off.

What I can see is bad enough—a wall of bodies pressing against the vehicle, camera flashes strobing like a rave from hell, faces contorted into shouts I can't quite decipher through the bulletproof glass. This is my life. Trapped in a rolling panic room, watching strangers try to capture my worst moments for profit.

"Charlie." Sage's voice is calm, measured, the tonal equivalent of a weighted blanket. "We've seen worse. Everything is okay."

I drag my gaze away from the window. Sage is sitting across from me in the spacious back seat, her tablet balanced on her crossed legs, looking as put together as she always does. I don't know how she does it. I've been stress-eating room-service pasta and crying into my pillow, and she looks like she just stepped out of a board meeting.

Seeing my anxious expression, she adds, "Just breathe."

"I'm breathing."

"You're hyperventilating."

She's not wrong. My chest is doing that thing where it feels like someone's sitting on it, and my hands won't stop shaking no matter how hard I press them against my thighs. The black leggings I'm wearing are already damp with palm sweat.

"And you said Taio's here?" I ask.

"Yes. He's two cars ahead, he's already loaded his cat onto the plane."

I cock my head to the side, the sweet detail distracting me from my borderline panic attack. "Aww, he's bringing a cat on tour?"

"Yes, let's find that charming and sweet, and not wildly inconvenient and gross," Sage tsks. "Private jets are not supposed to smell like cat restrooms."

"Cat restrooms?" I chuckle to myself. "You mean litter boxes."

"I mean cat ass," she grouches out.

"I love animals," I muse. "Did you know up until sixteen, Claire and I always had a gaggle of guinea pigs? At least four at a time, and we wouldn't travel without them. This one time we accidentally let two out in Dad's favorite jet that they just renovated." I belly-laugh at the memory. "There was so much guinea pig crap on the floor. He was livid."

Nate was a good sport with the guinea pigs, but the moment I left to pursue my dreams of stardom, and Claire moved out for college, he took them to a farm. An actual farm, not a metaphorical kill house. They live in a small, temperature-controlled barn. Happy as clams. Multiplying by the second.

"Charlie...I think Taio is a very nice man. But there's no version of this that ends with you two starting something—"

"Sage," I whine. "Stop. You're being judgmental. He told me why he's an escort and—"

"The escort part is not the issue." She clears her throat. "Well, not my only issue. Charlie, what Taio's dad did—"

"Is what *his dad* did. Not what he did."

"You know better than anyone what it means to live with the consequences of your parents' choices."

A sad reminder sweeps over me. "I didn't tell you about my bio dad's letter so you could use it against me in one of your cautionary TED Talks, Sage. That's not fair."

She puts her tablet aside and yanks me into a hug, kisses the top of my head over and over. "Sweetheart, that is *not* what I'm doing. I am just warning you, as someone who cares deeply about you, Taio is never going to be a man who wants to be in the spotlight for you, okay? He has too much baggage to see this as anything other than a job. I don't want you to fall in love with something that isn't there."

I pretend like her words don't cut me to the core. I've had a lot of time alone to create plenty of fictitious happily-ever-afters in my mind. Lately, Taio is the star in all of them. I don't like Sage reminding me that I need to live in the world and not in my mind. Not with the monsters I can't escape, and the heroes I conjure up to fight them away. "I'm not in love, Sage. He's basically a stranger. I'm not even into him."

She flutters her lashes at me, her sarcastic smirk indicating she doesn't believe me. "Well, good. I want us to end this tour strong, empowered, energized, *and without child.*"

"How feminist of you," I deadpan. "I'll get on birth control."

"Or just don't sleep with your staff." She shrugs. "Your call."

"No promises," I mutter just to spite her.

Sage doesn't sigh, but I can tell she wants to. "All right, I'm about to give the signal. Taio will exit first and approach our car. He'll open your door, help you out, and escort you and me through the little paparazzi crowd to the tarmac. The whole thing should take less than two minutes."

"Should I pull up my hood?" I nestle deeper into my sweatshirt, like a turtle retracting into its shell.

"No, we want you photographed. We want clear footage of you and your bodyguard doing his job. Protecting you. Being professional." She taps something on her tablet. "We need more organic images of you two together before we release the official statement. The more normal this looks, the more ridiculous the cheating narrative becomes. We're poking holes in all these trolls' credibility."

"By giving them more pictures?"

"By feeding them the pictures we want them to release. They'll be chomping at the bit, thinking they found more incriminating evidence of your affair, and all we need is for someone to use some common sense and ask, wait...does it look like that guy is just Charlie's bodyguard? Thank goodness for Taio's physique. Had you hit it off with the Danny DeVito type, this would've never worked."

I nod like this makes sense. It does make sense, intellectually. Sage is brilliant at this—at spinning narratives, at turning disasters into opportunities, at making the machine work for us instead of against us. But right now, all I can think about is the fact that in approximately ninety seconds, I'm going to see Taio again.

Taio.

Truthfully, I haven't stopped thinking about him since he left my penthouse four nights ago. I've been sitting cross-legged on my bathroom floor until three in the morning, writing lyrics on the back of room-service receipts with a half-chewed pencil. My hair's been in the same messy bun for so long it's now a biohazard that dry shampoo cannot assuage. For two entire days after Taio left that night, I locked the penthouse doors, ignored Sage's increasingly panicked texts, and survived on nothing but gummy bears and LaCroix. Not because I was having a breakdown like everyone thought—well, maybe a little—but because I was having a breakthrough. Something raw and powerful inside me cracked open. My fingers found melodies on the piano keys that were buried so deep inside, it took an excavator in the form of a six-foot-four, half-Japanese escort adonis to reveal. God, he's interesting. For once, I find my life *interesting*. I wrote a real song, the first in over a year, and it spilled out like I'd punctured an artery.

My label is going to hate it. It sounds nothing like the Charlie Riley they've invested millions into. Instead, it sounds like...me.

Paper hearts and frozen time
This stranger made his secrets mine
And I returned the favor
Just so I could claim him later
Hero in disguise
A prize that can't be mine.

I keep playing that night in my head like it's a movie I can't stop rewatching. The way he cleaned the mascara off my face with a warm washcloth. The way he listened—really listened—when I told him about my mom and the letter and all the lies I'd been living inside. The way he asked me to sing, and then looked at me afterward like I'd given him something precious.

Then there was the hug. That stupid, perfect hug that ruined everything and also might have been the best moment of my entire year.

I felt safe in his arms. I felt like I could breathe for the first time in months. And then the camera flashes started, and my whole world collapsed. Sneaking him out the service elevator like he was contraband, I honestly thought I'd never see him again.

"Charlie."

I blink. Sage is watching me with that knowing look she gets when she's about to say something I don't want to hear.

"Where'd you go just now?"

"Nowhere. I'm fine. I heard you."

"Okay, he's on his way. We just wait for the knock."

"Sage." My voice comes out smaller than I intended. "How did you convince him to do this? To upend his whole life for four months just to play pretend bodyguard for a pop star he barely knows?"

Sage is quiet for a moment. When she answers, her tone is softer than usual. "I didn't have to convince him."

"You...What do you mean?"

"I mean I showed up at his apartment ready to threaten him into compliance, and before I could even finish my pitch, he was already volunteering to help. He offered to make a public statement. To take the fall. To do whatever it took to make things easier for you." She shakes her head slightly, like she's processing it even now. "He's a born bodyguard. Willing to sacrifice himself to protect you."

A gentle warmth blooms in my chest, followed immediately by suspicion that crawls up my throat. "And how much are you paying him?"

Her expression doesn't change. "Does it matter?"

"Yes. It matters."

"Why?"

Because I need to know if this is real. Because everyone in my life wants something from me, and I need to know what he wants, but I'm also terrified of finding out. Because if he's just doing this for money, then that night on the balcony was a transaction, not a connection. And if he's not? That might be scarier. God, I don't think I can survive another person turning out to be less than I hoped, but I also don't know if I can handle someone actually living up to my expectations.

"It just does."

Sage studies me for a long moment. Then she reaches across the space between us and squeezes my knee. "He cares about you, Charlie. We all do. Just focus on that."

It's not an answer. But somehow, it's enough.

Knock, knock. Two firm thuds announce Taio's arrival.

My stomach does a backflip. Then a somersault. Then it just goes haywire, like a gymnast on crack.

"Charlie." Sage clasps my wrist. "Breathe. Smile. This is going to be fine."

The door handle clicks.

Light floods in, harsh, accompanied by a wall of sound—shouting, clicking, the roar of a crowd that's been waiting for this moment. I blink against the onslaught, momentarily frozen, my body refusing to cooperate with my brain's desperate commands to move. They're already yelling at me, some slurs, some pleas. A medley of "Charlie, you're beautiful, please look this way," and "The world is calling you a cheating whore. What do you have to say?" They butter me up before they cut me down. That's the routine. But this time...

Taio's here.

His broad, tall frame fills the doorway, blocking out the chaos behind him like a human shield. His hand extends toward me, palm up, steady as a rock. And when our eyes meet, he smiles. Not a professional smile. Not a practiced, publicity-ready smile. A real smile, warm and slightly crooked, like he's genuinely happy to see me.

"Hey, Tweety Bird. Nice to see you," he says, low enough that only I can hear. "Ready?"

Did he just nickname me? Oh, this is not the moment to swoon. Not in front of these accosting cameras.

I take his hand, trying to ignore the warmth in our touch and my nervous system short-circuiting.

His fingers close around mine, warm and solid, and I let him pull me out of the SUV and into the storm.

The noise is deafening. Cameras flash from every direction, a strobe-light assault that makes it impossible to see more than a few feet ahead. People are shouting my name—some in support, some in accusation, all of them hungry. I feel hands reaching toward me, brushing against my jacket, my arm, my hair, and I have to fight the urge to curl into a ball and disappear.

But Taio doesn't let me disappear. He keeps his hand firmly on the small of my back, guiding me forward, his body angled to block the rowdiest of the crowd. When someone gets too close, he smoothly redirects them without breaking stride. When a camera gets shoved in my face, he steps between us, creating space. He moves like water around obstacles, never stopping, never hesitating, always keeping me moving toward the tarmac. He does this like he's practiced.

"You're doing great," he murmurs near my ear. "Almost there."

I focus on his voice. On the pressure of his hand against my spine. On putting one foot in front of the other until the roar of the crowd starts to fade and the sleek white shape of the private jet comes into view.

The stairs unfold before us like a ladder to salvation. Taio guides me up, Sage close behind, and then we're through the cabin door and the noise cuts off like someone hit a mute button.

Silence. Beautiful, blessed silence.

I sag against the nearest surface, a lavish cream-colored leather seat that could fit two of me, and let out a breath I didn't know I was holding. My hands are shaking again. My heart is pounding. But I'm here. I made it. We made it.

"That was intense," Taio breathes out, stepping past me into the cabin. "Is it always like that?"

"That was tame in comparison," I tell him.

He lets out a low whistle. "How in the world do you get used to that?"

"I don't." I hold up my shaking hands. "Fake it 'til you make it, right?"

I crane my neck to examine him head to toe. He's dressed like a cat burglar who moonlights as a fitness influencer—all-black everything. Black slacks that somehow look both professional and ready for a parkour escape, a black T-shirt that clings to him like a barnacle, and a black athletic jacket that's fighting a losing battle with his shoulders, the zipper barely closed over his broad chest.

He looks different up close. Not bad different—just a brand-new canvas to admire. His jaw is stronger than I remembered. His eyes are a warmer brown. His lips are apple red. There's a small scar near his left eyebrow that I didn't notice before, and I find myself wondering how he got it.

"Welcome aboard, everyone." The flight attendant—a polished blonde in a navy uniform—gestures toward the cabin's interior. "Please make yourselves comfortable. We'll be departing shortly."

The plane is obscene. Even by private jet standards, it's ridiculous—a flying palace. The main cabin stretches out before us like a high-end living room, all cream leather and polished wood and ambient lighting that makes everyone look like they're in a perfume commercial. There's a full bar along one wall, stocked with bottles I can't pronounce. A sectional sofa that could seat six. Individual seats that recline into beds.

Sage moves past me toward the back of the cabin, already on her phone, barking orders at whoever's unlucky enough to be on the other end. Her assistant—a nervous-looking guy named Derek who I've met maybe three times—scurries after her with a tablet and an expression of uncontained panic. I don't even think anything is particularly wrong, he's just a bit squirrely. The flight crew disappears into the galley, tinkering like flight crews do.

And then it's just me and Taio, standing in the middle of this absurd luxury, looking at each other like two people who aren't sure what happens next.

"So," he says.

"So," I echo.

"Nice plane."

"It's my dad's. Well, one of them."

"One of the planes, or one of the dads?"

I laugh—a real laugh, surprising myself. "One of the planes. I only have one dad. Oh, wait. Actually, I guess now two. Am I allowed to claim a bio dad I've never met?"

"Most definitely."

I hold my elbows, rubbing them like a genie might appear. "I can't believe I told you all that within minutes of knowing you. I'm too much, huh?"

"You're not too much for me." He shrugs like it's a casual statement, but there's something distinct in his expression, like maybe he wants me to read between the lines. "For what it's worth, I'm glad you told me. It helped me understand."

"Understand what?"

"You. Why you were so..." He searches for the word. "Untethered that night? Like you were floating away and looking for something to grab on to. Like you really needed a friend."

I don't know what to say to that. It's too accurate. Too close to the bone.

"I did," I admit. "I do. But who can I trust? The song is 'No New Friends' for a reason."

"Lonely at the top?" Taio asks.

"And the middle. And the bottom too," I answer back. "I've been lonely all over the place."

He holds up his hand. "Condolence high five?"

My face scrunches up like I caught a whiff of something

sour. "Did you just offer me a high five?" I ask while staring at his massive palm, mere inches from my face.

"Well, I'd hug you, but that got us into a lot of trouble last time."

"There are no cameras in he—"

But the plane shudders slightly as the engines power up, cutting me off. The movement is my warning to get my ass into a seat and tie myself down with the seat belt like a roast chicken gets trussed up. Taio takes the seat across from me, facing me, his long legs stretched out into the aisle, his body relaxed in a way mine hasn't been in weeks.

"It's really nice to see you again," he says. That crooked smile is back, the one that makes my stomach do complicated things. I want to stay focused on his gorgeous face, but as the plane starts to move, I feel my insides floating around untethered, like a lava lamp.

My breathing starts to shallow, I can't help it. I can't control it. Sage must be busy bossing her assistant around, because she never misses takeoff with me. It's always either Claire, Spence, or Sage who hold my hands through this. I've always been and will always be a nervous flyer.

"Can you get Sage?" I whimper, too afraid to leave my seat as the jets really start to whir.

"What's wrong?" Taio asks, his face flooding with concern. "You look pale all of a sudden."

"Not a good flyer," I mumble. "Just takeoff and touchdown. In the air I'm okay." My words are coming out in short staccatos as I try to calm the raging flames of anxiety with cool-headed logic. "Sage, now, please?"

The plane jolts forward, trading its leisurely stroll for an all-out sprint.

"No time," Taio mumbles, quickly trading seats so he's right next to me. He folds my arm around his like twisted pretzels and holds my hand tightly. So tight the pressure is almost painful.

"Ow, that hurts."

"Oh come on, tough girl. Squeeze back. I know you have more endurance than that." But he lessens his grip just a touch. "Show me how strong you are."

"Not interested in your mind games, Taio. I know what you're doing."

He smirks. "I'll tell you what, if you can make me say 'ow' with that tiny bunny paw you're sporting, I'll...I don't know, what's something you want?"

"A kiss," I reply like a reflex.

He quirks a brow. "Had that one locked and loaded, did you?"

"Taio..." I whine as the front half of the plane starts to levitate. "I'm going to be sick."

"Shh, shh," he coos. "Just squeeze. As hard as you can."

I do. I squeeze his hand like I'm trying to crush it, until my forearm aches and my veins are bulging. It's actually exhausting, and from this day forward I will be in full support of arm wrestling entering the Summer Olympics. Fatigued, I have to take deep breaths, and my sole focus becomes making Taio squirm in his seat. I want that kiss. But he's barely flinching. I have to pull in my other hand, wrapping around the bottom of his, trying to double the amount of pressure.

I press with all my might and then his pinky finger twists, buckling under the pressure from both sides. "Oof," he huffs, shaking out his hand.

"That counts," I say, releasing the pressure. "*Oof* counts."

He smiles at me, his perfect dazzling teeth all giving me a standing ovation. "Great job, Tweety. That was ferocious."

I glower at him. "You're placating me. That didn't hurt, did it?"

"Like a chubby puppy falling into a bed of blankets. All soft."

"You're the worst," I grumble, shaking my head.

"Maybe, but you're breathing normal now, and we've already leveled out." He points to the window. I slide open the shade to see us dancing just above the clouds.

Understanding his game of distraction, I smile and nod in

gratitude. "Thank you. That was very nice, and far less stressful than the warrior speech Sage always gives me."

"Yeah, she's a little scary."

I let out a light laugh. "She's not a fan of your cat, hate to tell you."

"More concerning is that she's not a fan of me."

"Oh she is," I assure him. "This is Sage being nice."

"Dear God, I fear for her enemies."

I nod solemnly. "As do I. Try not to make that list."

He winks at me. "Noted. Now, if you're okay, I need to attend to the other lady in my life—which is a spoiled, overweight black cat, who's been mean-mugging me since I put him in a carrier."

I'm the lady in Taio's life now? Huh. I like how that sounds. Except, aside from his death-grip trust exercise, he seems like he doesn't want to get too close. I mean, I tried to undress in front of him, and we tossed around a vibrator like a hot potato, and now all of a sudden he's offering me high fives.

"Can I meet your cat?"

Taio's smile fades. "Absolutely. As long as you don't call him 'my cat.' He's a passerby. I just couldn't abandon him at my apartment for four months straight. And I didn't have enough notice to find a more permanent solution."

"Sorry, we did sort of pluck you from your life without warning, didn't we?"

Taio rises to his feet, having to duck his head to avoid the overhead storage compartments. "It's fine. It worked out. I'll go get Black Cat."

"What's his name?" I ask.

I have no idea why, but Taio rolls his eyes before heading down the aisle to the back of the plane storage area where his cat's carrier is probably buckled down for safety.

I let out a deep breath when I'm finally alone, letting the residual nerves fall off me like raindrops on a freshly waxed car. I always feel better when we're mid-flight. Up here in the sky, it's serene. I'm safe. Untouchable. At peace.

"Hey," Taio says, sending my heart rate right back to the moon. He leans over the outer seat, getting as close as he can.

"Jesus," I say to his face which is mere inches from mine. "Scared me."

"Sorry, I forgot. I owe you this." His lips graze my cheek, so soft, but they linger. My pulse surges, sending electric currents of curiosity through me like Frankenstein coming to life. The moment he pulls away, I replace his lips with my hand, trying to hold the warmth in place. "A deal's a deal. I'll be right back."

With that, he disappears again, leaving me far more confused than before.

He wants me?

He wants me not?

It was a kiss on the cheek.

But still a kiss...

I touch my cheek again, my smile growing.

Yeah, still a kiss.

Chapter 10

Taio

A dick-piphany?

Miami in February hits a man like a sucker punch of paradise after weeks of battling New York's frozen hellscape. The air wraps around you—thick, damp, and sticky, while your nostrils fill with saltwater, coconut sunscreen, and the unmistakable musk of old-money portfolios mingling with new-money Lamborghinis. I'm surrounded by the kind of wealth that makes even millionaires feel insecure.

The private resort where we're staying looks like something out of a Bond villain's real estate portfolio. A sprawling Mediterranean-style compound perched on the edge of Biscayne Bay, all terracotta roofs and white stucco walls and infinity pools that seem to spill directly into the ocean. Palm trees line the crushed-shell driveway like soldiers on watch duty. Exotic plants explode in violent shades of pink and purple over every available surface. The main house has seven bedrooms, a home theater, a wine cellar, and a kitchen bigger than my entire Brooklyn apartment.

I'm staying in the guesthouse, which is its own kind of absurd. Two bedrooms, floor-to-ceiling windows overlooking the bay, a bathroom with a rainfall shower and heated floors. Black Cat has claimed the entire king-sized bed as his personal territory and regards me with open contempt whenever I try to share it.

Three days into our Miami stay, and I've barely seen Charlie.

Not for lack of proximity—we're literally on the same property. But she's been swallowed whole by tour prep: rehearsals from dawn until dinner, vocal coaching, costume fittings, production meetings, the endless machinery of putting on a show for tens of thousands of people. My job, such as it is, has consisted primarily of escorting her from car to door and back again. Open the door. Walk beside her. Look intimidating. Repeat.

It's not exactly challenging work.

What *is* challenging is watching Charlie in her element and feeling like I'm observing a creature from another planet. Even my family's old money—the country club memberships, the summer homes in the Hamptons, the casual assumption that doors would always open for us—feels quaint compared to this. The Wilkes fortune, at its peak, might have bought us a nice vacation here. Charlie's world operates on a scale I can't quite comprehend. Private jets—plural. Compounds with names. Staff who exist solely to anticipate needs you didn't know you had.

I keep catching myself doing the math. The art on the walls. The cars in the garage. The casual way Sage ordered a helicopter to avoid Miami traffic yesterday. Each calculation is a reminder: even my past life, the one that ended when my father's empire crumbled, would never have been enough to impress a girl like Charlie Riley.

Not that I'm trying to impress her. I'm her employee. Her fake bodyguard. A prop in the elaborate theater production that is celebrity damage control.

But still. A man notices things. Especially when he's not feeling man enough.

I'm stretched out on a lounger by the guesthouse pool, pretending to read a book with Black Cat curled at me feet, obviously tanning, when my mind drifts back to yesterday's rehearsal. I'd been stationed in the back of the rented gym space, doing my best impression of a piece of furniture, when I overheard two of the backup dancers talking during a water break.

"Hopeless," the guy with arms like tree trunks muttered.

"Girl looked like a fish flopping on a dock."

Another dancer with a ponytail sharp as a dagger snickered. "I know. Like, how do you sell out arenas when you move like that?"

"Because nobody's paying attention to the dancing, babe. They're paying attention to the face and the voice and the sob story."

"Still. Embarrassing. I'd be mortified if that was me up there."

They noticed me watching and immediately clammed up, suddenly fascinated by their water bottles. I said nothing. What would I say? They weren't wrong about the dancing. Charlie's movements were technically correct but stiff, mechanical, like she was solving a math problem instead of feeling the music.

But hearing them talk about her like she wasn't a real person, like she was just a product to be critiqued...it made something hot and protective flare in my chest.

She's trying so hard. Can't they see that? Would they hold themselves to the standards they hold her to?

I toss the book aside. I haven't absorbed a single word anyway. My gaze turns toward the main house; my body follows suit when I can no longer ignore the rumble in my stomach.

I see Charlie, in thick sweats, dancing in the kitchen, her back turned. She's clueless that she has company. Her headphones are in, so she doesn't hear me slip in through the glass sliding doors. I move quietly, not wanting to disturb whatever creative process might be happening. I hear the music through her headphones—some bouncy pop track with a driving beat. She turns around but her eyes are closed, like she's trying to ignore the gift of sight to heighten her other senses. She's mouthing the lyrics, her body attempting the choreography she's been drilling all day.

She looks *determined*. Focused. Also, to be honest, a little bit like a baby giraffe learning to walk.

Her arms hit the marks a half beat late. Her hips don't quite commit to the movements. There's a shimmy that turns into more of a shudder. But God, she's trying. Every ounce of her concentration is poured into making her body cooperate, into forcing grace where it doesn't come naturally.

I lean against the doorframe and watch in silence. The song builds to a climax. Charlie attempts some kind of spin-to-freeze combination that ends with her stumbling slightly and catching herself on the island. The music fades. She stands there for a moment, breathing hard, staring at her own reflection in the window.

Then she slams her fist against the marble countertop.

"Fuck!"

She rips out her AirPods, spinning around, and freezes when she sees me.

I start clapping. Slowly. Deliberately. When she just stares at me, I add an earnest thumbs-up.

"Don't even. It sucks," she says flatly.

"It doesn't—"

"*I suck*. I'm a terrible dancer. Everyone knows it. The backup dancers hate me."

I hesitate, which is apparently enough of an answer.

"Oh my God." She drops her face into her hands. "They do, don't they? What did they say?"

"Nothing worth repeating."

"Taio."

"Something about a fish. And a dock. It wasn't clever."

She laughs, but it's hollow. "A fish. Great. That's exactly the vibe I'm going for. Sexy fish energy."

I push off from the doorframe and move into the kitchen, giving her space but making my presence known. "You're not as bad as you think. You're just in your head too much."

"Easy for you to say. You're not the one who has to dance in front of twenty thousand people tomorrow night."

"No, but I am the one who's watched you rehearse for three days straight. You know the moves. Your body knows the moves. You just need to stop thinking and start feeling."

Charlie snorts. "Feel the music? Really? That's your advice?

What is this, a dance movie from two thousand three? Because if watching *Step Up* will magically impart some wisdom from the universe, make some popcorn, buddy. I need all the help I can get."

"I'm serious. You're so focused on hitting every mark perfectly that you're forgetting to actually enjoy what you're doing."

"Hard to enjoy it when the music sounds like the soundtrack to a Disney Channel original movie." She hops up onto the kitchen island, her legs dangling. "That's the problem, Taio. The songs are juvenile. The choreography is juvenile. My whole brand is juvenile. I'm twenty-three years old, and I'm still performing music I wrote when I was sixteen."

"So?"

"So I'm never going to be taken seriously. I'm like Peter Pan—destined to never grow up. My career is basically over because everyone is bored of me. Nobody wants to watch a grown woman sing songs about first kisses and summer crushes."

I consider this for a moment. She's not entirely wrong—the pop landscape is littered with child stars who couldn't make the transition to adult artistry. But she's also catastrophizing, which seems to be her default setting.

"Those songs meant something to you once," I say. "When you wrote them?"

"Co-written. Which is code for my label takes my notes and censors me. My producers take my sloppy thoughts and transform them into something I don't recognize."

"But you chose to sing them. You connected with them enough to build a career around them."

She's quiet for a moment. "I guess. When I was younger, they felt true. Like they captured something real...things that feel obsolete now, but in the moment felt epic."

"Then go back to that place. When you're performing tomorrow, don't think about whether the songs are 'mature' enough. Think about the girl who first sang them and believed every word. Let each song serve its purpose. If that purpose is youthful joy—so what? There's plenty of time for you to grow up, Tweety. You don't have to rush it."

"Tweety because I'm short?" Charlie asks, flipping her long hair over her head, then collecting it into one bunch so she can lasso it all with a thick scrunchie.

"Tweety because you're my little songbird. Your performance at the Elusive was breathtaking. I'll never forget it," I say, full of genuine praise.

"The performance of a song that wasn't mine," she counters.

I take another step toward her. "You made it yours."

Charlie studies me with an expression I can't quite read. Then she smiles—a real one, small but earnest. "Know what I'm going to do, Taio Wilkes?"

"What's that?" I fold my arms over my chest, waiting to be impressed at the little firecracker standing barely over five feet in front of me.

"I'm going to believe every damn thing you tell me, so you better not lie to me...ever."

I hold up my pinky. "You have my word."

She laughs, and something in my chest loosens. "Okay, fine. So your advice—stop thinking, start feeling. Let the songs be what they are." She tilts her head. "But the dancing part—it's still a problem. You make it sound so easy. *Just relax. Just feel the music.* Like I haven't been trying to do that for literally years. It's not that easy. I mean, can *you* dance?"

"Sort of."

"Listening..." Charlie prods.

I should not say what I'm about to say. I know this. And yet—

"I know *one* dance that I've had to perform."

Charlie's eyebrows shoot up. "Oh?"

"A bachelorette party. A few years back. The client specifically requested a...performance. It was a whole *Magic Mike* kind of thing."

Charlie's face transforms. Her eyes go wide. Her mouth drops open. She looks like a kid who just found out Christmas is coming early.

"You learned a whole *Magic Mike* routine?"

"I dabbled." Oh, no. I don't like how she's looking at me like a starved coyote, ready to feast.

"Taio." Charlie hops off the island. "Do the dance."

"Absolutely not."

"*Do it.*"

"Charlie, it's inappropriate. The final move is me ripping off my pants."

"Uh-huh." She crosses her arms. "Do. The. Dance."

"No."

"Do it or you're fired."

I stare at her. "You can't fire me. Sage hired me."

"I outrank Sage. I'm the talent. The talent gets what the talent wants." She flicks her hair, which is silly because there's not one diva bone in her entire body. But she's grinning now, clearly enjoying my discomfort. "Come on, show me your moves. Or do I need to hit the ATM first?"

"Hilarious," I gripe.

"Taio," Charlie says, dead-ass serious.

"Charlie," I repeat, equally as serious.

We stare at each other across the kitchen. She's not going to let this go. I can see it in her eyes, and that stubborn set to her jaw—the barely contained delight at having found a new way to torture me.

I'm going to regret this.

"Fine. Get a chair."

Charlie

SOMETIMES CHRISTMAS MEANS pine trees decorated in lights and ornaments. Early morning warm cinnamon rolls to munch on while we dive into presents by the fire...And sometimes Christmas means a hotter-than-hell escort, who is so tall he could hunt geese with a rake, doing body rolls in his slutty little gray sweatpants.

Well, deck my halls and jingle my bells, because Christmas is right here in front of me.

Taio drags one of the dining room chairs into the center of the kitchen, positioning it with the back facing me. His black T-shirt clings to his chest and shoulders like it's trying to win a koala-hugging competition.

"I want it on record that this is basically quid pro quo," he says.

"Noted. Now dance, monkey, dance." I clap my hands together like they're cymbals.

He shoots me a look that says *I'll remember that*, then pulls out his phone and scrolls through what I assume is his music library. A moment later come the opening notes of "Rodeo (Remix)" by Lah Pat and Flo Milli. I specifically remember this song because everyone on TikTok was doing that trending dance that I couldn't decode to save my actual life. I learned the choreography and showed it to my social media manager who sweetly asked if we could just tuck that away for a rainy day.

I shake off the memory as I grab my phone. "Hang on, I can get this on the built-in speakers."

Taio rolls his eyes. "Of course this place has built-in speakers. Probably has a button that makes champagne spray from the ceiling and another that summons a tiny French man to feed you grapes." He turns off his phone as the intro explodes through hidden speakers with enough bass to make the fancy fruit bowl vibrate across the counter, transforming the pristine kitchen into what feels like the world's most expensive strip club.

"Sit." His tone is commanding, a glimpse of something gruff and animalistic, a side I know he's determined not to show me. Either way, I obey.

Taio positions himself behind the chair, hands gripping the back, and for a moment he just stands there, head bowed, waiting for the beat to hit.

Then he moves.

I wish I could make a joke to put us both at ease. Or maybe find the words to convey my genuine shock. But no, all I can do is drop my jaw and gawk.

He's fluid. That's the only word for it. Every movement flows into the next like water, his hips rolling in a way that makes my mouth go dry. He circles me like a predator, one hand trailing along the back of the chair, making the hair on the back of my neck rise, eyes finding mine and holding them with an intensity that makes my stomach flip.

This is not the reluctant bodyguard who's obviously parked me in the friend zone. This is something else entirely. *Hot.* Someone else entirely. Someone I really want to get to know.

He straddles the chair, legs spread wide, careful not to touch me, and then to my great horror and simultaneous glee, he does this thing with his hips that can only be described as obscene. His hands run down his chest, his abs, his thighs. He throws his head back. He bites his lip. He looks like sex personified, and I am having a *crisis.*

I grip the edge of the chair on either side, partly for support and partly because I need something to do with my hands that isn't reaching for him.

Taio's voice drops an octave. "Shift to the left, Charlie." His neck glistens with a thin sheen of sweat, each breath making his shoulders rise and fall as his hips carve figure-eights in the air. The muscles in his thighs flex beneath the thin fabric of his sweatpants, and I swear I can feel the heat radiating from him like a furnace, making my own legs tremble in response.

"Like this?" I croak, shimmying two inches.

"Good girl." He smirks, probably pleased he made me blush. I can feel the heat in my cheeks and I just *know* they are painted red.

He plants one heel on the open space on the seat, then shifts his weight, gyrating his hips, teasing me more and more, never making contact. And I'm sure he'd prefer to keep it that way, except at the worst possible moment, a tickle forms in my nose.

I try to hold it in, summoning inhuman strength to send this sneeze back down into the abyss of wherever sneezes form. Instead, the pressure pops, silently, causing an internal eruption and for my head to duck forward at the precise moment Taio thrusts, causing his semi to crash into my face. And I don't mean a gentle touch. An adorable accident. No, not adorable, because Taio's dick caressing my cheek is like getting your face fondled by an elephant trunk.

He stumbles backward, face frozen in horror.

"Oh my God." He backs up so fast he nearly trips over the discarded chair. "Oh shit, I'm so sorry, I didn't mean to—the choreography, it just—I forgot how short you are—"

I'm laughing too hard to respond. Full-body, tears-streaming, can't-breathe laughing. I fall out of the chair, one hand pressed to my allegedly assaulted nose, absolutely losing my mind.

"Charlie. Charlie, are you okay?"

"You—" I wheeze, trying to catch my breath. "You just—"

"I know. I know what I did. We don't need to say it out loud." He groans in agony.

I'm crying now, actual tears rolling down my cheeks as I try to hold my ribs, plagued with stitches from the hysterical laughter. "You really committed, man. I mean, I feel like I have to tip you now—"

"*Please* stop talking."

"This is the greatest moment of my life."

Taio drops into the dining chair I toppled out of, head in his hands, looking like a man who's seriously reconsidering all his life choices.

I finally manage to pull myself together, wiping my eyes with the back of my hand. Taio is still sitting there, radiating mortification.

"Hey. I think I get it now." I anchor my hand against his thigh and rise. Holding his face in both of my hands, I tilt his gaze up. "The part that's missing? It should be fun, right? Or funny at least."

"Yeah," he says, his controlled masculine temperament

returning. "You have a right to enjoy what you've built, Charlie."

"Thank you. What an epiphany. All from a pervy nose boop."

"Please don't call it a 'pervy nose boop.'"

"The face-to-crotch collision?"

"That's worse."

"A dick-piphany?" I offer.

"I'm going to walk into the ocean now."

I laugh again, lighter this time, and perch on the edge of the kitchen island across from him. "Seriously, though. That was really good. You're naturally athletic. I wish I was more like that."

We're quiet for a moment. The song has ended, replaced by silence that feels charged with something I can't name.

"Know what I want for you?" Taio asks, his eyes latching on to mine.

I'm tempted to make a joke, but the sincerity is scrawled across his face. "What?"

"I want you to be proud of being you. It's okay to love yourself, Tweety. You have plenty of ammo. You just need to pull the trigger of self-awareness. Of course the internet is coming for you at every turn. We love to throw rocks at shiny things. To envy what we can't have. To shun what feels unique. But the moment you stop giving a damn about fitting in their perfect little pop-star box is the moment you become unforgettable."

Unforgettable. It echoes through my mind like a promise, or a curse. Jury's still out.

"So," I say, when I can't bear the intimate silence between us, "what are we now?"

Taio's expression shifts to something more guarded. "What do you mean?"

"I mean, you just sweated on me a little while you were giving me a lap dance. Feels like we've crossed some kind of threshold."

"I'm your bodyguard. Same as before."

"Are you sure? Because you also just booped my nose with your dick."

He chokes on nothing. "Can we please retire that phrase?"

"Never. It's going in my memoirs."

"Charlie."

"Fine, fine." I hold up my hands in surrender. "Bodyguard and pop star. Very professional. Except for the part where you dry-humped my face."

"I'm going to need therapy after this."

"Join the club." I chuckle at his glowing cheeks. It's sort of adorable to see such a large man brought to his knees by a little embarrassment.

He rises to his feet, creating a gulf between our bodies that feels wider than the actual steps he takes. The temperature in the room seems to drop as I watch him rebuild the fortress around himself brick by brick—bodyguard mode reactivating despite the fact we've just crossed lines that no employee handbook would ever condone.

"Listen," he says, "about tomorrow night. The performance. I've been thinking."

"Dangerous activity."

"Maybe you should go rogue."

I blink. "Go rogue?"

"One number. Just one. Where you don't do the choreography. Where you just...stand there and sing. Let the music be enough." He shrugs. "Give yourself one moment in the show that's just for you. Something you can actually enjoy without worrying about hitting marks or looking like a..."

"Like a fish on a dock?"

"I wasn't going to say that."

"But you were thinking it."

"I was thinking you deserve to have fun up there. And if dancing isn't fun for you, then maybe don't dance. For one song. Let yourself perform like you did for me on that balcony. You looked so alive and happy."

I turn this over in my mind. It's not a bad idea. The show is tightly choreographed, every moment planned down to the second, but isn't it still *mine*? I can make a change. Isn't it time I start running my own damn show?

"Go rogue," I repeat. "I like it."

"Just don't tell Sage I suggested it. She already thinks I'm a corrupting influence."

"Aren't you?"

He doesn't answer. Instead, he moves toward the massive stainless-steel refrigerator and pulls out a bottle of some green smoothie concoction that looks like a liquified lawn.

"I'm going to go take a shower," he says, heading for the door to the guesthouse. "Maybe try to wash off the shame of the last fifteen minutes."

"Is that an invitation?"

He stops. Turns. Looks at me with an expression that's half exasperation, half something else. Something warmer like intrigue.

"Behave, Charlie."

"Why?"

I'm pushing. I know that. But I want to hear him say it. I want him to admit there's something here—this electricity between us, this pull that I feel every time we're in the same room.

But Taio doesn't cave. He just shakes his head, that guarded expression firmly back in place. "Let it go. You have a busy day ahead."

I pucker my bottom lip. "Can't resist me forever, Taio. I'm a solid seven! You don't turn down sevens with a bubbly personality."

"Text me the moment you need anything today." And then he's gone, the door closing softly behind him.

I sit in the empty kitchen for a moment, surrounded by marble and steel and the phantom beat of "Rodeo (Remix)" still playing through my mind.

The door opens again. Taio's head appears.

He holds up both hands, all ten fingers spread wide. "And for the record, you're a goddamn ten."

Then he's gone again.

I touch my face, feeling the heat in my cheeks, the smile I

can't suppress.

A ten. He thinks I'm a ten.

And he still walked away. Which means he's either the most disciplined man on the planet, or he's fighting this much harder than I am.

Either way, I'm screwed.

But maybe—*just maybe*—so is he.

Chapter 11

Charlie

All I know is I want him to stay.

The paper heart sits in my palm like a tiny origami grenade.

I'm sitting in front of a three-panel mirror, in my dressing room at the FTX Arena, surrounded by enough hairspray fumes to piss off environmental activists. I'm wearing a bedazzled leotard and it's clear the designer gave zero fucks about comfort. My hair has been teased, sprayed, and shellacked into submission. It might look nice but it's crunchy to the touch. My makeup could survive a nuclear blast. I am, by all external metrics, ready to perform.

Inside, however, I'm unraveling.

I unfold the paper heart carefully, the creases soft from years of handling. My mother's handwriting stares back at me—loopy and feminine, the kind of penmanship they don't teach anymore.

When you feel lost, remember: the stars shine brightest in the darkest night.

I wait for the words to land. To settle into my chest and fill the hollow space that's been growing there for weeks. To do what they've always done—anchor me, guide me, remind me that someone who loved me left behind a roadmap for moments exactly like this.

Nothing.

The words sit there, inert. Pretty but meaningless. Fortune-cookie wisdom dressed up in my mother's scrawl.

I fold the heart and reach into the box for another. The wooden chest is smaller than I remembered—or maybe I'm just picturing a pair of child-sized hands clutching to it like a lifeline. A talisman that holds all the answers to everything that matters. I pull out a pink heart this time, edges worn soft.

You are braver than you believe, stronger than you seem, and smarter than you think.

The first time I read that one, it landed deep. Then I learned it's literally a Winnie the Pooh quote. My mother plagiarized a cartoon bear to bestow her infinite wisdom.

Another heart. Yellow.

Dance like nobody's watching.

Painfully cliché. A little reminiscent of *Footloose*. And wildly ironic, considering twenty-some thousand people are about to watch me dance like Napoleon Dynamite in a leotard.

"You're going to wear those out."

I look up. Taio is leaning against the doorframe, arms crossed, watching me with that quiet intensity that makes my stomach do complicated things. He's in all black, as usual—the bodyguard uniform that somehow looks like it was tailored specifically for his tease of a body. What is the point of all those muscles if he insists on keeping them sheathed in clothing?

"How long have you been standing there?"

"Long enough to watch you shake that box like it owes you money." He pushes off the frame and moves into the room, settling onto the arm of the couch a few feet away. Close enough to be present, far enough to give me space. "What's wrong?"

"Pre-show ritual." I hold one up. "I do it before every single performance for good luck...well, except for New York, but we know how that ended."

"Why so many?" Taio asks, looking at the growing pile of

paper beside the box. "Those aren't working?"

I let out a laugh that sounds more like a sob. "Tonight nothing is working." I pull another heart from the box—blue this time.

The only person you need to be better than is the person you were yesterday.

"But what if the person I was yesterday was also a disaster?" I mutter, crumpling it slightly before smoothing it back out. Old habits. I can't bring myself to actually damage them, even when they're failing me.

Taio watches me pull another heart, then another, my movements getting more frantic. Shaking the box. Digging to the bottom. Searching for the one piece of paper that will somehow make all of this okay.

Follow your heart. Believe in yourself. Everything happens for a reason.

"Charlie." His voice cuts through my spiral.

I freeze, a fistful of hearts clutched against my chest like they might save me if I just hold on tight enough.

"Why are you so nervous?" He tilts his head, genuinely curious. "You've been doing this forever. You've performed hundreds of shows. What's different about tonight?"

The question hits somewhere deep. I set the hearts down, smoothing them against my thigh.

"I can't remember," I say quietly.

"Your lyrics or your marks?"

I stare at my reflection in the mirror—the glitter, the rhinestones, the perfect waves. The costume I didn't know would become my permanent identity, like a sparkly exoskeleton I can't shed. "I can't remember what I loved about this." The words come out hollow, echoing against the vanity lights that frame my face in surgical brightness. "I used to love music. Like, genuinely love it.

The way the bass line would climb up through the soles of my feet and settle somewhere behind my sternum. How a perfect bridge could make me weep. The electricity of an entire crowd breathing together in synchronized awe." I shake my head and watch the light catch on my hair, creating a momentary halo that feels like false advertising. "Now all I can think about is what could go wrong. What has already gone wrong. How, no matter what I do, or how hard I try, somebody is leaving disappointed. Someone hates me for existing. I can't win them all, Taio..."

"Of course not," he says.

I lift my gaze, his eyes are deadlocked on me, a look of anticipation on his face, like he's waiting for me to get to the punchline.

The ugly honesty takes over like it tends to do around Taio. "But I still want to. I want to be the girl that everyone likes. That everyone approves of. I want other people to treat me the way I'd treat them—with respect and grace, not like a glittery, soulless mascot, stuffed to the brim with confetti and bullshit. Is that really too much to ask?"

"If you only live to ensure everyone likes you, you'll never find the people who love you. But people have to know you to love you, Charlie."

He renders me speechless, his advice seeping into my bones like they are the last, secret commandment. *That's the key? Let people in? See who stays?*

Taio is quiet for a moment. Then he moves closer, settling onto the couch across from me. He pats the cushion next to him, inviting me closer. I sit and his hand finds the small of my back. The warmth of his palm seeps through the thin fabric of my costume, grounding me in a way the paper hearts couldn't tonight.

"You know what I think?" His voice is low, meant only for me. "I think you've spent so long performing for everyone else that you forgot the performance is for you too."

"For me?"

"Yeah." His hand moves in slow circles against my spine,

soothing the tension I didn't realize I was carrying. "Twenty thousand people in the crowd tonight, and you belong to yourself more than you belong to them. More than you belong to the label, or the brand, or the internet, or any of it." He tugs gently on a tendril of my hair. "Give yourself permission to perform for yourself. Not just for the crowd. Find one moment up there that's just yours, just a baby step toward remembering why you love this again."

Tears prickle at the corners of my eyes, threatening to ruin two hours of professional makeup work. "How?" I whisper. "How am I supposed to—"

The door bursts open.

Sage strides in first, tablet clutched to her chest, her expression carefully neutral. I know that look—it means she's about to deliver bad news. Marcus follows closely behind wearing his default expression of "calculating profit margins."

"Charlie." Marcus's eyes flick to Taio, then back to me. "Can we talk? *Privately.*"

Taio's hand stills on my back. I feel him tense, protective instincts kicking in, but he doesn't argue. He just squeezes my shoulder once and rises.

"I'll be right outside," he says quietly, like a promise.

The door clicks shut behind him.

Marcus pulls up a chair across from me, close enough that our knees almost touch. Sage hovers behind him like an impeccably dressed shadow.

"What's going on?" I ask, even though I can already feel it. That sick twist in my gut that means something bad is coming.

Marcus takes a breath. The kind of breath people take before they say something they know you won't want to hear.

"We've been talking—me, Sage, the label, the tour producers—and we think it's best if tonight's performance is...modified. To make it easier on you and on everyone."

My voice is calm over the thunderous beating in my chest. "Modified how?"

"We want you to lip-sync tonight."

The suggestion doesn't compute at first, just floats there, nonsensical, like he's speaking a language I don't understand.

"I'm sorry, what?"

"Your mic will be off. We'll have the usual back tracks, and the main vocals will be piped in from the studio recordings. All you have to do is move your mouth and hit your marks. The audience won't know the difference."

I look at Sage. She won't meet my gaze.

"You're joking."

"You've missed four shows, Charlie. You collapsed on stage in New York. The label is terrified of another incident, and frankly, so am I." Marcus leans forward, his tone softening into something that's probably supposed to be paternal. "This is to protect you. If something happens up there...if you freeze, if you panic, if your voice gives out—no one will know. You can just get through it. Fake it until it's over."

"Fake it," I echo robotically.

"Yes."

"You want me to fake my own concert."

"I want you to survive your concert." His jaw tightens. "Charlie, do you understand what's at stake here? The tour insurance alone is not enough. If you have another public breakdown, we're looking at lawsuits, canceled dates, sponsors pulling out. Your career can't take another hit right now. Not with the scandal, not with the press circling like sharks. We need tonight to go smoothly. We need you to be okay."

"And if I'm not okay, you'll just...play a recording of me being okay?"

I try to catch his gaze, so he has to look me in the eye when he tells me he doesn't think I can do this. Instead, Marcus hangs his head. "Essentially, yes."

"Sage?" I ask, helplessly. "Sage, look at me, please?"

She won't. Not for a long moment.

Then reluctantly, she turns her head, watching my lips

slacken into a heartbroken frown.

"I think," she answers carefully, "that we should do whatever gives you the best chance of getting through tonight. And if that means having a safety net—"

"A safety net. Right." I stand abruptly, my shins knocking into the coffee table in front of me. I rub the pain away until it's a distant memory.

"Charlie—" Marcus starts.

"No, I get it. I really do." I'm pacing now, my heels clicking against the floor like a metronome counting down to disaster. "I'm a liability. I'm a ticking time bomb. Better to just mute me. Put me on autopilot. Let the machine do its thing while I smile and wave like a trained monkey."

Sage scoffs heavily. "That's not what we're saying—"

"That's exactly what you're saying." The words explode out of me louder than I intended. They both flinch. "You're saying you don't trust me. You're saying I can't be trusted to do the one thing I've been doing since I was sixteen years old. The one thing I'm supposedly good at."

Marcus stands, hands raised like he's approaching a spooked horse. "We trust you, we do. But we also have a responsibility to protect you—"

"From myself?"

"From the pressure. From the expectations. From the sold-out arena who paid good money to see you at your best." He pauses. "And from the millions more who are waiting for you to fail so they can tear you apart."

The fight drains out of me. Because he's not wrong, is he? They're all waiting. The hashtags are still trending. #CheaterCharlie. #FakeBarbie. The internet has decided I'm a fraud, and now my own team wants me to prove them right.

"Fine," I hear myself say. The word tastes like ash. "Whatever it takes. Mute my mic."

Marcus sits back down, sagging with relief. "Thank you, Charlie. This is the right call. You'll see. Just go out there tonight and try to have fun."

I don't respond. I just turn to stare at my reflection in the mirror—the glittering, perfect, hollow shell of a pop star who's starting to make lying her coveted brand.

Taio's words echo in my head: *You belong to yourself more than you belong to them.*

But right now, I don't feel like I belong to anyone. Not even myself.

THE SMOKE IS thick enough to choke on.

I stand on the platform beneath the stage, waiting for my cue, surrounded by fog and darkness and the muffled roar of the crowd above me. The bass thrums through the floor, vibrating up through my heels, into my bones. Thousands of people are already screaming my name in anticipation.

The jitters are crawling up my spine, making me want to stop, drop, and roll. But I stay frozen, ignoring the pinpricks of nervous energy stabbing me everywhere at once.

The platform begins to rise. Slowly at first, then faster. The smoke parts around me like curtains opening on a show I'm no longer starring in.

Light explodes.

The crowd erupts in cheers.

And a polished Charlie Riley takes the stage like it belongs to her.

The next ninety minutes pass in a blur.

I hit my marks. I move my mouth. I execute the choreography with mechanical precision, my body doing what it's been trained to do while my mind floats somewhere above it all, watching from a safe distance.

"*Summer Nights*"—bounce, smile, shimmy, pretend this song about teenage crushes isn't mortifying to perform at twenty-three.

"*Electric Heart*"—strobe lights, hair flip, the complicated footwork sequence I've practiced but certainly not perfected. My lips move. The recording fills in the rest.

"*Dancing in the Dark*"—this one has a key change that I always loved hitting live. Now I just watch my pre-recorded voice nail it while I stand here, powerless, voiceless, fake.

The crowd doesn't know. That's the worst part. They're singing along, holding up their phone flashlights, screaming my name like I'm giving them something real. And I'm up here committing fraud, every smile a lie, every gesture a performance of a performance.

Between songs, I do the banter. The mic works for talking, just not for singing. So I tell them I love Miami. I tell them they're the best crowd on the whole tour. I ask if they're ready to party, and they roar back at me, and I feel nothing. *Nothing at all.*

"*Midnight Confessions*" comes and goes. No vocal runs. No octave showcase. Just me, mouthing words a different version of myself is singing, dancing steps someone else choreographed, being a person someone else invented.

The fish on the dock. The trained monkey. The perfect little pop star in her perfect little box.

By the time we hit the final number—"*Unbreakable*," the power ballad that's supposed to be my triumphant closer—I'm running on fumes. My face hurts from smiling. My feet are screaming in these heels. And deep in my chest, in the place where music used to live, there's nothing but static.

The last note rings out. The lights go down. The crowd erupts.

I stand in the darkness, breathing hard, waiting for the relief that's supposed to come when a show ends.

It doesn't come.

Instead, there's just emptiness. A show completed. A fraud perpetuated. Another night of being everything everyone else needs me to be.

The crowd is still screaming. *Encore, encore!* They want more. Of course they do—they always want more. More songs, more spectacle, more pieces of me ready for the snatching.

Usually this is where I wave, blow kisses, and exit stage left while the house lights come up.

But tonight, something snaps.

Maybe it's the paper hearts that failed me. Maybe it's the lip sync that stripped away my last shred of authenticity. Maybe it's the thought of going back to that dressing room and facing Marcus and Sage with their relieved smiles, their "see, that wasn't so bad" platitudes.

Or maybe it's Taio's voice in my head: *You belong to yourself more than you belong to them. Give yourself permission to perform for yourself.*

I turn and walk toward the grand piano, which is really just a performance prop. My band plays on the keyboard; this piano is purely for aesthetics...until tonight.

The crowd goes quiet. Confused. This isn't in the script.

I settle onto the bench. The leather is cool against my bare thighs. My fingers find the keys automatically, muscle memory taking over.

"Charlie." Omar's voice crackles in my earpiece. "Charlie, what are you doing? The show's over. You did it. Now exit stage left."

I ignore him.

Instead, I look toward stage right, where the sound director is standing with his headset and his mixing board. I catch his eye and beckon him closer.

He approaches cautiously, like I might bite.

"I need a working mic," I say.

"A—what?"

"A mic that's not muted." I hold out my hand. "Turn it on."

"I can't just—Marcus said—"

"Keep your eyes on me." My voice is steady. Certain. I don't know where this calm is coming from, but I'm not questioning it. "I'm calling the shots right now. Not Marcus. Not Sage. Me. Turn the mic on."

He hesitates. The internal battle shows in his eyes—the fear of disobeying Marcus versus the fear of disobeying me, right here, right now, in front of all these witnesses.

"*Turn. It. On.*"

He clicks a button on his belt. Nods once. "All right. You're live."

The moment the mic goes hot, there's a shift in my chest. My power, my voice, my purpose returning.

I adjust the microphone stand attached to the piano, angling it toward my mouth. Then I turn to face the crowd—all twenty-some thousand of them, phones raised, faces expectant, waiting to see what happens next.

"Hey, Miami." My voice echoes through the arena—eerie against the sudden dead silence. "I want to end this show with something a little different, if that's okay with you."

A scattered cheer. They're curious now.

"One of my sweetest memories as a little girl was sitting next to my dad, Nate, while he taught me to play the piano." My fingers drift across the keys, not playing anything yet, just touching. Remembering. "I was so impatient at first. I didn't want to play the classics. I was ready to be the next Hannah Montana, you know?" There's a low hum of laughter at the nostalgia. "But he was so patient with me, teaching me the fundamentals, so when I started to create, I always had something solid to fall back on. I've been playing piano for over ten years, but I don't think I've ever played for you guys live. No time like the present, right?"

The arena is dead silent. Waiting.

"I want to sing you one more song tonight. It's not one of mine—it's by an artist I really admire. And the reason I'm singing it is because someone very special to me once told me that I sang it like an angel. He was probably lying, but it lit me up the way he said it. It made me believe in myself a little bit more."

The crowd murmurs. I can practically hear them thinking: *Grayson. She's talking about Grayson.*

But my eyes find the wings, stage right, where a tall figure in all black is standing just out of the spotlight's reach. Taio. He's watching me with that quiet intensity, that same look he had in the dressing room, and even from this distance, I can see the question in his eyes: *What the hell are you doing?*

I smile. Just for him.

"This one is for someone special," I say into the mic. "But it's also for me."

I play the opening notes.

The song is "Stay" by Rihanna—the same song I was singing the night Taio first knocked. I was alone in that penthouse, having no idea that my life was about to come alive. The hero I didn't want to need was already on his way.

My fingers move across the keys, building the arrangement I've played a hundred times in private but never once in public. The melody is simple, haunting. A song about not being able to make someone stay. About needing them anyway. About the impossible ache of wanting something you're not sure you can have.

And then I open my mouth, and I sing.

Not the manufactured voice. Not the compressed, auto-tuned, producer-approved version of Charlie Riley that exists in studio recordings. The realest, rawest version of my voice on display with no armor. This is me. The real me. Not all of you will like it. *But who here will love it?*

The first verse pours out of me—rich and aching and alive. I let my voice crack where it wants to crack. I let the emotion bleed through where the producers would have smoothed it away. This isn't a performance. This is a confession.

I close my eyes and disappear into the music, letting the trance take over.

The arena falls away. The crowd falls away. The scandal, the headlines—all of it dissolves until there's nothing left but me and this piano and this song and the memories of all the times I've played it before.

Nate's proud smile. Spencer's teary eyes, her hand clutched over her chest. Claire's roaring cheers. Taio, looking positively hypnotized when he finally laid eyes on the girl behind the voice.

You belong to yourself more than you belong to them.

I understand it now. What Taio was trying to tell me. The crowd's not my enemy. My obsessive desire to please them is. When's the last time I cared about how I saw myself instead of how the world saw me?

It starts now.

This is mine.

This moment. This song. This voice.

Mine.

The bridge builds. I lean into the high notes, letting my voice soar in ways I haven't allowed myself in years. The runs I've been suppressing. The riffs I've been trained out of. All of it, finally free.

I pour my guts onto those keys—the bone-deep exhaustion that makes my limbs feel like concrete, the terror that claws at my throat every time I step on stage, the loneliness that has hollowed me out until I'm nothing but an echo chamber of other people's expectations. And still I sing, voice breaking, fingers trembling, while the man in the wings watches me bleed truth all over this beautiful, polished stage.

The final chorus approaches. I can feel the crowd holding its breath. So many people, suspended in silence, waiting for me to take them somewhere they've never been.

I open my eyes.

And there, just outside the spotlight, exactly where I left him, is Taio.

It's the perfect setup, because he can see my whole world, but they can't see him. My secret weapon. My revival.

And he's beaming like he's proud.

For a moment, our eyes lock. It's just us—two very broken people who somehow found each other in the middle of all this chaos.

I take a breath. I let it fill my lungs, my chest, my whole body.

And I pour everything I have into the final line. The words about someone being the reason, the only reason. About not being able to walk away. About needing them, wanting them, choosing them—not because you should, but because you can't imagine any other choice.

The last note rings out across the arena. My fingers lift from the keys. Silence.

For a moment, nothing.

And then the crowd explodes in a way I've never heard before.

The audience is on their feet, screaming, crying, stamping so hard the stage shakes beneath me. The sound is a wall—physical, overwhelming, the kind of noise that breaks through to your bones and rewrites your DNA.

I sit at the piano, trembling, barely able to breathe, and I feel something I haven't felt in years.

Alive. The high. The perfect hit of that drug of approval. Except this time I think it's my own approval which feels like a giant step forward.

I did it. I went rogue. I sang for myself. And somehow, impossibly, they loved it. And I think to myself, *Does it matter as long as I loved it?*

The lights are doing something strange now—shifting, flickering, creating patterns I don't recognize. The stage glows golden, and through my tears, I see faces in the crowd. Strangers, all of them, but in this moment they feel like family.

And then I see her.

Third row, center section. A woman with long blond hair and bright blue eyes, and a warm smile I'd know anywhere, because I see it every time I look in the mirror.

"Mom?" I whisper away from the mic.

She's standing there, clapping, tears on her cheeks, looking at me the way she used to when I was five years old singing into a hairbrush in her bathroom.

I know she's not real. I know it's the lights, the adrenaline, the emotional overload playing tricks on my brain. She died eighteen years ago. She's not here.

But for one perfect moment, I let myself believe in miracles.

"I love you, baby. Proud. I'm so proud of you." I enjoy the

hallucinogenic bliss of my mother's praise. The real validation I've been craving.

The vision fades. The crowd keeps screaming. And I sit alone at the piano on the biggest stage of my life, tears streaming down my face, broken and whole, more myself than I've been in years.

This is what it feels like to belong to yourself. Beautifully unhinged. An endless stream of options—some of them right, some wrong, but all worth experiencing.

"Charlie, are you ready? We're going to turn the lights off now." Omar comes through my earpiece.

"Just one more moment," I murmur, barely audible over the insatiable crowd. I breathe in the high one more time, the lights burning hot on my face, the salty tears teasing the corner of my lips, my chest rising and falling like there's not enough air in the world.

I meet Taio's eyes again and the world crystallizes into a single point of connection. My heartbeat thunders in my ears.

He slams his fist against his chest twice before thrusting it skyward, his face fierce with pride and something deeper—something that makes my skin burn and steals my breath.

The song lyrics sear through my mind like lightning, no longer just words but prophecies carved into my bones.

I'm not sure how to feel about it.
But somehow, something about him...
All I know is I want him to stay.

Chapter 12
Taio

Lies upon lies.

I watch Charlie play the final note from the wings, my chest so tight I'm not sure I'm breathing.

The arena is silent for one impossible moment—tens of thousands of people holding their breath in the dark—and then the moment Charlie lifts her hands from the keys, the crowd's response crashes over me like a tsunami. The roar vibrates through the floorboards and up into my bones. Their screams pierce my eardrums from every direction at once. Wave after wave of thunderous applause and foot-stomping that makes the metal scaffolding around me tremble. The kind of deafening, all-consuming noise that jumbles your brain and rewrites reality, leaving nothing but goose bumps and adrenaline.

And Charlie just sits there at the piano, tears streaming down her face, looking like someone who just discovered fire. *Her fire.*

It's been there all along, dormant, waiting. She just had to light that match. To claim a little piece of her life for herself.

She glances my way and I don't know what to do except slam my fist against my chest twice, then thrust it skyward. It's instinct, the kind of gesture that bypasses language entirely. *I see you. I'm proud of you. You fucking did it.*

She holds my eyes across the chaos, and what passes between us—I don't have words for.

Then the lights shift, the stage crew swarms, and reality reasserts itself. I'm pulled backward by a meaty hand on my shoulder.

"Sir, we need to move you to the secure corridor."

The arena's security team—actual professionals in actual uniforms with actual earpieces—surrounds me like I'm a package that needs delivering. They're efficient, coordinated, operating from a playbook that involves hand signals, code words, and years of training.

I'm a guy in a black T-shirt and worn shoes who follows Charlie around like a lost puppy.

The contrast is not lost on me.

"We'll escort Ms. Riley to you once she's cleared the stage," the lead guard explains as they usher me through the maze of backstage. "Private hallway, no public access. You take over from there until vehicles are ready."

Take over. Like I'm part of some security relay race, except everyone else is an Olympic athlete and I'm a guy who showed up in ten-year-old sneakers.

They deposit me in a corridor that looks like it's been triple-coated in epoxy. Shiny tile floors, clean, white walls, not a shred of decoration except a sad-looking analog clock mounted on the wall, displaying the wrong time. There's a fire exit at one end, a heavy door at the other. No windows. No cameras that I can see.

No witnesses.

The guards vanish toward the stage, leaving me alone with nothing but the distant thunder of the crowd vibrating through concrete. I press my hand against my chest where my heart hammers like it's trying to escape. My shirt sticks to my back. The corridor suddenly feels too small, too empty, like the calm before some inevitable storm.

Like I might actually combust if I don't see her in the next thirty seconds.

Like suddenly infatuation has turned to unwelcome possessiveness, because I'll admit, I don't like it when she's farther than arm's reach from me.

The heavy door swings open on the opposite side of the hallway.

And there she is.

Sweat-drenched, hair a frizzy halo around her face, chest heaving like she just ran a marathon. Her stage makeup is smeared. Her bedazzled boots are in her hands as she walks barefoot into the hall. She looks wrecked. Unpolished. Completely undone.

She's the most beautiful thing I've ever seen.

Our eyes lock. I watch the recognition hit her—me, here, alone, waiting...Her expression shifts. Something wild and reckless and beyond reason moves in.

She runs.

Full sprint, heels abandoned against the tile, stocking-covered feet slapping so hard against the floor it sounds painful. And before I can think, before I can prepare, before I can do anything remotely sensible, she launches herself at me.

I catch her. Of course I catch her. My arms wrap around her automatically, hauling her up against my chest as her legs lock around my waist. She's breathing hard, laughing and crying at the same time, and she smells like sweat and hairspray and something underneath that's just sweetly...her.

"That felt unreal," she gasps against my neck. "Taio, your advice. It was everything—"

And then she kisses me.

Her mouth crashes against mine with such force our teeth nearly collide. It's graceless and desperate, and exactly the way we need to be kissing. She tastes like salt and adrenaline and something forbidden I've been starving for. Her hands don't just fist in my hair—they pull, sending sparks of electricity down my spine that pool hot and urgent in my groin. When her mouth opens, her tongue slides against mine with deliberate, devastating intent. There's no hesitance, no hint at the fact that Charlie's inexperienced.

She's kissing me like it's the only thought in her head from sunup to sundown.

I kiss her back like a man equally possessed.

My hands grip her ass hard enough to bruise it, lifting her higher against me as I press her into the wall. The heat of her body burns through her sweat-soaked costume, and when my thumb grazes the sliver of bare skin at her lower back, she arches against me with a gasp that turns into a moan so raw it makes my blood roar. I can feel her heartbeat hammering against my chest, or maybe it's mine, thundering out of control as her legs tighten around my waist.

Our gasps and rustling clothes bounce off the bare walls, transforming this stolen moment into something that sounds obscenely public in the empty corridor.

This isn't just crossing a line. This is obliterating it completely.

This is real, and it's dangerous, and God help me, I'm no longer in control.

Her tongue slides against mine and I go weak. My will is completely, utterly useless. I press her harder against the wall, securing her so my hands are free to explore. One hand bracing beside her head, the other cupping the curve of her ass through her tights. My senses are on overload, it's all warmth and sugar, and pressure in the best way. Her hips are locked into mine, she has to feel my growing erection. She doesn't shy away. Instead her fingers are tugging at my hair, and the way she keeps making these tiny desperate sounds—

Voices.

Distant, but approaching. Footsteps echoing down the corridor.

Reality crashes back like a bucket of ice water.

I pull away. Set Charlie on her feet. Step backward so fast I nearly trip over my own legs.

She blinks at me, dazed, lips swollen, chest heaving. For a moment she just stares, like maybe I got hurt or caught on fire. But then I watch understanding dawn, followed immediately by disappointment.

"What's wrong?" Her voice is raw, wrecked from singing and kissing and God knows what else.

"I heard someone coming. I don't want to get caught."

The words land wrong. I know it the second they leave my mouth. Her face shutters, that vulnerability hardening into something defensive.

"Get caught," she repeats flatly. "Like I'm something to be ashamed of—"

"That's not what I—"

"There's nothing wrong with me liking you, Taio." She steps toward me, closing the distance I just created. Her hand lands on my chest, right over my heart, and I know she can feel it hammering. "We're just two people. That's it. That's all this has to be."

"Charlie—"

"Don't." Her eyes flash. "Don't you dare stand there and pretend there's nothing between us. I felt it. You felt it. I don't easily connect to men, Taio. So sorry if I'm coming on too strong. If you don't feel the same, I'll—"

"I'm not saying I don't feel...the same," I manage. "I'm saying it's complicated."

"So uncomplicate it."

"Charlie, your celebrity status and public *boyfriend* are just the massive cherry on top of that already impossibility that is us. Have you forgotten who I am and what I actually do?"

She's not backing down. If anything, she's getting closer, her hand still pressed to my chest, her eyes demanding answers I don't have. "I don't care, Taio. You're not some dirty little secret to me. You make me feel...good. So what's the problem?"

The problem. Where do I even start?

"The problem," I say slowly, "is that the only reason I'm here is to cover up a lie. Your lie about Grayson. My lie about being your bodyguard. Lie upon lie upon lie. Who wants that?" I shake my head. "That's not how happily-ever-afters begin, Charlie."

The fire in her eyes dims. I watch her shoulders drop, her

defensive posture crumbling into something smaller. Sadder.

"Don't I know it," she whispers.

And I understand, with sudden awful clarity, that she's not just talking about us. She's thinking about her mom and eighteen years of believing in a story that turned out to be fiction.

Lies upon lies.

Her whole life has been built on them.

"Charlie." I reach for her, guilt clawing at my chest. "I didn't mean—"

But the corridor door bangs open, and Sage and Marcus come barreling through like a two-person hurricane.

"*Charlie*!" Sage's yell echoes off the industrial walls. She's practically running, tablet abandoned somewhere, her carefully composed expression completely shattered. "Charlie, oh my God, actual tears. I had actual tears running down my face. I was standing there sobbing like a baby. I couldn't—when you started singing, I just—"

She reaches Charlie and pulls her into a fierce hug, squeezing like she's trying to physically transfer pride through osmosis. Over Sage's shoulder, I see Charlie's face—confused, guarded, waiting for the other shoe to drop.

Marcus hangs back for a moment, and when Sage finally releases her grip, he steps forward. His expression is strange. Soft in a way I haven't seen from him before.

"Charlie." He takes her by the arms, gentle but firm. "I'm an idiot."

She blinks. "What?"

"I'm an idiot," he repeats. "I was wrong. I was so focused on protecting the investment that I forgot what I should've actually been protecting." He shakes his head. "When it comes to following my dumb business advice or following your heart? Always trust your heart. Always. I should have trusted it from the beginning."

Charlie looks like she doesn't know what to do with this information. Like she's been bracing for a fight and instead walked into a surrender.

"Marcus—"

"No, let me finish." His grip tightens on her arms. "From here on out, we're building your vision. Not the other way around. You want to sit at a piano and sing covers for twenty minutes? We'll restructure the whole show. You want to write new music that sounds nothing like the old stuff? We'll figure out how to market it. It's time for you to take back what's yours. Your voice. Your career. Your life." He pauses. "I'm sorry it took me this long to see it."

Charlie's lip trembles. For a moment I think she might cry again but instead she throws her arms around Marcus, hugging him with the kind of desperate gratitude that makes my chest ache.

"Thank you," she whispers. "Thank you."

Marcus hugs her back, one hand patting her shoulder awkwardly. Sage is beaming, already tapping at her phone, probably drafting press releases about Charlie's triumphant return.

It's a victory. A real one. The kind of moment that changes trajectories.

But over Marcus's shoulder, Charlie's eyes find mine.

She doesn't look triumphant.

She looks broken.

A single tear slides down her cheek—silent, almost invisible in the harsh fluorescent light. She doesn't wipe it away. She just holds my gaze while Marcus murmurs reassurances into her hair, and I watch that tear trace a path down her face like an accusation.

You did this, her eyes say. *You kissed me like you wanted me and then you pulled away. You told me our foundation was cracked with lies. You reminded me that nothing in my life is solid. That I will always be a girl caged by others' criticisms and expectations.*

My feet ache to move toward her, to brush away that tear with my thumb, to whisper something comforting against her ear. I want to be honest that when she's close, everything else falls away and I feel something I thought I'd forgotten how to feel. And when we kissed, I was reminded what it was to ache for someone.

But I don't. I remain rooted in place.

I'm just the hired muscle. The human shield collecting six figures to blend into the wallpaper and never, ever touch the merchandise.

Seems I've failed spectacularly at the one job I was actually supposed to do.

Charlie finally looks away, burying her face in Marcus's shoulder, and I stand there in that bland corridor feeling the weight of every bad decision I've ever made pressing down on my chest.

I watch silently as our first kiss dissolves into a distant memory far too fast. Like it didn't even happen.

Chapter 13

Charlie

The kind of gentleman that holds doors, or my legs over his shoulders?

The sheets in this Miami mansion are obscenely soft. They have the kind of thread count that probably requires its own insurance policy—but I still can't get comfortable. I've been lying here for an hour, rearranging pillows, kicking off blankets, pulling them back on. My body is exhausted but my brain refuses to power down.

It keeps replaying the same five minutes on an endless loop.

His hands fisting in my hair. His mouth hot and desperate against mine. The low sound he made when I arched into him—something between a groan and a growl that vibrated through my entire body.

And then: the way he practically pushed me away. The cold air rushing in to fill the space where his warmth had been. The look on his face like he'd just committed a crime he couldn't take back.

My phone buzzes against the pillow, rattling me out of the memory. Claire's face fills the screen—a contact photo from two Christmases ago, both of us squeezed into matching ugly sweaters, her pregnant belly just starting to round under a reindeer with a light-up nose. Her smile in the photo is pure chaos, like she's mid-laugh about something only we would find funny. It was only a few weeks later that she lost the baby. I haven't seen her smile like that since.

I answer before the second ring.

"*I watched it.*" Claire's voice explodes through the speaker with the force of a small bomb. "Charlie, I've watched it like a gagillion times already. I have it saved. I have it bookmarked. I texted it to literally everyone I've ever met, including my dental hygienist, who now follows you on Instagram."

"You text your dental hygienist?"

"Yeah. Is that weird?"

"Super weird." I sink deeper into the mountain of pillows, letting her enthusiasm wash over me like a warm bath. "Which part was your favorite?"

"All of it. Every single part. But when you got on the piano. *Ugh, my heart.* The speech about Dad teaching you how to play. The way you just—" She makes an explosion sound, complete with what I imagine are accompanying hand gestures. "Your voice, Charlie. When you held that last note like you never wanted to let it go. You should've seen how the crowd was looking at you. You looked so at peace."

Something loosens in my chest. "It felt different this time. Being up there. Like I remembered why I started doing this in the first place."

"It was always in your DNA. Do you remember when we were twelve and you used to make me sit through full concerts in our living room?"

I laugh, the memory surfacing easily. "You said you loved those."

"I was a captive audience. Under duress. You'd set up all your stuffed animals on the couch, bring out the guinea pigs' cages. You just wanted as many bodies in a room as you could fit. I got up to pee once and you threatened my life."

I clear my throat. "I might've been a little intense."

She snickers. "My favorite memories. Just you, singing Mariah Carey covers, the guinea pigs squealing as your backup vocals. You were so happy. That's what you looked like tonight. Really, really happy. And you didn't even have to hog-tie anyone in the audience to get them to stay."

"I never once hog-tied you. You were free to leave."

"You would've cried." I hear her shifting, settling deeper into what's probably her own bed, thousands of miles away. "Besides, I was jealous."

The admission catches me off guard. "Jealous? Of what?"

"Of the way you had this thing. This gift. It just radiated out of you. Even when we were kids, anyone could see it. You'd open your mouth and suddenly every adult in the room was paying attention to you instead of me." There's no bitterness in her voice—just honesty, aged and softened by time. "I was stuck with my participation trophies and my solid B in drama class. I didn't have a creative bone in my body, and you were over there being *special* all the time."

"Please." I roll onto my side, phone pressed to my ear. "You were the pretty one. You had boys following you around like lost puppies from the time you were twelve. I couldn't even get Jason Mercer to look at me, and I had a crush on him for two years. And the first time he ever passed me a note in science class, know what it said? 'Is your sister, Claire, still dating Aiden'?"

"I don't remember getting that note."

"I also don't remember crumpling it up and putting it in the trash," I answer.

"Well, Jason Mercer was an idiot who peaked in middle school and now sells insurance in Kansas City. You dodged a bullet."

"Damn, how do you know that?"

"Bed rest is *so boring*. I've watched all of Netflix and Hulu. I've now moved on to internet stalking our old high school class."

"Riveting," I deadpan.

Claire's voice takes on a knowing quality. "And, by the way, what are you talking about? You had plenty of boys interested in you. You just never really wanted any of them back. It was just the chase for you."

The words land in a tender place, stirring up memories I'd half forgotten. Notes in my locker with phone numbers scrawled in nervous handwriting. Promposals I declined as gently as I could. The confused, wounded faces of perfectly nice boys who couldn't understand why I wasn't interested.

I never knew how to explain it to them. Something in me was always waiting. For a feeling I couldn't name. A recognition I'd never experienced. A special spark my mom practically prophesied. I wanted my first love to be fireworks, blimps in the sky, a perfect story to rewrite my life. I wasn't going to settle for giving it up in the back of an old Chevy after homecoming.

"It wasn't the chase. I just wanted big love. *Forever love.* Beauty and the Beast, the old couple from *Up*, Harley Quinn and Joker. You know the kind of love that becomes your whole world."

"I don't think you want what Harley Quinn and Joker have," Claire says. "Pretty toxic."

"The way he broke down prisons to save her—"

"After he basically put her there."

"Okay, and when he rescues her from that vat of acid?"

"After he pushed her in? Geez, Charlie, you're scaring me. Just say like Superman and Lois Lane."

I laugh. "Fine. All I mean is I wanted a guy who'd move mountains for me. I wanted a guy that I'd move mountains for, too. Just that monumental, kismet feeling. You know?"

"Yeah, I get that, sweetie. But that's not how real love works."

I beg to differ. "I kissed him tonight."

"What? Who? Grayson?"

"What? No. Grayson serves the purpose of a used lollipop stick."

"What do you do with used lollipop sticks?"

"*Exactly,*" I emphasize. "At the end of this tour, Grayson is no longer my problem. I'm talking about *Taio*...who I very much want to remain my problem."

"Taio..." Claire muses. "Is your...?"

"Bodyguard. Well, fake bodyguard. Real escort."

"Oh. My. Fuck. That's what the paparazzi actually got a picture of? You banging your bodyguard on the patio of Dad's hotel?"

"*No! Claire!* They got a picture of me...*trying* to bang my bodyguard on the patio. But he wasn't my bodyguard at the time. Just—"

"Your escort?"

"Not *my* escort. Just *an* escort. There was a mix-up. It was actually adorable. He was so embarrassed when I found the vibrator he brought."

Claire's silent for a moment. "Charlie, are you doing drugs? Like the hard stuff?"

"Claire," I growl into the phone.

"Well, I'm sorry. You're my little sister—"

"Barely."

"—and you're sitting here telling me you gave your virginity to an escort? After all these years of waiting for your big fireworks moment? Spence told me you were coming a little unraveled, but I'm getting ready to stage a family intervention."

"Claire Bear," I whine.

"I hate when you call me that."

"I know but it shuts you up." I put the phone on speaker and toss it on the mattress. Rubbing the side of my temple, I explain the only way I know how. "I didn't sleep with him, but I really, really like him. A lot. And our kiss was...everything. I've never had a kiss like that before."

"Aw, Charlie, you *like him*, like him? Then, that's great. Where is he now?"

"Hiding from me, probably," I admit. "I think I liked the kiss more than he did."

"Uh-oh. Did you go in with too much tongue?"

Well, shit. I didn't think of that. "How much is too much tongue?"

"If you can feel his tonsils, you're in too deep." She cackles at her joke.

"So helpful, sister. I'm so glad I shared this with you," I say, my response drenched in sarcasm.

"Okay, okay, I'm being serious now. I'm sorry. How can I help?"

I stare at my kneecap, tracing the small, California-shaped birthmark with my gaze. "I don't even know what I'm feeling. My life is so intense. Like constant sensory overload but whenever I'm around him it seems so simple. And I really like that. He makes me feel like a normal person. But I can't figure out his deal—if he's this sexual sensei who wants to rearrange my insides, or if he just wants to be my new best friend."

"Ah." She draws the syllable out knowingly. "What are the chances he wants both?"

"Men never want both."

"Men? Or you?"

Before I can answer, my bedroom door creaks open.

I freeze, staring at Claire's profile picture, heart catapulting into my throat. A shadow moves in the doorway, low to the ground, and for one wild, hopeful second I think—

Black Cat rockets across the hardwood floor like a furry cannonball with an attitude problem.

He makes a beeline for my bed, launches himself onto the mattress with an athletic grace that seems unnatural for a creature of his considerable roundness, and immediately begins kneading my stomach like he's preparing bread dough. His purr rumbles through my entire body.

I hold my breath. My eyes fix on the doorway. Waiting. Hoping.

But the doorway stays empty.

The hallway beyond is dark and silent. No footsteps. No voice. No Taio.

Just me and his cat and the echo of a kiss I can still feel on my lips.

Black Cat, utterly oblivious to my romantic disappointment, flops onto his back with the theatrical flair of a fainting Victorian maiden. His paws paddle the air expectantly, demanding tribute.

"Charlie? You still there?"

"Yeah." I swallow past something that feels embarrassingly close to tears and begin scratching Black Cat's exposed belly. He melts into a puddle of feline contentment. "Sorry. Got distracted. His cat just came in."

"His cat is there? Where is he?"

"Not here." I try to keep the disappointment out of my voice.

"Hmm." Claire files this information away. "Okay, Charlie, I'm just going to say something that may or may not make sense, but here's what I think. You've let everyone else's opinion of you mold, shape, and warp your identity for so long. That's not an accusation. I can't begin to fathom the pressure you're under, constantly. But you don't know who you are anymore. You don't know what you like. Your entire sense of self-worth is wrapped up in the comments on social media. I know the label, and Marcus and Sage, put all this pressure on the legacy you'll leave behind when you're gone, but what about the life you should be living while you're here? It's okay to want the simple things. Having a crush on a guy is a very normal thing."

"Those are my choices? Leave an everlasting legacy behind or actually enjoy the life I have now? You sound like the world's worst fortune cookie."

"I know." She's definitely grinning. I can hear it in every syllable. "But it's true. You can't rationalize your way to the answer, Charlie. You have to feel your way there. I know you've had tunnel vision since you were sixteen, but maybe it's time you live a little, too."

Black Cat repositions himself against my hip, his engine rumbling back to full speed. I stroke his fur absently, considering. *Is Taio worth the risk? And what exactly am I risking?* My reputation? Obviously. My sanity? Yeah, that's becoming more apparent. My heart? No, oddly enough that doesn't feel at risk. It feels safe.

Claire yawns, the sound stretching long and unashamed.

"You okay?"

"Yeah, God, I'm just exhausted. Growing a human is no joke. Not that I'm complaining," she quickly corrects. "I mean, I'm grateful—"

"Claire. It's okay to hate pregnancy. It doesn't mean this baby isn't the most important thing in the world to you."

"I complained a lot...the first time I was pregnant. Sometimes I think I—"

"No," I interrupt, knowing the unnecessary guilt she carries. "I love you, Claire Bear. Let's not think like that, okay?" I smile despite everything. "How's she doing in there?"

"Active. Opinionated. Already causing trouble." Claire's tone warms with obvious love. "Just like her aunt."

"I'll be there for the birth," I say, suddenly fierce. "I promise. No matter what. The moment you go into labor I will drop what I'm doing—"

"Charlie, don't be ridiculous. I know you have bigger fish to fry. The tour, the press. They barely give you time to pee—"

"*Claire*. I mean it. In a heartbeat."

"Your life doesn't work like that, sweetie. The machine doesn't stop."

"Then the machine can wait." I sit up straighter, disturbing Black Cat's comfortable position. He shoots me a look of pure feline disgust but doesn't relocate. "I missed Remy's first birthday party. I missed your bachelorette party. I missed when Grandpa was in the hospital after his heart attack. I've missed birthdays and holidays and random Tuesdays that turned out to matter, and I'm done. I'm done letting this career steal the things that actually count."

The line goes quiet. When Claire speaks again, her voice is thick with something I can't quite name.

"Charlie, what's going on? Is this all about your dad's letter? Spencer told me what you guys found. Have you reached out to him?"

"No," I murmur. "It's not about him." The truth is it's just about the life I could've had. A life that I think would have been filled with more peace and joy...all the beautiful simple things I can't seem to make room for in my world.

"Then what's it about?"

I sigh. "Getting my priorities straight, I guess. So, when I tell you I'll be there when my niece is born, I mean it. I promise you."

The silence stretches between us, heavy with eighteen years of complicated history. All the times I wasn't there. All the ways fame changed the shape of our family. All the distance I couldn't close no matter how much money or success I accumulated.

"Well." Claire's voice comes out rough, like she's fighting her own tears. "I guess this is a good time to tell you something."

"Tell me what?"

A pause, weighted with significance. "Justin and I have been talking about it for months. We wanted to name her something meaningful. Something that would keep her connected to you, forever."

My heart is doing something strange. Fluttering and clenching at the same time, like it can't decide whether to soar or break.

"We're naming her Charlotte." Claire's voice cracks on the word. "Lotti for short. So there won't be two Charlies in the family causing confusion."

I clap my hand over my mouth to catch the sob. I have to hold my breath because if I make even a peep, I'll unravel.

We breathe together for a moment, two sisters separated by thousands of miles but connected by something deeper than distance or time or the strange circumstances of our lives. I think about my mother—the paper hearts, the lies, the love that was real even when the stories weren't. I think about what it means to have my niece named after me. A little girl who will grow up knowing she's wanted, cherished, chosen.

A soft knock at the ajar door shatters the moment.

I jolt upright so fast my head spins. Black Cat's head swivels toward the sound with predatory interest.

"Hey," comes Taio's voice, muffled from behind the wood.

"Come in," I command and he pushes the door wide, but doesn't enter my room.

"Is that him?" Claire asks with zero stealth over the speakerphone.

I shush her. "What's up, Taio?"

"There he is," Taio says, glancing at the furry heap at the foot of my bed. "I was looking for Black Cat. He escaped during my shower and I couldn't find him anywhere."

I glance at the traitor currently sprawled across my duvet like a furry emperor surveying his kingdom. He blinks at me with exaggerated innocence. "You say he's not your pet, but you worry when he's gone."

Taio shrugs. "He's not native to Miami. I wouldn't want to abandon him in a foreign land. I'll happily kick him to the curb when I get back to New York."

I cock my head to the side and smile. "Your denial is getting out of control."

He whisper-laughs, awkwardly shifting his weight side to side like he doesn't know whether to stay or go. I decide to put him out of his misery. "Claire, thank you for telling me that. It means everything to me. Also, I want to be there when you tell Spencer the baby will be named after me and not her."

"Why?" Claire asks.

"I have a tiara and a sash that says 'Favorite Aunt' that I really want to parade in her face."

"Good grief," Claire grumbles.

"I love you, sister."

"Love you, too."

The call ends. I toss the phone aside and look up again.

Taio fills the doorway like a man who was specifically designed to fill doorways. He's changed out of his all-black bodyguard uniform into something softer—dark sweats that sit low on his hips, a tight, dark blue T-shirt that does obscene things to his chest and shoulders. His jet-black hair is still damp from a shower.

And he smells...good. *Really good.* Like he put on cologne before coming to look for a cat he almost certainly didn't lose.

"You're not sleeping?" he asks. "I figured you'd be exhausted."

I sink deeper into the covers. "I am, but I'm way too wired. It's like this after almost every performance—good or bad, I just sit here and play everything back in my mind, over and over. I'm powerless to stop it. When Claire's on tour with me, we always plan for midnight junk food, movies, face masks, pedicures, anything to tucker me out. Right now I'm on my own, and failing."

Black Cat yawns extravagantly, displaying an impressive array of teeth, and begins grooming his paw with aggressive disinterest.

I tuck my legs beneath me, suddenly hyperaware of my thin pajama shorts and tank top. "He can stay, by the way. I don't mind."

Taio hovers in the doorway, one hand braced against the frame, fingers drumming an uncertain rhythm. "And can I? Stay, I mean?"

"What do you mean?"

"I mean, are you mad at me?" The question comes out rough, scraping against something raw. "About earlier. The hallway. I wouldn't blame you if you were."

I weigh the possibilities in my mind. I could stretch this out—make him dangle in suspense a little longer, watch him fidget. The petty part of me is tempted. But exhaustion has worn down my edges, and there's something about the way he's standing there—all vulnerable and ridiculously good-looking—that's making it impossible to hold on to my righteous indignation.

"I'm not mad." I pitch my voice into my best imitation of a disappointed parent—the exact tone Nate used when we broke curfew or crashed the golf cart into the pool house. "I'm just disappointed."

The tension in his shoulders melts. A laugh escapes him, surprised and warm. "Fair enough." He takes a step into the room, then stops, like he's not sure he has permission to come further. "Are you hungry?"

As if on cue, my stomach releases a growl so loud and prolonged that Black Cat's ears flatten in alarm. I haven't eaten since before the concert—fourteen, maybe fifteen hours ago. The adrenaline kept me running, but now that it's drained away, I'm suddenly aware that I'm completely, desperately, would-commit-minor-crimes-for-food ravenous.

"Starving," I admit. "But it's past midnight. Nothing's going to be open. There are acai bowls in the freezer."

"You just had the night of your life. We need carbs and cheese."

"We?" I ask.

"Well, Claire's not here...I guess it's my job to tucker you out." His stupid, teasing smile appears. I'm beginning to think he likes this game.

"Any ideas?" I ask, fluttering my eyelashes, feeling stupid, but I'm too tired to flirt in any sort of productive way.

"Actually, yeah. Stay right here. Give me about an hour. I'm going to run out for supplies."

"Supplies for what?" I ask.

He winks at me. "It's a surprise."

I narrow my eyes at him. "Fine, but if you show up with any more sex toys, the rule is you have to use them."

He bursts out in laughter. "You're always on, aren't you? You make it hard to be a gentleman."

My smile turns mischievous. "You think you're a gentleman?"

"I'd like to be for you."

Again, cryptic. The kind of gentleman that holds doors, or my legs over his shoulders?

I throw back the covers and swing my legs over the side of the bed, making a point to stretch in a way that lifts my tank top just slightly. Taio's gaze dips for half a second—just long enough for me to notice—before he forces his eyes back to my face. I file that reaction away for later.

"All right, I'm ready to be wowed. Take your time, I'm going to take a scalding-hot shower first."

As if on command, Black Cat rises to his feet, ready to follow me into my en suite bathroom.

"You're not going to watch her shower, you little perv. Out, now." Taio points sternly to the hallway, and I swear on my life Black Cat laughs at him.

Despite his hissing protests, Taio marches across the bedroom and scoops up the cat like a naughty toddler. He plants a quick kiss on my forehead, which should feel nice but it sort of feels dismissive. And let's be honest, I'm ready to move past forehead kisses by now.

A thought strikes me as he leaves. I pad to the door on bare feet, poking my head out into the hallway. He's already halfway down the hall, Black Cat dangling from his grip, still snarling.

"Hey, Taio?"

He pauses, glancing back over his shoulder.

"Did you actually lose Black Cat?"

The guilty twist of his expression tells me everything I need to know before he even opens his mouth. "I might have sent him in first as a sacrifice to scope out the situation. He volunteered, enthusiastically. He really likes your bed."

"So...did you hear anything? While I was talking to my sister?"

He shakes his head, looking confused. "Nope."

"Okay, good. See you soon, then."

"Sounds good." He takes a step forward, then spins back around. "Oh, and, Tweety, before I forget. That kiss earlier? It was the perfect amount of tongue."

Chapter 14

Taio

Do you have a Looney Tunes fetish I should know about?

Taio has been gone for forty-seven years. Shocking, I know. But it's true. I'm now an old maid with silver-streaked hair and I most definitely missed the rest of my tour all because I was waiting on a boy.

I've checked my phone approximately nine hundred times, watching the minutes tick by while my hair air-dries into what will inevitably be a frizzy disaster. I should've blow-dried it. I should've put on something cuter than these old sleep shorts and this oversized T-shirt, yet another with Tweety Bird on it saying *I tawt I taw a puddy nap*. Terrible pun. Also, I think I own too many Tweety shirts.

I should've done literally anything other than sit here vibrating with anticipation like a golden retriever waiting for its owner to come home.

The shower helped. Lava hot, long enough to prune my fingers, steam thick enough to fog the entire bathroom and leave droplets running down the marble walls. I stood under the spray and replayed the kiss for the hundredth time—the way his hands felt in my hair, the desperate pressure of his mouth, the sound he made when I pressed closer. That low, rumbling groan that made me wet.

And then we took ten steps backwards with that stupid

forehead kiss. That patronizing little peck that felt more like a pat on the head than actual affection. Like I was a child being sent to bed after staying up past curfew.

I'm spiraling. I know I'm spiraling. But forty-seven years is a long time to get "supplies," and my brain has already cycled through seventeen different scenarios, ranging from "he got lost" to "he's reconsidering this entire situation and is currently booking a flight back to New York."

Forty-eight years now.

And now I'm battling glaucoma.

I've rearranged my pillows three times. I've scrolled through Instagram without actually seeing anything. I've gotten up to check my reflection twice, which is absurd because he's already seen me covered in sweat and stage makeup and post-crying puffiness. A little frizzy hair isn't going to be the dealbreaker.

A smell starts to drift under my door. Something warm and savory, with an undertone of spice that makes my empty stomach clench with desperate interest. I sit up straighter, inhaling deeply. Cheese, definitely. Something meaty. Peppers?

A knock at my door makes me catapult off the bed.

"Charlie? You decent?"

"Define decent," I call back to Taio, scrambling to arrange myself into something resembling casual nonchalance. I settle for cross-legged back on the bed, phone in hand like I've been casually scrolling instead of counting the seconds since he left.

"Clothed. Conscious. Willing to leave your room."

I'm at the door before he finishes the sentence, yanking it open to find him standing in the hallway with a barely suppressed grin. He's still in the same dark sweats and blue shirt, but now there's a small splatter of something light orange on his collar—evidence of whatever's creating that incredible smell.

"Follow me."

"Where are we going?"

"Living room. I made something."

The aroma intensifies as we walk down the hallway, and my

stomach responds with a growl so loud it echoes off the marble floors. Taio glances back at me with an amused quirk of his eyebrow but doesn't comment.

When I round the corner into the living room, I stop dead in my tracks.

Taio has transformed the space.

The massive sectional has been completely dismantled. Cushions form walls. Throw pillows create a plush floor. Sheets drape from the ceiling, anchored to a complicated system involving floor lamps, dining chairs dragged in from the adjacent room, and what appears to be a telescoping curtain rod wedged between two bookcases.

It's a blanket fort. A massive, elaborate, clearly-took-forty-seven-years-to-construct blanket fort.

LED candles flicker throughout the structure, casting warm amber light that makes the white sheets glow like something from a dream. The whole thing is maybe eight feet wide and six feet tall at its peak—big enough to actually move around in, not just crawl through like the forts Claire and I built as kids.

Inside, visible through the entrance flap that Taio has pinned back with what looks like a binder clip, is a spread that would make my nutritionist burst into a slew of curse words: bags of chips in multiple flavors, bowls of candy sorted by type, a towering stack of Double-Stuffed Oreos, a family-sized container of Goldfish crackers, gummy worms spilling out of their bag, and in the center of it all, a cast-iron skillet filled with something bubbling and golden that's clearly the source of the incredible smell.

"Is that...Rotel dip?"

"With chorizo." Taio looks almost shy, which is absurd given that he's approximately the size of a professional linebacker and could probably bench-press the sectional he just disassembled. "A throwback delicacy from dorm room days."

"I've never lived in dorms."

"Too fancy to slum it?" Taio asks teasingly.

"Are you kidding? I think I would've loved college. I never got a chance to go. Did you?"

He nods slowly, like the admission is very heavy. "Stanford. I lived in the dorms my first year. Sophomore through graduation I shared a two-bedroom apartment with my girlfriend at the time."

"Aw," I say, reaching out to rub his arm. "Another ex who broke your heart?"

"Same one. I've only ever had one girlfriend. I didn't even experience other women until I..."

"Became an escort?"

"Yeah," he breathes out.

I place my hands on my hips. "Can I ask an obnoxious question?"

Taio puts his hand on his hips, sweetly mocking me. "I prefer your questions when they're obnoxious."

"How'd you know you were qualified to be an escort if you'd only been with your girlfriend? Like what if you were really bad in bed and she didn't tell you?"

"Gee, thanks, Tweety. Sidebar question—do you have a Looney Tunes fetish I should know about because"—he tugs on the collar of my shirt—"you seem to have a lot of these."

"Just the two...and one Lola Bunny shirt. Another Elmer Fudd, because come on, who doesn't love that grouch? I also have a few *Space Jam* shirts and—" I hold my hands in the air. "Okay, you know what? Yup, I hear it now. That's a lot of Looney Tunes shirts."

Taio's eyes bulge to teasing proportions. "I'd say."

"Back to my question..."

"What do you want me to say? I've never had any complaints that I know about." It's like watching a tree blush. How is he so tall? Most of my barefoot conversations with him are me speaking directly to his pecs.

"That must've been so nerve-wracking."

Taio grumbles, a low bubbly gurgle from his throat teaming with reluctance. "It's not *that kind* of agency. Really. Rina hired us to be arm candy for events. That's it. She encouraged us to network and make friends. When you rub elbows with the upper financial echelon of humanity, sometimes there are opportunities. I didn't actually sleep with anyone until four months in."

"And Rina's okay with this?"

"We're grown men. There's not much she can do about it. Look—it's not my forever plan, okay? It's a means to an end."

I read the anguish suddenly shadowing his face. "Taio, do you think I'm judging you?"

"No."

"Then why are you being so defensive? Please understand if I'm asking questions, it's only to get to know you better."

"I just don't want you to see me as an escort. I mean, that's why you keep coming onto me, right? Because you think I'm some sort of sex Yoda that's going to get between your thighs and awaken you to a whole new world of magic and creativity? And then because of my gag order, there's no chance of public consequences for me being your practice fuck."

"That's not true." It comes out like a plea, my hands wrapping around his muscular forearms. "*Not true.* I don't care what the public thinks."

"No?" he asks. "Then why are you dating Grayson when you don't want to be?"

"It was a business strategy."

"That's the point. Your job capsizes your love life. Charlie, that's—"

"Not so different than what you do."

His eyes lift and he looks shocked, as if my declaration was a slap to the face. "What's that mean?"

"I mean we both would rather make room for work than love. Or are you going on jobs while still looking for Mrs. Right?"

"Definitely not."

"So, pot." I point at Taio, then myself. "Meet kettle. We have more in common than you think. And I don't see you as *just* an escort. I see you as..."

"What?" he prods, eyes full of anticipation.

"The guy who keeps showing up right when I'm about to give up."

He hunches over and hooks his arm around my shoulders, yanking me into a hug. "That's right." He kisses the top of my head. "And I'll keep showing up as long as you need me to."

Forever, is on the tip of my tongue, but it seems like a "pick me" response, so I redirect the conversation.

"So, what in the world inspired you to make a blanket fort?"

"I had insomnia as a kid. Bad bouts of it, from about nine to eleven. Sleepless spells that would last two weeks. It was miserable. I'd miss school. I was cranky and constantly saw double. The doctors wanted to pump me up with drugs but my mom was so worried about stunting my growth. I was a little small for my age."

My jaw drops. "You? Were small? *Ever*?"

"My growth spurt kicked in really late."

"Is it still going on?" I ask, genuinely curious. "Like right now, do you think you're still growing, because I'll be honest, the mechanics of this are already tricky. Another few inches"—I gesture between us—"and we become a ridiculous-looking couple."

I'm addicted to his smile, I swear. It takes up his whole face in the best way. "No, I think six-four is peak."

"Good. So your mom built you forts to help you sleep?"

"Not this big. My mom's theory was that I was overwhelmed and developing anxiety. My world felt too big and my brain couldn't figure out how to compute it. So she'd make these little spaces—forts, mostly. Sometimes just a closet with pillows and a flashlight. Anywhere small and contained to make the world feel less big. Said it helped reset my nervous system."

"And it worked?"

"Every time. I'd crawl in, she'd bring snacks, we'd talk about nothing important, and eventually I'd pass out." He runs a hand through his hair, mussing it slightly. "You said you couldn't sleep after shows. That your brain keeps running and you just lie there replaying everything. Figured it was worth a shot."

My throat tightens unexpectedly. I think about all the post-show nights I've spent alone in hotel rooms, wired yet exhausted, doomscrolling until my eyes burned. All the times I wished someone understood what it felt like to come down from that high with no one to catch you.

"This is the sweetest thing anyone has ever done for me."

"It was nothing." He shrugs, but I catch the softness in his eyes, the vulnerability he's trying to play off as casual. "Tomorrow I should probably go back to being professionally distant and emotionally unavailable."

"With no more hallway kisses?" I ask.

"No more hallway kisses."

"Cool. Can't wait."

"But we still have tonight." He gestures toward the fort entrance with exaggerated formality. "After you."

I duck through the entrance flap, and the world shrinks in the best possible way. Inside, the sheets filter the candlelight into something warmer and golden, transforming the sleek modern living room so it feels like a childhood memory I never actually had. The cushions beneath me are soft but supportive. Spices and sweetness and melted cheese perfume the air.

It's cozy. It's intimate. It's the least fancy thing that's happened to me in years, and yet this is the most luxurious feeling I've ever had. Seen. Supported. Dare I say...wanted? What kind of man builds forts for a girl he doesn't want?

Taio follows me in, folding his long body into the space with more grace than should be possible for someone his size. He settles across from me, the cast-iron skillet between us like a centerpiece, steam still rising from the bubbling dip.

"Careful," he warns as I reach for the bag of tortilla chips. "It's still hot. I literally just took it off the stove."

I scoop a chip through the dip anyway, blowing on it impatiently before taking a bite. The flavor explodes across my tongue—creamy cheese, spicy chorizo, the sharp kick of green chiles—and I actually moan.

"Mmmm. Oh my God."

"Good?"

"This is the best thing I've ever eaten. Oh fuck, it's so good it hurts." I dunk another chip into the dip, scooping out a greedy portion of cheesy, chorizo decadence. "So good," I groan again through a mouthful.

"Okay, this is getting a little pornographic."

I hand him a chip. "Dig in."

"I would but I'm afraid of losing a finger."

Another dip-loaded chip inches from my lips, I poke my tongue out at him. "I told you I was hungry."

"Yeah, but I thought you meant 'people' hungry. Not ravenous-little-a-T-rex hungry."

"Well, now you know I do not eat like a lady."

He laughs. "My new favorite thing about you. Actually, nope. Eating like Cookie Monster is still second to your Looney Tunes T-shirt shrine."

"Hilarious. Well, my favorite thing about you is the way you make cheese dip. What other hidden talents do you have in the kitchen?"

"Literally none. I can make exactly three things: this dip, scrambled eggs, and reservations."

I laugh, nearly choking on my chip. He grins, reaching for his own snack, and for a moment we just eat—passing the skillet back and forth, occasionally reaching for Oreos or handfuls of Goldfish to break up the cheese intake.

Black Cat materializes from somewhere, using his truly unsettling ability to appear out of thin air. He inserts himself between us as if this spread is for him. He immediately begins stealing Goldfish from the pile near Taio's knee, crunching them with aggressive satisfaction.

"Hey." Taio nudges him gently with his elbow. "Those aren't for you."

Black Cat ignores him completely, selecting another Goldfish with deliberate care and consuming it while maintaining direct eye contact. Dominance established.

"He's so obedient," I observe, reaching for a gummy worm. "You've done wonders as a cat trainer."

"I'm not fully convinced he's a cat. He likes walks, belly scratches, and has stolen my shower on multiple occasions. I think someone bred this dog wrong. I genuinely don't know why I keep him around."

"Because you love him."

"I tolerate him. There's a significant difference."

Black Cat, as if understanding the conversation, curls into a ball against Taio's thigh and begins purring at a volume that seems medically improbable for an animal his size. Taio's hand moves automatically to scratch behind his ears, completely undermining his protestations of mere tolerance.

Once my belly is comfortably protruding, I settle deeper into the cushions, pulling a throw pillow into my lap. The combination of food and warmth and soft lighting is already working its magic—I can feel the tension from the concert starting to unspool, the hum of anxiety in my chest finally beginning to quiet.

"So," Taio says, reaching for another chip. "Tonight. The concert. How are you feeling about all of it? Are you going to work in a piano performance for each stop moving forward?"

I groan, tipping my head back against the cushion wall behind me. "Honestly? I don't know. And I don't want to think about it. I'm sick of myself." I stare up at the sheet-draped ceiling, watching the candlelight dance across the fabric. "Tonight, I just want to talk about literally anything else. Tell me about you. Tell me something I don't know."

Taio is quiet for a moment, his hand still moving absently through Black Cat's fur. I prop myself up on my elbows to look at him—really look at him—and catch something vulnerable flickering across his face before he smooths it away.

"What do you want to know?"

"More about your mom." I sit up fully, crossing my legs beneath me and setting the throw pillow aside. "You said she moved after everything happened? Was that hard?"

The silence stretches long enough that I start to worry I've pushed too far, asked for too much too soon. But then Taio exhales slowly, setting down his chip and brushing the salt from his fingers.

"It was all so sudden." The words come out quiet, almost reluctant, like he's not used to saying them out loud. "I had a lot of guilt. All the nice things I had—my Bentley, my Stanford degree, my nice clothes and shoes. I can't stop thinking about who actually paid for all of it. But my mom didn't feel guilty. She was angry. She had no problem blaming my dad for what he did. She wanted me to do the same. To choose sides. To choose her."

"Why didn't you?"

"Because my mom's a wonderful human being. Her life will always be filled with love, friendship, and karmic blessings. I don't worry about her. My dad? I'm it. The only person left who still wants to see him get out and get better. My mom has everything. My dad has...me. It was the only choice."

"That's a lot of pressure to put on yourself."

"Maybe. He's my dad though, you know?"

"Yeah, I get it. Do you still talk to her?"

"Holidays. Birthdays. But no, not really. I think she's mad at me for staying. I think I'm mad at her for leaving. But I can only focus on one painful parental relationship at a time." He's staring at Black Cat now, fingers still moving through his fur in slow, rhythmic strokes. "Once Dad's out and on his feet, I do want to see her again. Clear the air."

The pain in his voice is so raw, so unguarded, that I have to physically stop myself from reaching for him.

"Taio, honestly? You have such a unique heart. I don't think anyone on this planet deserves you."

"Except for you, right?"

I flash him my most serious look. "Obviously. Because I'm perfect."

He chuckles warmly. "You definitely are." He waits for me to look at him, and there's something in his gaze that makes my breath catch. "You're easy to talk to, you know that? Dangerously easy."

"I'll take that as a compliment."

"It was meant as a warning."

"You don't like talking to me?" I ask.

"No, I do. Way too much. I can't seem to shut up when I should."

I let the moment sit, giving him space to decide whether he wants to keep going or pull back. He takes a deep breath of relief and I take it as an invitation to go deeper. Get closer.

"What about your dad?" I ask softly. "You said he's in Otisville. Do you visit?"

Taio's hand stills on Black Cat's fur. The purring continues, oblivious to the shift in atmosphere.

"Every other week." His tone has gone careful, measured. "I make the drive, sit across from him in that visiting room with the plastic chairs and the vending machines and the guards pretending not to listen. He's fidgety and paranoid. Otisville isn't a maximum-security prison or anything, but the lack of freedom is driving him unhinged. Sometimes I get glimpses of the man I remember from my childhood. The one who taught me to ride a bike, who took me to Yankees games, who told me I could be anything I wanted when I grew up. He's more grounded when I visit. I'm a little worried about missing visitation this week, but he'll be okay."

"You're missing visitation?"

Taio shrugs. "How can I be there, when I'm here?"

"I feel like an asshole now. I didn't realize what we were taking you away from—"

"Hey, I'm a grown man. I made a decision. And it's actually nice to have a break from it." He meets my eyes. "I've been on this mission. For years. Trying to pay back what he stole. The victims—the pension funds, the hospital, all those people who trusted him—I've been tracking them down. Sending money when I can. It's not much. A few thousand here and there. It'll never be enough to actually fix anything. But it's my constant obsession. It eats away at me. Since I got on the plane with you, I haven't been thinking about it as much."

"So you traded your dad's drama for mine?"

"Perhaps." He laughs bitterly. "But you're much more fun to look at."

"Glad to hear it." I reach up to smooth his hair, pretending like it's disheveled, but I actually just wanted to see how soft it is. Like silk weaving through my fingers. "Why are you so determined to pay back what your dad stole? Are they coming after you because he's in prison?"

"No, nothing like that. It's personal...like...some stupid part of me thinks that if I can undo enough of the damage, maybe he'll go back to being the person I needed him to be. Maybe I can restore our name. Put our family back together. Maybe this can all end in something other than just...destruction."

The weight of what he's carrying settles over me like a physical thing. Years of trying to clean up his father's mess. Years of hoping for a redemption that might never come. Years of loving someone who keeps disappointing him.

"Hope's not stupid. Hope is all we have. And a son fighting for his dad is such an honorable thing."

He doesn't respond for a long moment. When he does, his voice is a murmur that's soft and rough at the same time.

"Is it though? He hasn't apologized once. He doesn't regret taking the money, just getting caught. Money turns him into this cold reptilian. Sometimes I think..." He trails off, the sentence hanging unfinished between us.

"That he might actually be a bad person?"

Taio doesn't confirm or deny. He just sits there in the warm glow of the flameless candles, looking more lost than I've ever seen him. "I don't know. But someone has to take responsibility for the pain he caused. If not him, then...me."

"What's the total?" I ask gently. "The debt. What does he still owe?"

Taio's head snaps up, his expression shifting instantly from vulnerable to guarded. The walls slam back into place so fast I can almost hear them.

"Charlie, don't."

"I'm just asking. Maybe I could help. I have resources, and—"

"*No*," he says, sharp enough to make Black Cat lift his head and blink in sleepy irritation. Taio takes a breath, visibly forcing himself to soften. "Please. Don't ever go there."

"I wouldn't think anything of it." I reach for his hand, wrapping my fingers around his. "Taio, most of my relationships are transactional, that's how my world works. People do things for me, I compensate them. It's not personal. It's not charity. It's just how things operate at this level." I squeeze gently. "You've basically been keeping me sane this entire time. You saved my tour. You should be rewarded for that. Let me help with this humongous burden you're carrying."

"Rewarded." He scoffs, like the word left a bad taste in his mouth. "Charlie, no. I'm not going to take your money. I'm not going to let you pay off my father's debts like I'm some project you've decided to fix."

"That's not what I—"

"Every other relationship in your life can be transactional. Fine. That's your world, and I get it." His hand tightens around mine, his grip almost desperate. "But not this. This part is honest. I need that. I think you do, too."

My heart is so full I'm not sure how it's still fitting inside my chest.

"Okay," I whisper. "Okay. I won't bring it up again."

"Thank you."

We sit in the quiet for a spell, letting the intensity of the conversation slowly dissipate. Black Cat has resumed his Goldfish theft, crunching contentedly between us like he hasn't just witnessed a significant emotional moment. The LED candles flicker. Outside, distantly, I can hear the hum of the central air, the sounds of the massive house settling around us.

That's when I notice it.

A book, tucked into the corner of the fort near Taio's knee. Worn cover, soft pink, spine cracked from multiple readings. I know for a fact it's not mine—I read all my self-help books on my Kindle, and I definitely don't read anything with a cover that involves two people in a dramatic clinch.

"What's that?" I point.

Something fascinating goes on with his face. A flush creeps up his neck, splashing across his cheekbones and making him look suddenly, endearingly boyish.

"Nothing."

"Really? Because it looks like a very loved book with a very pink cover." I'm already reaching for it before he can stop me. "Is that...is that a romance book?"

"Charlie—"

Too late. I've got it in my hands now, turning it over to examine the cover. Two figures locked in an embrace—a woman with windswept hair, a man with a jawline sharp enough to cut glass. The title is in gold embossed letters. The tagline promises passion, heartbreak, and a love that conquers all.

I'm grinning so wide my face hurts. "Taio Wilkes. Do you read *smut*, as the kids these days call it?"

"The kids these days? You *are* the 'kids these days.'"

"True but I have the soul of a sixty-year-old."

He makes a grab for the book but I twist away, clutching the book to my chest. "Hey, whoa, stop."

"Give me my book, you animal."

"No way. This is my new favorite thing about you. Screw cheese dip. You read romance for fun?"

His face has gone fully red now, which only makes me more delighted. "Lots of people read romance. It's the highest-selling genre in publishing. There are statistics."

"I'm not making fun of you!" I protest, though I'm definitely still grinning. "I think it's sweet. Really. I think it's the sweetest thing ever." I soften slightly, clutching the book to my chest. "Why romance?"

He's quiet for a moment, the flush slowly fading from his cheeks as he realizes I'm genuinely asking. When he speaks, he sounds almost shy.

"I like the happy endings."

I pump my brows at him before shooting him a wink and clicking my jaw. "Happy endings. *Got it.*"

"I'm not talking about seedy massage parlors, Charlie. I mean actual happily-ever-afters. I find them cathartic."

The simplicity of the answer catches me off guard.

"I haven't had a lot of control over how my life turned out," he continues, not quite meeting my eyes. "My parents' marriage. My career. My dad's mess. My family's reputation. None of it ended the way it was supposed to. But in books like this..." He indicates said paperback still clutched to my chest. "...the good guys win. People find each other despite impossible odds. Love is enough to overcome all the obstacles and mistakes and misunderstandings. It's nice to believe that's possible, even if it's just for a few hundred pages at a time."

My heart clenches so hard I'm surprised it doesn't make a wheezing sound.

"I sing songs like that," I hear myself say. "The ones I love most are all about the experiences I've never had. Love that lasts forever. Being chosen. Finding someone who sees all the broken parts of you and decides to stay anyway." I hand him back the book. "I guess we're two peas."

"Two peas in a delusional pod."

"The best kind of pod."

He's smiling now—really smiling, not the guarded half smile or the professional pleasant expression he usually defaults to. It transforms his whole face, softens all the hard edges, makes him look younger and more open and achingly, stunningly beautiful.

"What's this one about?" I nod toward the book now resting in his lap.

And his dark eyes alight. He starts talking about the plot—a second-chance romance between two people who fell in love young, were torn apart by circumstances beyond their control, and find each other again ten years later—and I watch him transform into someone I've never seen before. His hands move as he describes the characters. His voice gets animated when he explains the tension, the miscommunications, the moment when they finally admit what they've been feeling all along. He's passionate about this in a way he hasn't been passionate about anything else in my presence.

"And the thing is," he's saying, leaning forward with enthusiasm, "they both think the other person moved on. They both spent ten years convinced they were the only one still holding on to something. And when they finally talk—really talk, not just the surface stuff—it all comes out. Every assumption, every fear, every reason they stayed away. And you realize the only thing keeping them apart was their own inability to be honest."

"That sounds painful."

"It's excruciating. But in the best way." He grins. "I'm about three-quarters through. The grovel scene is coming up."

"The grovel scene?"

"When one of them has to apologize. Make amends. Prove they've changed." His eyes are practically sparkling. "It's the best part of any romance. The emotional climax before the actual climax. There's something about a man begging on his knees, you know?"

I'm charmed beyond words. This giant man with his tragic backstory and his walls and his complicated relationship with physical intimacy, geeking out about fictional love stories like a kid discussing their favorite superhero.

It's the most attractive he's ever been.

"Will you read some to me?" I ask, before I can think better of it.

He pauses mid-sentence, the enthusiasm dimming slightly into surprise. "What?"

"Read to me. Just a little bit." I'm already repositioning myself, shifting closer to him on the cushions. "I want to hear the grovel scene. I want to know if they get their happy ending."

"Read to you? I thought we were trying to get you to sleep. This is riveting stuff," he teases.

"I will sleep. This will help me." I curl against his side, resting my head on his chest. His heartbeat is steady beneath my ear—strong and rhythmic, like a drum keeping time. "Please? Just until I drift off?"

I feel him hesitate. Feel the moment when he could pull away, establish distance, be the gentleman he keeps insisting he wants to be. The responsible choice. The safe choice.

Instead, his arm comes around me. His hand smooths back my slightly damp hair, fingers gentle as they work through the tangles.

"All right," he murmurs, his voice rumbling through his chest and into my ear. "But if you hate it, lie, because this is one of my favorites."

"I promise to lie so good," I say sincerely.

He chuckles. "If only you were capable of it. You couldn't lie to me to save your life. You know what? *That* is my favorite thing about you."

"You seem to have a lot of favorites."

He taps my nose before holding out his hand for the book. It opens with a soft crack of well-worn spine. He clears his throat.

And then he starts to read.

His voice is low and warm, wrapping around the words like they're something precious. He does different voices for different characters—subtle shifts in tone and cadence that bring the story to life in ways I didn't expect. The heroine is sharp-tongued and stubborn, wounded but hiding it beneath layers of sarcasm. The hero is gruff and guarded, protecting his heart behind the barricade of professional distance.

It sounds...familiar, somehow.

I let my eyes drift closed.

The candles flicker against my eyelids, painting the darkness in warm orange tones. Black Cat migrated to my feet at some point, his warm weight a comforting pressure against my ankles, his purr a melodic background hum. Taio's chest rises and falls beneath my cheek in a slow, steady rhythm. His hand continues to stroke my hair—absent, soothing, the kind of casual intimacy that feels more significant than any kiss.

The story washes over me. Tender moments. Heated glances. The slow, inevitable pull of two people who can't stay away from each other no matter how hard they try.

I don't remember falling asleep.

But I know, in the last moment before consciousness faded, I'd never felt safer in my entire life. The world felt so small and manageable, just me, Taio, and our definitely-not-for-keeps cat.

It all seemed...

So simple.

So peaceful.

Chapter 15
Taio

It was either this or BDSM.

I wake up alone, and for a disorienting moment, I have no idea where I am.

Sheets. Flameless candles, their LED flickers timed out. Goldfish crackers scattered across cushions like tiny orange casualties of war. A pink romance novel splayed open near my knee, spine cracked to the page where I must have finally stopped reading.

I sit up slowly in the fort, my neck protesting the angle I apparently slept in. At some point in the night, I must have shifted from sitting upright with Charlie against my chest to lying flat on my back, because I'm now sprawled across three couch cushions with a throw pillow wedged awkwardly under my shoulder blade. My phone has migrated to somewhere near my hip, buzzing insistently with notifications I've apparently been ignoring for hours.

I fish it out and squint at the screen.

12:47 p.m.

I haven't slept past noon since college. Maybe not even then—Alaina was an early riser who believed sleeping in was a moral failing, and her internal alarm clock became mine.

But last night I slept like the dead. Deep and dreamless and so complete that I feel almost hungover from the rest. My body is loose in a way it hasn't been in months. Years, maybe. The constant tension I carry in my shoulders—the hypervigilance that comes with always watching for threats, always calculating exits, always preparing for the next disaster—has dissolved into something resembling peace.

I think about Charlie falling asleep against my chest. The weight of her, slight but solid. The way her breathing slowed and steadied as I read, her body going boneless with trust. Complete trust. The kind you can't fake, the kind that only comes when someone feels genuinely safe.

She felt safe with me.

At some point I must have stopped reading and just...held her. Let myself exist in that moment without calculating the risks or cataloging the reasons it was a bad idea. Her hair smelled like whatever expensive shampoo stocked the bathroom—floral and sweet. Her hand had curled into my shirt like she was anchoring herself to me even in sleep.

It felt good. It felt like something I could get used to.

It felt absolutely terrifying.

I scrub a hand over my face and start scrolling through my phone, partly to distract myself from the direction my thoughts are spiraling and partly because I should probably check in on the outside world. The tour doesn't stop just because I built a blanket fort and caught feelings like some kind of lovesick teenager.

Instagram first. I don't post—my account is locked down tighter than Fort Knox, no photos, no followers except a few verified accounts I use to keep tabs on industry news—but I keep regular surveillance on the celebrity gossip pages that have been dissecting Charlie's every move since the scandal broke.

The shift is immediate and obvious.

Three days ago, every headline was some variation of "Charlie Riley's Balcony Romp" or "Pop Star's Secret Scandal" or "Is This the End of America's Sweetheart?" The comments were vicious—people who'd never met her confidently diagnosing her with personality disorders, addiction issues, attention-seeking behavior. The memes were everywhere. Her career was supposedly over, finished.

Now?

"Charlie Riley SLAYS Miami Concert: The Tour Is Alive!"

"The Moment That Made Us All Cry: Charlie Riley Goes Raw and Real"

"From Scandal to Standing Ovation: Charlie Riley's Big Comeback"

"Who Is the Mystery Bodyguard? Fans Are OBSESSED"

I click on that last one, morbidly curious. It's a compilation of photos and videos from the concert—Charlie at the piano, her face luminous with something that looks like joy and terror combined. Charlie taking her bow, tears still wet on her cheeks. Charlie being escorted through the crowd by a tall figure in black, his hand pressed protectively against her lower back.

Me.

My face is mostly obscured in the shots—caught in profile, hidden behind a shoulder, conveniently blurred by movement. The paparazzi got a few clearer angles, but nothing that would hold up to serious scrutiny. Nothing that would trigger facial recognition or link back to my other life.

Knowing Sage, that's not an accident. She probably had someone reviewing footage before it went live, flagging anything too identifying. The woman operates like a chess grandmaster, always thinking six moves ahead.

The comments on the bodyguard post are...something.

"okay but the bodyguard can GET IT"

"the way she looks at him in that backstage video?? ma'am

that is not professional"

"I would commit crimes to have five minutes alone with that man"

"charlie's bodyguard is giving very much 'I would kill for you and enjoy it' energy and honestly? goals"

I scroll past before I can read any more, feeling heat creep up the back of my neck. The narrative has shifted completely. The escort angle is dead—buried under an avalanche of new content, new storylines, new things for the internet to obsess over. The bodyguard story is holding. Charlie's performance overwrote everything else, gave people something new to focus on, something that painted her as triumphant rather than tragic.

Sage Hilston is a damn genius.

I keep scrolling. The tide has turned so thoroughly that I'm finding actual think pieces about Charlie's "artistic evolution" and "vulnerability as strength." One entertainment site has already published a retrospective of her career, framing the scandal as a catalyst for growth rather than a catastrophe. The comments are full of people supporting her continuation of the tour, claiming they "always knew she had this in her" and "never believed the haters."

The internet has the memory of a goldfish and the loyalty of a weathervane. Yesterday they wanted to destroy her. Today she's their queen again. Tomorrow, who knows? But for now, the tide has turned, and I'll take the victory.

I keep scrolling, switching over to Twitter—or X, or whatever they're calling it now. The trending topics confirm what Instagram suggested: #CharlieRiley is up there, but this time the associated tweets are glowing. Video clips of the piano performance have been viewed millions of times overnight. Someone's already made a fan edit set to emotional music that's racked up six figures' worth of engagement.

There's even a hashtag specifically for the bodyguard situation: #CharliesBodyguard. I tap on it against my better judgment.

It's mostly thirst tweets. Extremely creative thirst tweets, some of which describe acts that are probably illegal in some states. There are also conspiracy theories—people convinced I'm actually a secret boyfriend, or a planted actor, or some elaborate PR stunt designed to distract from the original scandal. One person has apparently spent several hours trying to identify me through analysis of the birthmark behind my ear, which is both impressive and deeply unsettling.

The most-liked tweet in the hashtag is a zoomed-in screenshot from backstage footage, catching a moment where I'm looking at Charlie while she talks to someone off-camera. My expression in the photo is painfully revealing. Soft in a way I didn't realize I was being. Obvious in a way that makes my stomach clench.

The caption reads: *"this man would walk through fire for her and you can't convince me otherwise."*

The replies are full of heart emojis and keyboard smashes and people tagging their friends with comments like "find someone who looks at you like this."

I close the app.

I should feel relieved. This is good news—great news, actually. It means the plan is working. It means Charlie's career is recovering. It means my presence here is serving its purpose, and when this is all over, I can walk away knowing I helped instead of hurt.

Instead, I feel something more complicated. And it has nothing to do with PR strategies or professional responsibilities or the carefully constructed boundaries I've been maintaining since this whole thing started. It has everything to do with the woman who fell asleep in my arms last night, trusting me completely, and how badly I wanted to stay in that moment forever. My entire locus of control has shifted. Who am I now? Apparently whatever she needs. A friend. A bodyguard. Her protector. Her confidant. A man who wants her way more than he'll ever let himself admit.

My thumb slides down the screen, pulling up a laundry list of notifications.

Charlie

Awake yet, sleeping beauty?

I check the timestamp. She sent it twenty minutes ago. There's a follow-up from three minutes later:

Charlie

I fed Black Cat.

Another follow-up fifteen minutes later.

Charlie

Okay, twice. I fed him TWICE.

I smile at my phone like an idiot.

Just woke up. What time did you get up?

Her response is immediate, like she's been waiting for me.

Charlie

Hours ago. Been very productive. Definitely not pacing around nervously.

Nervously about what?

Charlie

Come to my bedroom when you're functional. I have something to show you.

Should I be concerned?

Charlie

Yes. 

I stare at the devil emoji for longer than is healthy. In my experience, that particular symbol from Charlie means one of two things: she's about to do something chaotic, or she's about to do something that will test every ounce of my carefully maintained self-control.

Given our current trajectory, probably both.

I extract myself from the blanket fort wreckage, my joints popping in protest as I stand. The living room looks like a tornado hit a sleepover—cushions everywhere, sheets drooping from their ceiling anchors, the snack debris scattered across every available surface. I should clean this up. Put the sectional back together. Do something productive with the remnants of last night.

Instead, I head for the guest bathroom to brush my teeth and splash water on my face. If Charlie has "something to show me," I should at least be presentable for whatever fresh chaos she's cooked up.

The face in the mirror looks different than it did a week ago. More relaxed around the eyes. Less tension in the jaw. There's something almost soft about my expression that I'm not used to seeing—a looseness that wasn't there before. I haven't been thinking about my insurmountable problems with their haphazard solutions. I've been investing in a relationship that actually gives something back.

Charlie Riley is dismantling my carefully constructed emotional fortress brick by brick, and the most alarming part is how little I want to stop her.

I dry my face, run a hand through my hair in a futile attempt at presentability, and head down the hallway toward her bedroom. Past the kitchen where the Rotel pan is soaking in the sink. Past the windows showing off another aggressively sunny Miami afternoon. Past the spot where Black Cat is lounging in a patch of sunlight, watching my approach with an expression that suggests he knows something I don't.

"Kiss-ass," I mutter at him. "You only favor her because she overfeeds you."

He blinks slowly and goes back to grooming his paw. Zero loyalty when it comes to food.

Charlie's door is closed when I reach it. I knock twice, the sound echoing slightly in the quiet hallway.

"Come in."

I push the door open.

And stop breathing.

Charlie is standing in the center of her bedroom wearing a black teddy that looks like it was designed by someone who wanted to cause highway pileups. Lace and silk and strategic cutouts that leave approximately nothing to the imagination. The straps are thin as spider silk, looking like they might disintegrate if I stare at them too hard. The neckline plunges to somewhere around her navel, held together by sheer optimism and probably some kind of fashion tape. The whole thing barely qualifies as clothing.

She's also standing next to a chair—one of the decorative ones from the corner of the room, now pulled out to face the bed like a throne awaiting its occupant.

"Took you long enough," she says, with a confidence that almost masks the nervous energy vibrating beneath her skin. I can see it in the way she's holding herself, shoulders a little too straight, chin a little too high, hands clasped in front of her like she doesn't know what else to do with them. "Sit."

I don't move. I'm not entirely sure I can move. Every functional brain cell I possess has redirected its attention to the task of not staring at the way that lace hugs the curve of her hips.

"Charlie. What is this?"

"It's a chair." She gestures to it like I'm being particularly slow. "You sit in it. With your butt. I'm sure you've done this before."

"I meant—" I gesture vaguely at her entire situation. The lingerie. The staging. The obvious premeditation of whatever is about to happen. "This."

"Oh, this?" She does a little spin, and the teddy flares slightly at the hem, offering a glimpse of black underwear that matches. My mouth goes dry. "Do you like it?" I think she's trying to smile sexily but it's coming off like she's in pain.

"Are you okay? Did you sleep enough?"

"Yeah. Taio." She holds her palms to the ceiling. "I'm trying... to seduce you. I read a couple articles about how to get his attention and take your relationship to the next level." She shrugs innocently. "It was either this or BDSM."

I blink slowly. "Our relationship? Next level?"

She shoots me a cool glare. "Please. Sit. Down. I've been practicing this all morning. Just let me do my thing. Please?"

Oh, fuck me. I sit.

The chair creaks slightly under my weight—these decorative pieces aren't exactly built for function—but it holds. I'm positioned about six feet from the bed, giving me a clear sightline to what is apparently about to be a show. Charlie pulls out her phone, scrolls through something with the focus of a surgeon selecting their instrument, and a moment later music starts playing from the bedroom's built-in speakers.

The opening notes of "Gangsta Lovin'" fill the room.

"Old-school. Okay, I'm feeling it," I say, as she tosses the phone onto the bed and turns to face me with determination etched across every feature. "You really don't have to do this though. We can talk."

"We've been talking...a lot." She rolls her shoulders back, like she's preparing for an athletic competition. Cracks her neck side to side. Shakes out her hands. She looks less like a woman about to perform a striptease and more like a boxer entering the ring. "And plus, you gave me that whole speech about confidence and not caring what people think and being unforgettable..."

"Yeah, I have a feeling I'm never going to forget this." Except I'm staring at her in deep concern. "You sure this is how you want to go about *seducing me*? Because I know dancing isn't your favorite."

"It's fine. There's this stripaerobics instructor that does tutorials on TikTok. I watched her routine to this song like fifty times. I mostly learned it. It's going to be spectacular."

"I don't think spectacular is where this is heading."

"Rude." She points at me sternly. "No heckling from the audience. This is a supportive environment."

"My apologies. Please continue."

"Thank you. I will."

When the bass line throbs through the room, that unmistakable groove that's launched a thousand amateur stripteases, Charlie starts to move.

Move is a generous term.

What she's actually doing is a sort of aggressive hip sway that looks less like seduction and more like she's trying to dislodge something stuck to her lower back. Her arms come up over her head in what I think is supposed to be a sexy stretch, but the movement is jerky and uncoordinated, like a marionette being operated by someone who's never actually seen a human body in motion.

"How am I doing?" she asks breathlessly, attempting to body roll and mostly looking like she's experiencing mild gastrointestinal distress.

"You're doing great," I manage, biting the inside of my cheek hard enough to taste copper. "Very...athletic."

"Athletic wasn't the vibe I was going for."

"Sexy. I meant sexy. *Incredibly sexy.*" Maybe if I keep saying it, she'll believe me.

She shoots me a suspicious look but continues her routine, now attempting to incorporate my chair into her performance. The idea, I believe, is to drape herself seductively over the back of it while I watch in stunned appreciation.

What actually happens is she misjudges her balance, rolls off the back, and hits the ground with an audible thunk, then lets out a very unsexy "*ow, shit, motherfucker*."

I leap up only to find her clambering back to her feet. "You okay?"

"Fine. Sit back down." She rubs her hip vigorously, wincing before retreating back into position. "It's part of it."

"Injury is part of it?" I ask over the thumping music.

She ignores me, refocusing as the song swells into the chorus. Charlie makes her move toward me. This part is actually working—she's got a decent walk when she commits to it, all swaying hips and deliberate steps. The lingerie helps. The lighting helps. My pulse picks up despite the comedy of the situation.

She's beautiful, even when she's being ridiculous. Maybe especially when she's being ridiculous. Her complete commitment to this disaster makes my chest tight in ways I'm not prepared to examine.

She reaches my chair and does a slow circle around it, trailing her fingers across my shoulders as she goes. The touch sends sparks cascading down my spine, pooling somewhere low in my stomach.

"See?" she murmurs near my ear, close enough I can smell her perfume—warm and sweet and definitely new. "I can indeed be sexy."

"I never said you couldn't be sexy."

"Your face said it. When I fell. Your face was very judgy."

"My face was concerned for your safety. There's a difference."

She completes her circle and positions herself in front of me, so close I could reach out and touch her if I let myself. Which I won't. Probably. The teddy looks even more enticing from this angle, the way the lace stretches across her collarbones, the shadow between her breasts, the ridiculously dainty straps that look like they'd snap if I breathed on them wrong.

"Now for the grand finale," she announces, with the gravity of someone unveiling a grand work of art.

She whirls around, presenting me with a view of her back—the teddy dips dangerously low, exposing the delicate architecture of her spine, the dimples just above her hips—and attempts what I can only describe as an ambitious controlled descent toward my lap.

It is not controlled.

It is not even close to controlled.

Her knees buckle at an awkward angle. She overcorrects by grabbing the arm of the chair. Her center of gravity shifts catastrophically to the left. She pinwheels her free arm in a desperate attempt to regain balance, catches a fistful of my shirt, and ends up in a sort of sideways sprawl across my thighs that is approximately zero percent what she was going for.

"Nailed it," she says, from her position of tangled limbs and wounded dignity. "Exactly as planned."

I'm shaking. My whole body is shaking with suppressed laughter that I'm trying desperately to contain because she looks so earnest, so committed to pretending this went well, that the kindest thing I can do is play along.

She sits up, but stays cradled in my lap. I secure her, wrapping my arms around her. "Don't you dare laugh at me, Taio Wilkes."

"I'm not laughing."

"You're literally vibrating. I can feel it. The chair is shaking."

"That's...enthusiasm. For your performance." I press my lips together hard. "Very moving. Literally. A lot of movement happened."

"Was it hot?" She pouts her lips.

"Very hot," I answer automatically.

"Are you turned on?"

"Extremely." I try to mask my chuckle with a cough.

"You're the worst." Charlie buries her head into the crook between my arm and chest. "Why don't you want me? It's maddening."

"What makes you think I don't want you?" I tuck my finger under her chin and pull up until her gaze is on mine.

"We were alone last night. You had me all to yourself, and you didn't even try to make a move. I'm so confused. I don't know what you want."

The afternoon light filters through the curtains, catching the gold in her hair, the flush spreading across her cheeks and down her neck, the rapid pulse I can see beating at the base of her throat. Curled up in my lap, warm and soft, she's so close I can count the faint freckles scattered across her nose.

I think about how badly I want to kiss her.

And why I didn't last night...

"Charlie, last night, sleeping next to each other? That was the most intimate thing I've done with someone in a long time. It wasn't sex, but that was my way of telling you how I feel about you. I work in an industry where people try and fail every day to solve their problems with sex. I don't want to be your problem. And I don't want sex to be the solution. Because it doesn't last. Do you really want to be with the son of a felon who scrapes by as an escort? Don't you care about your reputation? Be honest."

"Do you really want to be with a broken pop star who's been so deadlocked on fame and success that she doesn't know how to function as a person? Because being with me means backtracking and going through all the firsts I missed while my head was in the sand."

I think about last night, how satisfying it was to hold her and be the reason she could rest.

For once I let myself say exactly what I want to. "Yeah, I do."

She nods. "Me too. So...what now?"

I slide my hands down to her waist, settling on the curve of her hips where lace meets silk meets warm skin. "What do you want to happen now?"

She's quiet for a long beat, processing. Her hands have come up to rest on my chest, fingers curling slightly into the fabric of my shirt. "I want you to take the lead. I don't know what I'm doing."

I widen my eyes at her. "Says the girl dressed up like this to give me a lap dance."

"It was a striptease," she argues. "And let's be honest, we both knew it was for comedy. I was just trying to get your attention, Taio."

"You have it." I trace the plunge line of the teddy from her collarbone down to her navel. She shudders under my touch. "You've had it all along. You know what the funny thing is?"

"Hmm?"

"You call it a striptease, but nothing came off." I hook my finger into the lace trim of her teddy and pull it aside, exposing one of her breasts. My eyes lock in on her nipple like a target's been identified. The music has faded—the song ended at some point and neither of us noticed. The room is quiet except for our breathing and the thunder of my own heartbeat in my ears.

I cup her breast before she can shy away, gently rolling her nipple between my thumb and forefinger until it's hard. Then I lean down to take her nipple in my mouth, gently suckling while swirling my tongue around its sensitive tip.

"How's that feel?" I blow gently on her wet skin, making her squirm.

"Good." She nods fervently like she's trying to convince herself. "I'm just nervous."

"Of course you are. It's the first time—"

"No, I'm nervous because it's you. I don't want to blow it or embarrass myself."

"And you thought leading with that performance was a good idea?"

She relaxes instantly. Her face turns to a scowl before she smacks my shoulder. "You ass—"

"I'm kidding. I just want you to relax. *It's me.* Don't worry about impressing me. Not that you need my approval, but I'm already awestruck, Charlie. There's nothing you can do to change that. I'm a man, obsessed. I promise you." I tuck her breast back into the teddy, covering her nakedness. She's too nervous. We need more time. But just when I think we'd be better served to have lunch and swap more childhood trauma stories, Charlie speaks.

"Would you be willing to go down on me?"

The directness of her question surprises me so much, I very uncharacteristically stammer. "I-I...um...yeah?"

"It's the one feeling you can't really replicate without a partner, so I've always been curious. Supposedly it feels really nice."

I clear my throat, regaining composure. "Yeah, it does."

"I'll repay the favor," she says awkwardly. "So it's fair."

"*Oh, Tweety,*" I say. "Remember how our relationship isn't transactional?"

"Well, I want you to get something out of it, too."

"Oh, I will," I say, almost warningly. "Here's what's going to happen," I murmur, my lips barely an inch from her ear. "You're going to go lie on that bed and get comfortable."

Her breath hitches audibly. "Okay."

"And then you're going to open your legs, close your eyes, and focus on all the details so you can really make this memory."

"Memory of what?"

"The best orgasm you've ever had."

Her gulp is obvious. Not of nerves, but of all the saliva pooling in her mouth. I like having that effect on her. I really like her wet, *everywhere*, for me.

"Okay, what do you get out of it, then? What do you want?"

I brush my lips against hers in a half kiss, before I usher her off my lap and point to the bed. Removing my shirt, I answer, "All I want is for you to come. *Hard.*"

Chapter 16

Charlie

I want to say his name, but I can't remember how talking works.

I've never been more aware of my own body than I am right now.

Every nerve ending is awake. Every inch of skin feels hypersensitive, like I've been wrapped in electricity and told to hold still. The silk of the teddy whispers against my thighs as I crawl onto the bed, and even that small friction makes me shiver.

Behind me, I hear Taio's footsteps. Slow. Deliberate. The sound of a man who knows exactly what he's doing and is in no rush to do it.

I arrange myself against the pillows the way he instructed—on my back, legs slightly parted, hands resting uncertainly at my sides. I feel ridiculous. Exposed. Like I'm posing for a photograph I didn't consent to.

"You're thinking too hard," Taio says from somewhere near the foot of the bed. "I can hear it from here."

"I can't help it. My brain doesn't have an off switch."

"It does. I'll show you." I look up to see his sly smile and my stomach swoops in anticipation.

The mattress dips as he climbs onto the bed. I resist the urge to squeeze my eyes shut like a kid waiting for a shot at the doctor's office. Instead, I force myself to watch him—shirtless now, all that warm tan skin and defined muscle moving toward me with predatory grace.

He's beautiful. Objectively, scientifically, undeniably beautiful. And he's looking at me like I'm something to revere. Something worth taking his time with.

"Hey." He settles between my legs, his hands coming to rest on my knees. The touch is gentle, grounding. "Look at me."

I meet his eyes.

"You trust me?"

I nod.

"You want me?" he asks in a sex-drenched drawl.

I nod again.

His expression shifts—it softens, deepens. His thumbs trace small circles on my inner knees, and even that innocent touch sends heat spiraling through my core.

"Good," he murmurs. "Now close your eyes."

I obey. The world goes dark, and suddenly everything else amplifies—the whisper of the air-conditioning, the distant cry of seagulls outside, the sound of my own breathing, shallow and uneven.

His hands slide up my thighs. Slowly. So slowly it's torturous. Fingertips tracing paths along my skin like he's mapping territory, memorizing every curve and hollow. When he reaches the edge of my underwear, he pauses.

"Still good?"

"Mm-hmm." It comes out strangled.

He unsnaps the teddy, exposing my underwear. I don't think you're supposed to wear this outfit with anything underneath. It was sent to me by some up-and-coming lingerie brand looking for celebrity ambassadors. But no one from my marketing team thought it was a good idea to get in bed with something so risqué. Now, here I am, riskier than ever, putting the merchandise to good use.

He hooks his fingers into the waistband of my panties. The fabric slides down my hips, over my thighs, past my knees. The cool air hits skin that's never been exposed to anyone like this, and I have to fight the instinct to clamp my legs together.

"Breathe," Taio reminds me, and I exhale shakily. He's right—I'd been holding it without realizing, my whole body locked up with anticipation. "That's it." His voice is low, warm, reassuring. "Just breathe. I've got you."

His hands return to my thighs, easing them apart with gentle pressure. I let him guide me, let myself be opened, and try not to think about how vulnerable I feel. How seen.

For a long moment, nothing happens. He's just...looking. I can feel the weight of his gaze between my legs, and my face flames with embarrassment.

"Taio—"

"Shh." His breath ghosts across my clit, and I nearly buck off the mattress. "You're so beautiful, Charlie. I can't wait to taste you."

Before I can argue or deflect or make some self-deprecating joke to cut the tension, or tease him to hurry up, his mouth is on me.

Oh.

Oh.

His tongue is soft, exploratory, the first brush more a question than a demand. I tense, because of course I do, and in response he hums, the vibration so light it makes my hips jerk in surprise. Embarrassment wars with pleasure, but the pleasure is winning, and he hasn't even really started.

Taio takes his time. Every lick, every kiss, is deliberate, reverent. He's not showing off or teasing me. It's like he's tuning an instrument, learning what makes the strings inside me shiver. He laps at me in slow, shallow sweeps, then presses his mouth down, sealing me in darkness and heat. The sensation is nothing like I expected—maddening and tender and somehow more intimate than I ever imagined sex to be.

My hands fist the sheets, nails digging tight enough to leave crescent moons in the fabric. I can't help it. My hips want to move but I'm paralyzed by how good it feels and how much I don't want to mess this up, to let myself be bad at receiving pleasure in front of him. I should be making noise, saying his name, maybe arching my back like every woman does in every movie ever, but I'm caught somewhere between wanting to disappear and wanting to let him see every inch of me unravel.

He pauses, just for a second, and lifts his head. I risk opening my eyes.

"Still okay?" he asks, voice thick and impossibly gentle.

I nod, then realize maybe he can't see me, so I make myself say, "Yes. Um, thank you."

He grins, and there's a little smear of my wetness glistening on the corner of his mouth. The sight of my arousal on his lips should make me want to die, but it doesn't—it makes my clit throb harder. He looks so satisfied, so proud, like he's just tasted paradise. Then he dives back between my thighs, his tongue delving deeper this time, his strong hands spreading me open so he can taste every slick fold. I feel the hot, firm pressure of his tongue circling my entrance before pushing inside me, fucking me with slow, deliberate strokes that make my inner walls clench desperately around nothing, silently begging to be filled.

I let out a sound, a weird half sob, half plea, and Taio groans in response, the vibration sending another bolt of sensation through me. "Oh, good girl, you're already singing for me."

He's paying attention, adjusting his rhythm, finding the edge where the pleasure turns sharp. He keeps me right there, hovering, holding me open and wet and desperate, until I'm not thinking about anything except the hot, slick way his mouth moves and the way his hand fits against my thigh, grounding me so I don't float away.

I dig my fingers into the sheets. I want to say his name, but I can't remember how talking works. The world is a tunnel and the only thing at the other end is Taio, and Taio's mouth, and Taio's hands bracketing my hips like handles on a carnival ride.

Somewhere between one heartbeat and the next, his rhythm changes. He finds a pattern—a pulse and flick that feels mathematical at first, but then he throws in a syncopation just to keep me off-balance. There's a pressure building inside me, every muscle banding tighter, a high-pitched note winding in my chest.

All I can do is gasp, fists knotted in the blanket, thighs trembling around his shoulders.

"Taio—" I try, but it comes out a whimper.

It's ridiculous—he's barely even started and already I'm right there, teetering on the edge like a cartoon character about to look down and realize there's nothing but air. I bite my lip, afraid of the noises clawing up my throat, but he just keeps going, relentless, gentle, the tip of his tongue circling my clit like he's drawing a map of my undoing. The tension builds and builds, everywhere at once: behind my knees, up my neck, in the soles of my feet. I'm going to come, I think. I'm really going to—

And then he stops.

I make an inhuman sound. Not broken, exactly, but not whole, either. I open my eyes just in time to see him wipe his mouth with the back of his hand, a wicked gleam in his gaze.

"Not yet," he says, voice rough with authority and amusement.

I want to argue, but I can barely form words. Instead, I pout, and he laughs—a low, satisfied rumble that pulses into my bones.

He flips me over like it's nothing, rolling me onto my stomach with hands both gentle and firm. I gasp, the shock of movement making me hyperaware of every inch of my body. All the places still tingling, all the places suddenly exposed. The silk teddy is bunched up around my ribs, my ass in the air, the backs of my thighs trembling.

"Keep your legs together," he instructs, and I do, feeling awkward and animalistic and so, so open.

He kneels behind me, large hands sliding up the insides of my legs. His thumbs spread me apart, exposing everything, and I almost choke on my own nerves. Then his mouth is between my cheeks, tongue darting between the tight lines of my body, and I lose whatever composure I had left.

He licks me from behind, slow and deliberate, sometimes flattening his tongue and sometimes flicking, sometimes just breathing me in. He eats my pussy like it's the only thing he'll ever taste again, and the new angle makes everything sharper, more desperate. My hands claw the sheets, my forehead pressed into the mattress, and I don't even bother to muffle the noises now. I'm crying his name, begging, and it doesn't matter. Nothing matters except the relentless, exquisite sensation of being devoured.

He slides a finger into me while he works my clit with his tongue, and I come apart, body going rigid and then melting, a hot flood of pleasure crashing through me so hard it makes my vision blur. I convulse, sob, and Taio keeps going, licking me through it, holding my hips so I can't squirm away from the overwhelming feeling.

I come so hard, I nearly collapse to the side, but Taio holds me in place, refusing to show mercy. He slides two fingers in easily, my arousal and my release now mixed into the most inviting potion, and now his fingers aren't enough. I want his pants off too. I want to get closer.

But another orgasm rips through me, jostling my brain. This time I scream. I thrash. Then I collapse onto the mattress, boneless and spent.

He climbs up next to me, planting a kiss on my shoulder, then nuzzles into the hair at the back of my neck. I'm still shaking.

"Was that good?" His tone is smug and gentle all at once.

"I can't feel my toes."

His pupils dilate until only a thin ring of brown remains, and his gaze drops to my lips, lingering there with an obvious hunger and my breath catches in my throat. "You're so wet right now, I bet you could handle me." He asks for my hand, and I let him guide me to the thick, hard bulge in his pants. He lets me try to map out his girth and length like constellations, but I can't make out the entire picture. Taio stands at least a foot taller than me, with hands twice the size of mine, but this defies proportion.

"How do you feel?" he asks. "We can slow down."

I shake my head. "I don't want to slow down."

Taio leans over and kisses me sweetly. His lips are gentle,

undemanding, but his hand travels up my thigh in a languid, intimate sweep. He palms the side of my hip, thumb stroking small, lazy circles there, like he's coaxing me open one inch at a time. He kisses around my mouth, my jaw, the shell of my ear—little pecks, like he's sampling. With every touch, I'm melting, my body turning right back to syrup underneath him.

"Charlie," he murmurs, and the way he says my name—low, like a prayer—makes me want to cry for no reason. "This isn't fucking, okay?"

"What is it?" I ask, confused.

"Something more. I promise you that. For your first time you should know this means a great deal to both of us."

I press my cheek into his shoulder and nod, not sure I'm ready for words yet. Slow, yes. Safe. I want to remember this, every second.

He slides his hand up my torso, pausing at my ribs, then cups my breast with a reverence that makes me forget how small they are, or their slight asymmetry. Taio touches me like I'm sacred. His thumb grazes my nipple, and my breath skips. He doesn't rush, doesn't pinch or grope or do anything movie-men do. He just holds, massages, waits for me to tell him what I like. The patience alone is enough to make my core clench.

He climbs on top of me, his weight on his hands and knees, his body a protective cloak around me. Then, he drops his hips, grinding against my naked center with his pants-sheathed hardness. The wave of aggressive need that washes over me is foreign. Something new and primal, like the only thing that matters is Taio's body melded into mine. He's way too big for this to be comfortable in any way, but it's okay. I'll take the pleasure. I'll take the pain. I'll take everything if it keeps me close to him.

"Tell me if you want to stop," he says, and I realize I'm still trembling.

I manage, "Don't stop."

He smiles, sweet and open. It makes me want to kiss him again, so I do, my hands threading up into his hair. It's so fucking soft. He groans into my mouth, shifting his weight so the tip of his cock nudges against my clit.

I run my foot along the back of his calf, testing the weight of his leg above me. He's solid, but not crushing. I feel small underneath him, but not at all powerless. If anything, I'm the one in control—he's the one waiting for my next move, holding himself back so I can catch up.

When he finally peels the teddy off my arms, he does it with slow, careful hands, leaving kisses behind on each new inch of skin. He doesn't comment on my body, doesn't make a joke or a compliment, just lets his hands do the talking. I can feel how much he wants me in every touch.

I'm trembling as I reach for his waistband. He bridges his hips so I can work the waistband of his bottoms down.

Then, the sound of voices...

We both freeze, wondering if we imagined it.

The sound fades, then returns. Definitely real, definitely happening.

Taio leaps to his knees, clasps his hands around my mouth, telling me with a finger to the lips to be quiet. His ears are perked, fire in his eyes, and I realize he's not worried about getting caught. He thinks there are intruders. Wordlessly, he lets go of my mouth and points to the closet. *Hide. I'll handle this.*

I reach up and place a hand on each cheek. "Taio, it's fine," I whisper.

His eyes are bewildered, probably wondering why I'm sabotaging his heroic sacrifice. "I'm responsible for you, Charlie. It's my job to protect you," he whispers. His eyes say don't fuck with him. He'll hog-tie and throw me in that walk-in closet himself if it means my safety.

Maybe Claire is right. I'm looking at Taio and right now he looks far more like Superman than Joker.

"My hero," I say. "But there's nothing to save me from. Those are my dancers. I invited them over. They have a key. It must already be two o'clock."

Taio's eyes shift left, then right. "Invited them over for what? To announce your deflowering?"

I chuckle underneath him, rubbing his strong forearms. "No. To team-bond. To make some performance changes. I...Well, you slept in really late, and I didn't know how the striptease was going to go. I didn't think we'd be doing this."

There's a loud splash. We both glance to the far window which luckily has the drapes closed. "They enter someone else's home and just immediately dive into the pool?" Taio asks.

"Apparently...I should get decent," I say. "Unless you want to make this quick."

"I do not," he deadpans.

He flinches when I gently pat against his erection. "What about this though?"

"Believe it or not, they do eventually deflate on their own."

I chuckle. "Rain check, then? Tonight? Can I buy you dinner as a thank-you?"

He bites his bottom lip. "I don't know. Just ate. I'm kind of full."

"I'm serious." I tuck my knees and roll to the left, out from under him. "We can order in. I used to live in Miami when I was little. I know where all the good street food is. Do you like Cubanos?"

"Then let's go out," Taio says. "Our first official date kicking off this situationship. Street food should be eaten fresh, on the street. We could do downtown Miami, or walk the beach after." His eyes dim when I don't match his innocent enthusiasm. "What's wrong?"

I scoot to the edge of the bed, wedging my heels into the frame so I can securely refasten the teddy. "I don't know if we can be in public like that without people being suspicious."

He shrugs one shoulder. "I'm your bodyguard. I'm supposed to be with you."

"I know but...I just want you to myself. Where I don't have to pretend or watch the way I'm touching you or looking at you. Let's eat in?" I ask again. "Whatever you want. My treat."

"Sure. I get it." *He says the right words.*

Taio climbs off the bed, then circles around to the other side where I'm sitting. He brushes his lips against my forehead. *He does the right things.*

But judging by the look on his face, I just hurt his feelings.

My heart sinks, the glaring obstacle between us, momentarily muted by a moment of delicious passion.

But now all that's left are two things:

The obvious truth that we can't be together. Not in a real way.

And the other obvious truth, which is—I want us to be.

Chapter 17
Charlie

And yes, this is absolutely a bribe.

February in Miami means bearable heat instead of the August inferno that would otherwise be slow-roasting us all. My dancers have colonized every inch of the pool area, their toned bodies draped across inflatable loungers, kicking up spray in the shallow end, or clustered around the poolside bar like they're afraid the free booze might evaporate if they don't claim it quickly enough.

I will fully admit, I'm not above bribery. I ensured the bar was replenished and the margarita machine is functional.

I adjust my oversized sunhat and take a deep breath. I've been standing at the edge of the pool deck for five minutes now, rehearsing what I'm going to say, trying to find the right words. The pizza should be here any minute—another bribe, because apparently my leadership style is "feed them until they're too full to be mad at me."

"Hey, everyone?" I raise my voice over the splash of water and the thump of whatever playlist someone's connected to the outdoor speakers. "Can I get your attention for a sec?"

The noise dies down gradually. Heads turn. Devon, my lead male dancer, paddles his float closer to the edge of the pool. Maura and Jasmine pause mid-conversation on the lounge chairs. Marcus—not my manager Marcus, dancer Marcus—sets down his drink and gives me his full attention.

Twelve dancers in total. Twelve people who've put their lives on hold for a year and a half to be part of my tour. Twelve people who've watched me struggle through choreography, stumble through rehearsals, and generally fail to keep up with the routines they execute flawlessly every night.

Twelve people who probably think I'm a joke.

"So," I begin, my voice steadier than I expected. "Pizza's on the way. Bar's fully stocked. And yes, this is absolutely a bribe."

A few laughs ripple through the group. Good. Laughter is good.

"I wanted to talk to you all about something. Something I probably should have addressed a long time ago." I take off my sunhat, because suddenly it feels like a barrier, something to hide behind. "I can't dance."

Silence. A few exchanged glances.

"I know you know this. I know there have been...comments. Behind my back, during rehearsals, probably in group chats I'm not part of." I hold up a hand before anyone can protest. "It's okay. I'm not calling anyone out. I'm just...acknowledging reality."

Devon pulls himself out of the pool, water streaming off his shoulders. "Charlie, we don't—"

"Let me finish. Please." I wait until he nods, then continue. "The truth is, I don't just struggle with dancing. I don't like it. I never have. When I was a kid, I wanted to be a singer-songwriter. Full stop. But somewhere along the way, the industry decided that pop stars have to be triple threats—singing, dancing, acting—and I got swept up in trying to be all the things I'm not. All the things I don't want to be."

Mia has sat up on her lounge chair, her expression unreadable. Jasmine is nodding slowly, like pieces are clicking into place.

"I've spent years forcing myself through choreography that doesn't suit me, and in the process, I've been holding all of you back." I gesture at the group, at these incredible athletes who could be headlining their own shows. "You put your entire lives on hold to support my tour. Your careers, your families, your own opportunities—all of it, on pause, to make me look good on stage. And I haven't been honoring that sacrifice."

The pizza delivery guy chooses this moment to appear at the side gate, looking confused about whether he's supposed to interrupt. I wave him over, and Marcus—again, dancer Marcus—and Devon gallantly jog over to help with the boxes.

"Anyway," I continue, once the pizza is safely deposited on the patio table, "I want to change things. Before the next show, I want to completely rework the choreography."

Now I have their full attention. Even the people who were still half floating in the pool have drifted to the edge, listening.

"I want to step back from the moves I can't keep up with. I want to focus on what I'm actually good at—singing, live, mic on, no more lip-syncing, no more backup tracks doing the heavy lifting." I meet their eyes, one by one. "And I want to give you all the space to actually shine. Solos. Features. Moments where the audience is watching *you*, not just using you as background decoration while I flail around pretending to know what I'm doing."

Jasmine's hand goes up, tentative. "You want us to have our own solos? On your tour?"

"It's not just my tour. It's our tour. Or at least, it should be." I step closer to the group, my bare feet warm on the sunbaked stone. "I've been thinking about what I want this experience to be—not just for me, but for everyone involved. And I realized I've been so focused on my own survival that I forgot we're supposed to be a team. The name Charlie Riley has to sell tickets, but the performance belongs to all of us."

"That's..." Devon drags a hand through his wet hair, looking genuinely thrown. "Charlie, this only exists because of you. You know that, right? It's okay for the headliner to want the spotlight to themselves."

"I've had all eyes on me for seven years. Where has it gotten me?" I shrug. "It's time to try something different."

Kenny, still floating on an inflatable flamingo, raises his

hand. "Can I say something?"

"Of course."

"When I got the call for this tour, I almost didn't take it." He paddles closer, his expression unusually serious for someone perched on a giant pink bird. "Not because of you. Because of the industry. I was tired of the glass ceilings. Tired of working my ass off in rehearsals just to be a blur behind some artist who didn't even learn our names. But my agent said your team was different. That you actually talked to your dancers, remembered birthdays, gave us security budgets, checked in and congratulated us after shows."

I blink. "I didn't know anyone noticed that stuff."

"We notice everything." Mia stands up, wrapping a towel around her shoulders. "You're the only artist I've worked with who asks how we're doing. Like, actually asks, and waits for an answer. That matters."

"It matters more than you know," Jasmine adds quietly. "I've worked tours where the headliner literally didn't know my name after six months. You knew my daughter's name after the first week. You asked about her dance recital."

My throat tightens. "Well, getting to play Poppy in an elementary school rendition of *Trolls* is a big deal."

"See?" Jasmine's eyes are bright. "That's what we're talking about. You care. And now you're asking us to step up and share the stage?" She shakes her head, smiling. "Charlie, we'd follow you into a burning building."

"Let's hope it doesn't come to that," I manage, my voice wobbly.

"The point is," Devon cuts in, ever the practical one, "we're with you. But I want to make sure you understand what you're proposing. Complete re-choreography in less than a week is ambitious. Some would say impossible."

"Yup." I meet his eyes steadily. "Total suicide mission."

There's a hum of agreement around the patio.

"Look, I'm not expecting perfection. I'm expecting effort.

Creativity. Willingness to try something new and fail and try again." I gesture around the pool. "This tour was supposed to be the biggest thing I've ever done. Instead, it's been a disaster from the jump. But maybe we can turn it into something bigger and better than revenue. Something we look back on that actually means something. Not just to the fans, but to us."

The silence stretches for a hot minute. I can feel my heart pounding, the vulnerability of what I've just said sitting exposed in the humid air.

Then Mia stands up from her lounge chair and starts clapping.

It's slow at first—almost sarcastic, and for a horrible second I think she's mocking me. But then Jasmine joins in, and Devon, and suddenly they're all applauding, and the sound echoes off the water and the white walls of the villa until it's basically a standing ovation.

"I'm so fucking in!" Kenny shouts from the back—he's one of the newer dancers. "I've got choreo ideas I've been sitting on for *months*."

"Same!" Mia is grinning now, her earlier unreadable expression transformed into something bright and eager. "I've got some routines that would break your back, Charlie. But Devon and I could own that stage—"

"Wait, wait." I hold up my hands, laughing despite myself. "Guys, I just want you to know, if you want an out, here it is. This is going to be a lot of work. We're talking complete overhaul, probably pulling all-nighters, definitely pushing ourselves harder than we have all tour. The show in Tampa is next week. That's not a lot of time to reinvent ourselves. So if anyone is not up for it... it's okay. Just let me know. You will still be compensated for your time with me."

"Yeah, who wants to be a little bitch?" Devon crosses his arms, but he's grinning, looking around the patio.

Not a single soul pipes up. No one retreats. No unsure expressions. They always had the fire. They just needed me to light the damn match.

All right. Here we go.

I glance around the group. "I believe in every single one of you. I'm asking you to believe in me, too. Believe that I can pull this off. Believe that we can create something better than what we've been doing."

The pool filter hums. A bird calls somewhere in the palm trees.

Then Devon raises his hand. "Fully in."

"Me too," Mia says immediately.

"Obviously," from Jasmine.

One by one, hands go up. Voices call out agreement. By the time the last dancer has committed, the energy around the pool has completely transformed—from lazy afternoon hangout to this pure, electric sense of *purpose*.

"Holy shit." I press my hands to my cheeks as tears prick at my eyes. I expected our ranks to shrink today. I didn't expect to feel strengthened. "You guys. I don't even know what to say."

"Don't say anything." Devon pulls me into a hug, his still-damp skin cool against my sundress. "Save those pipes for the performance. We can take the lead on the dance side."

More hugs follow. Jasmine squeezes me so hard I squeak. Marcus lifts me off the ground entirely. By the time they release me, I'm laughing and crying and feeling lighter than I have in months.

"Okay, okay." I wipe my eyes with the back of my hand. "Pizza first. Then we talk logistics. Sound good?"

The group descends on the pizza boxes like locusts, and the afternoon dissolves into a chaotic mix of brainstorming and pepperoni and arguments about which songs need the most work. I'm in the middle of it all, scribbling notes on napkins, fielding suggestions, watching these incredible people come alive with creative verve.

This is what it's supposed to feel like. A team. A family. Something worth fighting for.

Taio

I WATCH THE whole thing from the kitchen window.

From where I stand, I can see her by the pool, this tiny figure in an oversized hat and billowing sundress. She's laying herself bare, confessing doubts to people who dance behind her every night, who could so easily turn on her. Yet there she is, reaching out with open palms instead of clenched fists, asking them to catch her when she could have pretended to never stumble.

Then it happens—the dancers burst into applause, circling around her with open arms. I watch her face transform: first shock, then a trembling smile, then something luminous and grateful spreading across her features as she realizes they're still with her, all in.

My chest twists, warmth spreading outward until I'm smiling like a loon, alone in the kitchen, watching a woman I've known for less than a few weeks command the loyalty of an entire dance team through sheer vulnerability and authenticity.

This is what she does. She walks into rooms full of people who have every reason to resent her, and she wins them over by being exactly who she is. No pretense. No manipulation. Just Charlie, messy and imperfect and somehow radiant because of it.

I think about the book still sitting in my bag—the romance novel I'm three-quarters through, the one where the hero and heroine keep circling each other, kept apart by circumstance and fear and all the reasonable obstacles that make stories interesting. I've read dozens of these books. I know how they work. I know the beats, the tropes, the inevitable moment when everything clicks into place and the couple gets their happily-ever-after.

But standing here, watching Charlie through a window, I feel like I'm caught in the middle of a plot without any guarantee of how it ends.

The inkling is there. That spark I've envied, the one that only exists in fiction, the one I'd almost convinced myself wasn't real. It's small, but it's growing. Every time she laughs. Every time she says something ridiculous. Every time she looks at me like I'm the only person in the room.

I'm falling for her, one idiosyncrasy at a time. The realization should scare me more than it does. Instead, it feels inevitable, like I've been moving toward this moment since the night I knocked on the wrong hotel room door.

My phone buzzes in my pocket.

I pull it out, expecting Charlie, or maybe Sage with some tour update. Instead, the screen displays a number I know by heart but never saved as a contact.

Otisville Federal Correctional Institution.

My lungs bottom out, like an anchor suddenly dropped.

I step away from the window, moving through the kitchen and into the hallway where the noise from the pool party fades to a distant murmur. The phone is still buzzing. I could let it go to voicemail. I could pretend I didn't see it, didn't hear it, didn't feel the immediate clench of obligation in my chest.

I answer.

"You have a collect call from an inmate at Otisville Federal Correctional Institution. To accept charges, press one."

I press one.

"Taio?" My father's voice comes through the line, slightly distorted by prison phone quality but unmistakably him. That smooth baritone that used to read me bedtime stories, that commanded boardrooms and charmed investors, that told me I could be anything I wanted when I grew up.

"Hey, Dad." I lean against the hallway wall, closing my eyes. "How are you?"

"Oh, you know." A pause, weighted with unspoken accusation. "Same as always. Counting the days. Watching the clock. Waiting for someone to visit."

Here it comes.

"I checked the visitation schedule online. Your name isn't on tomorrow's list." His tone is carefully neutral, but I know it well. It's the one he uses when he wants you to feel guilty without having to explicitly accuse you of anything. "Did something happen? Are you sick?"

"No, I'm not sick. I'm in Miami."

Silence.

"Miami," he repeats flatly. I can hear the machinery turning in his head, that analytical mind that built an empire on calculated theft and betrayal. "What's in Miami?"

"I got a new job. It requires some travel." I keep my voice light, casual, like this is a normal conversation between a father and son. "I'll be back in New York soon. I'll get on the visitation schedule the second I'm back."

"A new job." The words land heavy with skepticism. "What kind of job takes you to Miami on such short notice that you can't even tell your father about it?"

"Private security. Personal protection detail." It's not entirely a lie. "Good money. Steady work. The kind of opportunity I couldn't pass up."

"Private security." He lets that hang there, and I can practically see him turning them over, examining them for weaknesses. My father never takes anything at face value. "For who?"

"I can't really discuss the details. Client confidentiality."

"Client confidentiality." A soft laugh, but there's no warmth in it. "You sound like a lawyer. Or like someone who's hiding something."

"Dad, I'm not hiding anything. It's just work. I'm under an NDA. I can't say more, especially not on a recorded line."

"Mmm." The sound is noncommittal, loaded. "And this work couldn't wait until after visitation? You know how much I look forward to seeing you, Taio. It's the only thing that gets me through these weeks. Sitting in that room, watching the clock, knowing you're coming...it's the one bright spot in this whole miserable existence."

His words land with surgical precision, right where they're

meant to—a direct hit to the center of my chest. I press my palm against my sternum as if to contain the spreading ache. Dad makes Otisville sound like Alcatraz, but I've seen the "prison" where he's serving time. All the calls may say Otisville, but he's serving at a Satellite Prison Camp. Barely there security. Dormitory-style housing. Recreation areas. A commissary better stocked than my corner bodega. The man who once owned three vacation homes now acts like sharing a bathroom is torture, as if the real punishment isn't the bars but the indignity of consequences catching up to him.

"Dad, I'm sorry. It came up suddenly. I didn't have a lot of choice about the timing."

"There's always a choice." His voice is gentle now, reasonable. That's the thing about my father—he can turn on a dime, switch from interrogation to understanding so smoothly you wonder if you imagined the sharpness. "But I understand. You have your own life to live. I can't expect you to put everything on hold for me forever."

"It's not like that—"

"No, no. It's fine. Really." He sighs, the sound of a man who's made peace with disappointment. "I'm not trying to make you feel bad, son. I just miss you. It gets lonely in here. The other inmates, they're not exactly intellectually stimulating company. And the guards—well, you know how they treat people like me. Like I'm still dangerous, still capable of...I don't know. Orchestrating a Ponzi scheme through the prison phone system."

Despite myself, I almost smile. "Are you?"

"Perhaps. Visit and find out." A hint of his old humor surfaces, then fades.

"How are you, really? How's the commissary? Do you need me to add more money?"

"I could use some, actually. They raised the prices on everything again. Coffee's up to four dollars a packet. Four dollars, Taio. For instant coffee that tastes like burned rubber."

"I'll transfer some tomorrow."

"And my prescription cream—the good one, for my back—they're saying I need a new authorization form. Some bureaucratic nonsense. I've filled out the same paperwork three times now, and every time it gets 'lost' in the system. I think the medical staff here actively enjoys watching me suffer."

"Your rash is still acting up?"

"It's spreading," he complains.

"I'll call them. I'll take care of it."

He sighs in relief. "What would I do without you, Taio? You're the only one who still believes in me."

"You have your legal team too—"

"The legal team believes in billable hours. They don't care about me. They care about the case, the precedent, the media attention. You're the only one who actually..." He trails off, and when he speaks again, his voice is thick. "You're the only one who still sees me as a person. Not a case number. Not a cautionary tale. You see me for what I am. A good father caught up in everyone else's misfortune."

I can't believe that's still his narrative. Like theft slipped on a banana and fell into him.

"You'll always be my dad. Nothing changes that. Family first."

His laugh is bitter. "Your mother used to say that. One day I'm her husband of eighteen years who she promised to stand by no matter what, the next I'm a stranger she can't wait to forget."

I close my eyes, pressing my forehead against the cool wall. "Dad, you lied to her for a long time. Mom went through a lot more than you realize—"

"I know, I know. The shame. The scandal. The way her friends looked at her." His tone grows mocking. "All that woman cares about is public appearance. She didn't care who was paying the bills as long as her ass was dressed up in Gucci and shoes had red bottoms. After everything I did for her, I thought, at least, she'd be loyal."

I exhale, giving up on the narrative. It's like trying to convince an early colonist that the world isn't flat. He lives the only story he's allowing himself to accept. "Well, I'm sorry it didn't work out that way. But you do still have me."

"Do I?" Another pause, heavy with meaning. "Suddenly you're in Miami. On some new job you couldn't even mention before today. Missing visitation for the first time in—how long has it been? Three years? I've never had to sit in that room and wait for someone who wasn't coming."

"Dad—"

"I'm not blaming you." His voice cracks, just slightly—practiced or genuine, I can never quite tell. "I'm just saying, I see the pattern. Your mother pulled away slowly too. First it was one missed visit. Then two. Then she stopped answering my calls. Then she moved to a different continent." He takes a shaky breath. "I can't lose you too, Taio. You're all I have left. The only person in the world who still gives a damn whether I live or die in here."

I know what he's doing.

I can see it clearly—the comparison to Mom, designed to trigger my deep-set fear of being like her. The fragility, calculated to make me feel protective. The implication that my absence is the first step toward abandonment, that one missed visit will inevitably become two, then ten, then forever.

It's manipulation. *It's textbook.* I've read enough about narcissistic parents to recognize every technique he's using.

And yet...it works.

"You're not going to lose me," I say to him. "I'll figure something out. Maybe I can fly back for a few hours tomorrow, do the visit, and fly back."

"You'd do that?" The hope sounds so genuine it makes my chest ache. "For me?"

"Of course."

"Taio." His voice warms, filling with that paternal pride that used to make me feel ten feet tall. "You're a good son. The best son a man could ask for. I don't deserve you."

"Dad, stop."

"I mean it. After everything we've gone through, you could

have walked away. Most people would have. Hell, most people did. Friends, colleagues, everyone who swore they'd stand by our family disappeared the moment the indictment came down. But not you. You stayed. You fought for me." He pauses. "You're still fighting for me."

"Always."

"I love you, son. More than you'll ever know."

"Love you too, Dad."

"Don't forget to call about my cream."

"Roger that."

The call ends with the prison system's automated click. I stand in the hallway for a long moment, phone still pressed to my ear, listening to nothing.

Through the window at the end of the hall, I can see a sliver of the pool deck. Charlie is gesturing animatedly, explaining something to her dancers while they cluster around the pizza boxes. Her laugh carries faintly through the glass—bright and genuine and completely unaware of the conversation I just had.

Two worlds. Two versions of myself.

I'm trying to move forward, but I'm always a hostage to *him*. To guilt. I'm serving a sentence for a crime I didn't commit.

But what choice do I have? Dad stole everything to dote on me. Doesn't that make me...complicit in a way? I don't know. I don't want to think about it anymore. I want to rewind the clock by an hour, catch the tail end of her goofy striptease, and re-experience the pure bliss of kneeling between her thighs and giving her something no man had given her before. I want to disappear into Charlie, if only reality would stop biting us in the ass.

And honestly, even if I could figure out a way to resolve my dad's issues, I'm no match for Charlie.

When is she ever going to proudly claim an escort as the love of her life? No one would see us in a tabloid and think—couple goals. They'll only see the scandal we are.

I pocket my phone and head toward the pool, toward the woman who makes me want to believe in happy endings...

Even when I know better.

Chapter 18
Charlie

I can really feel the boyfriend-ly support bleeding through the speakerphone.

He left.

I keep replaying it in my head—the way Taio appeared in the doorway of the pool house while I was mid-sentence with Devon about the bridge section of "Hypnotic." The way his face looked tight, closed off, nothing like the man who'd had me in his mouth three hours earlier. The way he said he needed to take a rain check for our date because of a "family emergency" without meeting my eyes.

"Take the jet," I offered immediately. "Marcus can have it ready in an hour."

"That's not necessary."

"It's a nineteen-hour drive to New York. Or like, three hours if you fly. Just take the jet, Taio. It's sitting there doing nothing."

"I already booked a flight." His voice was clipped. Professional. Like we were back to being client and hired help instead of whatever we'd become in that bedroom. "Red-eye leaves at eleven. I'll be back in a day or two. Stay safe."

A day or two. Like he was running to the grocery store instead of fleeing across the country.

I wanted to push. Wanted to ask what was really going on, why he suddenly couldn't look at me, why he was choosing a cramped commercial flight over the comfort of a private plane.

But the dancers were watching—pretending not to, but definitely watching—and something in Taio's posture told me this wasn't a conversation he wanted to have in public.

So I just nodded and said "okay, let me know if you need anything." I watched him walk back into the guesthouse to pack his bag. I got so distracted with the dancers and our new Herculean task, I didn't even register when he left.

And now it's two in the morning and I'm lying in my bed, staring at the ceiling, replaying every moment of the last twelve hours, trying to figure out where I went wrong.

It was the date thing. It had to be.

I suggested we order in instead of going out. I basically made it clear I wanted to keep us hidden, keep him secret. I know I hurt him. Something shifted in his face. I felt the distance open up between us like a crack in the earth.

Shit.

I treated him like a dirty little secret. Like an escort. The very thing he doesn't want to be when it comes to me.

No wonder he left. I bet there's no family emergency.

I roll onto my side, pulling a pillow against my chest like it might fill the space where he should be. The sheets still smell faintly like him, that cedar cologne, something warm and spicy underneath. There's a weight on my chest making every breath strained.

This is ridiculous. I've known him for what, a few weeks? We've shared exactly one sexual experience that didn't even technically count as sex. He has a whole other life outside of me. For some reason, I don't like that. Not that he has another life, just that I'm not a part of it.

I stare at my phone on the nightstand, willing it to light up with his name. It doesn't. Of course it doesn't. He's probably still in the air, crammed into a middle seat between a snoring businessman and someone's emotional support animal, deliberately choosing discomfort over accepting anything from me.

God, I'm such a mess.

The thing is, I get it. I understand why he'd be hurt. Everything people see of me is manufactured—from the boyfriend who exists only in photo ops to the sparkly persona that bears no resemblance to who I am when no one's watching. I've spent years polishing an image that doesn't even feel like me anymore. How could I ask Taio to step into this funhouse-mirror version of a relationship? What kind of person would willingly sign up for that?

But the alternative is...what? Going public with the escort I hired to pretend to be my bodyguard? Announcing to the world that America's sweetheart is dating a man whose job may or may not be legal? The headlines write themselves. The scandal would make the balcony thing look like a minor PR hiccup.

I could lose everything.

Then again...what exactly am I holding on to?

The thought surfaces unbidden, and I let it sit there for a moment, examining it from different angles. What am I so afraid of losing? A career that's made me miserable? An image that requires constant maintenance? The approval of millions of strangers who'd turn on me the moment I stop performing for them?

I think about Claire, pregnant and radiant, building a life that has nothing to do with fame or followers. I think about my dancers today, the way they lit up when I gave them permission to be more than background decoration. I think about Taio reading romance novels because he wants to believe in happy endings.

What if I just...stopped?

Not forever. Not dramatically. But what if, after this tour, I actually took the break I've been pretending I don't need? What if I took some time to figure out who Charlie Riley is when she's not performing for anyone?

The idea is terrifying and exhilarating in equal measure. I've been on since I was sixteen. Nearly a decade of constant visibility, constant output, constant pressure to be bigger, better, more. When was the last time I did something just because I wanted to? When was the last time I made a choice that wasn't filtered through "how will this affect my brand?"

I need to prove to Taio that I'm serious about him. That he's not just a convenient secret, a safe practice run before I find someone more publicly acceptable. But how do I do that when my entire existence is built around image management?

Maybe I start by dismantling the image.

My phone buzzes on the nightstand and I lunge for it so fast I nearly knock over the water glass beside it.

Please be Taio. Please be Taio. Please be—

Grayson Hemsley.

My insides twist like I've swallowed ice water too fast. Grayson's name pulses on the screen, demanding attention it doesn't deserve at this hour. My thumb hovers over the red decline button. It's two in the morning. What could he possibly want?

I can't resist the pull of the unknown. My thumb betrays me, sliding to accept.

"Hello?"

"Charlie. Hey!" His voice is bright, energetic, completely inappropriate for this hour. "Did I wake you?"

"It's two in the morning, Grayson."

"Right, right. Time zones. I always forget Miami's three hours ahead." His words slur slightly at the edges. "I'm in LA. Just got out of this...thing, and I was thinking about you."

The pause before "*thing*" stretches just long enough for me to fill it with images of perfume-scented sheets and lipstick on his collar.

"You were thinking about me." I say it flatly, not bothering to hide my skepticism.

"I saw the clips from your Miami show. The piano thing? That was actually really cool. I didn't know you could play like that. I didn't know you could sing like that."

I blink at my ceiling, trying to recalibrate. In the three months since our teams arranged this fake relationship, Grayson has shown approximately zero interest in my actual life. Our interactions have been limited to carefully staged photo ops, the occasional text coordinating logistics, and one deeply awkward dinner where we ran out of things to talk about before the appetizers arrived. Now suddenly he's calling in the middle of the night to praise my artistic choices?

"Are you drunk or on drugs tonight, Grayson?"

He laughs, but there's something forced about it. "Come on, don't be like that. I'm trying to be a better boyfriend here."

"No need. We're not actually dating, remember? This is a business arrangement. A mutually beneficial PR strategy. Your words, not mine."

"I know, I know. But we're supposed to be selling it, right? And I've been thinking—" He pauses, and I hear ice clinking in a glass. Of course he's drinking. "Maybe I haven't been pulling my weight. Like, I hear about your tour drama through TMZ instead of from you directly. That's not very boyfriend-ly of me."

"Boyfriend-ly."

"It's a word. I'm making it a word." He barrels on before I can respond. "Anyway, I wanted to let you know I'm planning to come out to your Tampa show. Make an appearance. Show some support. Do the whole loving boyfriend routine, really sell the thing."

My blood runs cold. "You're coming to Tampa?"

"My publicist thinks it'll be good optics. Ever since that bodyguard thing, we haven't been photographed together. People think we broke up and are keeping it a secret. Let me set the record straight at your concert." He makes a squeaky sound like he's pushing debris through his teeth.

"Grayson, it's not necessary—"

"It's already in motion." His voice takes on a slightly harder edge beneath the casual veneer.

I close my eyes, feeling a headache forming behind my temples.

"Unless there's some reason you don't want me there?" he asks. "You're not still messing with the help, are you?"

"The help? As in *Taio*, my friend?"

"Oh come on, Charlie. I know we stay out of each other's

business and stuff, but I know what you were doing on that balcony."

"I'm not sure if you're accusing me of something, but I don't say a word about the parade of women I know you keep lined up at your door."

He laughs, which is such a bizarre response to that. "But I'm way more subtle. You haven't had to clean up any of my scandals, have you?"

"Wow, Grayson. Classy. I can really feel the *boyfriend-ly* support bleeding through the speakerphone."

"All right, all right," he singsongs. "I didn't call to fight. I just called to let you know I'm here. If you need anything. We should be better friends, Charlie. What do you think?"

If Grayson Hemsley is my friend, then I have to stop calling Taio that. They are opposites. They should be kept on different hemispheres. They aren't even the same species.

"Okay, well, thank you, Grayson. That's really thoughtful. Always helps to have more friendly faces in the crowd."

"I mean, I'll be in VIP, right? I'm not going to watch your concert from the nosebleeds."

Prince Charmless, everybody.

"Yeah, of course. I'll let Marcus know. He'll arrange everything you need."

"Cool." His tone shifts, warming into something that almost sounds genuine, and I wonder if he's this good an actor or if there's actually a real person underneath all that Hollywood polish. "And hey, I really am glad the tour's going better. I know the last few weeks have been rough. It'll be nice to actually see you in person. Maybe grab dinner after the show?"

"Um, maybe. Yeah. If there's time."

We exchange a few more pleasantries—surface-level conversation about his latest project, some industry gossip about a director I've never worked with, speculation about awards season that I barely register. I make appropriate sounds at appropriate intervals while my brain spins out in twelve different directions.

Finally, mercifully, he says he has to go. Off to whatever LA after-party awaits him, whatever beautiful people are waiting to laugh at his jokes and validate his existence.

I let the phone drop onto my chest and stare at the ceiling some more.

Grayson Hemsley is coming to Tampa.

This is fine. Completely fine. I'll just juggle my fake boyfriend and the man I'm falling for in the same space while performing a completely revamped show that we're building from scratch in less than a week. No problem. Totally manageable. Not at all a recipe for catastrophic public humiliation.

I unlock my phone and do something I've done approximately forty times today: I open Instagram and navigate to Taio's profile.

It's exactly as barren as it was the last time I checked. No profile picture—just the default gray silhouette. No posts. No stories. Zero followers, zero following. The account exists solely as a placeholder, proof of identity without any actual content.

He could disappear tomorrow and there'd be no digital trace of him. No archive of selfies, no carefully curated highlights, no evidence that he ever existed in the public eye at all.

I'm jealous. Genuinely, deeply jealous of his ability to be invisible.

My entire life is documented. Every concert, every interview, every paparazzi shot of me getting coffee in sweatpants on a bad hair day. I exist in the public record whether I want to or not. There's no escaping the narrative because the narrative is everywhere, constantly being written and rewritten by people who've never met me.

But Taio? Taio could walk away from all of this and no one would even know he was gone. He could go back to New York, delete my number, pretend the last several weeks never happened. There'd be no screenshots to analyze, no comment sections to dissect, no digital breadcrumbs for obsessive fans to follow.

The thought makes me feel sick and sad and strangely envious all at once.

I close Instagram and open my messages instead. Our text thread is sparse—mostly logistics from the early days, then a few flirty exchanges once things started shifting between us. The last message is from him, sent right before his flight took off.

Taio

Boarding soon. I'll text when I land.

That was five hours ago. He should have landed by now. Should have texted. Should have given me some sign that he's okay, that we're okay, that the distance opening between us is just physical and not something deeper.

My thumb levitates over the keyboard.

Don't be clingy. Don't be desperate. Don't be the girl who can't go twelve hours without contact.

But also: don't be the girl who's too afraid to say what she feels. Don't be the girl who lets something real slip away because she was too busy protecting her image.

I start typing before I can talk myself out of it.

I miss you already.

I stare at those four words on my screen, finger suspended above them like a diver who's suddenly realized how far down the water really is.

I've stood on stages with enough people to fill a small city staring back at me. I've hit high notes on primetime TV while network executives held their breath. I've smiled for cameras knowing tomorrow my chin, my nose, my eyes would be outlined in red circles on gossip sites with headlines like "*Botched Botox.*"

None of that felt as nerve-wracking as this.

Send.

The message delivers. The little checkmark appears, confirming it's gone out into the world, winging its way to wherever

Taio is right now. Probably his apartment in New York. Probably exhausted from the red-eye. Probably wondering why he ever got involved with a pop-star disaster who can't even commit to being seen on a date with him in public.

I watch the screen. Waiting for the three dots that mean he's typing. Waiting for any sign of response.

Nothing.

I keep watching anyway, phone clutched to my chest, breath held like a swimmer about to go under. The screen dims. I tap it to keep it awake. It dims again. I tap again.

The minutes tick by. One. Two. Five.

Still nothing.

Maybe he's asleep. It's almost three a.m. Normal people sleep at three in the morning. It's not personal...

I hope.

I place my phone screen-down on the nightstand and try to reason with myself. He's asleep. He's handling the family crisis. He has better things to do than stare at message notifications like I do. I'll look again tomorrow.

But I don't sleep.

I lie there in the dark, listening to my own heartbeat, wondering if I've already lost something I barely had a chance to hold. *Fuck.*

Sleep won't come, so I gather my bedding and shuffle to the living room, to the blanket fort where Taio and I spent last night. A corner has collapsed; I tuck the sheet back under the couch cushion to fix it. Inside, I find Black Cat curled in the same spot where Taio had lain. The air in here still holds traces of his cologne. I settle beside the cat, pulling my comforter tight around me, making myself smaller and smaller until the world outside this fragile shelter ceases to exist. It's just me, this sleeping cat, and the ghost of yesterday's happiness now.

My eyes grow heavy. Against all odds, unconsciousness finally claims me.

Chapter 19

Taio

I'm not asking you to pretend. I'm asking you to let go.

The Carrington house looks different in February.

Last time I was here, it was summer. The lawn was brown and crispy from drought, the flowerbeds wilted, the whole property radiating a kind of exhausted defeat. Now, in the gray light of a New York winter, there's something almost hopeful about it. Someone's hung a wreath on the front door. The walkway's been shoveled clean. Through the window, I can see warm light glowing from the kitchen.

I can't move from the driver's seat. Five minutes tick by on the dashboard clock while I finger the edge of the check in my pocket. Fifty grand. Half of what Charlie's team promised me; the other half comes when I finish the job. But right now, this promise is all I have to show Anne that I haven't given up, that I'm still chipping away at the mountain of debt my father left behind.

It's not enough. It'll never be enough. But it's something.

I finally force myself out of the car and up the walkway. The doorbell chimes inside, and I hear footsteps, then the rattle of a chain being slid down.

To my relief, Anne opens the door. I didn't want to deal with Mr. Carrington's judgy stare tonight. Everything he thinks about me, I do too. Spoiled little rich kid whose dad fed him with the stolen fruits of labor. I get it. Doesn't mean I want to be reminded every five minutes.

"Taio. Honey, what are you doing here? Come in, it's freezing this morning."

She's wearing an apron dusted with flour, and I can smell something baking—cookies, maybe, or banana bread.

"I didn't mean to intrude."

"Nonsense. I just put coffee on. Mr. Carrington is out of town on business, and Joy is still sleeping." She widens her eyes. "Teenagers, right?"

"I'm assuming Alaina is—"

"She lives with her fiancé."

Huh. Interesting. *Why didn't that sting?* I keep waiting for the usual emotional pinprick every time I get information about Alaina, but for some reason, it just doesn't hurt.

I step through the door. "Whatever you're cooking smells delicious."

"Then you're just in time, honey. In, in, *in*." She waits for me to kick off my shoes, then ushers me through the living room to the kitchen nook. I slide into the booth side of the round table, my old spot.

Before I can blink, a large mug of warm coffee is beside me. Cream and sugar magically appear alongside. Anne was always the best host. I used to love dinners at her place. She and Mom used to cater holidays together. I miss them arguing over pretentious appetizers and color schemes for Christmas spreads.

The house is warm and smells like cinnamon. There are new throw pillows on the couch, fresh flowers on the side table, a few new pictures, and I think a new area rug by the front entrance, but otherwise, this is the second home I remember from my childhood and adolescence.

I'm so glad, at least, they got to keep the house. It was paid off. The one thing the bank couldn't seize.

"You look tired, honey."

"Red-eye flight."

"From where?"

“Miami. Work.”

Her eyebrows rise slightly, but she doesn’t pry. Instead, she pours herself a cup of coffee, then slides into the seat across the table.

“So what brings you here?”

I reach into my jacket and pull out the check. I set it on the table in front of me, then slide it across with two fingers like I’m making her a written offer. Anne looks at it but doesn’t touch it.

“Fifty thousand,” I say. “I know it’s not all of it, but I wanted to give you some peace of mind. I’ll have the rest in about three more months. In plenty of time for Joy to start school.”

Anne is quiet for a long moment. She picks up her coffee cup, takes a slow sip, sets it back down carefully.

“Taio,” she says finally. “I can’t take that.”

“Mrs. Carrington—”

“Anne. Please.”

“Anne.” I push the check closer to her. “This is yours. It was stolen; I’m returning it.”

“Your father stole it,” she interrupts gently. “Not you.”

“I benefited from it. Every year of my life, everything I had—it was paid for with money he took from families like yours.”

She shakes her head. “Honey. This has to stop. You dad has a hold on you like...” She exhales deeply. Scooting the check aside, she grabs both of my hands and squeezes tightly. “You are a separate person than your father. You don’t even look like him. You are your mother, hair to toes. You’re a good man. Stop living your life like a conman. Just because you were raised by one, doesn’t make you one.” She grabs the check and rips it in half. “I love you, Taio. Like my own son. *This must stop.*”

I inhale and exhale slowly to control the pressure of emotions. “I can’t just pretend it didn’t happen.”

“I’m not asking you to pretend. I’m asking you to let go.”

The words hit harder than I expected. I stare at the torn check on the table, at the money that suddenly feels less like restitution and more like a weight I’ve been carrying for no reason. “How?” I ask. "Tell me how."

"I wish I knew. I think it starts by letting go of the undeserved guilt. You want to know something funny?" Anne's voice softens. "When the truth came out about your dad, I thought everything was over. Richard had to go back to work after early retirement. We lost most of our savings. The extravagance that I felt we'd earned disappeared overnight. I spent months so angry I could barely function."

"You had every right to be angry."

"I did. But here's the thing." She leans forward, her eyes meeting mine with a glowing intensity. "The money being gone? It changed us. For the better."

I blink. "It did?"

"We couldn't make back what we lost, and money just became less important. Richard's home now. Really home, not just passing through between business trips. He's at every single one of Joy's volleyball games. We have dinner together every night. We talk." A small smile crosses her face. "We'd forgotten how to do that. Somewhere in the years of chasing more—more money, more status, more stuff—we'd lost each other. Losing the money forced us to find each other again."

"That's...not what I expected you to say."

"Life rarely goes the way we expect." She takes another sip of coffee. "Joy's decided to take a gap year, by the way. We sat down and talked about it. She's going to intern at a nonprofit here in the city, then attend a state school. Not because she has to—she got into NYU, you know. But because she wants to stay close. Because for the first time in years, her family feels like a family."

I don't know what to say. I came here expecting to hand over money and leave with my guilt slightly lighter. Instead, Anne is telling me that my father's theft somehow improved her life.

"I'm not saying what James did was okay," Anne adds, reading my expression. "It wasn't. He hurt a lot of people, and he deserves to be in prison. But I've made my peace with it. I've moved on. And I found the silver lining." She reaches across the table and puts her hand over mine one more time. "You need to do the same."

"I want to. But I don't know where to start."

"You start by putting that money back in your pocket. Metaphorically, of course. I sincerely hope that wasn't a cashier's check. In which case I'll fetch you some tape."

I laugh. "No, it wasn't."

The oven timer dings demandingly. Anne leaps up from the table, summoned to her baked goods. She pulls a square pan out of the oven and my head goes hazy with the rich aroma of cinnamon and butter and sugar. The last thing I ate was a slice of pizza at Charlie's pool party. I'm ravenous now.

Anne flips the pan, the square cake staying perfectly intact on the cutting board. She cuts a generous slice and serves me on a small white plate.

"I was supposed to let this cool, but I can hear your stomach growling, kid."

"Guilty," I admit.

She scuttles back to the kitchen drawers and rejoins me with a fork. Holding it out, she says, "You don't have to have all the steps. Just one at a time. First, you eat this delicious coffee cake I made from scratch, thank you very much. Second, you start thinking about what you want. Not what your dad wants. He got the prison sentence, not you, Taio. You're free. So go live your life. Not the life you think you owe people. The life you actually want."

What's the life I want? I'm not sure. But I know who I want in it.

I sink my fork into the corner of the coffee cake, watching as the crumb gives way under the tines. It's still steaming. I blow on the bite, then let it dissolve on my tongue. It's so good I almost want to cry. Anne is humming as she slices the rest of the pan, a motherly melody that I remember from sleepovers and finals week cramming. While she's distracted at the counter, I slip out my phone and pull up my texts with Charlie. I'm surprised to see a message from her—four hours ago. Somehow I missed it in the chaotic trance of late-night travel.

Charlie

I already miss you.

I type back quickly, sending my reply before I question its sappiness. Charlie needs sappy right now. Actually, so do I.

Me too. From the very moment I left you. Be back as soon as I can.

~

OTISVILLE IS A three-hour drive from the city, and I spend most of it replaying Anne's words in my head. By the time I pull into the parking lot of the satellite prison camp, I've almost convinced myself that this visit will be different. That I can tell my father about Anne, about what she said, about the possibility of letting go.

Almost.

The visitation room is the same as always—plastic chairs, vending machines, guards pretending not to listen. I find a seat and wait, watching the door where the inmates enter.

My father appears looking better than he has in months. His hair is neatly combed, his prison-issued clothes pressed and clean. He's even put on a little weight, which means the commissary money I've been sending is going to good use.

"Son." He pulls me into a hug—brief, firm, the kind of embrace that's meant to project strength rather than warmth. "You made it. I knew you couldn't let me down."

"I told you I'd be here."

"You did." He settles into the chair across from me, studying my face with that analytical gaze that's eerily close to a villain's smirk. "You look tired. Long flight?"

"Red-eye from Miami."

"Ah yes. The mysterious new job." His tone is light, but I can hear the edge underneath. "Private security, you said?"

"That's right."

"For someone important, I assume. If they're flying you around the country."

I hesitate. The smart move would be to deflect, change the subject, keep Charlie as far from this conversation as possible. But after everything today—Anne's words, the envelope still in my pocket, the strange lightness in my chest—I want to be honest.

"Yeah," I say. "Someone famous, actually."

My father's eyebrows rise. "Care to elaborate?"

"It's complicated."

"It always is." He leans back in his chair, crossing his arms. "But we have time. And I'd like to know what's keeping my son so busy he almost missed visitation for the first time in years."

Ah, the guilt trip—familiar territory. Subtle, almost affectionate, but unmistakable. He's making me feel bad about something I didn't even do. *I'm here, aren't I?* But I let it wash over me without responding.

"Her name is Charlie," I hear myself say. "Charlie Riley. She's my boss, but we're also kind of starting something...I don't know. She's incredible, really."

My father's expression flickers. Recognition. "The singer? Taio...isn't she a teenager?"

"She *was.* Five years ago." You can't really blame my dad for being out of touch. Even before he went to prison, he's not exactly Charlie's target audience.

"Huh. So you're working security for Charlie Riley. And you guys are a thing. *Wow.*" He says it slowly, like he's tasting the words. "That's quite a client. She's worth...what? A hundred million? Two hundred? Is she paying you well?"

"Dad..."

"What? It's just curiosity." He waves a hand dismissively. "But go on. You were saying it's become more than just a job?"

I move past the money comment. That's just how his brain works—always calculating, always assessing value. It doesn't mean anything.

"It started as security. Well, it started as something else entirely, but that's a long story." I take a deep breath. "The point is, I like her. A lot. I haven't had anyone since Alaina, so this is new. She's different but in a good way. She makes me feel like there's more to my life."

Silence. My father stares at me, his face unreadable. I can see him processing, sorting through implications and possibilities, trying to figure out what this information means and how it might be useful.

"More to your life," he repeats finally. "Meaning what, exactly?"

"Meaning just that. She sees me as more than...a bodyguard. She makes me happy." Well, I'm certainly not going to say escort, because we're in a prison and every word I say is likely being listened to.

The words take up residence between us. I've never said them out loud before—not to Charlie, not to Forrest, not to anyone. And now I've said them to my father, in a prison visitation room, surrounded by vending machines and plastic chairs and the distant murmur of other families having their own difficult conversations.

Maybe I'm more tired than I thought.

But something unexpected happens. My father's face softens. The analytical edge fades, replaced by, possibly, genuine warmth. His eyes get a little shiny, and he blinks rapidly like he's fighting back emotion.

"Taio." He leans forward, elbows on his knees. "That's wonderful."

"You think so?"

"Of course I think so. You've been alone for too long. Ever since you dumped Alaina—"

"She dumped me, Dad," I correct him.

"Same difference."

I'm so tired of him rewriting this narrative. "No, it's not. I bought a ring for her. She left me because you stole her family's wealth. I just want to be clear."

He glares at me for a while, angry that I brought up the storyline he hates—the truth. "Well, either way, Alaina was a shit friend. This Charlie girl sounds much better."

"Based on what?"

"She's rich for starters. You made a good choice there." He laughs, but I don't see the humor in it. "I'm kidding, Taio. Tell me about her," he continues. "What's she like?"

I hesitate, waiting for the catch—the manipulation, the angle, the way he'll twist this information to serve his own purposes. But he just looks at me, expectant and somewhat pensive.

"She's chaos," I say finally. "She's messy and impulsive and she says whatever she's thinking without filtering it first. She can't dance to save her life, but she sings like her whole heart is trying to escape through her throat. She's terrified of being seen and desperate to be known, and she doesn't realize those are the same thing. She's this enigma that I can't stop thinking about."

Dad's smiling now—a real smile, not the calculated one he uses in negotiations. "You've got it bad, kid."

"Yeah." I exhale. "I really do."

"And does she feel the same way?"

My fingers rake through my hair, catching on the tangles I've neglected since yesterday's flight. "I think so. It's complicated. Her world is a lot. Paparazzi, publicists, fake relationships for PR. She's got this whole machinery around her designed to control her image, and I don't know how I fit into that. Or if I even can."

"What do you mean, fake relationships?"

"She has a public boyfriend. Some actor. It's all for show; their teams arranged it to manage their images or whatever. But from the outside, it looks real." I shake my head. "That's the world she lives in. Everything is performance. Everything is strategic."

"And where does that leave you?"

"On the outside, mostly. Hidden. We don't exactly run in the same social circles. She has her celebrity life and I have my..." I search my brain trying to remember what my dad thinks I do for a living. "Gym trainer buddies?"

My father is quiet for a moment, processing. "That must be difficult. Being with someone who can't acknowledge you publicly."

Okay, that was smooth sailing. Apparently he still believes I'm a personal trainer.

"It's fine."

"Is it?" He quirks an eyebrow. "Because it sounds like you're describing exactly the kind of relationship that would make you feel used. Like she's embarrassed of you."

The observation slices closer than I'd like. "I don't think she's embarrassed of me. And yes, this is messy and complicated, but she's worth it. More than worth it."

My father nods slowly. "Then you try. You fight for it. That's what we do, Taio. What I've always taught you. We don't give up on the things that matter."

The irony of receiving relationship advice from the man who destroyed his own marriage isn't lost on me. But there's something genuine in his voice—something that sounds like the father I remember from childhood, before everything went wrong.

"I need to keep this quiet for now," I add. "The public doesn't know, and if it got out..." I shake my head. "It would be a whole thing."

"Of course. I understand completely." He mimes zipping his lips. "Your secret is safe with me. No one to talk to in solitary confinement."

I groan and point to the wall over his shoulder. "Dad, there's literally a potluck signup on the wall over there. You're not in solitary confinement."

We talk for another hour—about the lawyers, about the case developments I've been tracking. For once, he doesn't ask about Mom, or insist he's innocent. He just listens. Asks questions. Acts interested in my life.

"What about that cat?" he asks at one point. "Where's he while you're gallivanting around Miami?"

"He goes with us, believe it or not. Traveling cat. Right now, he's with Charlie, while I'm here. She's been taking care of him."

"You left your cat with her?" His eyebrows rise. "That serious huh?"

"Well, he's not *my cat.*"

"Whose cat is it?"

I'm getting really tired of explaining this, mostly because it doesn't make sense. "It's not the point. All I mean to say is I trust Charlie."

I hadn't really thought about it consciously, but leaving Black Cat with Charlie felt natural in a way it shouldn't have. Like I already trusted her too much, and assumed we were this cat-parenting team. Is that a good sign or bad?

"The cat likes her more than me I think," I admit.

"He's not the only one." My father grins. "Go on, tell me more. What's her family like? Does she have siblings?"

I talk about Claire—the pregnancy, her naming the baby Charlotte, the way Charlie's face lit up when she told me. I tell him about the dancers and how Charlie gave them the spotlight. About the blanket fort and the Rotel dip and the way she looked at me when she fell asleep with her head on my chest.

I don't tell him everything, obviously. Some things are private. But I tell him enough, and he listens with what seems like genuine interest.

It's nice. Suspiciously nice.

But I push that thought away. Maybe Anne was right. Maybe it's time to stop looking for the worst in people—even people who've given me plenty of reason to expect it. It feels good to just talk. And by the end of the visitation, I realized I've probably shared way too much.

"Dad, I really mean it. You can't tell anyone. Not the lawyers, not your friends in here, nobody. Charlie's whole world is delicate, and I don't want her business to get out and put her through hell—"

"Taio." He puts his hand over his heart, expression wounded.

"I would never betray your confidence like that. You're my son. Your happiness matters more to me than anything."

And God, do I want to believe him. *I almost do.*

When visitation ends, my father hugs me again. Longer this time. Tighter. He pats my back twice, the way he used to when I was a kid and he was sending me off to school.

"I'm proud of you, son," he says quietly. "I love you."

"Thanks, Dad."

"See you in two weeks?"

"Dad," I say, dropping my gaze to my shoes. "The upcoming tour dates are tight. It's hard to get back here between the shows. And Charlie needs me with her—"

"Taio," my dad says, stern-faced, arms crossed over his chest. "I'll see you in two weeks," he reiterates. "End of story. Family sticks together. Don't let some girl muddle what's most important, okay?"

Some girl? Wow, how quickly that perspective changed.

"I'll do what I can."

He holds up his hand before the guard escorts him out of the room.

I walk out of the prison feeling lighter in a way. The sky is gray and heavy with the threat of snow, the parking lot slicked with melting ice, but inside, I feel almost warm. Hopeful, even. A feeling I'd nearly forgotten how to have. Maybe it was the admission. Telling my dad I'm falling for someone. Maybe he can learn to respect that. As much as I have to let him go, he has to learn to let me go too.

I get in the rental car and start the long drive toward the city, toward the airport, toward a flight that will take me back to Miami and the woman I can't stop thinking about. I'm already composing the text I'll send her when I land. Something sweet. Something that lets her know she's been on my mind every minute we've been apart.

I'm so caught up in this unfamiliar optimism that I'm halfway to the airport before I notice my phone buzzing with a call from

Rina.

And just like that, everything changes again.

Chapter 20
Taio

Please tell me you're at the world's quietest airport.

"Taio. I'm glad I caught you."

Rina's voice is clipped, professional—the tone she uses when something important is happening. I pull over into a gas station parking lot, not trusting myself to have this conversation while navigating New York traffic.

"What's going on? Is everything okay with the agency?" I'm always worried my sudden exposure could have consequences for Rina and the team.

"The agency's fine. We're all enjoying your new headlines." A hint of amusement creeps into her voice. "Something about a thirst-trap bodyguard?"

I groan. "Please tell me you didn't see those."

"I saw all of them. I am your biggest cyberstalker. My favorite was the Twitter thread comparing your jawline to various Greek statues. Very thorough research." She pauses. "I have to say, when you told me you needed this sabbatical, I didn't expect you to end up on TMZ."

"That makes two of us."

"How is the pop star treating you? Everything going okay with the assignment?"

There's genuine concern beneath the teasing. Rina's always looked out for me, ever since I stumbled into the agency years ago, desperate and ashamed and looking for any way to pay off my father's debts. She gave me a chance when no one else would.

"It's good. She's good. Actually, that's kind of an understatement, but—"

"Save it." I can hear her smiling. "I can tell from all the pictures. You look at her like she hung the moon. It's cute."

"Like a manly cute though, right?"

"No. Not remotely. But that's not why I called." Her tone shifts, taking on an urgency I haven't heard before. "This is about your father."

My stomach tightens. "What about him?"

She takes a breath. "Something came across my desk a couple days ago. Some of my attorney friends spreading the usual drama. But a name stuck out to me."

"What name?"

"Bryan Wright. The forensic accountant who testified about the fund transfers. The one whose documentation was the cornerstone of the prosecution's case."

"I remember him." Wright had been devastating on the stand—calm, authoritative, armed with spreadsheets and bank records that made my father look guilty beyond any reasonable doubt. His testimony was what sealed the conviction.

"He's been caught falsifying evidence in three other federal cases over the past eighteen months. Major scandal. The DOJ is reviewing every case he ever touched."

I stop breathing for a moment. "What?"

"He was being paid off to cover up some bigger corporate scandals. He was purposely cherry-picking data, ignoring exculpatory evidence, drawing conclusions that weren't supported by the actual numbers." Rina's words come faster now, tumbling over each other. "Taio, if his testimony in your father's case was based on the same faulty analysis—"

"Then the conviction might not hold."

"It's grounds for appeal, at minimum. Potentially a new trial. And if the documentation he provided was fraudulent..." She trails off, letting me fill in the implications.

A new trial. The possibility of a reduced sentence. Maybe even release, with time served.

My dad could get out.

My body reacts before my mind can catch up—lungs forgetting how to work, fingers going numb against the steering wheel. I'm drowning in contradictions: part of me wants to call my father immediately, another part wants to throw the phone out the window and drive until I hit ocean.

"Taio? You still there?"

"Yeah. Yeah, I'm here." I drag my palm across my stubbled jaw, desperate for clarity that won't come. "What do I do with this information?"

The line goes quiet. The kind of quiet that makes you check if the call dropped.

"Rina?"

"I'm here." She sighs, and there's something heavy in it. "Taio, I need to be honest with you about something. And I need you to hear it as someone who cares about you, not as a judgment."

"Okay..."

"I've spent a lot of time with these case files. I know what your father was convicted of. I know the scope of it—the families he hurt, the lives he destroyed, the way he manipulated everyone around him for years." Another pause, and when she speaks again, her voice is careful. *Gentle.* "I think he's exactly where he should be."

Her words hollow me out from the inside.

"Rina—"

"I know. I know he's your father. I know you love him. And I'm not saying you shouldn't—family is complicated, and you don't get to choose who you're related to. But listen, your father is a grown man who made choices. Bad choices. Choices that hurt a lot of people, including you. And I think...I think sometimes the most loving thing you can do for someone is let them face the consequences of their actions. Even when it's hard. Even when it hurts. As far as the information I just gave you, I couldn't withhold that from you. But we can pretend this conversation didn't happen if you want."

Through the windshield, I watch strangers move through the gas station lot—a woman laughing into her phone, a man wrestling with a map, a teenager counting coins for a soda—all of them blissfully unaware that my entire world is being rewritten in real time.

"You think I shouldn't pursue an appeal."

"I think that's not my decision to make." The phone line crackles with her deliberate pause. "I'm simply telling you how I see it. What you do with this information is up to you. I'll support you either way."

"But you don't think he deserves to get out."

A long pause. "No. I don't. I think he's a man who's never faced a real consequence in his life, and prison is the first time anyone's told him no. I think if he gets out, he'll find new ways to manipulate, new people to hurt, new schemes to run. Because that's who he is." She exhales. "But I also know that's a terrible thing to say to someone about their father. And I'm sorry if it hurts."

It does hurt. It hurts like hell. But beneath the sting, I feel my shoulders drop a fraction, as if someone's finally lifted a weight I'd been pretending wasn't there. She's voiced the thought I've been swallowing down every time it rises to the surface—the dangerous idea that's been hiding in the corners of my mind during every prison visit.

Did Dad get what he deserved?

"I don't know what to do," I admit. "Part of me wants to pretend you never called. Just let his lawyers put two and two together if they stumble upon it. Maybe that's destiny? Let it happen without my involvement."

"You could do that."

"But I can't, can I? Because now I know. And *not* acting is still a choice."

"True." Rina's voice is sad. "That's the real bitch of it."

I sit there for a long moment, watching life unfold around me. A woman at the next pump curses under her breath as the nozzle sticks, while her toddler performs a slow-motion jailbreak from his car seat. Their frustrations seem so beautifully uncomplicated. What I wouldn't give to wrestle a stubborn gas pump and a squirming kid versus make the decision on whether or not to save my dad.

Backward or forward?

Right or wrong?

I don't know. But it's time to decide.

"Can you forward the information to his legal team?" I regret the decision the moment the words leave my mouth. "As soon as you can."

"Are you sure?"

"No." I laugh, but there's no humor in it. "I'm not sure about anything. But he's my father. And if there's a legitimate flaw in his conviction, he deserves to have it examined. Whatever I think about whether he should be in prison...that's not my call to make. That's what courts are for."

"Okay." Rina doesn't argue, doesn't push back. Just accepts my decision. "I'll send everything to Bradley Castellano this afternoon. He goes to Sean's weekly poker games." There's a bitter edge to her tone anytime Rina brings up her ex-husband. "I'll make sure they move quick."

"Thank you. And, Rina?"

"Yeah?"

"Thank you for being honest with me. Even when it's hard to hear."

"Always, Taio. Now go back to your pop star. I can't wait to hear more about your life through the gossip columns."

"Quit looking me up, Rina."

Her laughter ripples through the phone, earnest and rich. "No promises."

I sit in the parking lot for another ten minutes, trying to

figure out who I am and what I want.

Then I start the car and drive back to the city.

I can't fly to Miami tonight. There's too much to figure out. The lawyers are going to want to meet, likely to discuss an increased fee. An appeal? A potential whole new trial? *Shit.* That was hell the first time. Now we're begging to do it again. *But if it means his freedom*...I don't have a choice here.

I wrench the wheel around and head back to my apartment, where stale air and a layer of neglect wait to welcome me home.

It's almost midnight when I finally get home and call her.

She answers on the first ring, which means she was waiting. Probably staring at her phone the way I've been staring at mine, both of us orbiting each other across a thousand miles of empty space.

"Hey, you." Her voice is soft, sleepy, relieved. "I was starting to think you fell off the planet."

"Sorry. It's been a day." I sink onto my couch, suddenly exhausted. The apartment feels emptier than usual without Black Cat judging me from his perch on the bookshelf.

"Please tell me you're at the world's quietest airport," Charlie says sullenly.

I exhale. "I'm at my apartment. Missed my flight. I can't come back tonight."

"Dammit, Taio," she grouches out. "Okay, you know what? Let's just clear the air right here and right now. You're mad at me and you're punishing me."

"I'm doing no such thing."

"Then why'd you run away? The family emergency excuse was flimsy to begin with, and now you're not coming back? Look...I want to go on dates with you. In public. I want everyone to know how you make me feel but I need time. I can't just flip the entire script of my life overnight. And it's a little unfair for you to ask me to have all the solutions at once, because this is new for me too and—"

"*Tweety, stop.* I didn't run away. I...came back for visiting hours with my dad."

"Oh. Well...is he okay? Why did you say it was an emergency?"

"Because I didn't want you to think less of me. Running home because Daddy demanded it. I don't want you to think of me as a pushover. Charlie, nobody who knows my dad thinks I should have a relationship with him. I find myself hiding my loyalty sometimes, just to avoid a lecture."

"Oh, Taio. *He's your dad.* I can understand that. It's normal to love your parents fiercely. It's just hard when you grow up and suddenly you're the one protecting them. Or at least, you're protecting the version of them that you treasure the most."

"Hmm," I say, nestling deeper into my worn couch. "Are you talking about your mom?"

"Yeah. And I promise you this, Taio—if my mom were alive, the fact that I'm the product of an affair, or that she lied, or that she kept me away from my dad...would melt away. If she were here, nobody could keep me from her. I'd talk to her every day. I'd defend her against the world. We're not really in control of it."

"Right. Hardwired into our DNA or something?"

"Remember the night in New York, when you told me it was okay to be mad at my mom but I could still love her?"

"Yeah, I remember."

"You may have to take your own advice. It's okay to be mad at your dad, Taio. It's also okay to love him."

I exhale into the phone, feeling a small smile form despite everything. "Listen to you, all wise and centered. When did we switch roles? I'm supposed to be the one with all the emotional clarity."

"Well, that's the power of a Mel Robbins audiobook on double speed. I can't exactly make out what she's saying at this rate, but the words subconsciously saturate, you know?"

A soft laugh escapes me. The line goes quiet after that, but there's nothing awkward about it. Just a gentle calm between us. I close my eyes and focus on the sound of her breathing, steady and intimate across the miles, collapsing the distance for just a moment.

"What are you doing right now?" she finally asks.

"Staring at the wall trying to figure out my life."

"That sounds productive."

"Extremely. I've got the wall memorized now. Every crack, every scuff mark. We're intimate."

"Should I be jealous of this wall?"

"Absolutely. It's a very attractive wall."

Her laughter ripples through the phone, and the tightness in my chest finally uncoils. It's like taking the first deep breath after being underwater too long.

"So how come you can't come back?"

"Just delayed. I'm coming back to you. I promise."

She hums into the phone. "Say that again."

"I'm coming back to you. I promise," I repeat obediently, making each word deliberate and weighted. Each syllable feels like a vow, like something I can anchor myself to in all this uncertainty.

"Good. Then why are you delayed?"

"There's new evidence that might help my dad's case. Rina found it and forwarded it to his legal team. Now they want to meet with me tomorrow to discuss next steps."

"That's good, right? New evidence?"

"I guess." I stare at the ceiling, trying to find the words. "The evidence suggests the guy who testified against my dad might have falsified some of his analysis. Which means there could be grounds for appeal. Maybe a new trial."

"Taio, that's huge."

"I know."

"So why do you sound like someone just told you your dog died?"

Because Rina thinks he deserves to stay in prison. Because part of me agrees with her. Because I don't know if I want my father free or if I just feel like I should want it.

"I don't know how to feel about it," I admit. "I mean, am I his son or his enabler?"

Charlie is quiet for a moment. I hear rustling, like she's settling deeper into her plush bed.

"Tell me what you're actually feeling," she presses. "Not what you think you should feel. What's actually going on in your head?"

So I spill it all out like water through a broken dam. How Rina dug up dirt on Wright that could blow the case wide open. How the appeal might actually happen now. Then my voice drops lower as I admit the rest—how Rina thinks Dad deserves every minute behind those bars, how sometimes I catch myself wondering if she's right. The knot in my stomach when I think about sitting through another trial, watching those families glare at me from across the courtroom. The way I hate myself for not being the loyal son I should be, for feeling so damn tired of carrying his mistakes on my back.

Charlie listens without interrupting, which is unusual for her. When I finally run out of words, she's quiet for a long moment.

"Wow," she says finally. "That's...a relief."

"What?"

"I mean I felt like our emotional baggage was pretty mismatched in this relationship. But you just laid a lot of cards on the table. It's good. Now, I'm not just a taker. See? That's a lot of heavy stuff, Taio. Now I can be here for you too."

"This relationship, huh? And how would you define our relationship?"

"Budding," she says. "Hopefully."

"Oh, I think we're definitely budding." The relief of confession gives way to a different kind of tension. I picture Charlie in my apartment, wrapped in nothing but my stolen shirt, and suddenly the miles between us feel like a physical ache. My fingers twitch with the memory of her skin.

"So, tell me, are you in a Tweety shirt, or in that sexy black lingerie?"

"You know the answer to that, Taio."

"Tweety shirt. Got it."

"Actually, Elmer Fudd tonight."

"For shame, Charlie. Wearing another man while I'm over here missing you? Bad girl."

"I'll make it up to you when you come back. I'm not letting you out of my sight for at least a week. Just so you know. You're going to be so sick of me."

"Impossible."

"We'll see." She chuckles.

"How about you make it up to me right now?"

The question catches her off guard. "What? How?"

"Are you alone?" My voice drops, taking on a playful edge.

"Yes," she answers hesitantly.

"Where are you?"

"In the blanket fort," she admits. "I live here now. I have a forwarding address if you're interested."

"Cute," I say.

"I'm going to be sad when housekeeping rips it down. We head to Tampa tomorrow night."

"I'll build you a fort everywhere we go. I promise."

Silence.

"Charlie, you still there?"

"Yeah, I'm here. I'm just swooning."

I laugh lightly. "Well, take your time, I'll be here."

"Taio?"

"Yeah?"

"I really like you." Her voice has gone soft, almost fragile. "In a way I feel like I'm not in control of. You've been in love before. Does it feel overwhelming all the time?"

"Overwhelming?"

"We haven't known each other long. Why can't I remember a time when I wasn't thinking about you?"

"What do you think about?"

She laughs. "Nonsense. It's embarrassing. I don't want to tell you."

"Well, in that case, definitely tell me."

"You first," she commands. "Secret for a secret, right? Better make it juicy if you really want to know what I think about when it comes to you."

I breathe into the phone, nervous about what she'll inevitably pull out of me. "What secret do you want to know?"

"Have you ever fallen for a client before? Has sex ever turned into feelings for you?"

"Charlie...there's no good way to answer that question."

"How about with the truth?" she challenges.

"I've only fallen in love once, so no, in that regard, I've never fallen for a client. But there's always feelings when it comes to sex. Sometimes those feelings are friendship, protectiveness, or plain curiosity. But when you have sex...you should feel something. It bothers you, doesn't it?"

"I'm not jealous of your clients, Taio," Charlie says. "I'm a little jealous of Alaina."

"Why?" I ask thickly. As if I don't know.

"Because I know she was your first love...your first everything. I know she hurt you but she'll always have that spot in your heart. The way you'll always have a spot in mine."

I know we didn't go all the way, but in Charlie's mind, we've already shared something so sacred and intimate. It was a big deal. I should've stayed that night. Instead, I ran home when my dad insisted. *Fuck.* Things need to change. One scary admission at a time.

"You might not be my first, Charlie, but I have a feeling you're something much bigger." She could be the last woman I ever love. But that's not something you say over the phone. Instead, I let myself sink into the unfamiliar warmth spreading through my chest—this feeling I thought I'd never have again. For once, the weight of my past feels lighter than the pull of my future. For once, I have something I'm not willing to lose. "Now, your turn. What do you think about when it comes to me?"

"I think maybe my mom wasn't totally full of shit."

I laugh at her crassness. "What?"

"Love seems...worth waiting for. That's all. But I'm not saying anything else because I would surely scare you away."

"Doubt it. Try me..."

But she holds something back, guarding her heart with the careful restraint of someone who's read one too many articles about scaring men away with too much honesty too soon. "Black Cat sneezed and scared himself so badly he fell off the couch. It was comedic gold and you missed it."

"I'm devastated."

"You should be. It was a top-ten cat moment." A pause. "He misses you too, by the way. He keeps sitting in your spot in the fort and staring at the door like he's waiting for you."

"Tell him I'll be back soon."

Charlie's voice softens as she addresses the cat. "Hear that, you little chonk? Daddy's coming back soon and then you'll be restricted to two meals a day instead of the four I've been spoiling you with." There's a faint meow in the background—that distinctive raspy sound Black Cat makes when he's mildly inconvenienced. I can almost picture his glowing eyes narrowing to slits, his midnight coat puffed slightly at the spine, tail twitching in what could either be contentment or the prelude to a playful swat at Charlie's hand.

"Four meals?"

I smile despite everything, letting her voice wash over me. Even her rambling about the cat feels like medicine—something to soothe the raw places the day has left behind.

"What are you wearing right now?" I ask, then immediately backtrack. "Wait, that sounded like a line. I genuinely just want to picture you. The full scene."

She laughs. "Elmer Fudd shirt, as established. Fuzzy socks with little avocados on them. Hair in what can only be described as a chaos bun. No makeup. Probably some chip crumbs on my shirt from stress-eating earlier."

"You're beautiful."

"I literally just described a gremlin."

"Rose-colored glasses, baby. All I picture is perfection."

"Smooth." But I can hear her smiling. "What about you? Paint me a picture."

I look down at myself. "Jeans I've been wearing for two days. A T-shirt that's seen better decades. I haven't shaved since I left Miami, so I'm rocking what can generously be called 'scruff' and realistically called 'homeless chic.'"

"Hot."

"Really?"

"I mean, I'm picturing it, and yeah. It's kind of working for me. Is that weird to find your disheveled exhaustion attractive?"

"Concerning, maybe, but flattering."

We fall into easy silence again. I can hear her breathing, soft and steady, and I close my eyes and pretend she's here—curled up on the couch beside me, her head on my shoulder, both of us too tired to move but too content to care.

"Taio?"

"Hmm?"

"When you come back..." She trails off, and I hear a shift in her voice. A new vulnerability. "I want all of it. With you."

"Sex?"

"That too. But *all of it*. Is your heart available, too?"

"For you it is." I smile into the phone, the tension in my jaw releasing for the first time all day, the corners of my mouth lifting so wide they almost hurt. The screen grows warm against my cheek as I listen to her breathe. "We can try. You mean exclusive, right?"

She's quiet.

"Tweety, if you're nodding, I can't see you."

"Oh," she squeaks. "Yes, exclusive. Is that even possible? Can you stay with me for the tour instead of going back to—"

"Escorting?"

"Yeah. Just while we're dating. Which hopefully isn't short, but also—"

"Charlie, just ask for what you want."

She lets out a deep breath. "You to myself. I want you to myself."

"So you don't want your boyfriend sleeping with his clients?" I suck the air in between my teeth. "Tricky, tricky."

"Yeah. Faithfulness would be preferable," she deadpans.

"Coming from the girl who's actually dating another man."

"*Fake dating*," she says in a tone that makes me picture Forrest's daughter, Koda, in the middle of an indignant tantrum. "He's coming to the Tampa show, by the way."

"Oh good. Can't wait to meet him," I say dryly.

"It's just for the tour, Taio. It'll be over soon."

"Right." I nod along, jaw clenched so tight I can feel a muscle twitching beneath my skin. Every cell in my body rejects the idea of her with another man, even for show. My fingers grip the phone until they ache. But I swallow the jealousy burning like acid in my throat because Charlie's peace matters more than the primal voice inside screaming that she's mine.

"I guess it's not fair of me to ask you to quit your job when I still have to do mine."

"You don't have to ask, Charlie. I've been thinking about other things I can do. Actually, I've been thinking about asking Forrest a little more about the publishing industry. I have a minor in literature, believe it or not. He's on the agent side which isn't for me, but I was thinking I could get into editing. I read his girlfriend's Sora's early drafts and she says it's really helpful. I don't know if there's a lot of money in it, but there's a lot of joy."

"Taio...that's amazing. And such a good fit for you. How long have you been thinking about that?"

"Unofficially, since Forrest fell in love and moved out. More officially since we met."

"Yeah?"

"Yeah."

Her laugh floats through the phone, soft and warm as honey

in sunlight. "You've got it bad for me, Taio. Don't you try to deny it."

"It's not a secret." I smile back, picturing her—those lips that curve into a perfect Cupid's bow when she's pleased with herself, eyes the color of sunshine-filled blue skies, wide and expressive, framed by those unruly lashes she's always batting at me when she wants something. I can almost see the tiny freckle at the corner of her mouth that I've memorized like a secret constellation. She reminds me of all my favorite romance books rolled into one. She's all the best parts.

"When I get back, how about neither of us sleeps alone anymore?"

"That sounds really nice." She yawns, the sound muffled like she's trying to hide it. "Sorry. It's not you. It's just been a long day of rehearsals and emotional processing."

"You should sleep."

"I don't want to hang up."

"Then don't." I walk to my bedroom, turning off the hallway light as I pass. "Stay on with me. I'll be here when you wake up."

"You need sleep too."

"I'll sleep. We'll sleep together. Separately. You know what I mean."

She laughs softly. "Phone sleeping. Very modern romance."

"We're trendsetters."

More rustling on her end. I picture her burrowing into the blanket fort, pulling the covers up to her chin, Black Cat curled against her side. God, how I wish I was there.

"Taio?" Her voice is muzzy now, sleep pulling at the edges.

"Yeah?"

But her breathing has already started to even out, the slow rhythm of someone slipping under.

"Charlie?"

Nothing. Just soft, steady breaths.

I stay on the line for a long time, listening to her sleep, wondering what she was trying to tell me.

“Goodnight, Tweety,” I whisper to her sleeping breath. “I’m coming back soon. I promise.”

Chapter 21

Charlie

Win or lose, we still feast on tuna tonight. -Black Cat

I must've paced a mile by now. My legs are tired, I'm a little breathless, and I'm burning precious energy I should be saving for the stage.

Tampa's dressing room outshines Miami's in every way—mirrors that don't distort, lights that flatter instead of interrogate, a pristine couch unmarked by mascara-streaked breakdowns. I should feel at ease here, but my reflection stares back with wide eyes as I check my watch again.

Thirty minutes left.

I've done this so many times I should feel prepared. But tonight is different. Risky. The stakes have never been this high. We're attempting choreography we've only run through a handful of times. My dancers have solos that could launch or sink them. And my voice—my actual, unprocessed voice—will have nowhere to hide.

And in attendance? The critics, waiting to declare Miami a lucky accident.

I pause, fixing my sights on the giant mirror above the counter still riddled with the glam team's supplies. My hands are shaking as I reach for the familiar wooden box on my vanity—it's time to participate in the familiar pre-show ritual. My mother's words and warning, responsible for fueling all of my confidence, and eliminating my self-doubt. It's such a heavy burden for paper to hold.

I flip open the lid and freeze.

There are new notes inside. Folded white paper, crisp and fresh, tucked among the faded hearts like they've always belonged there.

You don't need these notes to carry you. The spark is inside you. Believe in your own magic.

Like a frenzied shark, I attack the next square note.

Win or lose, we still feast on tuna tonight. —Black Cat

I laugh despite myself, the sound wet and wobbly. When did Taio find time to do this?

The third note is just a single line:

You don't need to earn their love. You already have it. We're all just here to watch you shine.

The fourth:

Black Cat says break a leg. I told him that's a weird thing to say to someone you supposedly love, but he insisted.

And the fifth, tucked at the very bottom:

I'm right here with you. You're never alone.

—Your Taio

Your Taio.

I clutch the notes to my sternum, each inhale a battle against the knot forming beneath my collarbone. Taio must have planted these little paper lifelines before his flight, slipping them into my sacred box when my back was turned, certain they'd find me at my most vulnerable moment.

God, this man. He's the stuff of fairy tales.

I grab my phone and call him before I can talk myself out of it.

He answers on the second ring. "Hey, you. Shouldn't you be getting ready?"

"I found your notes."

A pause. Then, softer: "Yeah?"

"They're perfect. You're perfect. I just—" My voice cracks embarrassingly. "Thank you."

"You don't have to thank me. I just wanted you to know I'm thinking about you." He sounds tired. More than tired—exhausted in a bone-deep way that makes me want to fly to New York and wrap myself around him until he remembers how to rest. "I'm so sorry I'm not there."

"It's okay. Tell me what's happening with your dad."

"Charlie, you have a huge performance. *In minutes.* Let's stay focused."

I collapse into the plush velvet chair in front of the mirror, my reflection wavering as I settle. The pacing stops, but my knee immediately picks up the rhythm, bouncing against the underside of the vanity with a soft thud-thud-thud that matches my racing pulse.

"No, definitely distract me right now. What's going on with the lawyers?"

He sighs. "They've got me going through boxes of financial records. Years of transactions. They need me to identify which ones Wright's testimony specifically covered, because apparently I'm the only one who can explain where the money went on our end. I've been highlighting bank statements for days now." Another sigh, heavier this time. "It's taking so much longer than expected. My dad keeps finding reasons for me to stay for 'one more meeting' or 'one more review session.' I don't know what's legitimate and what's him just...wanting me here."

"He's nervous."

"So nervous. And desperate. If this appeal doesn't go through, I don't think he's going to recover." I hear the frustration in his voice, the guilt. "I wanted to be there tonight, Charlie. You have no idea how much."

"Hey." I keep my tone firm but gentle. "It's okay. You need to get this sorted out. I understand. And I have backup security—"

"That's not why I'm sad to miss it." His voice drops. "I wanted to support you. I want to be close."

My heart does something complicated in my chest. "I know. But you'll be in Atlanta next week, right? It's two back-to-back nights."

"I'll be there. I swear it."

"Good. Now tell me to have a killer show so I can go have a killer show."

"Have a killer show, Tweety." I can hear him smiling. "I'll be watching the hashtags. Make them lose their minds."

"That's the plan."

"And, Charlie?"

"Yeah?"

"Thank you for calling." He stops. Clears his throat. "Thank you for thinking about me."

My pulse stutters. "I'm always thinking about you, Taio Wilkes. See you on the other side, babe."

There's a pause, then: "Did you just call me 'babe'?"

I bite my lip, wincing at my own boldness. "Sorry—was that weird? I was just trying it on for size..."

A warm chuckle vibrates through the phone, his voice dropping to a register I've never heard before. "I've never been *babe* before," he says softly. "I like it."

I don't care if he can hear my sigh of relief. The scales between us still feel uneven. There's me, obsessing over his texts at three in the morning, analyzing every inflection in his voice. Then there's him, caring in that steady, measured way that normal, experienced people do. I catch myself sometimes, reel back the spiral of thoughts that threatens to consume me. But maybe that's what happens when you fall for someone for the first time. Maybe it's supposed to feel like...well, falling. Totally out of control.

"Well, okay, *babe*. I'll call you after," I manage. "With a full report."

"I'll be waiting."

The call ends, and I remain still, clutching the phone against my chest alongside his notes. My stomach still twists with that familiar serpent of stage fright, but beneath the cold knot of fear, a small flame of comfort has kindled—steady, warm, refusing to be extinguished.

I'm not alone. Even when he's not here, I'm not alone.

A knock on the door. "Showtime, Charlie!"

I tuck Taio's notes carefully back into the box, right on top where I can see them. Then I check my reflection one last time—sparkly bodysuit, hair teased to perfection, makeup that could best a hurricane...and then I head for the wings guided by the stadium's security team.

Time to give them a show.

The roar of the crowd hits me like a physical force.

Tens of thousands of people packed into the Tampa arena, a sea of waving phone lights and homemade signs bobbing above upstretched arms. The screaming hits me in waves—piercing shrieks that make my eardrums vibrate, then deeper roars that I feel in my chest cavity. The energy is electric, crackling through the air like lightning about to strike, leaving the taste of metal on my tongue. I can feel it in my bones, that familiar pre-show tremor that starts in my knees and radiates outward, making my fingertips tingle and my stomach clench no matter how many times I do this.

Devon appears at my elbow, already bouncing on his feet. Sweat glistens on his forehead—he's been warming up the dancers, running through the new formations one last time. "You ready?"

"No."

"Perfect. Neither are we." He grins. "Let's do this anyway."

The opening notes of "Hypnotic" thunder through the speakers, bass so deep I feel it in my ribs, and I take a breath, and step into the light.

The first thirty seconds are terrifying. At first I feel like an out-of-place marionette, not sure what strings to pull. I'm doing a lot *less* on stage. Without the intricate dance sequences I usually hide behind, I feel exposed. Naked, almost. Like the audience can see every flaw, every insecurity, every reason I don't deserve to be on this stage.

My earpiece crackles with the stage manager's voice, calling cues, none of them belonging to me. The lights are blinding. The crowd is a faceless mass of noise and heat. I start to drift away.

And then something shifts.

My vocals go silent as they are scheduled to, and Devon and Mia execute their first partner sequence—a lift that ends with Mia spinning through the air like she's defying gravity—and the crowd loses their minds. I hear the gasp ripple through the arena, the surge of cheers that follows, and suddenly I'm not the center of attention anymore. I'm part of something bigger. Part of a team.

The weight on my shoulders lightens. I find my mark and start singing. Really singing. I toggle between hyperfocusing on perfect pitch and letting myself get lost in the artful riffs. My voice is strong and confident. I can put my breath behind every single note because I'm no longer flailing across the stage. I'm actually proud of this performance.

It's the most alive I've felt on stage in years.

The crowd surges with me, rising and falling like a tide. Thousands of voices blend into mine until I can't tell where my sound ends and theirs begins—a vast, living organism with one heartbeat, one breath.

The set unfolds like a dream. Song after song, the dancers take their moments. During "Gravity," Jasmine performs a contemporary solo that tells the story of the song better than my lyrics ever could—all reaching arms and controlled falls and the kind of raw emotion that makes people forget to breathe. I watch from my platform at the back of the stage, voice steady on the mic, heart full to bursting.

When she finishes, the applause is deafening. I see tears on faces in the front rows. I see people clutching each other, moved in ways they didn't expect to be.

This. This is what I wanted. I needed something to get excited about again. I needed the people I inspire to inspire me right back.

Kenny's hip-hop breakdown during "Burn It Down" gets the entire arena on their feet. The energy shifts from emotional to electric, twenty thousand people bouncing as one, the floor literally shaking beneath my feet. I abandon my mark and just dance with the crowd, laughing, pointing at fans who are going absolutely feral, feeding off their energy until I'm sure I could run a marathon.

Marcus—*dancer Marcus*—pulls off a gravity-defying backflip sequence that earns actual screams. Mia and Devon's tango interlude is so sensual, people in the audience literally fan themselves. Every single dancer has their moment, their spotlight, their chance to show the world what they can do.

And somehow, impossibly, the show is better for it. I'm better for it. Freed from the pressure of carrying every second on my own shoulders, I can actually enjoy performing. I can connect with the audience instead of just surviving for them.

By the time we hit the final number, I'm drenched in sweat and my voice is starting to fray at the edges and I don't care. I belt the last chorus with everything I have, the dancers moving around me in perfect synchronization, the crowd singing along so loud I can barely hear myself.

The spark is inside you. Believe in your own magic.

Taio's note echoes in my head, and I scan the front rows until I find her—a teenage girl with bright purple hair, tears streaming down her face, screaming every word like they're keeping her alive. She's wearing a homemade T-shirt with my face on it, but it's not the polished promotional image. It's a candid shot—me at the piano in Miami, mid-song, eyes closed, completely lost in the music.

She made that. For me. Because that moment meant something to her.

I sing directly to her for the final verse, watching her face transform with the realization that I'm looking at her, seeing her, connecting with her across the chaos and the lights and the noise. Her hands fly to her mouth. She turns to her friend, pointing, disbelieving. When I wink at her, she literally crumples, knees giving out, caught by the people around her.

In her eyes, I see why I'm still on this stage after all these years. Not the billboards or bank accounts or headlines that fade by morning—but this silent conversation between two strangers who might never meet again. Her tears tell me she heard exactly what I needed someone to hear when I wrote those lyrics at 3 a.m., alone in my apartment with only a piano for company.

I want to be that girl again. Write new songs. Make new connections. Believe in something so much bigger than myself.

The song ends. The crowd explodes. Confetti cannons fire, showering the arena in glittering paper. I take my bow, chest heaving, ears ringing, heart so full I think it might burst.

"Thank you, Tampa!" I scream into the mic. "You've been absolutely incredible! I love you all!"

The cheers somehow get louder. I blow kisses to the audience, wave to the purple-haired girl who's now openly sobbing into her friend's shoulder, and make my way toward the wings. The dancers fall into formation behind me, all of us waving, all of us riding the high of a show that actually worked.

We did it. We actually did it.

The moment I'm out of sight of the crowd, Devon grabs me in a bear hug. "Holy shit, Charlie. Holy *shit!*"

"We did it!" I'm laughing and crying at the same time. "You guys were unbelievable. That was actually incredible."

The other dancers swarm us, everyone hugging everyone, a sweaty joyful pile of exhausted artists.

"That was the best show we've ever done," Devon says, pulling back to look at me with something like awe. "I've been touring for eight years. That was the best show I've ever been part of. Charlie, your vocals were stunning. You're officially not allowed to dance anymore."

"Thank fuck," I respond through chuckles.

The adrenaline is still coursing through me, making everything feel slightly unreal, like I'm floating a few inches above my own body. I break away from the group hug, needing a moment to breathe, to process, to come down from the high.

And then I see him.

A figure waiting in the shadows just offstage. Tall. Broad-shouldered. Familiar silhouette backlit by the glow of work lights.

My heart leaps into my throat. He came. He said he couldn't, but he came anyway. He surprised me—

I rush toward him, already smiling, already reaching—

"Charlie! There's my girl!"

The voice is wrong. The arms that wrap around me are wrong. Everything is wrong.

It's not Taio.

It's Grayson.

I go rigid in his embrace, my brain struggling to catch up with reality. Grayson. Of course it's Grayson. He told me he was coming. I knew he was coming. I just...forgot. In the chaos of rehearsals and the new choreography and Taio's notes and the phone call, I forgot that my fake boyfriend was flying in to play his part. Or maybe I didn't care.

"Amazing show, babe." Grayson pulls back just enough to plant a kiss on my cheek—firm and performative, the kind of kiss designed to be photographed. "You were great up there."

I force my face into something resembling a smile. "Thanks. I didn't know you were coming backstage."

"Surprised you." He grins, all white teeth and practiced charm. "Marcus got me in. Thought it would make for good optics."

Optics. Right.

Over Grayson's shoulder, black camera lenses glint like hungry eyes. Three, no, four photographers huddle in the wings, their equipment aimed at us like weapons. Each flash captures another millisecond of this performance we're calling a reunion, preserving our manufactured intimacy for tomorrow's headlines.

I am so tired of being watched.

But I know how this works. So I do what I've always done—I perform.

"I'm so glad you're here," I say, loud enough for the microphones to pick up. I slip my hand into Grayson's, interlacing our fingers like we've done it a thousand times.

"Wouldn't miss it." He squeezes my hand, and I wonder if he can feel how clammy my palm is, how much effort it's taking to keep my smile in place. "Come on, let's get out of here. I made dinner reservations."

Dinner reservations? It's well past ten and I am covered head to toe in body glitter.

We walk toward the exit together, hands clasped, picture-perfect couple. The backstage corridor stretches ahead of us, lined with production equipment and crew members who step aside to let us pass. Everyone's watching. Everyone's always watching.

I can see our images flickering on the jumbotron screens that flank the stage—the arena's cameras tracking our exit, broadcasting it to the thousands of fans still in their seats, still buzzing from the show.

Grayson waves to the cameras with his free hand, that practiced celebrity wave—elbow, elbow, wrist, wrist—that I've never quite mastered. He's good at this. Better than me, honestly. He makes it look effortless.

"Smile, babe," he murmurs through his teeth. "You look like you're being held hostage."

I adjust my expression, pushing more warmth into my eyes. "Sorry. Just exhausted."

"Let's get out of here. Your stuff is already in the car. We can go right home."

The photographers follow us all the way to the parking structure, cameras clicking like hungry insects. I keep my chin up, my smile bright, my grip on Grayson's hand steady.

But as we step out of the arena and into the waiting SUV, the door closing behind us with a soft thunk, all I can think about is the guy who isn't here. For the first time, it bothers me.

I don't want to go out to dinner tonight. I need sweatpants, and junk-filled charcuterie boards with warm, cheesy dip. I need my fort, to make the world small. I need my person.

Grayson's in the seat beside me, taking up space like he owns it, legs spread wide enough that his knee presses against mine. "So," he says, scrolling through his phone before even making eye contact. "What's up?"

"Not much. What's up with you?" I don't have the energy to inject enthusiasm into my voice.

"Oh, just hanging out with my girlfriend." He glances at me sideways, a slow smirk spreading across his face. "Ready for dinner?"

No, Grayson. I'm not ready for you to orchestrate every detail of my life. Also, I'm still buzzing like I was recently electrocuted and I'd really like to go back home, grab a bag of gummy bears, and spend six hours trying to fall asleep.

"I'm not really hungry," I tell him.

"There's a dress code, I think." It's apparent he's not listening to me but at least that's consistent. The *girlfriend* bit is not. And it's weird how handsy he's being.

"Grayson, did you hear me? I've been performing for three hours straight. Rehearsals have been nonstop for six days now. I really want to go to bed. Rain check on a meal?"

His smile fades. "Why? You got someone at your place waiting for you or something?" He lifts his brows accusingly. How do I know he means Taio? What is that angry glint in his eyes?

"Yeah. My very comfy bed and sheets."

He holds my stare long enough to make my stomach twist

into a pretzel. Finally, he relaxes. "Fine. Breakfast, tomorrow?"

"Okay," I agree. "That works. I'll text you when I wake up."

"I'll just pop by. Send me the address."

There it is again...What is that?

My phone buzzes from in my clutch. I pull it out, heart lurching.

Taio

Tweety. I'm speechless.

Taio

Proud of you. So proud.

"Who are you texting?" Grayson asks, reading the glee in my expression.

My gut, intuition, and better judgment all team up to form one clear instruction. Do not let Grayson know what's really going on with Taio. He probably thinks he was a hookup gone awry. From some primal place of protection comes this urge to keep Grayson in the dark how important Taio really is to me. "No one."

I tuck my phone away and press my forehead against the window glass, letting the coolness seep into my skin. Grayson's voice becomes background noise—something about a hotshot director, on-set gossip, Oscar predictions. My "mm-hmms" and "oh reallys" fall into a rhythm as automatic as my choreography. The Charlie Show continues, even with an audience of one.

But in my mind, I'm with someone else. Far away. We're having much better conversations. We're falling in love.

When we pull up to the rental property, Grayson wastes no time leaning in for a kiss. I turn my head at the last second, letting his lips land on my cheek instead. He looks at me like I spit in his face.

His lips twist into something between a sneer and a pout. "Okay, then."

"See you tomorrow, Grayson. Have a good night."

I get out of the car like it's on fire. I'm already calling Taio's number as I rush up the walkway, the screen's glow illuminating my face in the darkness. But I'm too late.

I call him once. Then twice.

But whatever has been keeping him away from me must have struck again.

He doesn't answer.

Chapter 22
Taio

Who the fuck does he think he is? He's sitting next to my girl.

Castellano & Associates sprawls across the top three floors of a Midtown high-rise that screams old money. The kind of place where the elevator buttons are polished daily and the conference rooms have actual fresh flowers. I've memorized every painting in the hallway, but this visit hits different. No more strategy sessions about my father's case. Just delivering these final documents, then walking away. I'm not going to let this consume my life again.

One trial was enough hell to last a lifetime.

I slide the stack of folders across Bradley Castellano's mahogany conference table. "That's everything. Bank statements, transaction records, correspondence—all highlighted and annotated like you asked."

Bradley nods, but something's off. He's not reaching for the folders. Neither are the two junior associates flanking him. They're all just...looking at me. With expressions I can't quite read.

"Great work as always, Taio," Bradley says carefully. "Very thorough."

"Thanks. So listen, I need to head out. I've got a flight to catch." I check my watch. "I'm afraid to ask, but how much is all this going to cost? The appeal, the new trial prep—give me a ballpark so I can start figuring out payments."

The silence stretches between us like a taut wire about to

snap.

Bradley's eyes dart to his associates, a silent message passing between them. The younger man shifts his gaze to the city skyline beyond the glass. The woman beside him begins clicking her pen rhythmically, studying its silver clip as if it is the most fascinating piece of equipment.

"All right. What?" I look between them. "What's going on?"

"Taio..." Bradley folds his hands on the table. "There's something we need to discuss. Has your dad contacted you about the appeal?"

"No," I answer honestly. "I think I had a missed call from the correctional facility, but it's not like I can call back whenever I please. Is something wrong with the appeal?"

"There isn't going to be an appeal."

The words don't compute at first. "What do you mean? The Wright evidence—"

"The Wright evidence is solid. Great catch on Rina's part. Under normal circumstances, it would absolutely be grounds for appeal." Bradley's jaw tightens. "But your father has now made that impossible."

"It's barely been a week." My stomach drops. "What did he do?"

Another exchange of glances. Bradley sighs heavily and slides a printed email across the table toward me.

"Your father sent this to our office three days ago. He very thoroughly outlined a *strategy* he wanted us to pursue."

I pick up the paper and start reading.

The first paragraph proposes bribing the judge who would likely be assigned to hear the appeal. The second suggests blackmail as a backup plan, complete with research my father apparently did on the judge's extramarital affair. The third paragraph—

I stop breathing.

The third paragraph names Charlie Riley as the financial backer for these schemes. He describes her as "my son's wealthy girlfriend" and suggests her "entertainment industry connections" could help identify additional pressure points.

"This is insane." My voice sounds far away. "Charlie has nothing to do with any of this. She doesn't even know the details of my father's case."

"We know that." Bradley's tone is gentle, which somehow makes it worse. "But your father put an illegal plan down in writing *to his counsel*. Our firm's protocol is to report it."

"Report it to who?" I ask. "What about attorney-client privilege?"

"That privilege is revoked for soliciting us in his illegal, fraudulent activity. We report that to relevant authorities: the Bar association, potentially the court." He pauses. "Taio, your father didn't just kill his appeal. He committed additional crimes in the process. Conspiracy to bribe a federal official. Conspiracy to commit extortion. And he implicated an innocent third party."

Third party? No. This is way more personal. *He implicated Charlie.*

"What happens to her?" I manage.

"Nothing, assuming she cooperates. The authorities will want a statement from her denying any involvement. On record. It should be straightforward—there's no evidence connecting her to any of this beyond your father's delusional email."

"On record," I repeat the words slowly. "Meaning public record."

"Eventually, yes. These things have a way of getting out."

The room tilts. I grip the edge of the conference table, knuckles going white.

Charlie's reputation. The thing she's been fighting to protect since the scandal broke. The thing that keeps her up at night, that drives every PR decision, every fake smile at Grayson's side. My father just painted a target on it. For no reason. For nothing. Nobody cares what the truth is once her name is attached to bribery and blackmail of a federal judge. She's going to be right back in the hot seat, insomnia, hair falling out, endless tears... because of me.

"What the actual fuck is wrong with him?"

"Taio, the thing about your father is that he thinks he's untouchable." Bradley's voice cuts through the fog. "He's spent his whole life believing he's the smartest person in every room. Even when he's catastrophically, demonstrably wrong. To this day he thinks he's above the law."

"No, to this day, he thinks he's above being a good person."

I think about all the years I've spent cleaning up his messes. The money. The visits. The emotional labor of loving someone who sees you as a resource to be managed. The guilt I've carried for not being a better son, a more loyal son, when the truth is I've been the only thing standing between him and complete self-destruction.

And this is how he repays me. By trying to drag down the one person who's made me smile again after all the hell he caused? That's how a father treats his only son?

"I'm done."

It comes out calm. Steadier than I feel.

Bradley blinks. "I'm sorry?"

"I'm done. With him. With all of this." I stand up, and for the first time in years, my shoulders don't feel like they're carrying the weight of my father's sins. "You guys can stop here. I'm not paying for this anymore. He can find another legal team. Another son. Another someone to manipulate. I'm out."

Maybe they should be advising me against abandoning my father, especially when he's about to go through the hellfire he personally ignited. But instead, all I get is a resounding, "We understand." Meaning I am the last person on Earth to have faith in my dad.

Except, I don't anymore. Now, he has no one.

"Do not contact Charlie until I get a chance to speak with her. This has to come from me. Then, her lawyers will be in touch." I'm already moving toward the door. "And, Bradley? Thank you. For everything. But I'm serious. I won't be coming back."

Bradley's eyes crinkle at the corners. "About damn time," he says, rising and extending his hand. I shake it, feeling the finality in his grip. "Good luck out there, kid. I hope life gets easier for you."

The elevator doors close behind me with a soft chime. The marble lobby gleams under my feet. As I push through the revolving door onto the busy sidewalk, each step carries away another ounce of my father's gravity.

He endangered Charlie.

I could forgive the money he drained from me. I could forgive the way he twisted my words, my thoughts, my feelings to serve his needs. I could even forgive the years where every phone call felt like a hostage negotiation. But dragging Charlie into his criminal schemes—using information I shared in a moment of vulnerability about the woman who is starting to heal what he hurt—that's where I draw the line. That's where James Wilkes stops being my father.

I'm free.

For the first time since this bullshit scandal started, I'm free.

LaGuardia is a zoo, but I don't care. I push through the crowds toward the ticket counter, phone already in my hand.

"First available flight to Atlanta," I tell the agent.

She types, frowns at her screen. "The next economy seat isn't until tomorrow morning, but I do have one first-class seat on a flight leaving in..." She checks. "Thirty-eight minutes."

"How much?"

She names a price that would have made me flinch a week ago. Today, I hand over my card without hesitation.

For years, every dollar I earned went to my father's legal defense. I've lived in a cramped apartment with secondhand furniture and worn sheets. I've denied myself vacations, nice dinners, anything beyond the bare necessities of survival. All so Dad could have the best lawyers, the fighting chance he never deserved.

Not anymore.

"First class it is," I say.

The agent smiles and prints my boarding pass.

As I head toward security, I pull out my phone and call Charlie. It rings. And rings. And rings.

Voicemail.

"Hey, it's me. I'm at the airport—I'm coming to Atlanta. I have something I need to tell you, but I'd rather do it in person. Call me when you get this."

I hang up and join the security line, phone clutched in my hand. The line moves slowly, giving me too much time to think. Too much time to scroll.

The photos from Tampa are still everywhere.

Charlie and Grayson leaving the arena. Her hand in his. His arm around her waist. That practiced smile she wears like armor.

I zoom in on one image—their interlaced fingers, his thumb resting casually against her palm. It's a small thing. Probably meaningless. But my brain won't stop analyzing it.

I pivot to find a woman standing behind me in line. Without thinking, I flash my phone screen at her. "Sorry, weird question—in your opinion, does this look like genuine affection or just a publicity stunt?"

She leans closer than necessary, perfume cloud invading my space as her gaze flicks between my face and the photo. "Charlie and Grayson?" Her lips curve into a knowing smile. "Oh, they're the real deal. Total relationship goals."

My expression sours instantly. "Right. Thanks for the input," I mutter, turning away before her lingering look can develop into something I have zero bandwidth to handle.

I pocket my phone.

All this time, my jealousy was just a low simmer, something I could easily rationalize away.

Now, standing in the security line with my father's betrayal fresh in my mind and Charlie's voicemail greeting still ringing in my ears, the simmer is starting to boil.

I make it through the checkpoint and head for my gate, trying her number again.

Ringing. Ringing. Voicemail.

"Charlie, it's me again. I'm about to board. I'll be landing in a couple hours. I really need to talk to you. It's important."

Still nothing.

I check Instagram. Nothing new from Charlie. But Grayson's account—

My thumb floats, indecisive, above his profile picture. I shouldn't do it. I know I shouldn't. This is digital masochism, the finger-pick at a scab I can't leave alone, the old itch demanding fresh pain.

I tap it anyway.

His latest story is a boomerang of the Atlanta skyline, posted twenty minutes ago. The caption reads: *In ATL with my girl. City of love or whatever.*

My girl? Who the fuck does he think he is? He's sitting next to *my girl.*

The next slide is a photo of two coffee cups on a hotel room table. His hand is visible at the edge of the frame, reaching for one of them. The implication is clear. Intimate morning. Shared space.

I know.

I know it's fake. Charlie laid it all out, swore on her life it's just business. She chose me. Wants me. Called me "babe" and confessed she's falling so hard it terrifies her. Her fingers dug into my skin when I was the one making her come. I can still feel the marks.

I know all of that.

But Grayson is there and I'm not. Grayson is posting possessive captions while I'm stuck in an airport. Grayson gets to have breakfast with her, be photographed with her, call her his girl to millions of followers while I leave voicemails that go unanswered.

I sprint to my gate as the announcement crackle over the

speakers. First class, now boarding.

I snag my sad little carry-on, full of dirty laundry. I don't even know where I'm headed. If she doesn't reach out before we land, I'll tear through every Hatcher-owned property in Atlanta until I find her. That's where she retreats when the world gets too close—wrapped in her father's empire like bulletproof glass. He's the only other man I'll allow near her now. The only other shield I can tolerate between her and the chaos my father just unleashed.

Charlie needs to know what my father did. She needs to prepare for the statement, the scrutiny, the inevitable headlines. But more than that—she needs to know that I'm here. That I choose her. That I'll fight for her in ways Grayson never would because he doesn't actually love her.

I could. Maybe I already do.

Only love could free me from the trap I've been in, right?

The realization settles over me like a truth that's been waiting to be acknowledged. This is the big one. The second chance I always secretly hoped for. My own happily-ever-after, living outside the pages. That's what I want, at least.

And I'm going to tell her. Tonight. In person. No more waiting.

I board the plane, settle into my first-class seat, and watch New York shrink beneath me as we climb into the clouds.

Atlanta is two hours away.

Charlie is two hours away.

And Grayson better enjoy his stupid artisan hot coffee while he can. Because once I get there, he'll be wearing it.

Chapter 23
Charlie

Oh yeah, tough guy? Come on. I'll give you the first swing.

Crystal chandeliers sparkle prismatic light across white tablecloths. The silverware handles are cut from crystal, too, looking more art than utensil. Every table is occupied by people who look like they stepped out of a magazine spread—perfect hair, designer clothes, the kind of effortless elegance that comes from never having to worry about money.

I hate it here.

Grayson sits across from me, looking annoyingly at ease in his tailored jacket and open-collared shirt. He's been talking for twenty minutes about some director who wants him for a prestige project, and I've been nodding along while my mind wanders to Taio's unanswered calls.

Two voicemails. I saw them when I got out of the shower, but by then I was already running late for this dinner and Grayson was pounding on my hotel room door. I'll call him back after. I'll explain.

"—and then Spielberg said—are you even listening?"

I blink. "Sorry. What?"

Grayson's jaw tightens. "I said, Spielberg personally requested a meeting. But sure, keep staring at your phone like a teenager."

"I wasn't staring at my phone." I set it face-down on the table to prove my point. "I'm just tired. It's been a long week of rehearsals. I thought you were taking the whole team out to dinner. The dancers, vocalists, Sage, Marcus?"

"What can I say? They were all busy." His stupid smirk is an admission of his lie. He set me up. "So how are you feeling?"

"Good, actually. I think I'm still kind of on this high. Tampa was—"

"Yeah, Charlie," he cuts me off. "The videos are everywhere. Very impressive."

He doesn't sound impressed. He sounds irritated. Like my success is somehow an inconvenience to him.

"Thanks," I say flatly.

My phone buzzes against the tablecloth. I turn it over automatically to glance at the screen—another notification from some social media app—and Grayson's eyes narrow.

"You need to stop checking that thing."

"I'm not checking it. It just buzzed." Except I open the notification that I was tagged in a picture of the very restaurant we're eating at. The caption? #noshamestalking #graysonandcharlie

My stomach drops. "Grayson. Did you post our location?"

"No. I just said where we were eating. What's it matter? Our followers?" He scoffs. "It's not like they can afford to get in."

I exhale, lips parted, the real-life version of the shaking-my-head emoji. "We talked about this. You can't keep broadcasting our location. It's actually dangerous. Not to mention the paparazzi are always aggressive to me. I hate it."

"Relax." He rolls his eyes. "They can't bring cameras inside. The maître d' practically strip-searched everyone at the door."

"That's not the point. When we leave—"

"When we leave, we smile and wave and give them what they want." He leans back in his chair, spreading his arms like he's addressing an audience. "That's how this works, Charlie. You want the fame, you deal with the attention."

"I don't want—" I stop myself. Take a breath. "I'm just saying, I like my dinners without an ambush waiting outside."

"And I'm just saying, you're acting like I committed a crime.

You need to calm down. It's a few Instagram stories. It's not a big deal."

Calm down. The phrase that has never, in the history of human communication, actually calmed anyone down.

The waiter appears with our entrées—some kind of architectural foam situation for him, a delicate fish dish for me—and I use the interruption to compose myself. This is fine. Two hours, maybe less. Smile for the cameras on the way out, then I can go back to my hotel and call Taio and pretend this evening never happened.

"So." Grayson waits until the waiter leaves, then reaches across the table to cover my hand with his. "I was thinking. After dinner, we could go back to my suite. Have a drink. Really talk."

I slide my hand away, reaching for my water glass. "I'm pretty tired, actually. Early call time tomorrow."

"You're always tired." His fingers find my knee under the table. "Come on, Charlie. Don't you think it's time we considered taking things to the next level?"

"There is no next level." I shift my leg away from his touch. "This is a PR arrangement, Grayson. That's all it's ever been."

His face flickers with anger, maybe, or wounded pride. It's gone so fast I almost miss it, replaced by that practiced smile.

"Right. The PR arrangement." He picks up his fork, stabbing at his foam sculpture. "The one where you get to use my name to boost your concert sales and I get...what, exactly?"

"You get the same thing I get. Good press. Visibility. That's the deal."

"The deal." He laughs, but it's mirthless. "You know what's funny? Before your scandal, I was the one doing you a favor. Dating America's sweetheart, elevating your brand. But now suddenly you're the hot commodity, and I'm just the accessory."

I stare at him. "That's not—"

"Haven't the tour sales like tripled? Your streams are up. You're trending every other day." He jabs his fork in my direction. "And where does that leave me? Following you around like a puppy, pretending to be supportive while you soak up all the attention."

"No one asked you to follow me around."

"Sage asked me. Your whole team asked me. 'Be visible, Grayson. Look supportive, Grayson. Post about her show, Grayson.'" His tone has gone acidic. "I've been doing everything they asked, and what do I get? My notifications are full of people calling me your arm candy. Asking what I bring to the relationship. Making fucking memes about how you could do better."

So that's what this is about. Not attraction. Not interest. Ego.

"I'm sorry the internet is being mean to you," I say carefully. "But that's not really something I can control."

"No?" He leans forward, eyes glittering. "Because it seems like you could control it if you wanted to. Post about me more. Talk about me in interviews. Make it clear that I'm the prize here, not just some supporting character in the Charlie Riley show."

"Grayson—"

"Do you have any idea what it's like?" His voice rises slightly, drawing a glance from the next table. "To be constantly compared to you? To have people analyze every photo, every comment, every interaction to see if I measure up? I'm a movie star, Charlie. I've been in this industry since I was fifteen. And now I'm being treated like your plus-one."

I should feel bad for him. On some level, I understand the frustration—the industry is brutal, and comparison is a knife that cuts everyone eventually. But shouldn't our shared commiseration be making us better friends instead of enemies?

"I think," I say slowly, "that maybe this arrangement isn't working for either of us."

His expression shifts. Hardens. "What's that supposed to mean?"

"It means maybe we should talk to our PR teams about winding this down. Finding a graceful exit."

"A graceful exit." He laughs again, that sharp, humorless sound. "You mean you want to dump me. Publicly. After everything I've done for your image."

"I'm not dumping you—"

"Save it." He throws his napkin on the table and signals for the check. "We have a contract. You want out? Fine. But don't think for a second I'm going to make it easy for you. I know things, Charlie. About your little secrets. Your bodyguard with the wandering hands."

My blood goes cold. "What are you talking about?"

"Please. I'm not blind." His smile is cruel now, all pretense stripped away. "The way you look at him. The way he looks at you. It's obvious to anyone paying attention. And trust me, people are paying attention. Know what they're saying? That you're either an idiot or a whore. Depends on who is pursuing who here."

"You're an asshole."

"I don't actually care, by the way." He stands. "Keep your secrets. Fuck your bodyguard. Do whatever you want. But if you try to make me look bad on the way out, I will bury you." He leans close, his breath hot against my ear. "Got it?"

I don't respond. I can't. My throat has closed around the words.

Grayson buttons his jacket with practiced fingers, and like flipping a switch, his face rearranges into the camera-ready smile that's launched a thousand movie posters. "Come on. Let's go. I've lost my appetite. Let's get this over with."

He's such a dickhead. What a complete and utter waste of space. I follow in tow because it's the only path to escape.

But I jump out of the frying pan right into the fire.

Outside, a feeding frenzy of cameras and microphones awaits us, more aggressive than any mob I've faced before.

They swarm the moment we step through the door—a wall of flashing lights and shouted questions and bodies pressing close. I flinch back instinctively, but Grayson's hand clamps around my wrist, pulling me forward into the chaos.

"Smile," he hisses. "You wanted attention. Here it is."

"Grayson! Charlie! Over here!"

"How's the relationship going?"

"Charlie, any comment on the tour? Are the rest of the dates locked in?"

"Grayson, is it true you're up for the Tarantino project?"

The barrage of questions melts into a single deafening roar. I'm blinded by the strobe-like assault of camera flashes, each burst leaving ghost images floating across my vision. Elbows and shoulders dig into my sides as the crowd constricts around us like a python, and the terrible realization hits me: there's no escape route. We're completely hemmed in.

"Grayson." I try to keep my voice steady. "This is too much. We need to get to the car."

He ignores me. He's posing now, one arm around my waist, pulling me against his side like a trophy.

"I want to leave," I insist again, pulling away, but his grip becomes punishing.

"In a minute."

A photographer collapses to the ground in front of me, his body flat against the pavement. The lens of his camera tilts upward, seeking the shadows beneath my hemline. My stomach turns as I realize what he's hunting for—an invasive angle no woman should have to endure.

"Hey!" I try to step back, but there's nowhere to go. "What the hell are you—"

And then, out of nowhere, a hand reaches down and grabs the shameless photographer by the collar, hauling him up off the ground like he weighs nothing.

"What do you think you're doing?" The voice is familiar. *Furious.* "You're fucking disgusting."

Taio.

He's here. In Atlanta. Standing in the middle of my nightmare, holding a paparazzo by the scruff of his neck like a misbehaving puppy.

"Who the fuck are you?" someone shouts.

Taio shoves the photographer away and turns to face the crowd, his body shifting automatically into a protective stance between me and the cameras. "Her bodyguard."

His eyes find mine and for a moment, everything else falls away. The flashing lights, the shouted questions, the hands reaching for me—all of it fades into background noise. There's just Taio, looking at me like I'm the only thing in the world that matters.

Then his gaze drops to my waist.

The waist that Grayson's still wrapped around like a python with a vendetta.

"Let her go." I've never heard three words sound more menacing. Even Grayson's ego doesn't want to stand up to the hulk-fire burning in Taio's eyes. Grayson releases me.

"We don't need you tonight," Grayson seethes. "In fact, you're dismissed."

Taio's expression doesn't change, but his eyes flash with a cold, lethal quality. He turns to Grayson, and when he speaks, his voice is dangerously calm. "You may not need me. She does. What the hell are you doing? You brought her into this shark tank, and now you're what—letting them feast?"

Grayson puffs up, clearly not used to being challenged. "Excuse me?"

"There's a perverted fuck on the ground trying to take photos up her skirt, and you were just standing there posing. You're supposed to be protecting her, and instead you're—what? Checking your reflection in the cameras? What kind of man are you?"

"I don't know who you think you are—"

Taio's jaw flexes as he steps forward, his shoulders squared. "I'm her bodyguard. That means I'm paid to care when someone puts her at risk." The space between them shrinks; he seems to wilt under Taio's gaze.

"I don't control this circus, man."

"Sure you do. You led them right to her with your location tags and your thirst-trap photos. You might as well have sent out invitations, and now you're posing while that creep tries to violate her."

"That's ridiculous—"

"Is it?" Taio's voice rises, cutting through the noise of the crowd. "How the hell do you think I found you guys? Because I tracked you here using your Instagram stories. If I could do it, so could every other bastard with a camera and a grudge. You wanted attention so badly you didn't care what it cost her. These are just cameras. What if someone showed up with worse? Do you ever fucking think?"

The paparazzi have gone quiet, sensing drama better than any tabloid story. Cameras are still flashing, but the questions have stopped. Everyone's watching.

Grayson's face has gone red. "Listen, buddy, I don't know what your deal is, but you need to back off. Charlie is my girlfriend. And you are now fired. This is none of your business."

Taio doesn't flinch. "Let me be abundantly clear. There will never be a time where her business isn't my business. Get what I'm saying?"

Grayson balls up his fist, the veins in his forearm bulging.

The crowd murmurs. Someone actually gasps.

"Oh yeah, tough guy? Come on. I'll give you the first swing. But you better kill me. Because when I swing, you die."

Standing there, they're like two different species. Taio's shoulders block out the light of the cameras, his frame hewn from intimidating strength. Grayson, with his cardio-sculpted gym physique, suddenly looks like a child playing dress-up. If fists start flying, there won't be a contest—only a reckoning.

"Taio, please don't." My fingers find his forearm, just a whisper of contact against his skin. I glare at the crowd surrounding us. "Would you guys please give us some space?"

They don't budge.

For a moment, I think Grayson might actually swing at him. His fists are clenched, his jaw tight, his whole body vibrating with suppressed rage. Instead, he turns to me. "Charlie, let's go." He holds out his hand.

The paparazzi erupt.

"Charlie! Who is this guy?"

"Are you and Grayson breaking up?"

"You let your bodyguard act like this and keep him on payroll?"

The questions come from every direction, overwhelming, inescapable. I feel myself starting to spiral, the old familiar panic rising in my chest. This is going to be everywhere. This is going to be the only thing anyone talks about. My reputation, my career, everything I've worked for—

"Charlie."

Taio's voice cuts through the noise. He's standing in front of me now, his back to the cameras, blocking me from view. In the eye of this hurricane, his gaze finds mine—an impossible calm.

"I'm sorry," he says quietly. "I know this isn't how you wanted things to go. I know you're scared about what happens next." He takes a breath.

"Taio—"

"But I'm done hiding. I'm done pretending. I don't want to be the secret you're ashamed of." His voice is steady, certain. "I'm getting rid of everything that comes between you and me. My father, my past, all the bullshit I've been carrying—it's done. And if you want me, I'm right here. If you want me to go"—he glances at Grayson—"I can do that too. What do you need from me?"

My heart is pounding so hard I can feel it in my throat. "There are cameras everywhere," I say with tears in my eyes.

He holds out his hand, palm up, an offering. "What do you say, Tweety? You want to do this for real?"

The flashes are blinding. The shouts are deafening. Every instinct I have is screaming at me to be careful, to think about the optics, to protect myself from the inevitable fallout.

But then I look at Taio—really look at him.

And it's so fucking obvious.

I reach out and take his hand. Fingers laced. The intentional kind of hand-holding that's unmistakable.

The crowd explodes. Questions, flashes, chaos from every direction. But I don't hear any of it. All I hear is Taio's sharp intake of breath, all I feel are his fingers interlacing with mine, all I see is the smile breaking across his face like sunrise.

"Want to get out of here?" he asks. I give a small, sure nod.

He breaks through the crowd, removing human beings like they are merely branches in the way of a new path. His body shielding mine, his hand never letting go. Cameras follow us, shouts chase us, but none of it matters. We push through to the street, where a taxi is waiting and then we're inside, the door slamming shut, the noise cutting off like someone hit a mute button.

For a moment, we just sit there. Breathing. Processing.

"You had the forethought to plant a taxi?"

Then Taio turns to me, and his expression is somewhere between wonder and disbelief. "No. I went in there with no plan. It was a lucky break."

We collapse into laughter, the tension draining from our bodies. Outside, camera flashes strobe against the windows like lightning in a storm, but inside this taxi, we've found shelter. Almost. In the rearview mirror, I catch the driver's wide eyes darting between us and the mob scene surrounding his vehicle, his white-knuckled grip on the steering wheel, probably wishing he could eject us.

"That was—"

"Childish? Reckless? A little over the top?" he fills in.

I place my fingers against his lips, hushing him with a gesture. "That was like a scene from one of your books. Like a fairy tale."

"Fairy tale?" he echoes, confused. "I just blew up everything. Your face is going to be everywhere tomorrow. They're going to find out who I am...and what I've done."

"Yeah, they are," I say, my heartbeat steady, my head cool.

"I'm so sorry, Charlie. Do you have any idea what's about to happen? The headlines, the speculation. They're going to start talking and never shut up."

I shrug one shoulder. "Let them."

"What?" he asks again.

The words surprise me even as I say them. But they're true. For the first time in years, I genuinely don't care what the tabloids say or what the internet thinks or what Sage is going to scream at me tomorrow morning.

I chose him. In front of everyone. And it feels like the first honest thing I've done in months. Maybe the first really honest thing I've done in my whole life. I just told the world where my loyalty lies, and damn does that feel good.

"Charlie." Taio cups my face in his hands, his thumbs brushing my cheekbones. "There's more coming. I have something I need to tell you. About my father. About—"

"Later." I lean into his touch. "Tell me later."

"But it's important. I don't want any more secrets between us."

"I know." I press my forehead against his. "Me neither. And I want to hear it. All of it. But we have bigger fish to fry at the moment."

He looks worried. "Being?"

"Well the world feels very big right now. And I have a massive penthouse in downtown Atlanta that came equipped with everything except—"

"A fort."

"Exactly. We'll deal with the shitstorm tomorrow. Tonight it's just you and me and nothing between us—no lies, no secrets..."

"No clothes?" he asks.

I give him my most serious look. "Oh clothes are most definitely not invited."

He's quiet for a long moment. Then he nods, pulling me close, wrapping his arms around me like he's afraid I might disappear. "You could do better," he tells me. "You know that, right?"

"Taio."

"Yeah?"

"Shut up and kiss me now."

His arms envelop me completely, a shelter against everything outside this taxi. When our lips meet, the cameras vanish, the shouting fades. The world beyond our fogged windows ceases to exist. It's just his heartbeat against mine, the warmth of his breath, and somewhere above the chaos, stars bearing silent witness to the start of something more.

This hero? He chose to be mine.

Steam clings to the bathroom mirror, softening my reflection into something impressionistic. I've been in here for forty-five minutes—longer than any shower requires, even one meant to wash away the frenzy of paparazzi flashbulbs and Grayson's venom and the weight of a thousand cameras capturing my impulsive choice to blow up my reputation.

I'm stalling. I realize that.

I rub my hair with the towel until it's just damp enough to curl at the edges. I consider blow-drying it straight, then decide to let it be. My reflection looks different. Softer. I uncap the lotion bottle, inhaling vanilla and sugar as I massage it into my arms with deliberate circles. Each stroke stretches time, though there's no real reason to delay what waits beyond the bathroom door.

Still, my hands are trembling.

It's not fear, exactly. It's something bigger. It's like standing at the edge of a cliff, knowing you're about to jump, trusting that the water below will catch you but still terrified of the fall.

I'm not about to have sex with some random guy. I'm not about to check a box or get it over with or prove something to anyone. I'm about to give myself—all of myself, the parts I've protected and hidden and saved—to Taio. The man whose bookshelves overflow with dog-eared romance paperbacks and whose fingers can transform bedsheets into castles. The man who stepped between me and a wall of flashing cameras, extended his palm toward mine, and proudly claimed me with no sense of self-preservation.

He stood with me when he could've stayed in the shadows.

I pause, lotion half absorbed into my forearm, and stare at my reflection through the dissipating steam. When did this happen? When did "I like you" become "I'm falling" become this quiet, certain knowledge that settles in my chest like a heartbeat?

I can trace it back to different moments: his handwritten notes appearing in my box when I needed them most; my triumph in Miami which felt shared between the two of us; or just hours ago, when his body became my shield against the enemy of flashing cameras and angry interrogations, his stance unwavering.

It was all of it. Every small moment building into something neither of us can ignore anymore.

I think about my mom.

She fell in love so many times. Not just with Spencer's dad. Not just with mine. I have vague memories from being little, watching her get ready for dates—the careful application of lipstick, the way she'd spritz perfume on her wrists and behind her ears, the nervous energy that made her seem younger somehow. Spencer would stay home to watch me and wish our mother luck. Maybe this was *the one*. She believed in love the way some people believe in religion. *Completely. Recklessly.* Over and over again.

And none of them stayed. Each departure left a trail of shattered vows, tissues stained with mascara, and the hollow echo of another failed romance. She'd straighten her spine, reapply her lipstick, and somehow, after enough time passed, her eyes would start to sparkle with possibility again.

I used to think she was foolish. Now I wonder if she was brave.

How do you know if it'll last?

That's the question I've been asking myself since I realized what Taio means to me. How do you trust something so fragile and new? How do you give someone the power to destroy you and have faith that they won't?

The truth? You can't.

Standing here in this steamy bathroom, trembling on the edge of something terrifying and beautiful, I realize something: you can't learn to swim by thinking about water. You can't understand love by watching other people drown in it. At some point, you have to leap.

And looking back at my mother's advice, all the little pieces, fragments of her lessons learned, stuffed into heart-shaped notes...I see it now with blinding clarity. I missed the point. She wasn't telling me to wait for love. She was screaming at me to love myself first, with the desperate urgency of someone who learned it too late. The truth burns through me: I'd pass this same raw, vital lesson to my own daughter with my dying breath. To Claire's daughter. To Remy and Eli. This is what's been bleeding beneath my music all along. I've been hemorrhaging inside not because strangers on the internet hated me, but because I couldn't look at my own reflection and see something worth protecting.

That all changes now.

I take a breath. Then another.

Then I pull on a non-Tweety tank top over my bra—soft cotton, thin straps, shielding half of my ass. I wear a simple pair of underwear. Nothing fancy. Nothing performative. *Just me.*

I open the bathroom door.

The living room space has been transformed.

I somewhat meant it as a joke, but Taio has built a fort.

No, not a fort. This is a palace—a cathedral of blankets and pillows and string lights, stretching from the massive sectional couch to the fireplace, where flames crackle and dance behind glass. He's raided every closet and linen cabinet in the place, constructing walls of Egyptian cotton and supports made from chair cushions and decorative pillows. Fairy lights, stolen from the patio, wind through the structure like captured stars, casting everything in a warm, golden glow.

It's ridiculous. It's magical. It's exactly what I need for this moment. It's nothing like I pictured for my first time. It's better.

I stand in the entryway, hand pressed to my chest, feeling my heart expand in ways I didn't know were possible. He did this for me. While I was in the bathroom overthinking everything, he was out here creating a sanctuary. A place where the outside world can't touch us.

Taio crawls out from beneath the canopy of blankets, and when he sees me standing there, his expression reveals a kaleidoscope of emotions—his eyes widening with relief, then darkening with want, his smile both shy and certain all at once.

"There is admittedly room for improvement," he says, like there's anything in my eyes but visceral adoration.

"It's a tall ask to improve upon perfection, don't you think?" My voice comes out small, still processing. I take a step toward him, and another. Slow, reticent steps, but still...*brave*.

"Is this tacky? I'm trying to be sweet, but maybe you want sexy. The *Magic Mike* version of Taio?"

I nod at him seriously. "Oh, I always want the *Magic Mike* version of Taio, but just so you know, sweet *is* sexy. I'm nervous." I point to the fort. "I really needed this. Thank you."

"I promised I'd build you one everywhere we go." He gestures to his creation with exaggerated pride. "You just let me know anytime the world feels too big, Charlie Riley. I'll shrink it for you."

A laugh-sob escapes me, releasing the knot that's been sitting in my chest. "My hero."

"Want to see the inside?" He holds aside a blanket flap like a doorman at a fancy hotel, and I duck through the opening into the heart of his creation. Inside, it's even more magical—layers of soft blankets covering the floor, pillows arranged into a nest, the firelight filtering through the fabric walls to paint everything in shades of amber and gold. It's like being inside a cocoon. Safe. Warm. In another world.

Taio ducks in behind me, and the fort seems to contract around us. Not in a suffocating way—in the way a blanket wraps tighter when you need it most. I can hear his breathing, count his heartbeats, feel the heat radiating from him though we're barely touching. The inches between us feel charged, alive with possibility.

"Hi," he says softly.

"Hi."

The air in here becomes charged, humming, like the moment right before lightning strikes. His shoulders are set at careful angles, maintaining those precious few inches of space even in our blanket refuge. Every movement feels deliberate—his hands resting on his knees, his chest rising with measured breaths. He's waiting. Watching. The ball is in my court, and we both know it.

"Taio. Come closer." I reach for his hand, pulling him to me. He exaggerates his movements as if I have the strength to yank this man anywhere. Yet, he slouches down and bumps his shoulder to mine playfully.

"Why are you nervous?" His free hand comes up to cup my face, thumb brushing my cheekbone. "Outside of the obvious, of course."

"I'm worried you won't like it. How can I make you happy when I don't know what I'm doing?"

His fingers thread between mine like roots seeking soil, and I grip his hand so tightly my knuckles pale. "You don't know what you do to me?"

"Not really."

He brings the back of my hand to his lips. "Let me explain. I used to tear through a book a day before I met you, and now I've read almost nothing in weeks."

"So I'm distracting?" I poke my tongue at him. "That's all you got?"

"You made me want my own story. That's everything, Charlie. The whole damn point. You gave me something no one else could. Freedom...from myself. So don't be nervous about making me happy, because you've already found a way to help me feel whole."

There is no appropriate response to that except a kiss.

I swing a leg over his lap, settling on top of him, and his hands hover at my knees, tentative. It's like he's afraid to touch me and break the moment. So I do the touching for both of us—palms on either side of his face, thumbs tracing the stubble at his jawline. I kiss him slow and soft at first, then deeper, letting my fingers map the familiar geography of his cheekbones and ears, the warm silk of his neck, the scar that interrupts his left eyebrow. He tastes like bubblegum toothpaste of all things, but before I can ask and accuse him of having a child's hygiene regimen, he slips his hands around my waist, anchoring me in his gravity, and I lose the impulse to be funny.

He kisses back like he's been waiting all day, which, given the suspense of the last few hours, he probably has. His lips are careful, reverent, but his hands aren't. They climb the curve of my back. I let him. His hands slip up, unhurried, exploring every inch of me through the whisper-thin cotton. Two fingers hook under the strap, dragging it down my shoulder, exposing the line where my neck turns soft. I tip my chin, baring more for him. He sets his mouth to my collarbone, teeth grazing, tongue following, then plants a kiss at the spot that pulses with my heartbeat.

He traces the edge of my bra, then pulls the cups outward, and his pupils blow wide. He hesitates for a beat, waiting for my permission. I give a small nod and he grins against my throat before pulling the tank up and off with such ceremony it makes me giggle.

"They're small, I know," I whisper as he unhooks my bra and tosses it aside. His hands cup me gently, fingers splayed across my skin, easily covering the entirety of my chest, and for a moment I can't help comparing myself to invisible others—women with curves that spill over palms, women whose bodies have left their imprints in his memory.

His careful restraint gives way to something hungrier, though still gentle. He pulls me closer, one hand sliding into my damp hair, and kisses me hard. "I'm sorry, babe. I was so focused on being good to you, maybe I should've been louder about how good I can make you feel."

He takes my breasts into his mouth, one by one, his tongue circling each nipple until they harden to tight peaks. He sucks gently at first, then with more pressure that sends electric currents straight between my legs. I gasp when he grazes his teeth lightly across one sensitive tip, and arch my back, fingers tangling in his hair to hold him there as he toggles back and forth, from one nipple to the other, leaving nothing untasted. "God, I want you. I love everything I see. You don't need to worry about descriptors like small or big, Charlie. The only one that matters is 'mine.' *You're mine.*"

I nod in agreement, relaxing my shoulders, no longer trying to hide from him. "I want to be yours."

He pulls back just enough to look at me, his eyes searching mine for any trace of doubt. Whatever he finds there must satisfy him, because he nods slowly. "Good."

"Can I?" I say, tugging at the hem of his shirt.

He pulls it off, and then it's my turn to stare. I've seen him shirtless before, but not like this—not with firelight dancing across the ridges of his abs, not with a thin sheen of sweat making his skin glisten, not with the muscles in his shoulders flexing as he leans toward me. The V-line of his hips disappears temptingly into his waistband, and my fingers itch to trace it downward.

He catches the flicker in my eyes, then in one motion, he shifts me off his lap and onto my back, so I'm pillowed by a mountain of down and enfolded by the fort's tented walls. Taio hovers above, caging me with his arms, and for a second, I can't breathe from how intensely he's looking at me—like he's working up his own courage.

The waistband of my underwear—the one piece of armor I have left—is easily conquered by his thumbs. He peels them down, slow, reverent. He trails them past my knees, tossing them behind him, and then brings his mouth to the slope of my stomach.

"Careful. I'm going to get addicted to this," I warn as his kisses trail south.

"Get addicted. I'm going to do it every single time."

He holds my hips, thumbs pressing into the hollows beside my hip bones as he works lower. His hot breath fans across my inner thighs, making me tremble. I lift my hips, desperate for his mouth, but he pins me in place with a firm grip.

He murmurs something incomprehensible, his voice rough with desire. His tongue traces a slow, deliberate path along the crease where my thigh meets my center, so close yet not close enough. I whimper, my fingers clutching at the blankets. When he finally drags his tongue through my slick folds and closes his mouth over my pulsing clit, the jolt of pleasure is so concentrated, I shatter instantly against his hungry mouth.

But he doesn't stop. Not for a second. Before I've even finished gasping out his name, he hooks two fingers inside me. The stretch is new, but his patience is infinite, his touch so careful I want to cry. He works them slowly, curling them just so, finding some hidden place that makes fireworks burst behind my eyes. My body is a live wire, every nerve ending burning for him, my limbs jittering in the warm enclosure of our bodies.

"I want to make you feel good, Charlie," he whispers, the promise so raw it reverberates deep inside me. I try to say yes, or please, or Taio—anything to let him know I'm still conscious—but the words collapse in my throat. All I can do is press my hips closer, seeking more.

He returns his mouth to me, lips sealing over the desperate ache at my center while his fingers keep working, soft and relentless. The pressure builds fast, then impossibly faster, and this time when I come it's not a shudder or a sigh but a tidal wave, a full-body surge that leaves me sobbing against his head, clutching his shoulders like I'll die if I let go. He stays with me through it, mouth and hands gentle and sure, coaxing every last ripple from me until all that's left is the afterglow, a trembling hush that fills every cell.

He crawls up to kiss me, and I taste myself on his tongue, sweet and unfamiliar.

We sit side by side, his arm around me, holding me close as if escape was on my mind. "Hey," he says, voice gentle. "We don't have to do more tonight if you don't want. You lead."

"Taio, I've been waiting for you for so much longer than you can imagine. I want more." I reach for his waistband, fingers bunching the elastic, and pull him close enough that he can see exactly how much I mean it. He shudders, a full-body tremor, like he's barely containing a hurricane.

I tug his shorts down, and he helps, kicking them off until they're lost among the pillows. I try to play it cool, but the look on my face must give away my awe because he laughs—low and a little nervous, so unlike the cocky veneer he wears for everyone else.

"You're like *big*, big," I say.

I mean, it's not like I've never seen a dick before. I'm not an alien. I've seen my fair share in health-class textbooks and in the sort of blurry, late-night internet research that's inevitable if you have even a passing interest in sex. But I've never had one unveiled with the explicit intention of encountering it, up close, with my own hands and mouth and eventually, actual body. And I've definitely never seen one like *this*.

I tug his briefs down with all the finesse of someone opening a stubborn jar of pickles. Taio's surprised grunt is half amusement, half arousal.

He's...intimidating. His cock springs free with an enthusiasm that can only be described as athletic, and for a heartbeat—maybe two—I just stare at it, realizing I am utterly unequipped for this phase of the journey. I have to recalibrate all my expectations. I mean, Jesus, is that what regular dicks even look like? Should I have trained for this? Is there like, a yoga pose for this? Will I survive it?

Taio chuckles again, but softer. "Hey. Hey, up here." He tips my chin so I meet his eyes. There's a blush in his cheeks, and vulnerability behind the grin. "Don't look so scared. We're going to go really slow."

I want to be smooth. I want to come up with some sultry

quip, but what comes out is, "It's just...a lot...of dick. You're bigger than The Detonator."

He smirks at me. "Have you been doing comparative research?"

I flush. Okay, I maybe tested the vibration. *Briefly. For science.* "I needed details for my five-star review. I was trying to help the company."

Taio laughs. "We'll come back to that. First..." He leans over and finds a black Trojan packet he stashed under some pillows. With a look that pins me in place, he tears it open with his teeth, never breaking eye contact as he rolls the condom over his length with practiced grace.

His hands find my knees and gently urge them farther apart, spreading me open beneath the fairy-lit ceiling of our fortress. Taio settles between my thighs, balancing his weight on his forearms so his face is level with my center. He watches, entranced, as if cataloguing every micro-tremor of anticipation, every flutter of my breath. The head of his cock nudges experimentally against me—not entering, just grazing the slick heat gathered there, smearing it back and forth with a patience that feels like torture.

He doesn't go in. Not all at once. Instead, he drags the tip up and down, teasing, gathering wetness, his mouth silently worshipping the shiver of my body. It feels like he's painting me, signing his name on every nerve ending. I bend toward him, eager, but he pulls back, grinning at my frustration.

"Just wait," he croons, so featherlight it almost undoes me. "I need you a little wetter." Then, instead of moving forward, he slides down my body, and I feel the rush of his breath, the damp warmth of his lips as he licks a slow stripe up my inner thigh and then *right* to where I need him most. Like he's the one addicted, the one who can't get enough, he licks again, and again, tongue working in purposeful, hungry circles, the kind of voracious you only read about in banned books.

I can barely think, let alone speak. Taio gets me so wet it feels like a trick of the body, a secret hack no one warned me about.

When he's finally satisfied—when my body's humming on some secret frequency only he can read—he kneels in front of my legs. With his palms cradling my calves, he gently folds both legs up, resting my feet on his chest. The look in his eyes, desperate and adoring and a little bit awed, might have made me self-conscious once. Now it just fuels the hunger.

He lines himself up, pressing the head against me, and waits. Like he wants another green light, a final "I want this." I curl my toes against his chest and nod, once, and he exhales through a shaky smile.

I brace for pain, or at least for the kind of discomfort all the articles warn you about, but when he starts to push in, it's not pain I feel. It's pressure, new and stretching my limits, but it's not bad. It's intoxicating in its intensity, a sensation that makes me arch against him, greedy for more. He works his way in slow, watching my face the whole time, eyes absorbing every wince and shiver and gasp like he's the world's most devoted scientist and I'm his only subject.

He pushes in deeper, *deeper*, with infinite restraint, and every millimeter feels like a homecoming to a place I never knew existed. I clutch the blankets at my sides and let my head fall back, the ceiling of our fort a blur of golden light. His thumbs stroke gentle circles as he buries himself, filling me until I'm stretched tight around him, until the world contracts to the two of us and the hush of our joined breath.

I'm so wet the slide is frictionless, and when he finally bottoms out, face flickering with awe and disbelief, he hovers there, motionless, like he's trying to memorize the feeling. For a long second, neither of us moves, lost in the intensity. My body pulses around him, an unspoken plea, and when I squeeze my thighs together, his composure cracks.

"Fuck. The things I want to do to you," he groans, low and guttural, and starts to move—slow at first, barely rocking his hips, as if he's scared I'll break. The sensation is more than I can process, every stroke measured and mindful, his cock gliding in and out with a relentless, careful rhythm. I can feel him shaking, fighting the urge to go faster, to claim me with the same hunger he showed with his mouth.

"Wait," I beg.

He drags out of me, slightly panicked. "Hurts?" he asks.

I shake my head, heart thundering. My fingers tremble as I reach for the latex barrier between us, peeling it away with deliberate slowness. His breath hitches as my fingertips graze his heated flesh, the condom discarded within our nest of blankets. I guide him back to my entrance, slick and aching. "I think it'll feel better like this. Is that okay?"

"That's more than okay." He watches my face—eyes grazing my parted lips, the flush I'm certain is staining my neck. He enters again, this time more daringly. Plunging as deep as he can go in one stroke. My walls stretch taut around his bare flesh as he claims me, completely. I'm drunk on it. I'm high on it. I am completely addicted to this, to *him*.

He pumps into me, harder now, the carefulness giving way to something reckless and urgent. I anchor myself to his biceps, fingernails digging in, as he rocks into me with increasing force; every thrust sets off a chain reaction inside me, friction and fullness and the sweet ache of surrender. I cry out—unrestrained, louder than I thought I'd be—and he answers with a guttural groan that vibrates through his chest into mine. His rhythm falters as he grips my hips harder, fingers digging into soft flesh, the tendons in his neck straining as the last threads of his control snap completely.

My body's already so primed I don't think I can last, but still, the release when it hits is shocking—ferocious and raw, a detonation that burns through my core and leaves me sobbing his name into the hollow of his throat. He comes right after, pulling out in the nick of time. His warm cum coats my clit like honey, a sinfully sweet sensation that makes my toes curl in appreciation. We're breathless, his forehead pressed to mine, both of us held together by sweat and heat and the shared knowledge that we will never be the same.

We collapse, half tangled in the blankets, and for a while neither of us moves. I listen to our breath, ragged and synched, and trace slow circles on his chest, grounding myself in the realness of his body.

Eventually Taio rolls onto his back, tugging me along so I sprawl across his strong, damp skin, my face pressed to the side of his neck. I can feel the thump of his pulse, wild and uncalibrated, as he cages me in with one muscled arm.

"Hi," he says softly.

"Hi." I've lost my bones. I'm floating. "That was..."

"Good?"

"I don't have words."

He smiles—that warm, genuine one that transforms his whole face. "Same."

"Ready for more? Or do you need a minute?" I tease, but the shiver that skates up my spine is sharp, a little too real. I'm unraveled, nerves shot through, every muscle limp, splayed in these blankets as if the fabric itself has fused me to the mattress. I'm done. Stripped bare in a way I didn't know was possible. I need more than a few minutes. I need a hibernation.

"Insatiable little thing. I've opened Pandora's box, haven't I?"

I chuckle against him. "Oh, you definitely handled my box."

My head bounces off his chest, his laughter deep and roaring.

"I feel so full," I say, my breath tickling his nipple. "Is sex always so...grounding? I feel like everything is so right. Is that the sex haze everyone talks about?"

His chin rustles the top of my hair as he shakes his head. "No, this is what it feels like when you're with the right person."

"Like you felt with Alaina?"

He jostles my shoulder, a silent warning to not invite our ghosts into our sanctuary. "No. Like I feel with you, Tweety."

Hmmm. I cuddle closer into him. He misinterprets my shivering for being cold, so he reaches to the side of me and pulls up a blanket, covering me and the intimate parts of him.

"Did you stash your book in here, or just condoms?"

He smirks. "Just condoms."

"Damn. I wanted to hear how it ends. Do they get back together?"

He kisses the top of my head three quick times before releasing me. To my dismay, he leaves our love nest, but returns with supplies a few minutes later instead of forty-seven years. Both hands loaded down with snacks, a book tucked under his arm, and a warm washcloth draped over his forearm like a butler.

The washcloth passes between my thighs with tender care, Taio's touch gentle as he tends to me. When he's finished, he tucks the bag of chips by my side, before settling back down. We're both still naked like it's normal. Like our bodies were meant to be skin against skin at all times. He pulls me into his embrace and cracks open the pink-covered book.

I drift off before he finishes the chapter, his voice a low rumble against my ear. The story blurs into background noise as his heartbeat becomes my lullaby.

My dreams swirl with fragments of him and the hero in the story—dark eyes crinkling at the corners when he laughs, the unexpected sweetness of his toothpaste-flavored kisses mixing with his woodsy cologne. In that hazy space between consciousness and sleep, one thought anchors me...

This hero?

He chose to be mine.

Water is wet. The sky is blue. Charlie fell for Taio.

Morning light hits the penthouse windows like a tactical assault, cutting sharp lines across the marble kitchen island where I've set up camp. The coffee maker gurgles behind me—some fancy European model with too many buttons that took me fifteen minutes to figure out—and my notepad is open, pen moving steadily across the page.

Charlie's still in the shower. I can hear the water running through the walls, and every few minutes, the muffled sound of her singing drifts through the bathroom door. Something from her new album, I think. The melody is familiar now, constantly woven into the fabric of my days with her.

I turn back to my task: replenishing her paper hearts supply.

She has two back-to-back shows in Atlanta, and knowing Charlie, she probably didn't pick just one. I bet she blew through all of the ones I snuck into her box before I left for New York. Time to restock the arsenal.

Tweety—

Remember: you're not performing for them. You're sharing yourself with them. There's a difference.

I tear the note free, fold it into a small square, and add it to the growing pile beside my coffee mug. The next one comes easier:

The voice in your head that says you're not enough? She's a liar. Don't trust her.

And another:

Black Cat and I are watching from the wings. Well, I'm watching. He's probably napping. But we're both proud of you.

I stare at that one for a moment, then add a small drawing in the corner—a terrible stick-figure cat with too-big eyes. Charlie will laugh. That's the point.

Your mom would be proud of you. I know I am.

The dancers have your back. Trust them to catch you—literally and figuratively.

My girlfriend is smokin' hot...Sorry, that one was for me.

—Your Taio

I pause, tapping the pen against my lips. These notes hold so much weight—words to carry her through the moments when the lights are too bright and the crowd is too loud and the doubts start creeping in.

In my old life, I showed affection through physical presence. Through protection. Through the careful maintenance of boundaries between client and provider that somehow still allowed for genuine care. But with Charlie, I've discovered something different. Words matter to her. Written ones especially—maybe because of her mother's paper hearts, maybe because she's spent so long having her words twisted and misrepresented by tabloids.

When I write these notes, I'm giving her something no one

can take away or misinterpret. Private truths, just for her.

The coffee maker beeps, announcing completion, and I pour myself a cup—black, no sugar, the way I've taken it since I was sixteen and trying to seem more adult than I was. The penthouse kitchen is absurdly well stocked; someone on Charlie's team clearly called ahead. Fresh fruit in a bowl on the counter, pastries from some local bakery, enough snacks to feed an army.

I grab a croissant and return to my notes, chewing thoughtfully as I consider what else to write.

A soft thump interrupts my thoughts, and I look up to find a familiar black shape materializing on the counter beside me. Black Cat settles his furry ass directly on top of my notepad, tail swishing with the supreme indifference of a creature who knows he owns every surface he touches.

"Hey, buddy." I scratch behind his ears, earning a rumbling purr. "Where were you last night? I didn't see you when we got back."

He blinks at me slowly, offering no explanation. Probably hiding somewhere, traumatized by the sounds coming from the blanket fort. *Smart cat.*

"I missed you while I was gone, you know. New York was lonely without your judgment." I run my hand down his spine and the vibration of his purr intensifies. "Charlie took good care of you, though. Four meals a day, I hear. You're getting spoiled, and honestly? Good for you. Enjoy being loved."

He head-butts my palm, demanding more attention. I oblige, working my fingers through the soft fur at his neck while my mind wanders to the life this cat must have had before we found him. Stray. Hungry. Probably kicked around by people who should have known better. And now here he is, living in penthouses and eating gourmet tuna, completely unaware of how dramatically his circumstances have changed.

Maybe we have that in common.

"You know what?" I say, studying his golden eyes. "I think it's time to name you."

He stares at me with the blank indifference of a creature who has never cared about human conventions and never will.

"I already have a Tweety in my life," I continue, thinking out loud. "So how about Sylvester? Keep the theme going. You've got the coloring for it—black and sleek. And you've mastered cartoon-villain energy."

The cat yawns, displaying an impressive set of fangs, then begins grooming his paw with absolute disregard for my poignant naming ceremony.

"Yeah, that's what I thought. You don't give a damn what I call you as long as the tuna keeps coming." I shake my head, smiling despite myself. "Fair enough. Sylvester it is. Welcome to the family, officially. It's small and new. But it's a good one."

I attempt to reclaim my notepad from beneath his furry body, but he's dead weight. I've learned cats have this peculiar skill that defies physics—they become twice as heavy when they don't want to move. I end up sliding the notepad out from under him inch by inch while he glares at me with the righteous indignation of royalty being disturbed.

"Don't look at me like that. I'm trying to write nice things for your other parent."

He does not seem impressed. I'm mid-battle with Bla—*Sylvester*—when I hear footsteps approaching. The bathroom door must have opened while I was distracted.

Charlie rounds the corner into the kitchen, hair still damp from the shower, wearing one of my T-shirts that hangs to mid-thigh. She looks soft and rumpled and utterly beautiful—the kind of beautiful that doesn't require makeup or styling or any of the beauty-armor she wears for the public. Just her, fresh-faced, rosy cheeks, freckles on display. So real.

"Morning," she says, padding toward me on bare feet. There's a slight hitch in her walk—a tenderness that makes heat creep up my neck when I remember why.

"Morning yourself." I catch her hand as she passes, pulling her close enough to press a kiss to her knuckles. "How'd you sleep?"

"Yeah." She pushes my shoulder. "You were gone when I woke up. What gives?"

I sigh. "Okay, remember that thing we need to talk about?"

A sly smile crosses her face. "Does it have anything to do with your father naming me in an illegal scheme to pay off a judge?"

My heart drops to my ass and throbs there. "Who called you?"

"Dad called me very early this morning. He oversees everything legal and finance for me. It's in his DNA."

My head droops. "Well, I've certainly made a great first impression on your dad."

"Oh you did," Charlie says enthusiastically. "He saw you grab a sleazy paparazzo by the scruff and nearly beat Grayson to a pulp. He says he's very much looking forward to meeting you."

The warmth settles in my chest. "That's a relief. So what now?"

"We'll do the Atlanta shows, then we'll fly to New York, give a statement. Easy-peasy."

"What if it gets out though?"

She arches an eyebrow, her lips quirking into a playful half smile. "The world will probably end. Real Armageddon zombie-apocalypse shit."

"You don't care?"

"I'll always be some kind of headline, Taio. Might as well give them something interesting to conspire about. I'm not mad, babe. I am...wondering how you are. I'm sorry about your dad. I'm so sorry he tried to use me against you."

I let out a heavy exhale. "He only knew because I told him how excited I was about us. How much you already meant to me. I didn't expect—"

"Shhh." Only when I'm seated are we eye level. She holds my gaze as she traces my frown lines with the tip of her finger. "It doesn't matter. I won't let you beat yourself up over this. You and me? We're a team now. We'll solve your problems like we did mine—together."

I gather her in my hands, tracing her silhouette. "How did you sleep?"

"Like the dead. Turns out orgasms are better than melatonin. Multiple orgasms? Basically a medical-grade sedative." She grins at my expression—somewhere between proud and flustered—then reaches past me to steal my coffee cup, taking a long sip. "Ugh, how do you drink it black? This tastes like punishment."

"It's an acquired taste."

"It's an acquired cry for help." But she takes another sip anyway, wrinkling her nose. "Okay. So." Her face shifts into something more serious, the playfulness draining away. "Are you ready for the reckoning?"

"The reckoning?"

"Sage is on her way up. She texted me while I was in the shower. Actually, she texted me approximately thirty-six times while I was in the shower." Charlie sets down the coffee cup and pulls out her phone, scrolling through what I assume is a parade of damage. "She's mad, Taio. Like, capital-M Mad. The kind of mad where she stops using exclamation points and starts using periods, which is how you know it's serious."

"How bad is it?"

"Grayson went nuclear on socials overnight." She turns the phone toward me, showing a screenshot of an Instagram story—Grayson's face, artfully lit, with a caption that reads: *Some people show you who they really are. Believe them the first time.*

"He's..." Embarrassed, wounded, and probably mortified. But that's not what I say. "...such a punk-ass bitch."

"Oh, it gets worse." She swipes to the next screenshot. "He's been liking comments that call me a cheater. Responding to DMs with cryptic bullshit that makes it sound like I was the one who did something wrong. And apparently"—she swipes again—"somebody, aka Grayson, gave an 'anonymous source' interview to TMZ about our 'troubled relationship' and my 'erratic behavior' and my 'inappropriate closeness with a member of my security team.'"

"All in less than twelve hours?"

"Celebrity gossip never sleeps."

"It should." My jaw tightens. "He took over the whole narrative."

"Of course. He's trying to make me look like the villain so he can play the victim." Charlie's tone is flat, resigned. "It's not even that creative. This is like, *Toxic Ex Playbook* page one. But it's working—the comments are already filling up with people calling me a slut and saying Grayson deserves better."

"Babe—"

"I know. I know it shouldn't matter what strangers on the internet think. But it does matter, because those strangers buy tickets and stream songs and determine whether I have a career next year or not." She sets the phone face-down on the counter, like she can't stand to look at it anymore. "Sage is going to want a strategy. A spin. Some way to make this look like anything other than what it was."

I consider this for a moment, turning over the options in my mind. "I mean, she could probably spin it. Make it look like just a fight between you and Grayson—a lovers' quarrel that got heated. You called your bodyguard to pick you up because things got tense. The confrontation outside the restaurant was just me being overprotective, doing my job. We can say the handholding was comfort, not romance. Doesn't have to be a whole thing."

Charlie's quiet. Too quiet. She's staring at the counter, fingers tracing patterns on the marble.

"What?" I ask.

"I don't want to spin it." She meets my gaze, and there's something new in her expression. Something steely and resolved that I haven't seen before. "I'm done, Taio. I'm done with strategies and lies and carefully curated narratives that make me look like someone I'm not."

"Okay..."

"For years I've been letting other people tell my story.

Managers deciding what version of Charlie Riley the world gets to see. A publicist orchestrating fake relationships to boost my image. Stylists dressing me in things I'd never choose for myself. And every time something real happened, every time I felt something genuine, I had to bury it because it didn't fit the brand." She takes a breath, steadying herself. "I'm tired of being a brand. I want to be a person."

"You've always been a person to me."

"I know. That's why I fell for you." She says it simply, like it's just a fact of the universe. Water is wet. The sky is blue. Charlie fell for Taio.

"So what are you going to do?"

"Tell the truth," she says, like it's obvious. Like it's easy, even though we both know it's anything but. "You and I are together. Grayson and I were a PR arrangement that's now over. That's it. That's the whole story. The world wants answers, and I know social media is probably imploding right now with theories and speculation and people demanding to know who you are and what's really going on." She squares her shoulders. "But it's not my job to supply them with a convenient story. I don't owe them a performance of my personal life."

"What about the fallout? The headlines? The—"

"Will happen regardless of what I do," she cuts me off gently. "If I spin, they'll eventually find out the truth and call me a liar. If I stay silent, they'll fill in the gaps with whatever narrative is most damaging. The only way to actually control this is to...not. Let the chips fall where they may. As long as we're good, my world keeps spinning."

I stare at her, warmth expanding in my chest. This is the woman who, just weeks ago, was terrified of what the tabloids might say. Who built her entire existence around managing public perception. Who hid a relationship rather than face the messiness of real love.

And now she's choosing truth. Choosing authenticity. Choosing us—out in the open, consequences be damned.

"You're sure about this?" I ask, not because I doubt her, but because I need her to know I'll support whatever she decides. "Because once you say it out loud, there's no taking it back. Your whole life changes. My life changes. We become a story that other people get to have opinions about."

"We're already a story. We have been since those cameras caught us hugging on the balcony in New York." She reaches for me, fingers curling into the front of my shirt. "The only question is whether we let other people write it, or we write it ourselves."

"Then I'm with you." I cover her hand with mine. "Whatever you need, however you want to handle this—I'm with you."

"Even if it means your face is going to be everywhere? Even if people start digging into your past?"

The question lands heavier than she probably intends. My past. My father. The escort work that paid for years of legal bills. All of it waiting to be discovered by anyone with enough motivation to dig.

"Even then," I say, and I mean it. "We'll face it together."

She leans in, pressing a soft kiss to my cheek, lingering there for a moment like she's drawing strength from the contact. "It's too early to say it, but you know what I want to say."

"Who told you it's too early to say it?"

"*Cosmo, CosmoGirl, Vogue,* and also that Disney Princess quiz I've taken about thirty times."

"Well they don't—wait, what? Thirty times? Why?" I squint at her, baffled.

"Because, I want Belle. I keep ending up as Rapunzel. It's bullshit."

The genuine anguish in her face makes her ten times more adorable than I can bear.

"You can be whatever princess you want. I'll call you Belle. What prince do you think I'd be?"

"Beast, obviously." She gestures to my whole frame. "You're massive."

"Well how about this? Beast loves Belle. And we can bring

that into the real world whenever you're ready. Just know when you say it, I'll be ready to say it right back."

Black Cat—well, Sylvester now—ruins our sweet moment, managing to smack Charlie's arm and my elbow in one quick kitty-strike.

"Oh I'm sorry," she coos in that ridiculous high-pitched voice people use with babies and animals. "I didn't greet my kitty overlord this morning. Where are my manners? Good morning, handsome." She scratches under his chin, earning an enthusiastic purr. "Did you have your breakfast yet? Has Taio given you your second breakfast?"

"Second?"

"Such a smart, handsome boy. Yes you are. Yes you are," she continues.

The cat looks insufferably smug, as if he understands every word.

"Hey," I mention, "I finally named him."

"Oh?" Charlie's hand pauses mid-scratch. Her voice has gone carefully neutral in a way that immediately makes me suspicious.

"Sylvester. You know, because I have a Tweety, so it seemed fitting—"

"Sylvester," she repeats slowly. A fleeting mix of mischief and sheepishness sweeps her face, like a child caught with one hand still in the cookie jar but not quite sorry about it.

"Yeah. It fits, right? A black cat, always scheming, probably plotting to eat a small yellow bird—"

"Sylvester is a tuxedo cat."

"And?"

"Never mind. Same difference. It's a great name." Her voice is too bright. Too agreeable. She's doing that thing where she smiles too wide and won't quite meet my eyes. "He looks like a Sylvester. Very distinguished."

I narrow my eyes. "Charlie."

"What?"

"What aren't you telling me?"

She bites her lip, clearly wrestling with something. Even the cat looks between us with the detached interest of a creature who knows drama is unfolding but can't be bothered to care. He yawns pointedly, as if we need to become aggressively more entertaining, fast, if we want him to stay.

Charlie huffs out a breath, shoulders dropping in defeat. "I may have...already named him."

"Already named him."

"Like, a week ago. Maybe longer." She winces. "I've been calling him Toothless."

"Toothless." I stare at her. "Like the dragon?"

"Well it matches more than Sylvester!" She says it defensively, like this is a completely reasonable choice. "He's all black with big eyes and he does this thing where he retracts his claws when he's happy, just like Toothless retracts his teeth in the movie. And I know there's probably thousands of black cats out there also named Toothless, but it *fits*, okay? He responds to it and everything. He looks up when I say it. Well, sometimes. When he feels like it."

I'm laughing before she finishes. Full, belly-deep laughter that shakes my shoulders and makes my eyes water. Charlie swats my arm, but she's grinning too, the tension of the morning temporarily forgotten in the absurdity of the moment.

"Maybe we should let him pick," I say.

"Good call. Sylvester?" Charlie calls. Nothing. "Toothless?" she says in a tone that is far more honey-sweet, trying to stack the deck for her pick. Still, nothing.

"Black Cat," I gruff out. His ears perk, he catches me in his periphery in a look that says, *you rang*? "Oh damn. Damage might be done, Charlie."

She shakes her head in defeat. "We now have a black cat, that's named Black Cat. Sure...let's roll with that."

I don't care what we call the damn cat. I just like how she said *we*.

The cat in question yawns enormously, displaying all of his very much present teeth, then hops down from the counter and saunters toward his food bowl like this conversation is beneath him. His food dish sits empty, yet there he perches beside it, eyes narrowed to hostile slits that silently communicate we have failed at our most basic duty as his human servants.

This is what I want, I realize. Not just the big dramatic moments—the declarations and the confrontations and the passionate nights in blanket forts. But this. The small, mundane intimacy of a shared morning. Coffee she hates. A cat with two names. The easy rhythm of two lives beginning to intertwine.

"Hey." I catch her hand, tugging her back toward me. She comes willingly, a pastry in her hand, crumbs already on her lips that I plan to kiss away. "Why me? You've met a lot of strangers. Why did you keep me?"

She nods knowingly. "Mostly because all the other escorts that came before you were incredibly disappointing—"

"Charlie," I growl. "Be serious for me. For once."

She smiles. "Remember the night we met?"

"Of course."

"I begged my mom that night to send me a sign. A message from beyond of whether to give up or keep going. I didn't expect her answer to come in the form of a behemoth of a man carrying a two-pronged vibrator that could double as a jackhammer, but you ask the universe for gifts, you don't really get to pick the packaging."

A chuckle escapes me, soft but genuine. "So you think your mom sent me."

"Maybe. Maybe not. But all I know is that night I was paying attention. On any other night, maybe I would've let you slip away."

I hold up my coffee mug. "Well, cheers to your mom."

"Yeah," Charlie says with a distant look in her eyes. "Cheers to my mom."

The doorbell buzzes—sharp and insistent. Sage, here for the reckoning.

Charlie takes a deep breath, straightens her spine, and pulls away from me. But she pauses at the threshold of the kitchen, looking back with an expression that makes my chest ache.

"Thank you," she says quietly.

"For what?"

She smiles, soft and certain. "For being someone worth blowing up my whole life for." Doubling back, she kisses my forehead. "Would you get that? I'm going to go put on pants."

"How about you answer the door and I go put on your pants?"

She snorts in laugher. "Eventually you'll learn that Sage is on our side."

"Doesn't make her any less scary," I mutter as I stand up, my eyes following Charlie as she disappears down the hallway to safety.

The doorbell buzzes again, but I double back to my writing pad to jot down one more note before I forget.

I love you, Charlie Riley.

I fold the note carefully, add it to the pile, and head toward the sound of voices.

Time to face the music.

Chapter 26

Taio

So who is better? Me or The Detonator?

The bathroom door is cracked open, steam curling through the gap like an invitation I'm not sure I should accept.

It's the morning of the first Atlanta show, and Charlie has been in that bathtub for over an hour. She's probably decompressing. Sage didn't leave until the evening, after they'd spent six hours arguing about social media strategy. Or rather, Sage argued. Charlie just kept saying no.

No statement. No spin. No feeding the beast.

"People need to hear your side," Sage insisted, pacing the living room like a caged animal. "Silence looks like guilt. It looks like you have something to hide."

"I don't have anything to hide anymore," Charlie replied, calm as still water. "The truth is out. Taio and I are together. Grayson and I were never real. If people want to believe his version, that's their choice."

Sage looked at me like I might be able to talk some sense into her client, but I just shrugged. Charlie made her choice, and I'm not about to undermine it. Even if part of me wonders whether silence is really the best approach when Grayson is out there poisoning every well he can find. The man has been relentless—new posts every few hours, each one more passive-aggressive than the last.

But Charlie's done performing. And honestly? I think that's

the bravest thing she could do.

I push the bathroom door open slowly, announcing my presence. "Hey."

Charlie is submerged up to her shoulders in bubbles, head tipped back against the rim of the tub, AirPods in. Her eyes are closed, but there's nothing relaxed about her. Her jaw is tight. Her shoulders are creeping toward her ears. One hand grips the edge of the tub like she's bracing for impact.

Whatever she's listening to isn't helping.

I crouch beside the tub and touch her arm gently. She startles, eyes flying open, then relaxes when she sees it's me.

"Sorry." She pulls out one AirPod. "Didn't hear you come in."

"I noticed." I settle onto the bath mat, back against the wall, close enough to touch her if she wants but not crowding. "What are you listening to?"

"Nothing. Just white noise. Rain sounds. Trying to drown out my own thoughts." She pulls out the other AirPod and sets them both on the edge of the tub. "It's not working. My brain is louder than any rainstorm."

"Want to talk about it?"

"Not really."

"Charlie." I say her name like a gentle push. "I can see you spiraling from here."

She sighs, sinking deeper into the bubbles until they reach her chin. "I'm fine. I just need to get through today. The first show after is always the worst."

I reach over and brush a strand of wet hair from her forehead, tucking it behind her ear. "What's wrong, baby?"

She's quiet for a long moment. The water ripples as she shifts, drawing her knees up to her chest like she's trying to protect her vital organs from an attack she can sense coming.

"I'm scared," she finally admits, her voice small.

"Of what specifically?"

"Everything. Nothing. I don't know." She lets out a hollow sound that's more like a sob dressed up as a laugh. "The internet is having a field day right now. Grayson's narrative is winning because he's the only one talking. People think I'm a cheater, a slut, a liar—pick your favorite insult, I've seen it in my mentions. And tonight I have to walk out on that stage and pretend like none of it matters."

"It doesn't matter. Not really."

"It does, though. Because those people bought tickets. They're going to be in that arena, thousands of them, and some of them are going to be angry. They came to see America's sweetheart, and instead they got..." She shakes her head. "What if someone heckles me? What if someone throws something? What if—" She stops, swallowing hard. "What if someone is so angry about what they've heard that they decide to do something about it?"

The fear in her eyes guts me. This isn't about reputation anymore. This is about safety. About the very real possibility that some unhinged stranger might decide to make a statement at her expense.

"Hey." I shift closer, taking her hand under the water. "Look at me."

She does, reluctantly.

"I'm going to be there tonight. Right in the wings, watching every second. If anyone so much as looks at you wrong, I'll handle it. That's literally my job, remember?"

"I know. I just..." She squeezes my hand. "I can't get out of my own head. Every time I close my eyes, I see worst-case scenarios. My brain won't stop running disaster simulations."

I study her face—the tension in her brow, the way she's chewing her bottom lip, the shadows under her eyes that tell me she hasn't slept well despite our activities last night. She's trapped in her own anxiety, and no amount of reassurance is going to logic her out of it.

She needs a distraction. A reset. Something to pull her out of her head and back into her body.

"Charlie." I keep my voice casual. "Where's The Detonator?"

She blinks, thrown by the subject change. "What?"

"The vibrator. I know you still have it. Where is it?"

A flush creeps up her neck, visible even through the steam. "Why?"

"Just curious."

"It's..." She hesitates, suddenly fascinated by the bubbles surrounding her. "It's in my underwear drawer."

"Is the battery charged?"

The flush deepens. "Fifty-fifty chance."

A grin spreads across my face. "Oh really?"

"Shut up."

"I'm not saying anything."

"You're smiling. That's saying something."

"I'm smiling because I find it incredibly sexy that you've been using it." I lean closer, my lips near her ear. "Tell me, how'd it perform? Is it better than me?"

She pretends to gasp. "No. Of course not." Then she clears her throat. "Very close second though."

I press a kiss to her forehead and stand. "Don't move."

Her underwear drawer is exactly where I expected—top right in the massive walk-in closet. I find The Detonator nestled between silk and lace, already freed from its packaging just like she said. The thing is even more ridiculous up close, all curves and buttons and promises of destruction.

When I return to the bathroom, Charlie has shifted in the tub, sitting up straighter, the water lapping at her breasts. Her nipples are hard—from the cooling water or anticipation, I'm not sure. Probably both.

I hand her the toy and settle back against the wall, making myself comfortable. "Show me."

She takes a breath, then another, working up her courage. Her fingers find the button, and The Detonator hums to life with a low vibration that I can hear even from here. She starts slow, tracing the toy along her collarbone, down between her breasts, circling each nipple until she gasps.

"Lower," I tell her.

She obeys, dragging the vibrator down her stomach, beneath the water's surface. I can't see what she's doing anymore, but I can see her face—the way her lips part, the way her eyes flutter closed, the way her head tips back against the porcelain tub.

"That's it." My voice has gone rough. "Just like that."

Her hips shift beneath the water, chasing the sensation. A soft moan escapes her throat, and my cock throbs in response. I palm myself through my sweatpants, not hiding it, letting her see what she's doing to me.

She opens her eyes and looks at me, pupils pried wide with panic and anticipation. "Do you want me to put it in?" Her voice is almost apologetic, as if she's bad for wanting to be watched.

"Yes," I say. I want her greedy, I want her ruined.

"Do you want me to use both?" The Detonator is two-pronged, a joke and a challenge, both ends curved like a cartoon villain's mustache. I can't believe she's asking, and I can't believe how badly I want to see.

"I want you to do what you like, baby."

Charlie's hand trembles a little. "I want to try. I don't know if I can," she says. "How?"

I grab the bath oil sitting on the tub ledge and pour it into my hand. Understanding where I'm going, she lifts The Detonator out of the water, and I thoroughly coat both heads. I bring my mouth to her ear. "Turn over."

She blinks at me, skin already slicked with sweat and steam. "What, like—"

I nod. "Hands and knees. We'll go slow, okay?"

There's a beat where I see her hesitate, considering the strangeness of the position, the exposure, but then her eyes flick to my face, and she does it—knees tucked under her, elbows braced on the white porcelain, head bowed. Her ass breaks the surface, bubbles sluicing off and making rivers down the small of her back. I stare openly, shameless, at the way her body curves, the twinge of muscle in her thigh as she steadies herself.

"Beautiful," I tell her, and she laughs, a nervous edge to it.

"You're a pervert."

"You love it," I answer, and swirl the bath oil between my fingers, warming it. Tightening my fist, I let it drip slowly down her ass crack, and she twitches, a little giggle escaping. "That tickles," she mutters, but it doesn't sound like a protest.

I knead the oil in, circling her rim with the pad of my thumb, and she makes a strangled little sound, burying her face in her crossed arms. I keep going, slow and easy, letting her get used to it. When her breath evens out—when I can see the tension start to melt away from her shoulders—I position the toy.

The tip of The Detonator glides between her folds, bumping gently against the swelling flesh there. I watch her back arch, see her knees spread wider for leverage. Charlie's legs look almost too long for the tub, like she's trying to outrun her own nervousness. I guide her hand so the toy is right where she wants it, the soft silicone nosing forward.

"Breathe," I remind her, and she does, a shuddering inhale that echoes off the tile. The first slick inch slides in, and she gasps, her spine flexing like an animal startled in the woods. I steady her hip with one hand, not to restrain, just to show her I'm here.

"It's intense," she says, muffled by her arms.

"You're doing so good, baby. When you're ready."

She pushes back on the toy, tentative at first, then with a little more force. The curve of it disappears into her, and she whimpers, head turning to the side so she can see my reaction. I hold her gaze, daring her to keep going.

The second prong hovers above her ass. She bites her lip, uncertain, and for a moment I think she's going to stop. But then she shifts, lifting her hips, exposing herself to me without any pretense of shame.

"Try it," she mouths. Barely audible.

I oil the second end again, fingers shaking because I've never wanted anyone the way I want her right now, and I can't afford to lose control. I press it to her, applying the barest pressure, just enough that she knows what's coming.

Charlie shudders at the sensation, a tremor running the length of her spine. I watch her hands flex on the porcelain—knuckles white, fingers spread, gripping the tub for dear life. There's no sound but the quiet slosh of water and the hiss of her breath, then a small, startled giggle that surprises both of us.

"Too much?" I ask, already easing off the pressure, but she shakes her head, forehead against her arms.

"No, just—" She rolls her hips back, insistent now. "Go slow?"

I do. I work the head of the toy against her, letting the angle and the oil do most of the work. Charlie starts to rock, just barely, like she's searching for the sweet spot between pain and pleasure. Her body tenses, then shudders, the ridge of muscle under my palm jumping with each new inch. When the toy finally seats itself, she lets out a gasp, high and desperate.

"There it is," I murmur, my voice a gravel road, and I trace the knobs of her spine with my palms, claiming each vertebra with a touch that feels both tender and feral.

I thumb the control, and the vibration doubles. Charlie's breath stutters. She breathes a sound that's not quite a sob, not quite a laugh, just pure sensation. The water sloshes as she pushes against the toy, chasing the friction.

"Fuck, Taio." Her voice is ragged, the syllables brittle. "I can't—it's too—"

She comes hard, a soundless scream that snaps through her body like a circuit blown. Every muscle tenses, her thighs clamp and then tremble, and the only thing keeping her from submerging is the way she claws at the enamel. The bubbles die around her, replaced by ragged breaths and the tremor of aftershocks. I ease a hand up her slick back and rest it there, a silent anchor, steadying her as the quakes taper off.

She releases a whimper that is, somehow, both relief and embarrassment, and buries her face in the crook of her arm. Still kneeling, still split wide by the toy, but softer now—like she's let go of something she didn't know she was holding.

"Holy shit," she gasps, voice hoarse. "I think I left orbit." She relaxes.

"We're not done, baby."

Slowly, carefully, I pull out The Detonator, dipping it in the tub before setting it aside. She looks back at it like the thing might bite her if she turns her back. And we were only on the third vibration level. She's still trembling, her body loose and wrung out, when I shuck my clothes and climb into the tub with her, kneeling behind. The water has gone tepid but neither of us cares. The inside of her thighs is slick with oil and warmth, and when I grip her hips she arches back into me, greedy for more.

There's no teasing. No buildup. I line myself up and slide in, slow at first, but the gasp she lets out—sharp and surprised—shreds my resolve. I thrust all the way, buried to the hilt, and she sobs my name into the back of her hand.

The grip of her pussy is unrelenting, and I fuck her hard, the slap of wet skin loud as it echoes in the bathroom. Her fingers clutch the edge of the tub until they blanch. Each panting breath fogs against the bathroom tile. I bite down on the curve of her shoulder, not quite gentle, and she moans, pushing back against me with more hunger than I expect.

"God, Taio," she cries. Her voice is shredded, each syllable a tremor. I palm her ass and spread her wider, angle deeper, until the world tunnels down to the heat and friction and the way our bodies crash together. There's nothing else but now. Even my name sounds different when she says it this way—urgent, primal. She's never needed me like this before. I never want her to stop needing me like this.

I bottom out inside her and lose all the words in my brain; I can only make sounds. My hands clamp down on her hips, too rough, but she makes a noise like she loves it, and that's it, I'm done. The first pulse tears through me, white-hot, and I pull out just in time to paint her back with it—hot, shuddering, an obscene string of syllables torn out of my throat. Her ass is a canvas, and I make my mark, streaks of me sliding over her slick skin, chasing the trails of bath oil.

Charlie is panting, arms trembling, still holding herself up with the last dregs of dignity, but barely. Her hair is a mess, tangled and wild and sticking to her damp shoulders. She laughs—just a breath, really—and sags down with her face buried in her arms, ass still in the air. I kneel behind her, breath sawing in and out of my lungs, both hands steadying her so I don't slide down and drown us both in the aftermath.

After a minute, she peeks up at me, her smile dazed but wicked. "You're an animal," she whispers, and it's the highest compliment.

"Don't move," I manage. My arms are jelly, but I grab the hand shower and, as gently as possible, hose her off. The water is barely lukewarm so she squeals and twists, but makes no effort to get away. When I'm done, she waggles her butt at me and grins, then sinks back into the cloudy water with a satisfied groan, floating on her post-orgasmic high.

I slide behind her and pull her against me, her back to my chest, her body all but immobile in the aftermath as I cradle her in the water. Her head lolls onto my shoulder, her hair wet ropes across my jaw, and the heat of her skin radiates through to the hollow of my throat.

With my free foot, I nudge the lever for the water, and the faucet shrieks, then coughs out a fresh, scalding stream. Bubbles collapse and swirl; the water turns milky with oil and whatever was left of her resolve. She doesn't say a word, just lets the new warmth pour over her knees. The bathroom fills with the sound of running water, overwhelming the tiny huffs of her breath.

I kiss her on the shoulder, on the mole by her neck, on the nape of her hairline where the skin tastes like sweat and whatever intoxicating perfume she's been hoarding since the tour's start. She sighs, not so much content as liquefied. I wrap myself around her like a question mark—not so tight she'd feel trapped, not so loose she'd think I'm letting go. With Charlie, it's always been this dance of holding on while leaving the door unlocked. But she always stays.

She starts to talk, and I recognize the effort it costs her—like dragging words up from the bottom of the tub. "I feel like...I don't know..."

I press my lips to her temple. "Shhh," I whisper, the sound melting into her damp hair. "Just float for a minute. Let your mind go quiet." My arms tighten fractionally around her. "I've got you." Her exhale is long and deep, tension draining from her limbs until she's boneless against me, as if my words have found a secret switch beneath her skin.

After a while of quiet, I kiss the top of her head. "So who is better at making you come? Me or The Detonator?"

She looks over her shrugged shoulder as a mischievous smile grows on her face.

Then she leaves me answerless, pretending to suddenly fall asleep, fake snoring noises and all.

Chapter 27

Charlie

I choose you. In front of everyone. No more hiding.

The final note hangs in the air like a held breath.

Thirty thousand people crammed into this stadium. Thirty thousand strangers who came here tonight not knowing what to expect. Not knowing if the rumors were true. Not knowing if the woman on stage would be the sweetheart they remembered or the scandal they'd just read about.

For two hours, I gave them everything I had. Every song, every dance, every ounce of energy in my body. I didn't hold back. I didn't perform a carefully curated version of myself. I just...was. Messy and imperfect and completely, terrifyingly passionate.

And now there's a moment of silence. A brief clarity as I stare out into the sea of spotlights. I zero in on the magnitude of it all.

One heartbeat. Two.

Then the world explodes.

The roar hits me like a physical force—a wall of sound that vibrates through my chest and steals the breath from my lungs. A buffalo herd of people on their feet, screaming, clapping, crying. The noise is so loud it becomes its own kind of silence, a white-hot rush of approval that drowns out everything else.

I stand center stage, chest heaving, sweat dripping down my temples, and I let it wash over me. The lights. The sound. The overwhelming, impossible love pouring from every corner of this arena.

They showed up. Despite everything. Despite Grayson's poison and the tabloid headlines and the internet's cruelty. They showed up, and they stayed, and now they're on their feet telling me it was worth it.

I wasn't sure this would happen. In that bathtub this morning, running disaster simulations, I imagined a hundred different versions of tonight. Hecklers drowning out my vocals. Signs with cruel messages held up in the crowd. A cold, polite reception that would confirm every fear I've ever had about being unlovable once people saw the real me.

Instead, I got this.

My dancers surround me, faces split with matching grins. Mia grabs my hand, squeezing hard, tears streaming down her cheeks. Kenny pulls me into a sweaty side hug, laughing into my ear. The backup vocalists are bouncing, high-fiving each other, basking in the glow of what we just accomplished together.

It was our best show yet. Not because the choreography was flawless or the vocals were pitch-perfect—though they were, *they really were*—but because something shifted tonight. Some invisible barrier between me and the audience crumbled, and for the first time in my career, I wasn't performing *at* them. I was sharing *with* them.

That's what Taio's note said. Today's selection from my box of paper hearts.

You're not performing for them. You're sharing yourself with them. There's a difference.

He was right. He's always right.

I turn toward the wings, searching through the chaos of stagehands and crew members until I find him. He's standing just offstage, exactly where he promised he'd be, and he's cheering harder than anyone here. His hands are cupped around his mouth, amplifying his voice, and even though I can't hear the specific words over the roar of the crowd, I can read his lips.

That's my girl.

My heart splits wide open, raw and real and unstoppable.

My feet are moving before I make the conscious decision. I'm running across the stage toward the wings, my heels abandoned somewhere near the drum kit, my bare feet slapping against the smooth surface of the stage. The crowd's cheers shift, confused, curious, as they watch me sprint toward the shadows.

Taio's eyes go wide when he realizes what I'm doing. He shakes his head, holds up his hands, mouths something that looks like *Charlie, don't*—but I'm already there, my fingers closing around his wrist, and I'm pulling him into the light.

He resists for exactly half a second. Then he lets me lead him, stumbling slightly, onto the stage.

The jumbotron catches us immediately. Our faces, twenty feet tall, projected onto screens throughout the arena. Taio freezes in the spotlight, his shoulders hunched toward his ears, hands dangling awkwardly at his sides like they've suddenly grown too heavy for his arms—a deer caught not just in headlights but in the collective gaze of thirty thousand pairs of eyes.

But while he's nervous, I've never been more sure and confident in my life.

I reach up, cup his face in my palms, and I kiss him. PG-style.

It's not a long kiss. It's not a passionate, movie-style declaration. It's soft and sweet and simple—a press of lips that says everything I've been too scared to say out loud. *I choose you. In front of everyone. No more hiding.*

The crowd loses its damn mind.

The noise is somehow even louder than before—a tsunami of screams and whistles and stomping feet that shakes the stage beneath us. I pull back from the kiss and look up at Taio, and his expression has shifted from terror to wonder, like he can't quite believe this is really happening.

"Hi," I say, though he can't possibly hear me over the chaos.

"Hi," he mouths back. Then, quieter, just for me: "You're unhinged."

"You love it."

"I love *you*."

The words hit different when they're said on a stage in front of thousands of witnesses. They hit like a promise. Like a vow. Like the beginning of something that can't be taken back.

I grab his hand—properly this time, fingers interlaced, the way we hold hands behind closed doors—and I turn us both to face the crowd. The jumbotron shows our clasped hands, zoomed in, undeniable. There's no spinning this. No PR strategy that could explain it away. This is exactly what it looks like.

Charlie Riley, making a choice. Me, claiming Taio publicly, permanently, in front of the whole world.

The cheers don't stop. If anything, they intensify. I scan the audience, looking for the anger I was so afraid of, the judgment, the disappointment. But all I see are smiles. Phones held high, capturing this moment. Hands waving, tears flowing, voices screaming their approval.

They're happy for me.

These strangers who don't know anything about my life except what they've read in headlines—they're *happy* for me.

I didn't need this. That's the thing I understand now, standing here with Taio's hand in mine and the love of my fans washing over us. I didn't need their approval to make my choice. I would have chosen him anyway even against the advice of every publicist and manager and well-meaning friend. I would have chosen him even if the world hated me for it.

But God, it's nice to know they don't.

It's nice to know that authenticity doesn't have to mean isolation. That being real doesn't automatically mean being rejected. That somewhere out there, in the masses of people who have the privilege of living simple lives with beautiful, simple things, are still those who cheer me on through my chaotic, public, messy, complicated...but beautiful life.

And at the end of the day, they're rooting for joy. Theirs. Mine. We just need more of it, as much as we can get.

My mom would have loved this. She would have cried,

probably. Squeezed my hand too hard and told me how much she loved me. Maybe...I was enough. Me and Spencer. Maybe that big, magical love I thought she missed was there all along. Through her daughters, who keep her memory alive every day.

I hope you're watching, Mom. I love you.

Taio squeezes my hand, pulling me back to the present. The crowd is still cheering, still celebrating, but the energy is shifting—softening into something warmer, more sustained. They're not just excited anymore. They're witnessing something. They know it, and we know it.

I lean into Taio's side, resting my head against his shoulder for just a moment. Tomorrow there will be headlines. Tomorrow there will be think pieces and Twitter discourse and probably a very long conversation with Sage about "re-managing the narrative." Tomorrow, everything changes.

But tonight, I'm just a girl on a stage, holding the hand of the man she loves, finally free.

"Thank you, Atlanta!" I shout into the microphone, my voice cracking with emotion. "Thank you for being here. Thank you for believing in me. Thank you for..." I look at Taio, and he's looking back at me with so much love it makes my chest hurt. "Thank you for letting me share the best pieces of me."

The cheers swell one final time as we walk offstage together. Hand in hand. Out of the spotlight, into the shadows, toward whatever comes next.

I spent my whole life performing. Pretending to be someone I wasn't. Hiding the messy, complicated truth behind a practiced smile and a perfect image.

But the best performance of my career was the one where I stopped performing altogether.

The one where I just let myself be loved.

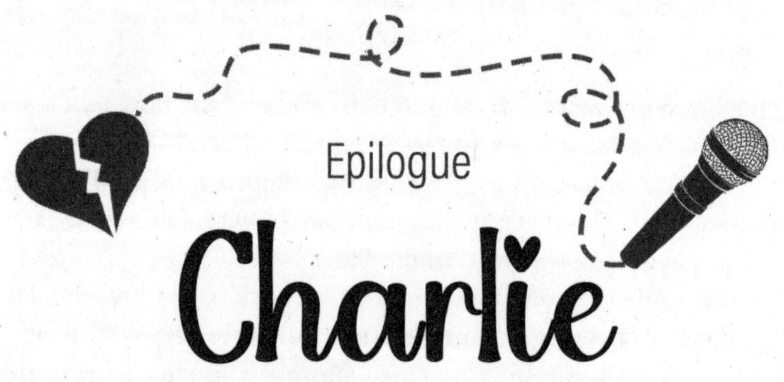

She's going to be extraordinary.

Five Months Later

The pizza is the size of a tire.

I'm barely exaggerating. Taio and I are sitting in a red vinyl booth at Gio's, a hole-in-the-wall pizzeria three blocks from my Vegas apartment, and the thing taking up most of our table could double as a spare for a midsize SUV. Cheese bubbles in golden pools across the surface. The pepperoni has gone crispy at the edges, curled into little cups of grease. It's the kind of calorie-dense masterpiece that makes my soul sing hallelujah—a hot, cheesy monstrosity that would make my nutritionist clutch her pearls. I want to propose marriage to this pizza after weeks of chicken breast, quinoa, and kale smoothies during tour rehearsals.

"This is obscene," Taio says, lifting a slice that immediately begins to droop under its own weight. He has to fold it in half just to get it to his mouth. "I love it."

"Gio's doesn't believe in moderation."

"Gio's believes in cardiac events."

"Same thing."

I grab my own slice and take a bite that's probably too big, cheese stretching in long strings from my mouth to the pizza. Very dignified. Very pop star. If the paparazzi could see me now—sauce on my chin, hair in a messy bun, wearing shapeless cream-colored sweats—they'd have a field day.

Taio's dressed in my favorite color on him—a hunter-green Henley and black pants. He looks handsome and sophisticated. Obviously he missed the memo where we were supposed to be bridge trolls *together.*

The bell on the door chimes as more patrons join the restaurant. By instinct, Taio and I both look toward the door. *Nothing.* We're unnoticed as the pair makes a beeline to the hostess stand.

A couple walked in ten minutes ago and did a double take when they spotted me, but they just smiled and went to their table. An older man at the counter glanced over, seemed to recognize me, and then returned to his calzone without comment. That's Vegas for you. Celebrities are furniture here. You notice them, maybe appreciate the design, and then you move on with your life.

It's blissful.

"Okay." I wipe my hands on a napkin and reach for my phone. "Are you ready?"

Taio groans. "Charlie..."

"You promised."

"I promised I'd listen. I didn't promise I'd be helpful."

"Just try." I pull out my AirPods and hand him one. "I need actual feedback, not just you telling me everything is perfect."

"But what if everything is perfect?"

"Then you're useless to me."

He grins and tucks the AirPod into his ear. "I've been called worse."

I queue up the first track—a stripped-down piano version of "Hurricane Season" that I recorded last month in a studio the size of a closet. No production. No backup vocals. No dancers or lights or spectacle. Just me and an old Steinway and whatever truth I could pull from my chest.

The opening notes fill my ear, and I watch Taio's face as he listens with casual interest, at first, then his focus sharpens, his head tilting slightly the way it does when he's really paying attention.

The vocals come in. My voice, raw and unprocessed, carrying the melody without any of the usual studio polish.

I dove into the deep end, aimed for the ocean floor
I let the waves block out the noise
But what I thought would drown me
Taught me how to breathe

Taio's hand finds mine. He squeezes once, twice.

The song ends. Silence hangs between us for a moment.

"Well?" I prompt. "The lyrics are shaky, but I like the melody. Needs a little more time in the lab. A good producer."

He shakes his head slowly. "Can you take a moment, Tweety? Before you start nitpicking? Charlie, you made this. It's beautiful."

"Thank you, babe. But that's not feedback. That's a compliment."

"It's both." He pulls out the AirPod and sets it on the table between us. "That bridge note? Goose bumps." He rubs his forearm. "The piano's haunting. Your voice is raw. It's perfect. It's ready."

"So no constructive criticism at all..."

"Okay, fine. I think maybe you should consider..." He pauses dramatically. "...recording more songs exactly like that one."

I throw a balled-up napkin at his head. "*Useless.*"

"Not true. I'm arm candy, baby. That's my whole job now." He catches the napkin and tosses it back. "Speaking of which—I heard back from two more authors this week. One's got a fantasy trilogy she wants some developmental help with, and the other is working on a historical fiction project set during the Gold Rush."

"That's...good, right? Do those interest you?"

"Well, I told them both I'm taking some grammar refresher courses first. It's been a while since my literature classes, and I will be honest—'who' and 'whom' still eludes me, but yeah. I'm interested in helping. Maybe taking some inspiration from my girl and seeing if I can monetize my passion."

"I know the difference between 'who' and 'whom.'"

He lifts a brow. "Really?"

"No. Not at all. You know, you don't have to come to Europe with me. If you want to go back to New York and work on your stuff for a while? I feel like my tour has stolen both our lives."

He kisses the side of my temple. "It gave me life, Tweety. We're finishing this thing together. You and me. Until the final performance. And beyond."

I have a month off. A little time of reprieve before we take the leap over the ocean and start the second phase of the tour. We chose to come back to Las Vegas, stay close to Claire with the baby due any day now.

I smile. "And beyond," I echo, looking forward to the quiet after the storm. More normalcy, more magical, yet regular moments like this one. Just sharing pizza with the man I love.

My phone buzzes on the table, interrupting our moment. I glance at the screen and feel my heart do a little skip when I see the name.

Dylan Perry

The message preview shows a wall of lowercase text, and I'm already smiling before I even open it.

"Who's that?" Taio asks, reading my expression.

"My brother." I swipe to open the message. "He found something. Said he wanted to send it over."

Taio wraps his arm around me, sliding in closer so he can see the screen. His hand settles on my lower back. He does this thing where he taps out a little rhythm with his pinky finger, like he's playing a tiny piano on my spine. It's his secret code for "I'm here." Whenever anything pertaining to my biological dad surfaces, his fingers start their silent concert against my vertebrae. It's still a sensitive subject.

I stalled for months after finding my mother's letter. I debated, back and forth—what was worth knowing, what was better to let go. But in the end, curiosity claimed me, like Black Cat and the can of Cheez Whiz he massacred. And also like the big, cat-cheese incident we now call the Kansas City "shitsplosion," it came with consequences.

More heartbreak.

Liam Perry died six years ago. He was survived by his wife of thirty-two years and his two sons. Also, by the daughter he didn't get to know He's gone, but it doesn't mean I can't still get to know him—or at least that's what my new half brothers, who were more welcoming and loving than I could've hoped for, said to me. For now it's just video chats and text messages, but we have plans to meet.

Dylan

hey so i was trying to dig up pictures for you and found this box of old paperwork in dad's desk. most of it was tax stuff but there was one that i think you should see.

Dylan

i asked mom if it was okay to send and she said yes. i think she feels bad about not wanting to meet you. she's just not ready yet. but she wanted you to have this.

Dylan

it's from your mom.

The lack of capitals still drives me bananas. Every text looks like a stream of consciousness that forgot to get dressed before leaving the house. But I've learned that's just Dylan—thoughtful, rambling, and completely incapable of locating the shift key. Our older brother Tyler, thank goodness, texts in complete sentences with proper punctuation. Dylan is the one who asks me for music and movie recs and sends me bizarre recipes like those spaghetti chili hot dogs that most definitely don't look "fire." Tyler, being more protective, sends simply check-in texts paired with articles about travel fatigue and homeopathic remedies. His wife is a wellness coach and doula and has an herbal remedy for *literally everything.*

I love it. I love having brothers who text me about random things. I love that six weeks ago we were strangers, and now they're part of my life like they've always been there.

Another message comes through—this one an image. I tap to expand it, and suddenly I'm looking at a photograph of a handwritten letter. The paper is yellowed with age, the ink slightly faded, but the handwriting is unmistakable.

My mother's.

I'd know it anywhere. The slight forward slant. The way she curved her lowercase "y"s.

"Is that..." Taio's voice is soft.

"Yeah." My throat tightens. "It looks like it's from her. To him."

I zoom in on the image, and together, we read.

Liam,

I've been staring at this blank page for three days, trying to find the right words. There aren't any. There's no right way to say what needs to be said, so I'm just going to say it plainly and trust that you'll hear what I mean.

What you did was wrong.

I know you know that. I could see it on your face every time you looked at me during those last few months—the guilt eating you alive. You loved me. I believe that. I still believe that, even now. But love isn't enough to build a life on. I learned that the hard way, with men who came before you, and I refuse to learn it again.

Forever love is built on trust. And I can't trust you. Not because you're a bad man, but because you made a choice that broke something between us that can't be repaired. You made me into something I never wanted to be. Now, I'm complicit in hurting your family.

Here's what I need you to do, Liam. Not for me—for yourself. For your sons.

Tell your wife the truth.

Be a man. Confess what happened. Beg for her forgiveness if you have to. Fight for the family you already have, the one that existed before I came along. Those boys deserve a father they can be proud of, and right now, you're not that man. But you could be. It's not too late to become someone worthy of their respect. You just have to do the work.

As for me and the baby—we'll be okay.

Thank you for the savings account. I wasn't going to accept it, but I've decided that's my pride talking, and my pride doesn't get to make decisions for my child. I'll use it to give her the best life I can. And it will be a good life, Liam. I'll make sure of that.

This baby is wanted. I need you to understand that. Whatever circumstances brought her into existence, she is not a mistake. She is not a burden. I'm going to spend every day of my life making sure she knows how much she's loved.

But now, if you really love me—and I think you do, in your own broken way—you need to let us go.

Move on. Be a better husband if you still can. Be a good father to your sons. Live a life that matters. And maybe, someday, a long time from now, we can look back on our time together and remember what was beautiful instead of what was shameful.

I won't contact you again after this. Please don't try to find me. It's better for both of us if we close this chapter and start fresh.

Thank you for the gift of this child. I mean that. She's going to be extraordinary.

I already love her more than I knew was possible.

Goodbye, Liam.

—Bettany

The letter blurs. I realize, distantly, that I'm crying.

Taio's arm tightens around me, pulling me against his chest. I bury my face in his shoulder and let the tears come—not sad tears, not really, but something more complex. Relief. Recognition. A grief I didn't know I was still carrying finally finding somewhere to go.

This baby is wanted.

She is the greatest gift I've ever been given.

She's going to be extraordinary.

"She loved you so much," Taio murmurs into my hair. "She really, really loved you."

"I know." I pull back, wiping my eyes with the heel of my hand. "I always knew. But it's different, seeing it. Hearing her voice again, even if it's just on paper."

"She sounds strong. Like someone who knew her worth."

"She was." I look at the letter again, at my mother's familiar handwriting, at the words she chose so carefully. "She made mistakes. A lot of them. But she wasn't weak. She wasn't some tragic figure who couldn't survive without a man. She chose herself. She chose me. And she never looked back."

I can't believe I ever thought my mother wasn't whole because she never ended up with her Prince Charming. She had two. In me and Spencer. My mother wasn't weak, she didn't miss out on love. We were it. Her daughters were her big loves. The ones she waited for, the ones she fought for.

"Hey." Taio tilts my chin up, meeting my eyes. "You okay?"

I think about the question. Really think about it.

Five months ago, I was drowning. Scandal, heartbreak, a carefully constructed life coming apart at the seams. I didn't know who I was without the performance. I didn't know if anyone would love the real me.

Now I'm sitting in a vinyl booth with pizza grease on my fingers and my mother's letter on my phone and a man who thinks my stripped-down piano recordings are perfect even when I need him to find flaws. I have a dad who chose me, sisters who would die for me, and new brothers I'm excited to get to know. I have an album to finish and a tour to complete and a whole life stretching out ahead of me—messy, complicated, entirely my own.

"Yeah," I say, and I mean it down to my bones. "I'm okay."

More than okay.

I'm thoroughly, completely, extraordinarily loved.

Just like she always wanted me to be.

Playlist

"Paper Hearts" - Tori Kelly

"Stay" - Rihanna, Mikky Ekko

"Gimme More" - Britney Spears

"Just Like Fire" - P!nk

"Jaded" - Miley Cyrus

"mine" - Kelly Clarkson

"Baby It's You" - JoJo

"Tell Me You Love Me" - Demi Lovato

"The Only Exception" - Paramore

"Dangerous Woman" - Ariana Grande

"Nonsense" - Sabrina Carpenter

"Beautiful" - Christina Aguilera

"Lose You To Love Me" - Selena Gomez

"The Life of a Showgirl (feat. Sabrina Carpenter)" - Taylor Swift

Acknowledgements

To Mr. Cove, for carrying me through this book. For being on the bandwagon. For drinking the Kool-Aid. For reminding me every single day that the magic was still there even when I couldn't see it. You are my rock, forever.

To Michelle, my incredible editor, who listened to me create a sound, responsible plan to write this book...then watched me abandon that plan swiftly. It never matters what walls I hit, what waves consume me, you're right there with me every step of the way. Thank you for editing all five versions of Charlie and Taio's story. You're more than an editor, you're one of my favorite friends, and the cherry on top is you, unlike me, actually know when to use "who" and when to use "whom." Bless you.

To Valentine, for being the voice of reason I desperately need. Thank you for every ledge you've talked me off, every spiral you've interrupted, and for pushing me forward even when I'm digging my heels in. You make me braver than I am.

To E.N. for the daily reminders to keep going even when I thought I lost the plot. Thank you for encouraging me to be my dorky, head-in-the-clouds, heart-in-the-fairytales self. This story couldn't have happened without your support.

To Aga, and all your vibrant energy and enthusiasm. For making the stories in my heart come alive with your art. Thank you!

To Judy for working so hard on this story, bending over backwards to accommodate all the curveballs life has thrown at me. Thank you for being the calm to my chaos.

To Meredith and the entire Page & Vine family, for your endless patience for this book. For giving me all the time and space I needed to find my muse again. The triumph of writing "the end" is definitely a shared one. Thank you for continuing to believe in me and my stories.

About the Author

Kay Cove, a Korean American, *USA Today* and Amazon bestselling author, known for Camera Shy, is a wife, boy mom, and accidental entrepreneur. After (surviving) a career in HR she ultimately decided to pursue her dream of becoming a published author. She writes contemporary romances filled with angsty characters, green flag MMCs, and witty banter.

She currently resides in Georgia with her husband and two sweet—albeit rambunctious—little boys. When she's not writing she can be found drinking copious amounts of coffee and watching true crime documentaries—all while keeping her tiny humans alive.

Some of her works include the Lessons in Love, PALADIN, Real Life, Real Love, and Off the Books series.

Also by Kay Cove

Lessons in Love

Camera Shy

Snapshot

Selfie

Real Life, Real Love

Paint Me Perfect

Rewrite the Rules

Owe Me One

Sing Your Secrets

First Comes Forever

Paladin

Whistleblower

Tattletale

Snitch - Coming 2026

Canary - TBD

Off the Books

Role Play

Paper Hearts

Gray Area - Coming 2026

Sweet Spot - Coming 2026

New York
She wanted to write a bestseller.
She wasn't ready for the plot twist.
Role Play
USA TODAY BESTSELLING AUTHOR
KAY COVE
Role Play
KAY COVE

Role Play

She wanted to write a bestseller. She wasn't ready for the plot twist.

Being an indie romance author was supposed to be a dream come true. But after publishing umpteen books, I still haven't "made it" and now I'm just waiting for the dark cloak of insignificance to completely snuff out my career.

I decide to roll the dice on a marketing guru who swears he can yank me out of obscurity. But after a frantic search for "book boyfriend material" and an unexpected bar encounter, I accidentally blow my entire budget on an escort.

You're beautiful. You're worthy.
You're mine.

CAMERA SHY

KAY COVE

Camera Shy

"A man is going to treat you how you treat yourself. So please, for the love of God, act like a queen."

I was expecting a ring on my thirtieth birthday. What I didn't see coming was my boyfriend and business partner dumping me because he couldn't bear the idea of our bland sex life for the rest of our lives.

When an opportunity arises to spend my summer in Las Vegas, I stumble upon my hot new neighbor and his photography studio. We strike a simple deal.

He's the teacher, and I'm his student.

My lesson is learning to love the body I have. In exchange, I'm going to save his business. I have exactly one summer to unearth the most confident version of myself before I go home and return to reality.

But after a passion-fueled summer, I'm not sure of who I am anymore, and it's clear that the worst heartbreak of my life might still be yet to come.

You're right where you belong.
With me.

SNAPSHOT

KAY COVE

Snapshot

Be loud. Lean in. Take your seat at the head of the table. I want the whole room to know that when my wife speaks, it's time to sit down and listen.

Thanks to my reckless roommate, I'm about two skips away from being homeless. Temp jobs aren't paying the bills, and now I have to cancel the scuba diving trip I can no longer afford.

At least I'll be spared from my instructor's tempting smile and rock-hard abs. Dex is wonderful, but he's only ever treated me like a friend...a really good friend. In fact, when he hears I'm having money problems, he comes up with a way we can help each other.

In a clever scheme to ensure her jaded, love-doubting grandson didn't end up alone, Dex's grandma left her company to Dex's...wife. Except he isn't married. Until me, that is.

Now I'm suddenly the CEO and majority shareholder of a billion-dollar cruise corporation. I'm unprepared, and the sharks in the boardroom are scarier than the great whites in the water. But the plan is simple. Play the part for a year, hand the company back over to Dex, then get divorced. Easy. In exchange, I'll never have to worry about money again.

But it's not long before I realize the company is in danger and a lot of people need my help. And now that I'm acting like the boss, there's a look in Dex's eyes I've never seen before. Something more than friendly... Because when he calls me "wife" lately, it doesn't seem like it's for show.

You're not just a reason.
You're the only reason.

SELFIE

KAY COVE

Selfie

Don't settle for a man who tells you he loves you. Choose one who shows you.

When my mom passed, I made her a promise that I'd take care of my little sister.

Then I find out my fiancé tricked me into draining her trust fund. There's only one thing to do—make it right. At all costs. It's my job to protect her...and I failed.

Luckily, I come across a job opening as an executive assistant in a new state. Between the generous salary and a place to stay, it's a no-brainer. Time to start over.

The only problem is that my new boss is a nightmare. The job description left out the part about working for Las Vegas's biggest billionaire bosshole. And the worst part? He's trying to get rid of me.

But Nathan Hatcher is dead wrong if he thinks his permanent scowl and impossible tasks are enough to make me quit. I only need to survive one year to secure the salary advance. Besides, what's far scarier than my boss is the idea of letting my mom and sister down.

But it's not long before I realize that there's a fine line between hate and lust. A tragic secret lies behind Nathan's broody stare, and the man I loathe may want me more than he hates me.

Even worse? With the way my heart races every time he enters a room...I seem to want him too.

PAGE
&
VINE